Table of Contents

Acknowledgements

A thanks to my editor Annie Jenkinson and my cover artist Adrian Cuevas for their hard work in making this book a reality and giving you the reader the best experience we could provide.

And a special thanks to my mom who helped me overcome Dyslexia and made me want to write and tell stories, without her none of this would have happened.

(https://www.artstation.com/shupeipa)

Chapter 1: Blessing of War

I grabbed my toolbelt, tossed it into the rusty bed of my truck, and got into the driver's seat. My left hand grabbed the steering wheel, a rag tied around my knuckles from where I'd scraped them when I'd punched a wall. Catching sight of my dark, angry eyes in the rearview mirror, my hand reached up to adjust its odd angle. It was broken, secured in place with duct tape now constantly falling off, but I didn't have the money to replace it.

By now, I was hot, sweaty, and tired, mentally and physically. It had been a long day filled with the usual bullshit and I just wanted to go home, shower, and play video games for a few hours. I didn't mind the work, but like every other job, it just took one asshole to ruin your entire day and make you consider bringing a gun to work the next time you showed up.

Sighing, I put my truck in reverse, backed onto the street, and headed home.

Opening the door of the rented downstairs apartment, I took off my boots and went into the bathroom, stripping out of my clothes which were soaked with sweat from the July heat.

Under the blissful, steaming hot water, I lathered my hair and body with soap, letting the torrent rinse it off me. Then I turned off the water, letting the excess moisture drip off me before grabbing a towel and drying off. Next, I wiped the steam off the bathroom mirror and looked at my long, dark, sodden hair. The mirror was still cracked from when I'd punched that too a few months back, the fissures throwing my features off, giving me an exaggerated, violent appearance. I quickly ran a comb through my hair, which hung down over my forehead and nearly to my shoulders.

A cut was in order, but laziness kept insisting I put it off.

On the underside of my chin, the stubble was starting to grow into a full beard, and I winced upon touching a faint bruise acquired in a fight with a coworker last week. There were bags under my sunken, dark brown eyes from lack of sleep too, from going to bed way too late and waking before dawn. These only served to make my eyes look even darker. Then there was my nose, slightly crooked from the many times it had been broken in fights I'd gotten into as a kid. A scar adorned my lip, busted open back in high school.

I rolled my neck, its vertebrae cracking satisfyingly.

Having donned boxers, gym shorts, and a T-shirt, I finally stepped out of the bathroom.

But wait—what?

There was someone in my goddamned living room! My first thought was, *where's my gun?* I had left it in its case under the bed, too far away for me to grab it. My second thought was that the person was a woman, and my third thought: *she clearly isn't human.*

My mind tried to overlook the fact that she had an extra pair of freaking arms, and her eyes were red, not as if she was wearing red contacts. No, blood red with an inner glow that some shitty costume contact lenses couldn't explain away.

"What the fuck are you doing in my house?"

"Greetings, mortal," the woman-thing said. "Please try to keep your fear to a minimum. I am not here to harm you."

"What do you want? What are you?" I edged toward my bedroom. Could I get to my gun before this thing got to me?

She wore armor made of some reptile's hide and metal plates, and she was strapped with at least half a dozen swords. Her skin was as white as paper but stained with dirt.

No, those were bloodstains.

Oh, shit! There is an alien, sword-wielding psychopath in my apartment!

I moved closer to my bedroom door.

"I am here to make you a proposal. I am Kelesa, Goddess of War and Conquest."

"What kind of proposal?" I asked. *That's right, Mark, keep the crazy sword-wielding alien talking. Just a few more feet...*

"Please stop trying to go for your weapon," Kelesa told me.

Shit! She can read my mind. I had not properly dried myself and was freezing.

"I require a champion to serve me. I am offering you the chance to gain all you have ever desired," Kelesa said, placing my gun on the coffee table in front of the couch.

"Why me?" I asked, the only question I could think of at that moment.

"There is nothing special about you," Kelesa said.

Ouch! That hurts!

"I have already asked four others in several different worlds, but they turned me down. If you do also, I will simply ask one of a thousand other candidates," she continued.

"Is that why you're covered in bloodstains?" I asked.

Kelesa looked down, seeming surprised.

"Oh, that's not from this." She said it as if absently dismissing the thought from her mind. "No, I simply wiped the memory of our meeting from their mind and went elsewhere. It would be against the rules to kill a potential candidate."

She could be lying, but I have no reason to disbelieve her.

"What does being a champion mean?"

"The world I am from has many gods. Every five hundred years, we each may select a champion who aligns with our ideals. These champions engage in a contest. Whichever one wins will become a new god in the pantheon of their patron god."

"You said you were the Goddess of War and Conquest. How do I align with your ideals? Shouldn't you be asking some African warlord?" I asked.

"I have tried such people in the past, but their methods have always failed me. I am experimenting with something new, looking for someone with the traits of a great warrior but who is more adaptive and less set in their ways."

"And how do I fit that?" I asked, somewhat curious.

"I have looked through your memories. You have some combat training, some leadership potential, a desire for power, and a bloodthirstiness you have always been forced to suppress," Kelesa said, her voice the exact tone you would use to praise someone for building orphanages and feeding the homeless.

"And what do *I* get out of this?"

"Otherworldly powers and the chance to ascend to godhood and gain immortality," Kelesa said, smiling, revealing jagged shark-like teeth.

"What kind of powers?"

I forced my mind to overlook her fangs in order to preserve my sanity.

"You will be given three of your choice. They will not be immensely powerful at first, but you can gain more and increase their potency with effort, time, and bloodshed. You will also be given a fourth power of my choosing."

"Any three powers of my choosing?" I asked, pushing this critical issue.

"Yes, but be warned, powers such as instant death or time travel are god-level powers. It would be best to choose something to help enable you to survive in your early stages," Kelesa warned me.

I thought about her words. Hadn't I always wanted magic powers? Who didn't, but at the same time, this sounded dangerous. She had implicitly warned me I might die if I became her champion. That said, what did I have going for me here? A shitty job that I came home from, day after monotonous day, only to escape into video games and pretend I did have those magic powers. Through video games, I could become someone else. I wanted to matter, to be powerful and significant. Now, I had a chance to escape my humdrum existence and acquire magical powers for real, to become a champion, someone to be feared and respected.

There was a chance all of this was not real. I could be in a coma or the unwitting stooge of some elaborate prank by a TV show that had broken into my house. But if it was real...

"What does it mean to be your champion? What do you want from me?"

"That's easy," Kelesa told me with her shark grin. "I want you to win at whatever cost."

"Then, I accept," I said, instinctively, without hesitation. I couldn't pass up this opportunity, even if it did have some strings attached.

"Good," Kelesa said, stepping forward and pulling a curved knife from her belt.

I almost had a heart attack when I realized this goddess was several feet taller than me and coming at me fast with a knife. Before I could do anything, she slashed a line across the palm of her hand and mine. Then she joined them together.

***

I felt space warp around me as I was yanked out of my apartment, finding myself standing on what looked almost like a ziggurat. All around the pyramid's base were corpses pierced with weapons as far as the eye could see in an endless aftermath of battle.

The flapping of wings and the cawing of birds created a white noise in the otherwise silent landscape as crows and other carrion eaters devoured the flesh of the slain.

"Where are we?" I asked, struggling against retching due to the all-pervading stench of death.

"This is my realm," said Kelesa, grabbing a chalice. "Now kneel."

I dropped to my knees as if someone had shoved me.

Kelesa raised the chalice above my head and poured a thick, red liquid over me.

I shivered and felt the blood quickly soaking through my clothes and skin.

Congratulations!
You have been chosen as the Champion of Kelesa, Goddess of War and Conquest. You have received the blessing of Kelesa, the Blessing of War (Mortal).

Blessing of War (Mortal): You are the mortal embodiment of war and carnage. You regain 3 Stamina and Mana per second to fuel you as you carve your way through the battlefield.

I blinked as the text superimposed itself over my vision. But it disappeared as soon as I finished reading it

---

You have been granted the ability Dominion by your godly patron as part of your pact.

Ability gained.
Dominion (Rank 1): Several times per day equal to your Spirit Attribute, you can, as a spoken command, force a creature not bound by another creature into your service. A creature may choose to serve you willingly or attempt to resist by opposing their Mind Attribute against your Spirit Attribute. You can, at will, see the Abilities and Attributes of any creature under your Dominion. You may have a maximum number of creatures under your Dominion, equal to your Spirit Attribute x2.

Cost: 1 Mana per creature.

Upgrade this ability to increase how many creatures you can dominate per day and the multiplier for how many you can dominate at any given time. Each upgrade increases your Spirit Attribute by 1.

I blinked as I looked at the ability. *Ok, that is definitely an evil power.*

"Are you evil?" I asked, though as she possessed the title 'Goddess of War and Conquest,' that realization should probably have struck me sooner!

"That is an entirely subjective question," Kelesa said, amused rather than offended. "Do I consider myself evil? No. Do others? It depends. In the world you are going to, the gods are divided into those who revere civilization and those who revere chaos. I am a goddess of chaos; I revel in and enjoy it. Those who revere civilization consider me evil, but ironically to oppose me, they must engage in war, the very concept they claim is anathema to them."

I supposed that was as good an answer as I would get.

"How do I choose my powers?" I wanted to know.

"First, you must choose a new name. Names have power in my world. This is why we gods typically choose those from other worlds as our champions since no one here will know your true name. Never tell it to anyone; consider it dead to you from now on. I will help with that."

"It's not like I was that attached to it anyway," I said. Then, I thought: this wasn't like picking a name for some video game where I could just go around calling myself Yuri Nator or Ben N. Syder or some other joke name. I was apparently now in the service of an evil or at least bloodthirsty goddess. Anyone (or anything) I encountered would therefore have certain expectations of me. I would need something imposing and easy to remember. I thought about all the games I had played and the books and movies I'd seen.

"Mordred," I decided, going with one of the better-known villains. It also started with an M, so was similar enough to Mark for me to quickly get used to it.

"Very well, Mordred," said Kelesa.

My head was suddenly dizzy, and I sat on a square, stone block as everything became foggy and hazy around me. What had happened? I had just changed my name to Mordred and suddenly could not remember my real one! I looked back through my memories, but everyone had called me Mordred for as long as I could remember. Hadn't they?

No! That was impossible because I did just recall picking it only moments ago.

"What did you do to me?" I asked as the haze began to dissipate.

"I erased your first name from your memories," Kelesa explained impassively. "It wouldn't do to change your name only for someone with a mind-reading ability to pluck it from your thoughts."

"How much have you messed with my mind?" I asked, afraid of the answer. "Was it even my own decision to become your champion?"

"I have only altered your memories and thoughts once," Kelesa stated. "It is against the pact we gods made to force or coerce someone to become our champion. I also don't want to alter your mental state. In the past, I used to be very hands-on with my champions, but it never ended well so that clearly wasn't the right route. I have learned it is best to offer only occasional, subtle guidance and let you forge your own path."

"What is the pact you mentioned with the other gods?" I asked.

If she was messing with my thoughts, I could do nothing about it.

Kelesa sat on another stone block in front of me. "Long ago, the first gods created a system to create champions to settle disputes between us. We are able to guide our chosen champion to do as we need as long as we stay within its restrictions. Tell me what powers you want, and I will convert them through the System into your abilities."

I thought for several minutes about what I wanted to be able to do.

Fireballs were cool but limited, and any situation that didn't call for absolute obliteration would turn one of my three powers into a useless ability. Invisibility had some practical and exciting possibilities but didn't interest me much. Flight? That might make me an easy target for archers. Ultimately, I decided to go with my powers the same way I'd gone with my name and make a decision based on movies and mythology. What sort of powers were wielded by the bad guys in my video games and movies? I thought of black knights, villains, and warriors and knew just what to pick.

"I want Telekinesis. The ability to pick up people and objects with my mind and move and throw them at will," I said.

"A versatile ability," Kelesa said, momentarily staring into empty space.

A shimmering silver and light blue ball of energy appeared in the air before me. Then, it moved toward my chest and soaked into it.

Telekinesis (Rank 1): You can, at will, lift 1 object or creature weighing 30 pounds or less and move it within 50 feet of your body; or 3 objects or creatures weighing 10 pounds or less and move them within 50 feet of your body.

The speed and power of objects are based on your Spirit Attribute.

> **Cost: 1 Mana per 10 small objects/sec; or 1 Mana per large object/sec.**
>
> **Upgrade this ability to increase the number of items, their weight, and the range at which you can move them.**
> **Every upgrade of this ability increases your Spirit Attribute by 1.**

As soon as the words appeared in my vision, they blinked away and something else appeared beneath them.

> **You have absorbed the remains of a divine wraith which has bonded to your Spirit Attribute and will fuel and guide your soul's mutation when you pass the Mortal limit for your Spirit Attribute.**

I was somewhat disappointed I wouldn't be able to force-choke people right out of the gate, but remembered Kelesa telling me that abilities would start off weaker and need to be upgraded. I could still do a lot with this; I could throw spears and rocks at my enemies, and once upgraded, the ability would let me do even more. The second notification was weird.

"What does this mean about me absorbing the remains of a wraith and my soul mutating?" I asked. "Also, what does it mean by Mortal limit for my Attribute?"

"There are six ranks. The first is Mortal, which you are now. The limit for a Mortal Attribute is twenty. Once all your Attributes are past twenty, you will enter the Veteran rank. From there, it proceeds to Hero, Exarch, Hierophant, Demigod, and the ultimate rank, God.

"I want a passive ability to see into the future to avoid surprise attacks and be able to predict my enemies' attacks," I said, wondering how weak this ability would start.

Kelesa said nothing this time but stared into space as she interacted with the System and did whatever god thing was giving me my powers.

Then, something else materialized in front of me.

This time, it was a black-faceted eye like that of a spider or fly. It dissolved into mist.

Before I could protest, it hit my eyes, passing harmlessly through, filling me with a clarity of vision I had never before experienced.

> **Ability gained. Foresight (Rank 1): You passively see 3 seconds into the future and know what will happen to yourself and the space within 9 feet of you at all times. This ability is based on your Perception Attribute.**
>
> **Increasing it will increase the time you can see by 1 second per rank in Perception above 10 to a maximum of 15 seconds in the future.**
>
> **This is a passive ability, costing 1 Mana/sec.**
>
> **Upgrade this ability to increase how far you can see into the future and how far around you can see. Every upgrade to this ability increases your Perception Attribute by 1.**

I dismissed the notification and read the next one that popped up.

> **You have absorbed the eye of Fate Spider, which has bonded to your Perception Attribute and will fuel and guide your eyes' mutation when you pass the Mortal limit for your Perception Attribute.**

I clutched my skull, becoming engulfed by an excruciatingly intense headache. I was totally unprepared for it; the first two abilities hadn't done anything like this.

I gritted my teeth, but already, the pain was beginning to fade. But now, disorientation set in as I saw double around me, like watching two screens playing the same movie but not in sync with each other. The dizziness faded, and although I was still aware of it, I could push the double image out of my mind.

It was like going nose blind or stepping into a pool of water, overwhelming and freezing at first, but once you were all the way in, you didn't notice it anymore. It simply ebbed away.

"What was that?" I asked.

"Abilities that directly affect you will have an impact on your body when you gain or upgrade them. Try to be in a safe place when you do so, or you may be killed while you are vulnerable," Kelesa warned me. There was no sympathy in her voice. Neither did she seem amused, more that she was devoid of humor. It occurred to me that her previous withholding of information had not been for her own entertainment.

My physical and mental discomfort was a matter of supreme indifference to her.

Looking at the ability in my mind again now that I had recovered, I was happy with it. Whilst it was not insanely overpowered, this was about what I had expected to be able to do. It would act as both a defensive and offensive ability if I could use it correctly.

"For my last ability, I want to move faster and have sharper reflexes," I said.

There was no point in being able to see into the future if I couldn't move fast enough to take advantage of it.

Kelesa nodded and stared into space again.

A massive scale the size of my hand appeared. It was black, but the edges of it glowed red-hot. It turned to mist, similar to the eye-spider, passing right through my skin.

Ability gained.

Heightened Speed (Rank 1): You move faster and can react more swiftly. Instantly, your body acts and can move at max speed without needing to build up momentum. The speed at which your body can move is increased by a multiple of 2.

This is a passive ability, costing 1 Stamina per second, and will cost more Stamina in combat depending on how fast you move.

Upgrade this ability to increase how fast you can move. Every upgrade of this ability increases your Speed Attribute x2.

I nearly fell over as the ability hit me. It felt as though snakes were burrowing through my muscles, and my heart was racing as if I'd just consumed thirty energy drinks in a row.

My entire body shook and spasmed, pins and needles pricking me all over.

Eventually, the feeling subsided, although my heartbeat remained faster than before. I sat up too quickly and had to pause to regain my equilibrium. Pushing myself up more slowly, I was now more controlled, trying to account for the effect of the increased speed on my body.

You have absorbed the scale of a world wyrm, which has bonded to your Speed Attribute and will fuel and guide your fast-twitch

> **muscles' mutation when you pass the Mortal limit for your Speed Attribute.**

"Wow," I said, clearly able to feel the results. "I feel like I could run a dozen marathons."

"Well, you cannot," Kelesa informed me. "Although faster, you lack high enough endurance to keep up your speed for long periods."

"Then how do I raise my other Attributes?"

"You can spend rank points equal to the rank of the ability you are trying to upgrade or directly spend them on the Attribute. Although the second option will only raise your attribute, it is less efficient than raising your Attributes through your abilities," Kelesa told me. "Before you ask, there are several ways to gain rank points. First, you can complete objectives related to your patron."

> **Quest gained.**
> **Blood and Souls (Repeatable): Kill 5 monsters or humanoids. Current progress: 0/5. When you complete this quest, you will gain 1 rank point. The next quest will require double the number to be completed but will award double the rank points.**

> **Quest gained.**
> **Whip and Chains (Repeatable): Conquer 5 monsters or humanoids by bringing them under your Dominion. Current progress: 0 out of 5. When you complete this quest, you will gain 1 rank point. The next quest will require double the number to be completed but will award double the rank points.**

"So, is everyone in your world just trying to kill and enslave everything?" I asked, apprehensively looking over my quests.

"Not all, but as the Goddess of War and Conquest, my quests will be related to my domain. The God of Smiths' quests will have his followers craft swords and armor while the God of Thieves will require his champion to steal certain items worth particular amounts."

So even my quests are evil? I shrugged.

There was nothing to do about it now. I had already signed up without reading the small print, evidently. "You said there were other ways to gain rank points. This seems easy at first, but I will have to massacre and enslave entire cities to keep gaining rank points from it?"

Kelesa nodded. "The second method is to kill others like yourself—known as the Gifted— who have also earned rank points. Each time you do so, you will gain half their total rank points, and there is a one-in-five chance of gaining one of their abilities, although it will adapt to suit you when you acquire it."

"And how many people like me are there? How many other chosen are there?"

"There are over seven hundred Gods of Order, each with a chosen champion," Kelesa said. "But they are not the only ones with powers. Abilities are hereditary, although your children will inherit only a few of your abilities based on how many their parents have when they are conceived. You cannot pass on your Dominion ability since that is only given directly by me.

"There are thousands of descendants of the champions over the millennia. They have bred like rabbits even if they do kill each other by the score to gain higher ranks. Also, any common man or beast can steal abilities if they manage to kill one of the Gifted."

"So, there are thousands of Gifted I have to look out for as well as the other champions?" I said. "What are my actual chances of winning this thing?"

"Poor," Kelesa said with a vicious smile. "There is a reason I am trying to switch up my method of selecting champions. Those I have chosen in the past have been over zealous in their bloodshed. When we first began this game, there were six gods, I being one of them. Two others revered chaos and three more who revered civilization stood in opposition to us. Over time, numbers of civilization-revering gods have increased dramatically but now, only fourteen gods are on the side of chaos."

She smiled and waited for my feedback. But I was still listening, so she continued, "You see, the problem with chaos is we make individually powerful champions... But, how shall I put it..? You really don't play nice with each other. I approve, of course. Who wants a champion who will bend the knee to the other? Still, the champions of the Gods of Civilization band together and will choose leaders from amongst themselves *democratically*," Kelesa said, the last word escaping her mouth as if she'd had to swallow a fat garden slug.

"You're saying I have to worry about hundreds of champions ganging up and coming to kill me?" *How badly have I screwed up by accepting this job?*

"Not all will live long enough even to reach you. The world you are entering is dangerous, filled with monsters in scale and fur and some in human skin. There is war and famine, and many will not be able to adjust to it. Royal families will take from the chosen for breeding.

"A champion like you will produce powerfully Gifted children. But yes, you should know your enemies and prepare for them, grow in strength, and find artifacts, powerful servants, and allies. Above all, though, never hesitate to kill. Amongst the gods of chaos, I am one of the most hated because although I have only ever had one successful champion, every last one has left a deep and lasting mark. You will be considered one of the biggest targets."

"You're not painting a very bright picture for me," I said. "It's not sounding very enticing."

"Life is painted in shades of blood and shit," Kelesa responded bluntly and without sympathy. "So, I would make sure you are the one with the paintbrush in your hand."

Suddenly, I realized something, casting my gaze downwards. "I'm barely dressed." I was still wearing a pair of gym shorts and a T-shirt. "I get some starting equipment, right?"

Kelesa reached into space. One of her arms seemed to disappear, and then suddenly produced a backpack which I recognized as the one I used for backpacking and hiking. She pulled out a drawer from my dresser and then another drawer, tossing them on the ground.

I quickly put on black cargo pants, two pairs of socks, and running shoes.

The shoes were ragged, and I looked at them disapprovingly. I had meant to get around to replacing them but had kept putting it off.

"What about weapons?" I asked, hoping she'd toss me my Glock pistol.

"We are forbidden from letting champions bring any weapons from their worlds," Kelesa told me, reading my mind. "However, we can each create one artifact for our champion. I suggest you create a weapon to help you survive."

Maybe I could get a lightsaber or a mini railgun? Or maybe some armor, a suit like Iron Man's, or a breastplate that deflects attacks back at whoever hits it.

"The artifact must be within limits like your powers," Kelesa said, glimpsing casually through my thoughts.

Ok, so a magic tank is out of the question.

Could I still get the lightsaber or some other weapon or piece of armor? No, every champion will probably pick something similar, which means I could just take it from them whenever we fight. In any case, there must have been so many champions in the past, so who knows how many artifacts are hidden away somewhere?

Looking down at my shoes again, I came to a decision.

These shoes probably wouldn't last a month of constant use and this world most likely didn't have nice concrete roads like my native world. I remembered hearing somewhere about people on those survivor shows in which they were forced to start with nothing.

The one thing they all wished they had was a pair of modern shoes. I didn't know if that was true, but I wasn't looking forward to going anywhere without practical, contemporary footwear. *Actually, let's raise the ante here.* "I want a pair of magic boots, something with a multiplier on my Speed attribute and the ability to teleport a few dozen feet," I said.

"You're sure you don't want a weapon?" Kelesa asked, seeming disappointed.

"I'm guessing most of the other chosen in the past have picked weapons, so they must be out there to find, so I should pick something that other people wouldn't have chosen."

Good reasoning, surely!

"Very well. It's your choice. Picture the item in your mind, and I shall try to create it as you imagine," Kelesa instructed.

I closed my eyes and imagined a pair of knee-high boots.

There was a thought to fold the tops over to create a cuff I thought would look nice, like a swashbuckling swordsman's footwear. I pictured thick cord laces up the front, solid rubber soles with good grip, a steel protective toe, and a steel guard over the back of the heel.

I kept the image in my head, focusing on the details as hard as I could.

"It is done," Kelesa said. "I have added some features of my own. I hope you don't mind."

I opened my eyes. There, right in front of me, was a pair of obsidian black boots resting on the ground. They appeared to be made from some reptile skin , similar to what Kelesa's armor was made from. It was a detail I hadn't imagined, but they looked all right.

I reached out and grabbed them.

Boots of Midnight Wind (Artifact: Rank 5): Gives a +2 bonus to the wearer's Speed Attribute and gains an additional +1 bonus for every 10 ranks you have.
You can double your Speed Attribute for 10 minutes with a cooldown of 1 hour. Duration and cooldown period are reduced and increased by 5 minutes every 15 ranks. You have a max of 1-hour duration and a 5-minute cooldown.
Once per minute, at the cost of 15 Mana, you can teleport 30 feet to a place you can see. The range is increased by 5 feet, and the cooldown is reduced by 5 seconds and increased cost by 1 Mana to a minimum of 5 Mana.
Created by the Goddess Kelesa for her champion Mordred, these boots are made from the hide of a black dragon with a mithril alloy for the toe and heel guard.
These boots are infused with the power of Kelesa's will and are indestructible except by another deity.

Weight:	4 lbs.

"Nice," I said, ditching my running shoes and putting on the boots. They fit perfectly, and I almost felt as though I was walking on air. I could feel the increase in my speed and could only imagine the effect of my Speed Attribute being doubled.

"I have another question: how am I supposed to win? What's the goal?"

"You are racing to Godhood. You need to raise all your Attributes to 600," she said with a viciously gleeful grin.

"I need to raise my abilities to Rank 600?" I asked disbelievingly.

"Rank 20 is the max level for abilities, apart from the divine ability that I gave you," Kelesa said. "You will need to unlock and earn more abilities to raise all your Attributes or spend rank points on your Attributes directly. Also, you will need to find items or pieces of monsters to absorb when you unlock new abilities. I provided the three for you today.

"Your Dominion ability is divine, and so it doesn't count, but for every ability, you need to absorb a treasure of some kind to fuel the changes made to your body. If you don't have one, then the System will pull the closest available rare material to you. This, however, will have a distinctly adverse effect on your physical prowess."

I had a myriad more questions but at that moment, could only summon one.

"What happens now?"

"Now, I send you out to kill and conquer," Kelesa said with another shark smile. "There is a place I know that should give you an excellent start... If you can survive it."

"That doesn't sound..." I began, but Kelesa pushed me backward, and I fell through a portal. She tossed my backpack and clothes after me, and the portal shut.

"Son of a..." I began, but the portal closed, and I could hear Kelesa's laughter no longer.

***

Arthur took Viviane's hand and she pulled him through the portal. They emerged on the shores of a beautiful lake, a ring of mountains surrounding them.

The goddess looked at her champion, her golden hair flowing down her back.

She was wrapped in a spotless white dress and wore a silver breastplate molded to her chest and showing her curves. Her wide eyes were pure blue, the naiad features of her original race evident. A singe rapier hung at her hip.

"Your ancestor served me well," she said. "Even though he did not win the game of the gods, he came very close. More importantly, he upheld my beliefs and vindicated my choice in choosing him as my champion."

"You honor my ancestor," Arthur said, bowing.

"He too was polite," she said, smiling. "I am glad to see his sword still serves his family well."

Arthur felt the weight of the heavy two-handed sword on his back. He had been given Excalibur by his father, King Arthur, when he had turned sixteen some two years ago. He still marveled at the wonder of the blade but turned his focus back to the goddess.

"He was my first champion, and very important to me," Viviane said. "When he died, I promised him I would pick one of his descendants as my champion. Some of my peers in the pantheon have called my oath reckless but seeing you now, I do not regret it."

"I will not let you down," Arthur promised.

"You are a native to our world and born with abilities, so I cannot grant you new ones beside my divine ability," Viviane said. "However, I can give you an artifact. Your family already has many lesser artifacts in their armory, but this one will be yours alone, tailored to your needs."

"I want an amulet to reduce the effects of going beyond my abilities," Arthur said.

"A wise choice," Viviane agreed. "You already know the divine ability and are preparing to fully utilize it. This is good, and you will need it. You will battle against dragons as did your ancestor. You will encounter monsters the size of castles, but you will find your greatest foes are the ones who walk on two legs."

Chapter 2: Mark of Cain

"… bitch," I said, looking up toward where the portal had been.

I looked about the place into which I had been shoved. It was almost pitch black, but light emanated from somewhere, allowing me to see faint outlines. The air was damp and smelled of mildew and decay. Stone coffins filled the room. A dark tunnel revealed stairs leading downwards opposite a set of massive stone doors.

"Looks like a crypt," I said and was instantly on alert.

I had played enough games to know that crypts typically meant undead, and Kelesa had implied that wherever I was going was dangerous.

First things first: what do I have?

Answer: only my hiking backpack and a pile of clothes. What did I have in my backpack? I opened it up and looked inside. It contained a first aid kit, a small camping coffee pot, a bag of beef jerky, an empty canteen, a roll of paracord, a box of strike-anywhere matches, a pocketknife, a compass, and a sketchbook with a case filled with pencils. In addition, a sleeping bag and a small cast-iron frying pan were tied to the top of the backpack.

Apparently, the pocketknife didn't qualify as a weapon. *Fair enough. I'll be better off punching things than trying to use it to stab something.*

It could have been much worse, but I was still pretty defenseless.

The only offensive ability I had was my Telekinesis. I rolled up my clothes to take up less space as I stored them in my backpack, stuffing it to the brim.

First, I need to find a weapon. Come on, this is just your tutorial. You've played enough games to figure this out.

Was there anything around that could be considered a weapon? There was nothing obvious. Then, I looked at the coffins and realized what I had to do.

Straining, I pushed as the stone lid slowly ground back before toppling and cracking on the floor. No skeletons or zombies rushed out to kill me, although I did find an inanimate skeleton inside the coffin but nothing of genuine interest.

There were some rings on its bony fingers, and I slipped them off. They appeared to be made of gold and silver. I might be able to sell them if ever I found a settlement.

There were some valuables inside the next coffin: rings, bracelets, necklaces, a small jade statue, and even a small pouch of coins.

On the sixth coffin, something interesting finally turned up.

The occupant had been a warrior and buried with all his armor. Unfortunately, the armor was rusted to shit. One gauntlet was rust-free, and I picked it up.

Gauntlet of the Soldier (Right hand).
   Type: Armor. Rarity: Uncommon.
   Increases damage with one-handed weapons by a minor amount. When paired with another gauntlet of the same type on the opposite hand, it will increase damage with two-handed weapons by a moderate amount. Durability: 9/10.
   Made from common steel and empowered by a novice enchanter.

Great! The first magical item, and it only reinforces that I don't have a weapon!

So frustrating! Hmm, was my decision to not start with a weapon as my artifact not as clever as I'd thought?

I dismissed my doubts. There was no point worrying about it now, stuck with what I had.

Grabbing the skeletal arm, I yanked off the gauntlet. After shaking out the last finger bones from the glove and all the corpse dust, I tried it on. I now had a piece of armor that covered my hand and wrist, something to amplify my damage if I could find something to use as a weapon. So, I continued to open coffins, wincing with each crash. There was an abundance of loot, just none of it very useful to me. My backpack was getting heavy from the weight of all the jewelry too, but I was still decidedly unarmed.

Finally, another body turned up, the corpse of someone who had been a warrior, the armor once again all rusty apart from the shin guards. They weren't magical but had stood up better to the ravages of time. My artifact boots were indestructible and already covered my shins, so this was another bust. A rusty warhammer rested alongside the skeleton.

As I held it, the system automatically identified it for me.

> **Raven's Beak. Type: One-handed weapon. Rarity: Common. A non-magical one-handed weapon, excellent at piercing armor. Durability: 6/10.**
>
> **Additional effect: inflicts tetanus.**
>
> **Any creature hit with this weapon that fails a toughness check will be infected with tetanus, suffering poison damage until they die or receive treatment or healing.**

Whatever system the gods had created had let me identify the weapon but for some reason, not the leg armor. The reason why was unclear, and it probably didn't matter.

I gave it a few test swings, familiar with hammers thanks to my work in construction, and it felt comfortable in my hand. Tucking the hammer in my belt, I continued to open the coffins. All I found, however, was some more jewelry and two rusty daggers in even worse condition than the warhammer. And soon, all the coffins were empty.

I looked around. It was now time to explore the tunnel or what lay beyond the set of stone doors. Looking down the tunnel, I had to decide against it, unable to see in the dark and lacking any way of producing light. Also, if there were any undead here, they would almost certainly be loitering down there. I had no interest in fighting the undead in the dark.

That left the door... It didn't budge an inch when pushed against, despite straining with all my might; still, the mighty door refused to shift. I kept at it for half an hour and eventually stopped to rest, leaning back against the door to keep an eye on the tunnel.

"So, I have to get through that tunnel, somehow," I told myself, just to hear a human voice and break the oppressive silence.

My eyes closed as I took a quick nap, a tremor reverberating through the door. I sat up, adrenaline jerking me to full wakefulness. The tremor came again, my eyes fixated on the door, watching as it trembled. While trying to get out of here, I hadn't considered that something or someone else might try to get in.

"Maybe they're friendly," I said to myself.

If you can survive, Kelesa had said.

"Probably not." Sighing, I pulled out my warhammer.

Crack! The sound echoed through the tomb, the stone beginning to shake particles of loose dust as the door trembled. *Crack!* The stone started to spiderweb. *Crack!* A wide hole opened, but there was no visibility as a cloud of dust filled the air. Coughing sounded from the other side, making me duck low behind a coffin in case they decided to shoot in blindly.

The dust cleared and a huge man stepped into the room, carrying a massive maul with a wooden head bound in iron bands, a metal pole at the base.

About a dozen other people followed him in and stared around the crypt.

"Someone already looted it," a male voice complained.

"Impossible. You all saw it was sealed," a woman said.

"Quiet, all of you!" the man with the maul commanded, his voice deep and gravelly. "We don't know what's in here."

Risking another glimpse, I studied their leader.

Quin Varis. Gifted Human/Humanoid. Mortal. Rank: 4.

The text appeared as I studied him. *So, he's a Gifted. What exactly does Rank 4 mean?*

The number at the end of a Gifted's description indicates their accumulated ranks in various abilities. A single question mark at the end of a creature's name or species indicates a Mortal-ranked Gifted with ranks below double digits.

?? indicates a Gifted with at least 10 or more rank points.

You can see the number of rank points of any Gifted with fewer rank points than yourself. It will be harder to determine the rank of those higher than yourself without a higher Perception Attribute than the opposing creature's Spirit Attribute.

We're roughly on the same level then, but there's no telling how experienced he is. Maybe it's possible to talk my way out of this. I slowly stood up, setting my warhammer where I could quickly grab it, and raised my hands placatingly.

"Hello there," I said, trying to sound friendly.

"An undead!" a man screamed as they loosed an arrow at me.

I didn't even flinch; my foresight told me the arrow wouldn't come close. The bow appeared so crude, as if someone had just chopped down a tree, stripped the branches, and added a string. Now that I looked, most of the weapons were crude, apart from the leader's maul. They had sharpened sticks in place of spears, and absurdly basic bows with hides draped over them in place of any armor.

Quin looked me over and smiled. "A bounty hunter! Looks like I'll earn myself some new rank points really quick!"

There goes diplomacy! I watched as Quin tensed.

I grabbed my warhammer just before teleporting in the instant Quin pounced on me.

The maul obliterated the coffin by which I'd been standing. I appeared in the doorway, and one of the men stabbed me with a wooden spear.

My reflexes kicked in before I could think, my warhammer caving in his skull.

It was a strange sensation; having always believed I'd feel something when killing a person—horror or shock at least—it was perturbing to grasp only a mixture of fear and something hot in my chest.

> **Quest updated.**
> **Blood and Souls (Repeatable): Kill 5 monsters or humanoids.**
> **Current progress: 1/5. Every time you complete this quest, you will gain 1 rank point. The next quest will require double the number to be completed but will award double the rank points.**

My head shook in irritation as the text blocked my vision. "Turn off quest notifications during combat," I ordered, and the text disappeared.

Quin turned and saw the corpse by my feet, his face twisted with anger. "Armor of the Earth!" he commanded, and stone flowed up his legs, forming plate armor over them as well as his torso, arms, and head.

He charged me while I still had thirteen seconds left before being able to teleport again.

Activating the speed increase on my boots, my entire body vibrated.

Quin's maul swung horizontally, the weapon creating a breeze with the force at which it moved through the air as it passed above my head.

I'd somehow matrix-dodged it.

So, I have speed and reactions on my side, whilst he has durability and power on his. I leaped to the side, foreseeing an arrow going through my chest.

And he has other people on his side.

Feet pounding on the rocky ground, I was upon the archer who shot at me in a second, my arm lashing out, caving in his skull, the warhammer splattering blood and brain matter everywhere, red and purple, green in places, hideous to see.

Standing outside the crypt now, my eyes cast around to see another two-dozen people, all brandishing crude weapons and wearing rags.

"Fight me, you bastard!" Quin shouted, chasing after me.

There surely must be a time limit on that armor, I thought, hurtling headlong at a group of three spearmen, finding myself intercepted by Quin and striking the ground before him, sending up a cloud of stone shrapnel.

Next, I dove behind a tree, stones cutting through my shirt, digging into my skin.

He still has ways to hit me, even without the speed to catch me.

As the thought hit me, a burst of inspiration came, a counter too.

With a mental maneuver, I teleported into the middle of the grave robbers and hit a spearman in the back of the head, spinning and hitting a woman's chest.

Quin roared and rushed to them but couldn't use his shrapnel trick without hitting his people. "Duck!" Quin yelled, and everyone around me fell.

He can't be trying it again…

He did not try it again, and instead, threw his maul. It spun horizontally, metal shaft and wooden head twisting through the air.

My eyes gaped wide with shock as the maul spun toward me like a death frisbee. My foresight told me I couldn't move out of the way fast enough, so I dropped too.

A spearman lunged at me with a dagger as the maul passed us overhead.

I blocked it with my gauntlet, but my balance was off, and another man grabbed my warhammer which I struggled to pull free.

Quin was getting closer.

Abandoning my warhammer, I rolled out of reach of the hands that had tried to grab me and sprang to my feet, tugging one of the looted daggers out of my boot and the other out of my belt, holding them in both hands. I stuck close to Quin now, ducking his attacks and trying to stab through a joint in his armor. None of my attacks penetrated his defense. The stone armor gaps seemed designed to prevent such attacks.

Arrows flew in our direction. It seemed the bowmen were not concerned about hitting Quin due to his impenetrable armor. Those arrows, however crude, would still be nasty for me to get hit with since my armor consisted of a cotton T-shirt and cargo pants.

My teleport came off cooldown, and I transported myself next to two archers, stabbing them in the back with my daggers. Wow, did that feel good!

Success per se felt good—until my targets dropped, and I couldn't pull my daggers free, the shoddy blades caught in the ribs of my foe.

"Fuck!"

I ran, Quin quickly closing the gap between us again.

I was all out of weapons now.

"Come on! you know karate. Time to put it to use!" I said aloud, trying to psych myself up. *Yeah, you took karate… five years ago, and it's going to do jack shit now*, another part of me retorted, but I did my best to ignore it.

---

1 rank point gained.

Someone had bled out, and I'd gained a rank point, but I'd need one more to upgrade any of my skills. I turned to the few dozen people forming a line and charged them.

I didn't have a weapon but moved as fast as a train.

They tried to form a wall of pikes.

I went low and flew across the ground, my momentum carrying me into the middle of them. Finding my feet again, I leaped up, and hit a man in the throat. His neck broke with an audible crack, and my knuckles echoed the sound with the force of the attack.

I maintained my speed, ignoring the brutal hand pain, spinning into a circle-kick whereupon the armored part of my foot collided with a woman's temple, caving in three inches of her skull. I kept punching and kicking, losing track of how many times I had to punch with my bare hands before they died. My knuckles were bleeding and broken, and there was a pain in my thigh from where one of the wooden spears had struck me.

Suddenly, I turned as my foresight gave me a warning and ducked Quin's attack. My killing spree felt as though it had taken minutes but likely had been less than a dozen seconds.

I rolled and grabbed a wooden spear, ramming it into the gut of a man already prostrate on the ground. I ripped it out and stabbed down again a dozen times before the wooden spear broke off inside the corpse.

2 rank points gained.

Ducking under Quin's next strike, my body screamed for me to stop and rest. I noticed a green bar at the bottom of my vision which I guessed indicated Stamina, flashing as it approached empty. I spun under the next attack, running back into the crypt.

"I hope I get your teleport ability when I kill you," Quin taunted as he followed, but he had lost sight of me when I'd entered the crypt.

He thinks my teleportation is an ability!

I had not used my only combat ability yet.

Crouching behind a coffin, I hid from his line of sight.

"Assign two rank points to Telekinesis," I whispered. There was a burning feeling around me, like standing beside a warm fire as my ability ranked up.

Telekinesis (Rank 2): You can, at will, lift 2 objects or creatures weighing 50 pounds or less and move them within 70 feet of your body; or up to 6 objects or creatures weighing 15 pounds or less and move them within 50 feet of your body. The speed and power of objects are based on your Spirit Attribute.

Cost: 1 Mana per 10 small objects/sec; or 1 Mana per large object/sec.

Upgrade this ability to increase the number of items, their weight, and the range at which you can move them. Every upgrade of this ability increases your Spirit Attribute by 1.

Quin stomped into the crypt. "All of you, stay out. This kill is mine!" he ordered as he angrily searched for me.

I lifted six rocks into the air and hurled them at Quin's head with as much force as my ability would allow, feeling no remorse as Quin staggered, my hurled rocks thrown with the force of a major league pitcher, hitting his head in rapid succession. He charged into the crypt, smashing coffins as he went, destroying any cover I could use. He found me and raised his maul high, clearly with the intention of bringing it down and turning me into paste.

I raised two huge chunks of rock and hit Quin in the back of his knees.

He staggered but remained on his feet, then grabbed a chunk of stone and tossed it at me.

I ducked, and the stone shattered behind me, the fragments striking me in the back. I began lifting rocks with the power of my Telekinesis, again hurling them at Quin as fast as I could, dodging and rolling out of the way as he relentlessly pursued me.

Quin's armor began to crack, but I could feel myself tiring; my Endurance wasn't high enough to support my Speed. I hit Quin in the back of the knee with a rock the size of his head, his armor shattering. I hit the same spot again with three smaller rocks the size of apples, hearing the bone crack.

Quin fell to his knees but didn't stop using his maul like a crutch as he hounded me.

Fuck this!

I lifted two massive rocks and dropped them on Quin's head.

He staggered from the sudden heavy impacts.

So, that encouraged me to raise two more and drop them again.

His helmet shattered, the blow sending Quin collapsing to the ground.

I gasped for breath as I continued the fight, no Mana left, but there was still Stamina. I lifted a rock with my hands and staggered toward him to stand over Quin, the hot feeling in my chest rising. This time, I raised the stone above my head and brought it down with all my strength. There was a sickening crunch as blood splattered the ground, rubble all around us.

---

2 rank points gained.

Blood and Souls (Repeatable): Kill 20 monsters or humanoids. Current progress: 1/20. Every time you complete this quest, you will gain 4 rank points.

The next quest will require double the number to be completed but will award double the rank points.

A stone the size of my thumb floated up from the ground before me, dissolving into mist and flowing up my nose. It felt weird as if I should sneeze, but I couldn't.

> **Congratulations! Ability gained. Compress Earth (Rank 1):** You can fuse dirt and stone together into a more durable, heavier material that can be shaped. You can currently fuse a 1-foot-square section of earth and common stone. Your compressed stone has a Hardness rating of 4; your compressed earth has a Hardness rating of 2. The precision of detail with which you can sculpt is based on your Mind Attribute.
>
> Cost: 1 Mana per 1-foot square.
>
> Upgrade this ability to increase the amount you can compress, its durability, weight, and the materials upon which you can use it.
> Each upgrade increases your Mind Attribute by 1.

When I dismissed the notification, another one popped up.

> **You have absorbed an uncut Greater Diamond which has bonded to your Mind Attribute and will fuel and guide your soul's mutation when you pass the Mortal limit for your Mind Attribute.**

I probably should have absorbed something better based on what Kelesa had told me, but I had no time to prepare for this. I dismissed the notification, and another one popped up.

> **You have completed a hidden objective and earned a title. Objective: Kill your first Gifted with an improvised weapon made of stone.**
>
> Reward. Title: Mark of Cain.
>
> *Mark of Cain: Your damage dealt with stone weapons is increased by 1 stage.

I dismissed the notification, wondering just how many had piled up while I had been fighting.

> **You have completed a hidden objective and earned a title. Objective: Kill at least 5 humanoids with no weapons.**

Reward. Title: Bloody Pugilist.
*Bloody Pugilist: Damage dealt directly with parts of your body, such as hands and feet are increased by 1 stage.

I dismissed these new titles, not even sure what they were or even what they did, and no new notifications popped up.

Why didn't it give me his armor ability? Also, is that how difficult it is to fight someone only two ranks higher?

I thought through my following actions as I panted, recovering from the battle. *Ok, I have one rank point. Where should I put it?*

"What are my current Attributes?" I asked the System.

Mordred, Champion of Kelesa. Gifted—Humanoid/Human. Mortal. Rank: 50.			
Available rank points: 6.			
Might:	12	Mind:	9
Speed:	12 (+2) =14	Perception:	8
Toughness:	11	Spirit:	15
Endurance:	10	Power:	10
Maximum Stamina:	56	Maximum Mana:	51
Stamina Regen:	11.2 per second	Mana Regen:	11.4 per second
Abilities:			
Dominion (Rank 1), Telekinesis (Rank 2), Heightened Speed (Rank 1), Foresight (Rank 1), Compress Earth (Rank 1).			
Blessings:			
Blessing of War (Mortal).			
Titles:			
Mark of Cain, Bloody Pugilist			

"Ok, I have excellent Speed and Spirit, but my Perception and Mind are low. I could increase my Perception but won't benefit from its increase until it hits fourteen," I said, reasoning aloud. "I could increase my Endurance to let me use Heightened Speed longer, but no ability I have will increase my Endurance. Two of my abilities benefit from Spirit.

"Telekinesis was the only power that let me win that last fight. But I'm one point short of being able to rank it up."

A sound emanated from outside; the others were still alive! I looked around for weapons to use, having lost all mine in the battle. I lifted Quin's maul and five rocks with my Telekinesis. As I slowly exited the crypt, the speed boost from my boots had ended, and it felt like the biggest sugar crash I'd ever had.

There were ten surviving brigands left, two women and five men. They had three bows drawn on me and a small phalanx of spears. They looked at me with terror when they saw Quin's maul. The three archers launched their arrows.

Three of the rocks dropped from my hands, instead reaching to grab the arrows midair, deftly turning their points toward the grave robbers.

"We surrender!" one of the women shouted, dropping her bow and raising her hands.

The others glared at her and didn't drop their weapons.

"There's more of us than there are of him," said a man with a spear.

"He killed Quin," another man reminded him. "You really think you can beat him?"

"I only really need five of you," I said. "You have five seconds to drop your weapons."

"Fuck this!" one of the men said and charged me.

Quin's maul spun and splattered the man's brains across the ground. Another threw his spear, and three arrows shot forward, taking him in the throat and neck.

Another turned to run, so I struck him in the back, grinning as he collapsed.

Blood and Souls (Repeatable): Kill 20 monsters or humanoids. Current progress: 4/20. When you complete this quest, you will gain 4 rank points. The next quest will require double the number to be completed but will award double the rank points.

The seven remaining dropped their weapons and raised their hands in surrender.

"Dominion," I said.

The seven brigands cried out in pain. In agony, they reached for their necks where marks had suddenly appeared around the base of each, white and like brands.

They revealed the pattern of a chain.

Quest updated. Whip and Chains: 1 rank point added.

Whip and Chains (Repeatable): Conquer 5 monsters or humanoids by bringing them under your Dominion. Current progress: 2/10. When you complete this quest, you will gain 2 rank points. The next quest will require double the number to be completed but will award double the rank points.

"You will serve me now," I said. "Prepare a camp and fire."

The survivors turned and ran into the forest. *Will they run off,* I wondered? I wasn't exactly sure how this ability worked. Ten minutes later, they reappeared, shaking and sweaty. Some carried packs while others lugged firewood. They began to set up camp, pitching tents.

I was thirsty and hungry. I looked around and saw gravestones all over the crypt, the only building in the clearing. A few trees and bushes grew among the graves, and it was clear this land had been abandoned long ago, the names on the gravestones not even legible anymore.

Wandering into the forest, I discovered a stream and bent down, cupping water and drinking, I felt some strength return, briefly wondering about sickness from the water, but I didn't have time for concerns like that with monsters and people with superpowers walking around. If I got sick, I'd deal with it as it came along.

I returned to the crypt, found my backpack buried among the rubble and pulled it out. Taking out the bag of jerky, I ate a bit before returning it to my pack.

Returning to sit in the light of the setting sun, I fixed on watching my captives, subjects and vassals, still unsure what to call them yet.

They set up camp with ragged tents and a rough campfire, with stones around fallen and broken branches and chunks of wood. They lit the fire and huddled around it, the ominous shadows of the night already darkening the clearing.

I got up and walked over to the fire, my vassals eyeing me the way you would a grizzly bear, making no sound or sudden movements as I sat on a large stone across from them.

"Who are you people?" I asked.

They were silent for a while, and I watched as the brand along their necks began to glow, and they twisted in discomfort.

"We're bandits!" one of the two remaining women finally exclaimed.

I reasoned that the brand must cause them more and more pain the longer they disobeyed or didn't try hard to comply with my orders.

"If you are bandits, you are not very good ones! Quin was the only one among you with any real weapons," I said.

"Quin sprang most of us from prison," said another woman. "He killed a noble in his sleep to steal his abilities, then used his powers to overwhelm the guards and break us out. We fled into the woods and have been hiding out here for about a week. We found this crypt and were going to search it for treasure."

"What do you want from us?" one of the men asked. "Are you a bounty hunter?"

I considered how much to tell them.

I don't think they could betray me even if they wanted to.

"I am Mordred, champion of Kelesa," I announced.

When I said the goddess' name, the bandits shuddered and made some ward against evil.

I laughed inwardly. "I want you to do as I command. As long as you follow my orders without complaint and without trying to escape or twist my words, I will protect you."

"Yes, Warlord," they mumbled, bowing their heads.

***

Guinevere rode at the column of a head of horses. Almost ten score knights rode behind her, all of them Knights of Camelot. She let out a sigh. This was overkill, even thirty royal Camelot Knights being enough to turn most armies, but the King had insisted she bring them with her. He wanted to protect the alliance that her marriage to Arthur would bring between their two houses. Her father, Merlin, hadn't wanted her to marry Arthur, but she had gone with it nonetheless, to keep stability in their kingdom.

"Guinevere," one of her knights said, riding up to her.

"You will address the Duchess Guinevere by her title or as Lady Guinevere, or you will not address her at all," Lady Kira said beside her.

Lady Kira was a healer. Guinevere's father had assembled an entourage for her and insisted she take them. More coddling she didn't need or appreciate.

"I've known Sir Kallin my entire life," Guinevere said. "He has every right and my permission to address me by my first name."

"But propriety…" Lady Kira said.

"We are on the border of the Cursed Forest," Guinevere said. "There isn't a town within a day's hard ride of where we are. These are the lands of barbarians, so if we can't have a little impropriety here, then where can we have it?"

"We've been following your lead," Sir Kallin said. "But we've been getting closer and closer to the Cursed Forest. Shouldn't we be heading north to the Old Road?"

"No," Guinevere said. "Going around the Cursed Forest adds another month to the journey. There isn't a man here below Rank Fifty. We'll ride straight through."

"The horses won't like that," Sir Kallin said.

"What's the point in having Gifted horses if we aren't going to use them?" Guinevere asked. "We waste valuable monsters on getting them abilities; the least they can do is ride through a damn forest once in a while!"

"Lady Guinevere!" chided Kira, shocked.

"My apologies," Guinevere said. "It's been a long day. We'll camp here tonight before heading into the forest tomorrow."

"What if monsters attack?" Sir Kallin asked.

"I hope they do," Guinevere said. "We could all use a bit of exercise and a new ability or two."

"There are worse things than monsters in those woods," Kira said. "What if a myrmidon raiding party decides you'd be a good wife for one of their warriors, or the hell dragon flies out of the forest… or worse, a chaos spawn uses us as rank fodder? What then?"

Guinevere rolled her eyes. "You're being melodramatic! The hell dragon has never flown out of the Cursed Forest, and he wouldn't be stupid enough to attack an army of Camelot knights. And as for a chaos spawn… Really? None of the Chaos gods would be foolish enough to set one of their champions this close to Camelot and Lunara; they know it would be suicide for them as soon as we found out about them."

Chapter 3: Ghoul Rot

Three champions stepped through portals into the capital of Lunara.

One was a tall man with broad shoulders, a fur cloak wrapped around his shoulders, and he also wore leather pants and boots, but no shirt. He wielded a pair of gauntleted bracers etched with green florescent runes, a pair of four-inch claws protruding from the gauntlets' knuckles.

Then there was also a woman with auburn hair and feathered wings the same color as the hair growing from her lower back.

She was lean, wore fur and leather armor, and carried a bow made of ivory with silver etching and blue, glowing runes. She stepped forward, looking around wearily.

The third figure was another man, almost as tall as the first but built like a rapier instead of a bear. He carried a spear longer than he was tall, a nimbus of golden light surrounding its shaft and head, and he wore a mixture of chain and plate armor.

They had appeared in a temple, and people stopped and looked at them in shock and fear. The spear-wielding man stepped forward, raising a hand to calm the crowd.

"Do not be afraid, people! I am Torvin, Champion of Galdren, God of the Charge & Chivalry."

The man in a fur cloak and wearing the clawed gauntlets stepped forward. "I am Jamis, Champion of Artrix, God of Barbarians and Bears."

The woman stepped forward and gave the nod to the two men.

"I am Mira, Champion of Jastrin, God of Archery and Hawks."

An elven woman with long silver hair braided down her back and wearing the garb of a priestess stepped forward. "We welcome the Allies of Order to the Temple of Luren."

Torvin turned to the other two champions. "My patron told me to find other champions to ally myself with and form a party."

"Artrix told me the same," Jamis said. "We should compare our abilities later and see how we can best fight alongside each other."

"There are two other champions here in the city," the High Priestess said. "They were chosen from the people of this world and were told to come here and wait for their companions. We have been expecting you for some time now."

"Then we should meet our new companions," Mira said, slinging her bow across her back. "I look forward to hunting down the Champions of Chaos with them."

***

The bandits went to sleep in their tents, several lying empty as they had belonged to their now-deceased companions, leaving us with plenty of room. I took one of them, the largest, and I assumed it had belonged to Quin. I rolled out my sleeping bag and sat down.

After collecting my daggers and warhammer, I had the bodies of Quin and the bandits dumped in the forest. My arsenal now included Quin's maul, but other than that, the entire camp was barely armed. I lay down but could not find sleep.

I grabbed a rock and held it in my hand. "Compress Earth," I said.

I watched as the rock, the size of a grapefruit, shrank to the size of a grape, its color darkening until it was almost obsidian. I tried to mold it and created a shape resembling an icicle, stabbing its point into another rock. They smashed together, but the tip of the stone only dulled slightly instead of breaking like an ordinary rock would have.

I molded the rock again, giving it edges which were jagged but now resembled a spearhead instead of a tiny stalagmite.

The Mark of Cain status struck me as ominous and weirdly connected to Christianity, which I was pretty sure wasn't a thing in this world.

Nevertheless, it enabled me to increase my damage with weapons made of stone by one stage. I didn't know what a damage stage even was, but more damage was always good. I wasn't sure if I'd get much use out of Bloody Pugilist, even with it increasing my damage; using fists instead of weapons didn't make much sense.

I kept working on my stone spearheads, thinning the edges, adding more and more stone to strengthen the point of the spearhead to cut and puncture without breaking or shattering.

They each weighed around seven pounds, their surfaces glossy smooth, making them look like blades fashioned in glass.

Grabbing all the rocks I could find in the firelight around the camp, I began turning them into stone spearheads. Having eventually made about a dozen, I finally felt tired enough, so I slipped into my sleeping bag and fell asleep.

A scream ripped through the air, jolting me awake. I rolled out of my sleeping bag and grabbed my warhammer and a handful of stone spearheads, then stepped out of my tent to see a humanoid bending over one of my vassals, ripping into his neck with its teeth.

It looked up when I stepped out of my tent, revealing its luminescent, milky white eyes.

I hit the zombie over the head with my warhammer, pounding its skull into the dirt. Eleven more stumbled into camp, and I launched the stone spears at them. They took them all through the face and collapsed. I waited, but no more undead appeared.

> **Blood and Souls (Repeatable): Kill 20 monsters or humanoids. Current progress: 16/20. When you complete this quest, you will gain 4 rank points. The next quest will require double the number to be completed but will award double the rank points.**

The notification appeared, and I waved it away. Looking at the now extra-dead undead, I realized they were some of the bandits I had killed yesterday. I looked around for the others I had killed, but nothing happened; these were the ones that didn't have their skulls caved in. I wondered if I could use this to farm my Blood and Souls quest. I could kill creatures, making sure to leave the skull intact, then wait for them to return as undead... then kill them again!

A groan sounded behind me, and the man on whom the zombie had been feeding began pushing himself to his feet. I smashed his skull in and looked around.

> **Blood and Souls (Repeatable): Kill 20 monsters or humanoids. Current progress: 17/20. When you complete this quest, you will gain 4 rank points. The next quest will require double the number to be completed but will award double the rank points.**

I turned to the four vassals looking at the pile of corpses, their eyes wide with fear.

"One of you must always be on watch while we sleep. Wake me up if anything else comes by. Oh, and do get rid of these corpses. I can't stand to look at them."

I went back to bed, not feeling too bad about not participating in taking watch. After all, I was the one who would do all the killing, so I needed to be at my best.

***

I woke up when sunlight began poking at my eyes. I groaned and wandered into the forest to take care of my business, splashing water on my face from the creek and filling my canteen. I returned to the camp and saw the four remaining survivors; they looked thin, weak, and scared. Pulling out the sketchbook from my backpack, I sat down, looking them over and surveying them. My Dominion ability had been activated, and I could analyze them, writing down the essential details.

Maria Cartwright (Vassal). Status: Pregnant.	
Mind:	7
Might:	8
Speed:	10
Toughness:	10
Endurance:	11
Perception:	12
Spirit:	8
Abilities:	n/a

She had a higher Perception than me but nothing special in her other Attributes. She was pregnant, but that was an issue for another day.

I looked at the other woman and analyzed her.

Carla Baker (Vassal). Status: Pregnant.	
Mind:	8
Might:	7
Speed:	11

Toughness:	9
Endurance:	10
Perception:	10
Spirit:	9
Abilities:	n/a

Again, nothing special.

The biggest man in the group had a bushy, black beard. I unconsciously rubbed my chin and the stubble there, realizing I didn't have a razor. I examined the man.

Fentren Smith (Vassal).	
Mind:	8
Might:	14
Speed:	10
Toughness:	12
Endurance:	12
Perception:	8
Spirit:	9
Abilities:	n/a

Better stats overall; excellent Might, and better Toughness and Endurance than I had. He could be a decent fighter if given better equipment.

I examined the last man.

He was built like a fencepole, but there was some strength in his lanky arms.

I got tired of writing down their powerless stats. These were just people who had been useless against me, and I had shown up to this world a few hours before and hadn't been wearing any armor. Maybe they would have other uses.

"What are your abilities?" I asked them.

"We don't have any abilities, my lord," Carla answered.

"Ok, let me rephrase that," I said. "What skills do you have, you know, professionally. Can you cook, sew, hunt… those kinds of things?"

"I can hunt," said Jand. "I was caught poaching deer. I can gut, clean, dress my kills and work with hide."

"I can cook, clean, and sew," Carla said. "I used to work for a nobleman's wife. She accused me of stealing her jewelry and had me thrown in prison."

I wrote down her skills, but didn't care why she'd become an outlaw.

"I worked in a tavern," Maria said. She chose not to reveal why she had been arrested.

"I was a smith," said Fentren Smith. "A horse I shod threw its rider and broke their neck, and I ended up taking the blame for it."

I wrote down their skills, then, collected their spears and used my ability to fuse some stone spearheads, making lighter versions for them. These, I attached to the wooden shafts by letting the stone flow up and then tighten around it. "Your tasks today are these," I said. "Jand, I want you to take someone with you and hunt and bring back food. Carla, you're on cooking. Maria, forage for berries and other stuff we can eat. Fentren, you take someone, stand guard, and work on getting rid of the bodies. Take them farther into the forest or something. I'm going to explore the crypt more. If you get attacked, hide in there."

I left them to their tasks, gearing up with my two rusty daggers, warhammer and maul. I emptied my backpack of clothes and left behind my skillet and coffee pot, then ventured into the forest, found some stout sticks, took clothes from the dead bodies, and made torches out of them. Lighting the fabric took some effort, but eventually, I had a usable torch.

Descending into the crypt, it was not necessary to go that far down the tunnel before I came to a stone door. I pushed at it, expecting it to be impassible like the last time, but this one slowly shifted and opened, allowing me to look out over a large burial chamber.

There was no light except for that from my torch.

A gaunt figure stepped into the torchlight. I was looking at the undead, its eyes a luminescent, milky white, but its movements were faster, and it seemed more intelligent than the unthinking undead from last night.

I readied my warhammer, holding the maul with my Telekinesis.

The ghoul charged me, and a dozen more emerged out of the darkness.

My swing with the maul was a sweeping blow instantly whisking three ghouls off their feet, their bones snapping with the force of the impact.

After this, I retreated slowly while my body blurred, ducking and dodging with my warhammer, lashing out to snap bones and crush a skull here and there; the maul was swinging like a power hammer, crushing ghouls into piles of bones and paste.

Only blows to the head were final; anything less and they returned to their feet.

The wounds did affect them. They were slower with crushed ribs and often, they only had one usable arm after I'd snapped some bones.

My speed kept me alive.

The ghouls were way more threatening than the bandits, their mindless aggression somehow a more effective tactic than careful coordination.

It was probably because they didn't care whether they died or were injured.

I was at the door when finally, the last remaining ghoul was dead. I panted with exertion even though I hadn't activated my boots. My heart, racing with effort, skipped several beats.

Quest updated. Blood and Souls: 4 rank points added.

Blood and Souls (Repeatable): Kill 40 monsters or humanoids. Current progress: 7/40. When you complete this quest, you will gain 8 rank points. The next quest will require double the number to be completed but will award double the rank points.

I now had two rank points to use, considering saving them but decided against it.

The fights were brutal, and I should ensure I could survive the present before worrying about the future.

"Increase Telekinesis by one rank," I said with five available rank points to use.

Telekinesis (Rank 3): You can, at will, lift 3 objects or creatures weighing 90 pounds or less and move them within 190 feet of your body; or up to 12 objects or creatures weighing 25 pounds or less and move them within 90 feet of your body. The speed and power of objects are based on your Spirit Attribute.

Cost: 1 Mana per 10 small objects/sec; or 1 Mana per large object/sec.

> **Upgrade this ability to increase the number of items, their weight, and the range at which you can move them.**
> **Every upgrade of this ability increases your Spirit Attribute by 1.**

I could raise my other abilities, but would need two more rank points before it could be Telekinesis again. There came a stirring from deeper in the cavern and I steadied my breathing. It might be possible, soon enough, to earn sufficient points to upgrade my skills.

I threw my torch forward and watched three dozen ghouls emerge from side passages in what I now realized were catacombs. No way could I fight them all on my own, but I refused to run. So, I raised my left hand, focusing on ten of the ghouls.

"Dominion," I said.

Quest updated. Whip and Chains: 2 rank points added.

Ten of the ghouls stopped their charge and stiffened.

I felt them try to resist the ability, but my Spirit crushed down on them.

The other ghouls, oblivious to my actions, rushed past the ten over which I'd taken control.

Readying myself for the fight, I was rolling my shoulders and adjusting the grip on my weapons before leaping over a stone sarcophagus, placing it between us, then smashing down with my warhammer into the skull of the ghoul on my heels.

The ten taken over rushed in, setting upon the others from behind.

They turned, surprised.

I took advantage of their shock, stepping into their midst, cracking and caving in skulls, my arm aching as I refused to let it rest.

Quest updated. Blood and Souls: 8 rank points added.

I kept fighting, even as the notification appeared.

More ghouls appeared. They saw the ones controlled by me fighting the others, but without being able to tell who was on whose side, they just sat on each other and at the height of their fecklessness, even tried to sit on me! The lack of the ghouls' ability to communicate with each other imbued the battle with an element of chaos.

I smashed in skulls, but one ghoul bit down on my leg, the thickness of my boot preventing its evil gnashing teeth from penetrating my skin. This encounter, however, delayed me sufficiently to enable another to approach and latch onto my arm.

Alongside the strikes from my warhammer, my stone spearheads were sent on their lethal mission. With pinpoint accuracy, they pierced through rotten flesh and bone.

Finally, the battle ended. All the ghouls on which I had used Dominion had died in the fight. I would only be able to use that particular ability on another five creatures today.

> **Whip and Chains (Repeatable): Conquer 20 monsters or humanoids by bringing them under your Dominion. Current progress: 2/20. When you complete this quest, you will gain 4 rank points. The next quest will require double the number to be completed but will award double the rank points.**

I dismissed the quest notification, and my other quest update notification appeared.

> **Blood and Souls (Repeatable): Kill 80 monsters or humanoids. Current progress: 13/80. When you complete this quest, you will gain 16 rank points. The next quest will require double the number to be completed but will award double the rank points.**

I panted and moved back up the tunnel, then sat down.

By now, my nose had become insensitive to the smell of gore and rot. I had twelve rank points to spend, and needed to upgrade my abilities if I wanted to live. I could upgrade Telekinesis twice, but it would cost me nine of my twelve rank points.

"Screw it," I grunted. "Raise Telekinesis by two ranks," I told the System.

There was a burning sensation all around as my ability increased alongside my Spirit Attribute.

> **Telekinesis (Rank 4):** You can, at will, lift 4 objects or creatures weighing 150 pounds or less and move them within 110 feet of your body; or up to 24 objects or creatures weighing 40 pounds or less and move them within 100 feet of your body. The speed and power of objects are based on your Spirit Attribute.
>
> **Cost:** 1 Mana per 10 small objects/sec; or 1 Mana per large object/sec.
>
> **Upgrade** this ability to increase the number of items, their weight, and the range at which you can move them. Every upgrade of this ability increases your Spirit Attribute by 1.

I felt time almost pause as a new notification appeared in my vision.

> **Congratulations! You have raised an ability to Rank 5. Please pick an additional effect for your ability from the list below:**
>
> - **You can now crush an enemy with your ability. You deal a moderate amount of damage each second to a creature suspended by your Telekinesis. The damage is increased slightly for every point in Spirit you have above 10.**
>
> - **You can now suspend 3 objects, weighing 230 pounds or less, to levitate motionless in midair for no Mana cost.**
>
> - **You can levitate yourself slowly at a rate of 5 feet per second. You cannot levitate any other objects during this time.**

Despite an ominously developing headache, I felt excited as I looked over the options. I got the sense that I needed to choose quickly. Only one of them did any damage, the others being utility effects. The ability to levitate myself seemed cool. Still, it was slow, and I couldn't levitate any other objects while doing it. The no-Mana cost for suspending objects midair seemed like something I would take if trying to be a human crane.

In the end, there wasn't any real choice, so I went with the first option.

> **Telekinesis (Rank 5):** You can, at will, lift 5 objects or creatures weighing 230 pounds or less and move them within 130 feet of your

> body; or up to 48 objects or creatures weighing 60 pounds or less and move them within 130 feet of your body. The speed and power of objects are based on your Spirit Attribute.

> You can now crush an enemy with your ability. You deal a moderate amount of damage each second to a creature suspended by your Telekinesis. The damage is increased slightly for every point in Spirit you have above 10.

> Cost: 1 Mana per 10 small objects/sec; or 1 Mana per large object/sec.

> Upgrade this ability to increase the number of items, their weight, and the range at which you can move them. Every upgrade of this ability increases your Spirit Attribute by 1.

Force choke unlocked. Nice.

I marveled at the number of objects I was now able to levitate at once. It should be quite a sight to see! I imagined slinging around 48-stone spears, beginning to search the coffins. I came upon a rusty axe, a sword, a small pile of gold and silver jewelry, and another rust-free gauntlet. I picked it up, reading its description as a notification popped into my vision.

> Gauntlet of the Soldier (left hand). Type: Armor. Rarity: Uncommon. Increases damage with one-handed weapons by a minor amount. When paired with another gauntlet of the same type on the opposite hand, it will increase damage with two-handed weapons by a moderate amount. Durability: 8-10.

> Made from common steel and empowered by a novice enchanter.

I put the gauntlet on and continued searching, exploring the passages of the catacombs, looking through the alcoves and finding a few odds and ends but nothing of note, just some jewelry, and a few coins. Descending another set of stairs, there was another stone door. I pushed against it and it opened to reveal a cavern.

This cave was not pitch black like the catacombs.

There was an opening at least a hundred feet up in the ceiling where sunlight streamed through, giving the cavern some light.

The air was wet with humidity and smelled of earth and fungus, and water could be heard cascading from a hole in the ceiling. The cave in the crypt had created a deep pond at its back while open coffins lined the walls of the alcoves.

I got close to the pond and looked inside.

Here, the water reflected the light, and I could see nothing inside.

Stepping back, I commenced tapping the surface of the water with a rock. A creature exploded out of the water, a ragged corpse with long hair floating about it.

The creature levitated, its hellish, unholy wail making my blood run cold. There came the desire to flee, but I stood my ground, launching a shower of stone darts toward it.

Now, the creature raised its arms. A bubble appeared around it, and all the darts bounced off. It moved toward me, staying in the shadows as it moved slowly through the air.

I focused my attention on it, and a notification appeared before me.

> **Melera Wanderlust. Gifted—Undead/Ethereal. Rank: 6.**

My hammer rose and fell as I attacked again and again.

Finally, the bubble popped, and the stone darts pierced into her. The wounds closed as soon as they were made.

> **This creature can only be harmed by light-based attacks or magical weapons.**

My face twisted into a grimace; should I have picked a weapon as my artifact? I had one other ability that might work on her. "Dominion," I said, feeling the undead resist. It bucked against my will like a wild horse, but eventually, the brands appeared around its neck, and it began to tremble as it succumbed.

> **Quest updated. Whip and Chains (Repeatable): Conquer 10 monsters or humanoids by bringing them under your Dominion. Current progress: 1/10.**
>
> **Every time you complete this quest, you will gain 1 rank point. The next quest will require double the number to be completed.**

I could feel the wraith trying to break free and was becoming increasingly concerned that it might succeed in doing so. With some indignation, I remembered my ability and that it could be opposed with a strong Spirit. "Move into the light," I commanded.

The wraith tried to resist, the brand around its neck glowing brighter and brighter. Eventually, it began to move forward, its form twisting and smoking as the light touched it. It withered and finally popped, becoming a shower of dust falling to the ground.

---

3 rank points gained.

Blood and Souls (Repeatable): Kill 80 monsters or humanoids. Current progress: 14/80. When you complete this quest, you will gain 16 rank points. The next quest will require double the number to be completed but will award double the rank points.

I dismissed the notification and another popped up.

You have completed a hidden objective and earned a title. Objective: force an undead to leave the mortal realm.

Reward. Title: Exorcist.

*Exorcist: Your damage dealt against undead has increased by 1 stage, and your damage against ethereal undead has increased by 2 stages.

I moved forward cautiously to the edge of the pool using my Telekinesis, feeling around in the water, seeking to grab any object touched by my power of levitation; I began lifting everything out, finding bones, rocks, and a few fish, which flopped to the ground.

Eventually, I pulled out a dark, round, steel shield.

"Finally, some boss loot!" I said, picking up the shield.

Shield of the Vengeful: Whenever struck with a melee attack on your shield, a moderate amount of the damage taken is reflected through the weapon to the arm of the attacker. Durability: 13/15.

Made from a shadow-steel alloy and enchanted by a journeyman enchanter.

I slipped on the shield, the leather straps still in good condition despite having soaked in water. I searched the pond further but only found a skull engraved with runes, a gem set into its forehead.

Gravecaller (Cursed Item): Any intact corpses within 3 miles that are unblessed by a priest will rise as undead at midnight. They will remain animated until 2 hours before daybreak. They are drawn to the location of the skull but will return to their resting place before dawn and de-animate if not destroyed and they do not find the skull. If they find the skull, they will advance to a higher level of undead.

Forged from the skull of a Gifted with Necromancer abilities, the enchanter of this item is unknown, but their power has tapped into the lost abilities of the owner of this skull.

Ah, right! That explains the undead from last night,

After examining the skull in my hands, I then put it in my backpack, thinking that possibly, I might be able to use it to farm for XP or against my enemies somehow. I left the crypt, carrying the fish pulled out of the pond and the other items I had acquired.

The decrepit axe I gave to Fentren so he could cut wood, keeping the rusty sword myself. Jand had caught a few rabbits, and Carla made them into a stew with some wild onions that Maria had found. She took the fish and gutted them, beginning to fry them in the pan.

I took the time while we waited for dinner to cook to make more stone spearheads. Looking at Quin's maul, I saw the wooden head had split and warped after its repeated use.

The iron bands had burst open at some point too, the head barely holding on. I removed the wooden head and looked at the steel rod pole, finding it hollow but strong.

Then I gathered some rocks and began to work.

"Compress Earth," I said and began to mold the stone around the top of the shaft, creating a new head for the maul, focusing and smoothing out the rock until a new glossy black maul head had been made. One side was flat, the other tapered to a sharp point for cracking armor.

I threw the Maul, which obliterated a small tree.

The head of the weapon hit the tree at its base and splintered it, and all that remained was a stump as the tree groaned and collapsed, the sound of its disintegrating branches snapping like firecrackers. I called the maul back. It slapped into my hand as I held it aloft.

Of course, I wasn't holding it. My hand was just wrapped around while my Telekinesis held it, suspended. The maul now weighed about a hundred pounds.

I let it fall to the ground and decided to look over my stats.

Mordred, Champion of Kelesa. Gifted—Humanoid/Human. Mortal. Rank: 50.			
Available rank points: 6.			
Might:	12	Mind:	9
Speed:	12 (+2) =14	Perception:	8
Toughness:	11	Spirit:	18
Endurance:	10	Power:	10
Maximum Stamina:	56	Maximum Mana:	64
Stamina Regen:	11.2 per second	Mana Regen:	12.6 per second
Abilities:			
Dominion (Rank 1), Telekinesis (Rank 5), Heightened Speed (Rank 1), Foresight (Rank 1), Compress Earth (Rank 1).			
Blessings:			
Blessing of War (Mortal).			
Titles:			
Mark of Cain, Bloody Pugilist, Exorcist			

I had rolled my shoulder with the loot taken from the crypt and was now holding my arm, wincing. The adrenalin and excitement had faded and the pain from the wound was now at the forefront of my mind.

I looked down at my arm, seeing black veins from the jagged teeth marks on my forearm.

"That can't be good," I said.

Hurrying out of the crypt, I went to the river to clean the blood and rotten flesh off me.

I washed my wound, being sure to remove all the filth, not wanting to be taken down by any infection. The wound was clean, and I wrapped it in a torn shirt from my bag but the black veins still extended from the teeth marks.

And as I looked at the veins, a notification appeared in my vision.

You have been infected with Ghoul Rot. Purify your body to remove the infection.
Ghoul Rot: Spreads through the entire body before causing the flesh to rot and turning the infected into an undead. Time until full infection: 7 days.

"Great... a zombie infection!" I grunted.

How to purify me?

There'd be a priest who could do it, but I doubted I had time to find one. I had seven days left to find a way, so I asked my local guides, returning to camp and locating Jand.

"I need a way to purify myself. What do you know about it?" I asked.

"A priest can easily perform a purification ritual," Jand said. "Or you could make a potion with herbs."

"Ok, that last option sounds better," I said. "What kind of herbs?"

"I don't know," admitted Jand. "But you have access to the System. You can analyze plants and find ones that can help you."

"Thanks," I said and looked over his shoulder, seeing the two rabbits hanging from a cord over his back. "Do you need anything?"

"A proper bow would be helpful, my lord," Jand said. "But I've set some snares in the area for catching small game."

"When you're done, take some of the others and clean out the bodies in the crypt," I advised. "Make sure not to get infected. We'll sleep there tonight; it will be easier to defend."

I returned to the woods, scanning every plant I came across.

Nothing popped up, which I had learned by now meant the item was mundane. Only equipment or magical things had ever shown a display when I analyzed them. I kept moving, carefully taking note of landmarks as I searched for anything that might help me.

I began looking for some herbs and plants, eyeing a red-leafed plant that grew like clover, and the System opened a prompt for me.

> **Red Yarrow. Type: Medicinal. Rarity: Uncommon. Yarrow that has grown powerful on ambient Mana is given potent healing properties. Eating this will cause damaged flesh and muscle to knit together and regrow rapidly. When mixed with water, it will also help to rapidly replenish blood loss.**

A healing potion plant!

I began picking it, using a T-shirt and piling the yarrow on it. Once I'd gathered sufficient leaves, I folded the shirt and shoved it back inside my backpack. I kept moving, scanning for new plants before coming across a patch of dark green fennels with bright orange and red around the edges of their leaves.

> **Cauter Fennel. Type: Medicinal. Rarity: Uncommon. Fennel that has gorged on fire essence and been planted in iron-rich soil. When dried and exposed to iron or blood, the leaves will instantly flash-burn. This is done to spread their seeds. These leaves are used in medicine for cauterized wounds.**

I gathered the fennel, taking only the leaves and leaving their roots behind so they could regrow. I stored them in another T-shirt which I folded and returned to my backpack. I'd have to find better containers for them later or have my vassals make something.

Keeping on moving, I soon passed a river that fed into a small lake, then followed a stream that issued from the lake and flowed down a cliff into a grotto. I looked down and saw a patch of pale-blue, semi-translucent petaled flowers, analyzing them from my vantage point, and the System opened up a notification.

> **Purity Lilies. Type: Medicinal. Rarity: Rare.**
> **Lilies that are used for removing corruption in their environment or brewed into a tea to clear adverse effects and purify the body. Extremely rare, they only grow in areas with massive amounts of Mana.**

I started to look for a way down, then saw movement in the grotto below. Crouching, I looked like a lion with red fur and black stripes.

As if on cue, an actual lion then emerged through a curtain of vines from a cave. As soon as I saw it, a notification appeared in my sight.

Adolescent Nemean lion. Gifted—Mage Beast/Nemean Lion. Mortal. Rank: 12.

That's adolescent? I thought in stunned amazement. *It's the size of a freaking horse.*

I kept still, watching as the lion drank from the stream and disappeared into the cave beyond the curtain of vines.

Nemean lion, I thought. *If it's like the Nemean lion from earth mythology, then it's basically immune to physical attacks. Hercules strangled it to death, but I've no chance of that.* I kept thinking. Strangling was just a way to suffocate something, but there was more than one way to do that: drowning… smoke inhalation… buried alive…

Neither could I fight it. I could try to sneak down and grab the flowers.

I looked at the cliff walls of the grotto. There was no way to climb those quickly. I'd be dead if the lion came out when I was down there. It was a little lower than my current range for teleportation, too, so that was also a no-go.

Moving back, I kept exploring, mulling the problem over in my mind. For now, I would keep looking for another solution to reverse my infection. I moved around the grotto, searching for another entrance that the lion might use. The grotto's walls were around fifty feet high, so I doubted it had left that way. I kept exploring and found it around a hundred yards from the grotto. There was a shorter cliff and a jagged, open cave mouth. The bones and remains of its prey were scattered around the area. I circled to get a view inside the cave.

It extended for at least fifty feet, appearing to open out past the entrance, but I couldn't see much in the darkness. I explored the top, finding lots of boulders and a circle of stones around a large flat rock in the center, like a crude version of Stonehenge. I found some mushrooms, and the System gave me another notification.

> **Black Rot Mushrooms. Type: Poison. Rarity: Rare. Grows only in places where blood or necromancy magic has seeped into the soil. These mushrooms are lethal to ingest, causing the intestines to swell and eventually burst, spreading a noxious rot throughout the body. Complete body failure results and the rot seeps out, further propagating the mushrooms.**

The mushrooms had a foul smell, and I was careful not to touch them as I harvested them.

I didn't use a shirt this time, instead using Compress Earth to create a jar.

It occurred to me unhelpfully that I could have done this before for my other herbs, still getting used to having my powers.

After this, I fashioned a lid, sealed the mushrooms inside, and stored them in my backpack.

I could poison the lion but the only problem would be the smell of the mushrooms—absolutely foul. I needed to find a way to somehow disguise the reek or keep the beast from smelling them so that he ate them.

That way, I might be able to kill it without a seriously dangerous fight.

I kept searching until I spotted a creature that made me smile, a plan starting to formulate in my mind. A skunk was nibbling at a blackberry bush.

I used Telekinesis and grabbed the creature.

"Dominion," I said and felt the creature's will instantly dominated by mine. I waited, but no prompt for my quest appeared.

Apparently, it did not consider animals worthy of progress in my quest.

Carrying the skunk, I brought it back to the crypt. Now, the plan was really beginning to take. I remained quiet and acutely vigilant, soon spotting a small herd of deer.

Using my stone spearheads, I brought down two of them, a buck and a doe. I set the skunk on my shoulder and levitated the two deer beside me.

When I arrived back in the camp, my vassals had set up a fire in the roof. They had cleared out the rubble, creating a barricade, and pitched a few tents around a fireplace. The smoke rose to the ceiling, blackening it with soot.

I set the deer aside, giving the doe to my vassals to prepare while I let the other lie undisturbed. Compress Earth proved useful indeed, and with it, I made a set of a dozen bowls, plates, spoons, and two-pronged forks. The stone dishes and utensils were stacked by the fire. I created a large serving bowl and poured out the hot soup from my coffee pot. Taking it to the river, I washed it out thoroughly and filled it with water.

I used Compress Earth a lot and decided to upgrade it, having enough rank points to get it to Rank Two.

"Raise Compress Earth to Rank Two," I told the System.

Compress Earth (Rank 2): You can fuse dirt and stone into a more durable, heavier material that can be shaped. You can currently fuse a 2-foot-square section of earth and common stone. Your compressed stone has a Hardness rating of 4.5; your compressed earth has a Hardness rating of 2.5. The detail with which you can sculpt is based on your Mind & Perception Attributes.

Cost: 1 Mana per 1-foot square.

Upgrade this ability to increase the amount you can compress, its durability, weight, and the materials upon which you can use this ability.

Each upgrade increases your Mind Attribute by 1.

I felt a slight headache as my skill increased, and my Mind Attribute went from nine to ten, making me glad of the elevation. Based on games I had played in the past, ten was average.

Having a below-average mind was not favorable; I guessed it was equivalent to intelligence. I didn't feel smarter, but maybe my thoughts were coming to me faster? I would need to increase my Perception at some point since that was my lowest Attribute, but I'd worry about that later when I had the points to spend.

I used compress Earth and created two dozen bottles the size of my fist, fitting them with stone corks and then heating the water in my coffee pot. When it was boiling, I added the red yarrow which quickly dissolved in the water, turning it a deep, thick crimson. I let it boil, then cool and poured out the thin, syrupy mixture into the different bottles.

With my supply of health potions seen to, I began to work on my master plan. The skunk had been resting in my tent, gnawing on some meat I'd given it.

Taking the skunk, I took another bottle, held it up to the animal's ass, and pressed. The skunk released its pungent odor, some of which emanated into the air but was mostly contained by the bottle. Sealing it up, I set the skunk down. The subscription-sized pill bottle was full. I placed it with my other potions and took a bowl of rabbit stew, seasoned with wild garlic. The food was surprisingly good considering our limited available resources.

"We will be attacked again by undead around midnight," I told my vassals, watching as they paled. "One or two of you keep watch and wake me when you see them."

I went to bed early, letting the skunk wander around our camp. It acted like a cat and curled up on my pile of clothes, its belly round from the meat on which it had gorged itself.

The nagging itch and pain in my forearm made it challenging to fall asleep immediately, but I did so after a couple of minutes.

Chapter 4: Survivor

Jamis, Torvin, and Mira sparred on the training ground of the castle.

Princess Helen was another champion who had joined them along with her bodyguard, Felrick, another champion chosen by Kilpso, Goddess of Protection and Safety.

Helen was the champion of Luren, Goddess of the Moon & Healing.

Wooden and copper training golems rushed them as they fought together, learning to work as a team.

"You are Champions of Order," Drill Sergeant Heldark barked at them. "Your strength is your allies. With them, you can face any of the Champions of Chaos who believe they are stronger on their own and are too selfish to work with others. This makes them weak!"

Jamis stepped in front of the wooden golem, protecting Mira as she fired arrows from her bow, each taking down a target.

Felrick carried a huge tower shield and stoically held off a dozen golems as they attempted to batter him.

Helen ensured she kept Felrick and the other melee fighters on their feet, letting out her occasional lance of silver light to obliterate a golem.

"You may be tempted to rush into the Cursed Forest but being dropped into that hell hole and just picking a fight with every Gifted beast and creature you come across will get you killed," Heldark barked at them. "I've been told if you impress me today, you'll be given a quest to go after some real prey. So, work together and show me what you got!"

They kept fighting as more and more golems surrounded them.

Eventually, the battle was done, and Heldark nodded approvingly. "Good. You're ready to start hunting. Tomorrow, I want you to head to the nearby mountains. A bear wandered out of the Cursed Forest and murdered a hunter's family. It's laired up in the mountains. Take some horses to the foot of the mountain. Find and kill the beast."

The five champions nodded. Sweaty and tired, they headed for the baths. Afterwards they would explore the city, their work done for the day.

***

Helen and Mira stepped into the bath, each wearing a bracelet that covered their body in mist, preserving their modesty. These baths were for the Gifted and weren't separated by gender, the bracelets being handed out to both sexes to allow everyone to use the baths in comfort. Mira still looked uncomfortable, blushing slightly as she stepped into the steaming water, her wings unconsciously wrapping around her.

Jamis lounged against the other side of the massive bath, the water piping hot but not enough to burn. It was designed to help passively raise a person's natural toughness over time. "I like these baths," Jamis said. "We didn't have anything like this in my clan."

"What kind of world did you come from?" Torvin asked.

"My world has more technology than this," Jamis said. "But only the mech priests are allowed to use it. The machines turned against us long ago, so even though I grew up surrounded by the old machines, we were never allowed to use them."

"Is that why you came here?" Helen asked.

"Yes," Jamis said. "I didn't have much opportunity back home; I was the youngest of my household in a large clan. There was no space for me even with my skill in brawling. When Artrix offered me the chance to be his champion, there was little need to overthink it."

"The risk of being killed in battle didn't bother you?" Mira asked.

"Did it bother you?" Jamis asked with a shrug. "Why did you choose to become a champion?"

"I've always been a hunter," Mira said. "But it's not a role women are encouraged to take in my world. I was weaker than the other hunters in my aviary and there is no System in my world. I could therefore never become as strong as them. I want to become stronger so that I can be better at helping others. What about you three?"

Torvin ran a bronze scraper down his arm as he cleaned himself.

"I was a soldier. I'd been riding horses all my life. When the war started in my homeland, I was conscripted. In the last battle, I lost my legs when my horse died under me, and I was trampled. I suppose I was lucky to live, but there's no use for a cripple in my world. When Galdren offered to give me back my legs and for me to become more than just a common soldier... Well, like you've both said, it wasn't much of a choice."

"Still, I don't resent him for choosing me. He could have chosen anyone. He gave me a second chance," Torvin said. "And I think I can make a difference. As a champion, I can fight on the front lines, so others don't have to be conscripted or suffer like I did."

"I've been chosen to be a champion since birth," Helen said with a shrug. "My mothers have been serving Luren as priestess for generations. She was always going to choose one of us to represent her; I've been prepared for this all of my life."

"Do you resent not having a choice?" Mira asked.

Helen laughed. "Of course, I had a choice, but what fool would turn down becoming a champion? Unless they are some god of Chaos, we get the opportunity to become ambassadors of the gods to the people. Not only that, but there is also the ultimate chance of becoming gods ourselves."

"I suppose I'm similar to Torvin and Helen," Felrick said. "I've been a prodigy among the royal knights since I was a child, assigned to protect Helen as just a young boy. When Kilpso gave me a choice, I took it so I could better protect her and others. I don't think I'm going to win this game, but I want to fight to make sure the right one does."

***

I was shaken awake by one of my vassals. Sighing, I rolled out of bed and levitated a few dozen stone spearheads. They were each as hard as iron, nine inches long and sharpened to a needlepoint. I went to the entrance of the crypt where a small horde of skeletons and zombie animals approached us: raccoon, deer, wolves, and a bear.

Smaller creatures scuttled over the ground. I launched attack after attack, standing in the doorway, stomping down on the little undead who tried to chew through my boots.

The skeletal bear reached me.

It was missing some of its bones, but its frame was still massive.

Ducking under a swipe, I smashed down repeatedly with my warhammer until its skull finally broke. My foresight warned me of an attack, and I brought my shield to bear, breaking the charge of an undead stag. Its antlers skittered off and broke on impact with the metal of my highly effective shield. I stepped forward, shattered its skull, and continued fighting.

It took around ten minutes for me to kill everything. There were so many of the little undead animals although, usefully, they died with one strike.

> **Blood and Souls (Repeatable): Kill 80 monsters or humanoids.**
> **Current progress: 57/80. When you complete this quest, you will**
> **gain 16 rank points. The next quest will require double the number**
> **to be completed but will award double the rank points.**

Panting from the exertion of battle, I had spent nearly every point of Stamina and Mana I possessed, dismissing the notification after briefly checking the numbers. I wasn't sure if the tiny undead counted toward the total, and I'd lost count of how many I'd killed.

Surprisingly, my title for Bloody Pugilist had been helpful after all, in stomping down on the little freaks. The acquired increase in damage from Bloody Pugilist and Exorcist practically made them explode when I kicked them.

I went back to bed and fell asleep much faster, this time from exhaustion.

***

The next morning, voices could be heard. I rolled out of bed and my vassals gave me a bowl of venison stew in return for me grunting thanks, not being a morning person. Invigorated by the wholesome breakfast, I took my newly acquired bottles, then grabbed the entire body of the buck and prepared to kill the lion. I sat above its cave and patiently waited.

I had changed the shape of the bottle of skunk odor; it was now spherical and as thin as an eggshell. The skunk bomb was ready, and all I had to do was wait.

It took around four hours, but the Nemean lion finally wandered out of its den.

I stayed pressed flat to the ground and using my Telekinesis, hurled the skunk bomb. It jerked its head at the last minute but was too slow. The stone shell broke over its face, drenching it in fetid skunk odor. The lion went ballistic, tearing all over the clearing.

It bashed its head into trees and knocked over the smaller ones as it tried to paw the disgusting smell out of its face.

Meanwhile, I didn't move an inch. Any sound or movement now could get me killed.

So, I waited until the lion fled back into its cave and kept waiting. Finally, I levitated the buck's body to the ground near the cave's entrance. I had slit its belly open and packed it with the Black Rot mushrooms. Now that the Nemean lion couldn't smell them, I hoped it would eat the buck and poison itself. I tried to think of a back-up plan, but didn't have anything else that could kill it, briefly regretting not choosing Force Lightning as one of my abilities but quickly turning my attention back to the clearing, waiting.

I wasn't a patient person, able to feel the rot spreading through me, the black veins extending even further from the bite mark on my arm.

Even though I technically had six days left, I didn't think I'd be operational for that long. I needed to purify the rot from my body… quickly.

It was almost nightfall before the lion exited its lair and looked around warily.

I froze.

It sniffed and snorted irritably, batting at its nose. As it looked around, it spotted the body of the buck then circled the carrion four times before getting closer, sniffing and snorting. Finally, it bit down, dragging the buck's body back into its lair.

Sighing, I slowly got up, and left.

I would have to come back in the morning and look it over.

After washing the dirt off me in the river, I returned to the camp. I missed hot showers, but had to admit to having fun despite the infection that if uncured, would kill me in a few days. I took another bowl of venison stew with added wild corn.

We also had pastries made of bread leaf and filled with wild berries.

The leaf was surprisingly thick and tasted like bread in itself, making it seem like a chewy naan. I ate my fill, letting the skunk have my leftovers, and took myself off to bed.

Awake again at midnight, I sighed, rolling out of my sleeping bag.

This time, it wasn't even a dozen skeletons. I appeared to have already culled the majority of the possible undead in this area. All that remained to deal with were a single wolf, a few deer, and a couple of undead raccoons, also some weird animals I couldn't identify from their remains.

Blood and Souls (Repeatable): Kill 80 monsters or humanoids. Current progress: 77/80. When you complete this quest, you will gain 16 rank points. The next quest will require double the number to be completed but will award double the rank points.

Frustrated at not completing my quest tonight, I went back to bed, falling asleep almost instantly.

***

I woke before dawn the next day and tried to get back to sleep, but the pain in my arm wouldn't let me. I sighed again, getting up and preparing my gear, ensuring I had all my weapons and potions. I heated up a bit of stew, ate it, and headed out.

The sun rose as I hiked the four miles through the forest back to the Nemean lion's lair.

Cautiously, I approached the cave's entrance, straining to hear what was inside. As I crept slowly forward, I was listening intently for any clues to the outcome of my plan.

Entering the cave, I looked around, barely able to see in the darkness. There was a sliver of light and I moved forward, stopping when I saw the lion lying on its side.

I held my breath and watched, but its chest did not move.

I let out a sigh and kept moving, pushing aside the curtain of vines and entering the grotto. Taking out a jar, I gathered the petals from the lilies and shoved them into my backpack.

On turning around, I nearly had a heart attack.

The Nemean lion stood there shaking, a deep growl rumbling out of its chest. Its eyes were bloodshot and its body trembled. Its menacing growl was momentarily broken by a cough before it snarled and lunged for me. Rolling under it, I felt the claws from its hind legs raking across my back. I pushed through the pain and ran, activating my boots, then teleported to the mouth of the cave and kept running.

The lion was on my heels and let out a roar.

I stumbled and rolled, the roar knocking me off my feet, leaving my mind fuzzy and stunned. My thoughts cleared just in time to roll out of the way as the beast pounced down on me. Its claws were long and dug into my chest. A huge paw slashed across my face, nearly taking out my eye. It elicited a gasp from me, feeling the claws deeply piercing the flesh between my ribs. Then it jumped off me as a stone spearhead struck it in the side of the head, narrowly missing its eye.

Rolling to my feet, I pressed a hand to my chest to slow the bleeding. Blood ran down the left side of my face from the long gashes inflicted by the claws. My teleport came off cooldown, and I darted forward, narrowly dodging another pounce from the lion.

Next, I charged toward the lake, jumped in and started to swim. The speed bonus from my boots apparently also applied to swimming, and I was moving out across the lake, kicking with my feet as I reached for the potions in my backpack.

There was a splash and I risked a look behind to see the lion swimming toward me. It was sinking quickly but was able to keep its nose above water as it paddled toward me.

I kicked out faster, my hand finding one of my health potions.

In my wake, the water reddened, my head going fuzzy. I uncorked the potion and chugged it down, getting a mouthful of lake water in the process. I swallowed, but it made me cough and splutter for air. Soon, however, I felt the wounds in my chest closing. The bleeding slowed without stopping completely, but the fuzziness in my head subsided.

Something clamped onto my foot, making me turn to see the Nemean lion sinking underwater while firmly latched to my boot, determined to take me with him.

"Dominion," I tried, feeling my ability impact the lion, but it slid off, unable to take hold as it resisted me, its will refusing to be bent to mine.

I took a breath, then went under.

The lion thrashed.

My ankle twisted, but my boots were an artifact, and its teeth couldn't pierce them. I held my breath, feeling my lungs burning.

The light in the lion's eyes faded, its grip on my boot loosening as it finally drowned. Evidently, the poison had ultimately taken its toll.

---

6 rank points gained.

Blood and Souls (Repeatable): Kill 80 monsters or humanoids. Current progress: 78/80. When you complete this quest, you will gain 16 rank points. The next quest will require double the number to be completed but will award double the rank points.

I kicked upwards desperately, my vision going black. Almost at the surface, it was possible to hold my breath no longer, the inhaled water flooding my lungs. Somehow, I made it, coughing up what seemed like gallons of the lake. I was still bleeding too.

The wounds across my face and chest had still not closed. There was a blinking notification in the corner of my vision; I opened it up.

> **You have been affected by a Laceration ability that prevents wounds from closing and healing. Stop the bleeding before you die. Time until death is 2:30 minutes.**

It seemed I had just bought myself some time with which to fend off imminent death. Pushing aside the panic, I felt around in my backpack, managing to find what I was looking for. Opening one of the jars I had made, I took out the cauter fennel, packing it into the three wounds on my chest and biting back a scream as a burst of fire flared up, burning my flesh. The pain was intense, but the blood stopped pumping out. I packed the cauter fennel into the gashes across my face, unable to bite back screams as the healing fire flashed through me.

It scorched my fingers as even the blood there was enough to ignite the leaves.

I waited. Five minutes passed. I was still alive.

> **You have completed a hidden objective and earned a title. Objective: Survive a mortal blow that prevents healing.**
> **Reward. Title: Survivor.**
> ***Survivor: You are resistant to death itself. Mortal wounds are less effective on you and require higher damage stages to occur.**

Exhaling pure relief, I lay on the shore, panting, staying there for almost half an hour before standing up, wincing from the pain in my ankle.

Finally feeling strong enough, I swam down to the bottom of the lake and grabbed the lion's tail. I dragged it toward the shore but it took multiple trips, moving the lion bit by bit. Eventually, I was able to drag half of its body up onto the beach.

I tried to skin it, but my knife refused to even prick its skin. I took its paw and awkwardly used it on its other limb to open up the flesh. A claw came away as I yanked. Razor sharp, it ripped through the skin on my palm, making me howl profanity into the air.

Then, I drank another potion. Soon, my palm healed and my ankle felt slightly better, but I still felt some deep bone bruising.

> **Nemean Claw. Rarity: Rare. Hardness: 12. Taken from the body of a Nemean lion, this is the only thing besides an artifact capable of damaging its hide.**

I used the lion's claw to skin it, heaving it over as I pulled off its hide. When its coat was clear, a notification prompt popped into my vision. I opened it.

> **Nemean Lion Hide. Rarity: Epic. Hardness: 12. Taken from the hide of Nemean lion, this hide possesses the latent power of its former owner and is immune to any weapon not made from Nemean claws or an artifact.**

I washed the blood and flesh off the hide and collected the other claws from its corpse. I cut it open and pulled out its heart; it wasn't fleshy but was still hot and hard like a rock.

> **Iron Heart. Type: Material. Rarity: Rare. This is a trophy from a Gifted beast and has a wide variety of uses, from alchemy and smithing to absorption when gaining a new ability.**

I stored the heart in my backpack and went back to the corpse, cutting through its flesh quickly and removing its skull.

> **Nemean Skull. Type: Material. Rarity: Rare. Hardness: 8. The skull of a Nemean lion, like all the bones of the beast, is especially hard.**

I chopped the rest of the body into sections, thankfully able to levitate its whole body which weighed as much as a draft horse. I went back to its lair and lit a torch. There was nothing in there apart from a few cave paintings of men hunting a massive, scaled beast.

Leaving the cave, I returned to the lion's body to grab my stuff and donned my backpack, grabbing the bloody skull and slinging the hide around me.

It was still tacky and raw, but was the only armor I had except for gauntlets and boots. So, I returned to camp wearing the red-striped lion pelt.

My vassals looked at me and blanched, turning away quickly.

I dropped my stuff, went to the river, and saw my reflection in the water. Black scabs in three lines covered the left side of my face. They extended from my forehead over my eye, which had narrowly escaped being blinded, almost down to my chin. I felt the inside of my mouth where the claws had ripped through. The wounds had healed faster than usual but would definitely leave a scar, especially since I'd had to cauterize them.

I washed the blood off and returned to camp, spreading out the Nemean hide and making a flat scraper from stone. I pulled the brain from its skull and started to boil it in a stone pot with a small amount of water. Then, I scraped off every inch of flesh until only the pelt was left. I poured boiling water over the hide, scouring off the blood and everything but the hide itself. After that, I spread the brain mixture over the hide, not sure what I was doing, but I knew that the brain was somehow used for tanning and figured I should let it sit for a while.

My brush with death had been exhausting, but I tried to overcome my fatigue for now and looked for my vassals for more information.

"Where can I find other Gifted?" I asked.

My vassals looked at each other. "The lord of this land and his family have the Gift. They have powerful earth magic."

"Right. Quin killed one of them for his powers, didn't he?" I asked for confirmation of something I already knew.

They nodded.

"If you're thinking about trying to fight them, I'd advise against it," Jand said. "They're powerful and have lots of guards and other protections. Quin killed a cousin while he was sleeping in a tavern. It was a lucky opportunity, but you can't count on that luck again."

"And if you kill one, the rest of the family will come to hunt you down," Fentren added.

"Aren't there any Gifted who are easier targets? Or, at least ones without many allies to come to their defense?"

They were silent.

Then Maria spoke up. "There is the Bandit King," she said. "He's a Gifted with supernatural strength and durability."

"He also has many men under his command," warned Jand.

"That's more of a bonus than a disadvantage," I said. "How far away are they?"

"A week and a half through the Cursed Forest," Jand said.

"Is that the name for this forest?" I wanted to know.

Maria nodded.

But Jand shook his head. "I believe that it's officially called the Cursed Forest on the maps, but my great-grandmother referred to it as the Forest of the Ancients."

"Very well. Rest up. Tomorrow around midday, you will guide me to the Bandit King," I commanded.

I went to bed, leaving them to sort out the intricacies of the watch between themselves.

There were still some things I wanted to do before sleeping, so I lay back on my sleeping bag, the skunk snuffling and curling up beside me. I had to make a decision.

I could either raise Telekinesis by one rank or raise Compress Earth by two ranks. While in combat, I made much use of Telekinesis. The stone spearheads were, however, a big part of my damage output, so increasing their quality could help a lot. I also wanted to raise it to Rank 5 and see if all abilities got an additional effect at this rank.

My mind was made up. I made the decision.

"Raise Compress Earth by two ranks," I told the System.

Compress Earth (Rank 3): You can fuse dirt and stone into a more durable, heavier material that can be shaped. You can currently fuse a 4-foot-square section of earth and common stone. Your compressed stone has a Hardness rating of 5; your compressed earth has a Hardness rating of 3. The detail with which you can sculpt is based on your Mind & Perception Attribute.
Cost: 1 Mana per 1-foot square.
Upgrade this ability to increase the amount you can compress, its durability, weight, and the materials upon which you can use this ability. Each upgrade increases your Mind Attribute by 1.

A throbbing headache pierced my skull.

Compress Earth (Rank 4): You can fuse dirt and stone into a more durable, heavier material that can be shaped. You can currently fuse an 8-foot-square section of earth and common stone. Your compressed stone has a Hardness rating of 5.5; your compressed earth has a Hardness rating of 3.5. The detail with which you can sculpt is based on your Mind & Perception Attribute.
Cost: 1 Mana per 1-foot square.
Upgrade this ability to increase the amount you can compress, its durability, weight, and the materials upon which you can use this ability.   **Each upgrade increases your Mind Attribute by 1.**

My headache turned into a migraine. It was as if a gnome had started jackhammering away at the inside of my skull. I groaned and clenched my teeth, the pain terrible, but nothing compared to the claws which had pierced my lungs.

Thankfully, the pain was as brief as it was intense. My work done for the day, I sighed and closed my eyes. Lying back on my sleeping bag, I fell asleep instantly.

Chapter 5: Feral Barbarian

Mira crouched down in the snow and studied the tracks she had managed to find.

"It's a day old," she said. "It leads further up the mountain. It's likely gone to lair for a few days to digest its meal."

Jamis looked west over the mountain to where the edges of the Cursed Forest began. "What do you think is in there?" he asked.

"It's filled with bandits, monsters, and barbaric tribes," Helen answered, looking down at the forest with derision. "They live there because they aren't welcome anywhere else and would rather live as animals than embrace civilization."

"Barbaric tribes?" Jamis asked, raising an eyebrow.

"She means the myrmidons, not people like your old clan," Felrick said. "They are the people of Kelesa, Goddess of War and Conquest. And obviously, they worship her, which tells you pretty much all you need to know about them."

"Maybe it tells you! You forget we're not from this world," Torvin said.

Felrick sighed. "It means they are savages in the truest sense of the word. Not all of them, of course. Some of their tribes have become civilized. The clans that hold to their old ways live in the wilderness, constantly at war with each other and frequently raiding towns and villages bordering the forest. They steal women, Gifted children, goods and cattle."

"They sound like trouble. Why hasn't your kingdom dealt with them?" Torvin asked. "I'm sure a few royal knights could rout them."

"They are all Gifted," Helen said bitterly. "Only those with the Gift are allowed to reproduce in their society. They breed their warriors and train them to feed off the beasts of the woods. While the royal knights are stronger than all except maybe their chieftains, they simply have more Gifted than we do."

"It's best to let them fight amongst themselves," offered Felrick. "The forest is land contested between the Kingdom of Dracon and Camelot anyway, so us making a move could be seen as a land grab which could start a war."

"Maybe with Dracon," Helen argued. "I'm related to Prince Arthur. We'd find a diplomatic way to resolve the issue."

"That sort of issue only gets resolved through a marital alliance, and he's already getting married," Felrick said. "I've only met Guinevere a few times, but she isn't the sort to allow her husband to take multiple wives or mistresses."

"We should get moving before the wind gets rid of any more tracks," Mira said, interrupting the conversation. "We've already camped on this freezing mountain once, and I certainly don't want to do it again."

She led the party up-mountain, following the tracks before the icy wind could blow them away. Her wings flapped now and then, throwing off the snow that clung to them and keeping them from freezing.

***

This time, no one woke me up in the night. I'd removed all potential undead in the area.

This earned me a full night's rest but also meant I didn't progress my quest. It was still early, and I took out my journal and sketchbook, removing my shield and the cursed skull and beginning to draw them in my sketchbook.

I had always liked drawing, and was careful to copy the runes exactly.

Whatever they meant, I was sure they were crucial for the enchantments, and I wanted to learn how to make them.

As I held up the skull and finished copying its runes, a notification popped up.

Quest gained. Death's Curse: You have encountered a powerful, cursed item that causes the dead all around it to rise. The System has awarded you a quest to deal with this curse. Find a way to remove the curse, destroy the item, or seal it away where it will no longer be a threat. Reward: Knowledge of the Old Magic.

This was new, the first time I had attained a new quest. This one said it was from the System and not a god, unlike the ones I got from Kelesa. The reward was interesting but raised some questions, such as what was the Old Magic, exactly?

The quest had offered itself to me while I was examining the runes, so I had to guess that they were somehow linked. Or were they? This was merely blind supposition.

I stowed away my sketchbook and went over to where I had set the Nemean hide to cure. There, I wiped off the remaining brain matter mix that hadn't dried and hung the hide over the fire like a tepee before cutting down some extra pine boughs for smoke, putting them on the fire. I knew that smoke and brain matter were somehow linked to tanning, but the specifics eluded me. Again, I felt as if I was making up so much of this as I went along.

I took the bones of the Nemean lion, having had Jand and the others take all the meat off the night before. They'd been drying the skeleton which had left me with a nice shiny stack of clean bones to choose from. I grabbed a leg bone, a little over three feet in length.

Taking the claws of the Nemean lion, I gathered some loose rock and set to work, using Compress Earth as the binder and fixing the claws out along the bone, so they created a spiked club. I picked it up and tested its weight.

It was heavy, weighing around five to six pounds, three heavier than my warhammer.

A notification popped up, and I quickly read it.

Nemean Club. Type: Club. Rarity: Rare. Hardness: 8. A savage implement, fashioned from a stone. Ability: The claws and bones of a Nemean lion. This weapon retains the hardness of the creature from which it was made and the effect of one of its abilities has transferred over. The claws of this club will inflict the Laceration condition on any creature they puncture.

*Laceration: Targets' wounds do not close when healed and will continue to bleed until the bleeding is staunched or the effect removed.

I would need to practice with this to get used to the weight. In so doing, I would hopefully also naturally raise my Might Attribute.

We started to pack for our journey, rolling up and storing our gear.

There was a problem when it came to carrying it since most of the people to whom the stuff had belonged were now dead. I fixed the problem by storing most of the items in a few of the canvas tents, tying them up like knapsacks and levitating them beside us.

I took the Nemean hide off the fire and washed it off in the river, rubbing some ash, animal fat and mint leaves together for a soap before hanging it over one of the tents I was levitating, and then we set off. Jand led us vaguely north. He didn't really know where we were going, but he was the closest thing I had to a guide at that moment.

I had to slow down to not outpace my vassals, my boots propelling me several yards with each stride. I kept a lookout for more herbs to use. I'd made a tea last night, and the black veins on my arm had completely disappeared. Based on the fact that my life had been saved several times by these plants, I would probably need more.

I found some more Red Yarrow and made sure to gather as much as possible whenever I came across a patch of it.

Scanning for more plants and materials, I asked Jand about the local flora and fauna.

He showed me a patch of bread leaf, and we stopped to gather it for our supplies.

Bread Leaf. Type: Nutritional. Rarity: Common.

A large, soft-leafed plant whose leaves are thick and nutritious, it has a flavor similar to that of a flat wheat bread. It can be cooked, causing it to rise slightly and ease its digestion. Four leaves will give enough sustenance to a medium-sized creature for one day, but most animals cannot digest this plant and so avoid it.

We kept moving, stopping after we'd been hiking for five hours. I could see my vassals were exhausted, and I scouted for a place to camp. Finding a cave set into a cliffside, I cautiously approached it, having wrapped myself in the Nemean pelt, also carrying my warhammer and club. The cave wasn't too deep, only around fifteen feet.

I brought my vassals to the cave, and they started to set up camp while I went exploring. I would swing my club as I walked, then let it rest when my arm got tired. I kept practicing as I looked around, scanning for any new herbs and eventually finding a patch of what looked like violets, but their flowers were bulbous, and their violet striped with blue.

> **Violet Nullifier. Type: Medicinal. Rarity: Uncommon.** The flower
> bulbs of this plant, when consumed, absorb toxins and poisons in the
> body. One bulb is enough to purify the entire body of a medium-
> sized creature. Creatures should wait 10 minutes between uses, or
> the flower will begin to excise other parts of the body.

I created another jar and gathered around forty of the bulbs from the patch, persisting in hunting and dropping to the ground when my Foresight flashed a warning. Something flew down from the tree and snapped its teeth at my neck before soaring up and landing on the branch of a tree. I wheeled around and looked up at a bizarre creature.

> **Alpha Gliding Wolf. Gifted—Mortal. Beast/Canine. Rank: 15.**

A gliding wolf? And it's a higher rank than the Nemean lion, I thought disbelievingly. Then again, it also said the lion was an adolescent. The alpha's limbs were different from those of a regular wolf, and its paws were wider with hooked claws that it used to grip the tree. Its fur was a greenish brown, providing camouflage amongst the upper branches.

Its eyes were wide and round like an owl's, with massive pupils and bright saffron irises. My Foresight activated, showing the back of my neck being ripped open, and I dodged to the side as another wolf whizzed past me.

"Dominion," I tried on the alpha, but again, as with the Nemean lion, there was little or no impact. "Why isn't this working?" I growled.

> **Gifted are highly resistant to all forms of mind control, mental
> manipulation, and control effects. To weaken their resistance, defeat
> in battle is usually required.**

Surprised by the System's information, I spun to the side, lashing out with my club and managing to score deep jagged cuts in the wolf's side as it attempted a glide-by attack.

"Not much point to that then," I grunted. "I'd rather have the rank points right now."

I levitated Quin's maul, having started to take it everywhere with me. I used my club instead of my warhammer and my shield, the Nemean pelt hanging over me like a poncho or serape, protecting my torso and upper arms.

The alpha howled.

I felt a sudden spike of searing pain in my head, its intensity almost driving me to my knees. I resisted the sonic attack and levitated two dozen spearheads, launching them at the wolf. The creature jumped into the air, emitting a gust of wind from its body, sending it rocketing toward me. I slashed out with my club, but the alpha rolled in the air under my weapon and lashed out with its teeth, nipping my thigh and ripping out a chunk of flesh.

Through gritted teeth, I barely contained a scream, spinning my maul, catching another gliding wolf that had tried to sneak-attack me from behind.

Another rushed me, but I teleported fifteen feet away to give myself a chance to catch my breath. The wolf landed where I had been and looked confused for a moment before my maul shattered its spine, and it lay on the ground, whimpering.

I leaped forward and smashed down with my club, ending its suffering.

After this, I warily eyed the trees.

1 rank point gained.

The wolves blended in with the trees. My low Perception made it hard for me to spot them, but now and again, I caught a flash of yellow eyes.

I rolled to the side as the alpha attacked again, letting loose another howl to try and stun me as it lunged in from behind. I whirled and deflected its jaws with my shield.

It yelped as the shield retaliated, damaging it with its reflective ability.

Although I lunged forward, it was only possible to inflict a minor wound on its foreleg before it soared back into the trees. Then, three wolves came in from behind.

I dodged one while another leaped onto my back and tried to savage my shoulder, its teeth audibly cracking on the Nemean pelt. I felt the crushing force of its jaws. It didn't pierce my skin, but blunt force-crushing damage was not pleasant either.

One dodged my club while another darted in and bit at the back of my knee.

I felt a sharp spike of pain, my leg starting to drag. Swearing, I grabbed a potion I kept in my pocket. Tucking my club under my arm, I downed the potion fast, dropping the bottle and leaping to the side as the alpha attacked me again. The wounds closed, and I breathed heavily, getting a little pissed as the fight dragged on.

I focused on one of the wolves, and the System prompted me again.

Gliding Wolf. Gifted—Mortal. Beast/Canine. Rank: 2.

Are they all Gifted? I wondered. *Probably. If rank points are 'XP,' then they'd all get a share whenever they take something down. Something like me, for instance...*

I rolled to the side again, and shield-crashed into the wolf, ringing its skull. I lashed out with my club and ripped into its neck.

Another alpha came in from the side and bowled me over.

We rolled on the ground as it tried to rip my throat out, others quickly joining, swarming all over me. Two bit down on my boots, and I could see them frantically shaking their heads as they tried and failed to get through artifact leather.

I held apart the alpha's jaws and focused on the objects I was suspending.

The alpha tried to dodge, but my hold on his jaws now served to keep him in place as the maul smashed down on his back, three stone spearheads piercing his side.

The wolves holding my legs yelped, also skewered by spearheads.

I shoved the alpha off me and teleported five feet, managing to land firmly and pausing for breath.

---

10 rank points gained.

Quest updated. Blood and Souls: 16 rank points added.

The rest of the pack didn't run the way I thought they would but rushed me in one mad frenzy. I shielded my front and put my back to a tree. Filled with my own rising fury, I met their aggressive charge. The next minute was a blur, a mad scramble to kill and stay alive as I spent every point of

Stamina and Mana. I had to kill the pack as they ripped at me. One of them managed to pull my cloak off, and they bit and clawed at my flesh.

---

13 rank points gained.

I came to, heaving for breath on the ground. I drank a potion and felt my head grow clearer, but a few of the larger wounds didn't fully close. Sighing, I pulled out some cauter fennel I had chopped up and packed it into my wounds.

Again, I bit back the searing agony as I felt the flashes of heat cauterizing my wounds. I was drenched in blood, uncertain sure which was mine and which had come from the beasts. I drank another potion to recover my lost blood and shakily stood up. Draining though it was, the battle had also bestowed on me a wealth of rank points to spend.

Blood and Souls (Repeatable): Kill 160 monsters or humanoids. Current progress: 3/160. When you complete this quest, you will gain 32 rank points. The next quest will require double the number to be completed but will award double the rank points.

I need to start working on my other quest, I said to myself, picking up my cloak and dismissing the notification.

You have completed a hidden objective and earned a title. Objective: Kill at least 10 creatures with a weapon made from a beast you have slain.

Reward. Title: Feral Barbarian.

***Feral Barbarian: The damage you deal with weapons made of bone is increased by 1 stage.**

I had acquired another title that increased my damage with a certain material. I had various titles like that, so how could I get them to combine to be more effective?

On dismissing the notification, a new one popped up.

The eyes of the Alpha Gliding Wolf flew out of its skull, hovered before me, and turned to a mist which seeped purposefully into my own eyes. I winced.

Ability gained. Bestial Senses (Rank 1): You can activate your senses to smell, hear and see more clearly, picking up the sound of a feather landing or the smell of footsteps on a day-old trail. Your hearing, olfaction, and sight are magnified x2 while this ability is active.		
Cost:	3 Stamina per second.	**Cast Time:** Instantaneous.
Upgrade this ability to increase the magnification of your senses. Each upgrade to this ability increases your Perception Attribute by 1.		

As my Perception increased, there was a pain like a needle jabbing into the back of my eyes and a ringing in my ears. The sensation faded, and I looked over my new ability before dismissing it.

You have absorbed the eyes of an Alpha Gliding Wolf, which has bonded to your Perception Attribute and will fuel and guide your eyes' mutation when you pass the Mortal limit for your Perception Attribute.

"I'd have preferred some sort of flight ability," I grumbled but took my win, glad I'd attained at least one ability from the fight, considering the number of Gifted creatures I'd killed. I now had forty rank points at my disposal. Whilst it was a significant number, I already knew it would be used up incredibly quickly. Just to increase Telekinesis once would cost me six rank points. If I spent every point I had, I could increase it to Rank Ten right now. I was tempted to do that, but realized I should probably increase my other abilities.

Compress Earth was one away from Rank Five, and I might get a new effect for it.

Foresight played a crucial role in all my fights and I should upgrade it, something that would also help to increase my Perception above ten.

For now, I deferred it, levitating the bodies of approximately sixteen wolves.

The wolves were light; I guessed they had to be able to glide even if they were magical, and only the alpha weighed more than a hundred pounds. I carried the dead pack back to camp and set them down for my vassals to skin and harvest. As far as I could tell, their pelts weren't magical, but they could probably still be useful.

I left them to their work and found a stream noticed while taking a walk. I began to scrub off the blood from my embattled body, finding the water freezing cold, but quickly getting used to it. It turned a reddish brown as dried blood flaked off my skin and clothes.

Next, I returned to camp, letting my cloak hang to dry; we'd be attacked again by undead tonight and needed to prepare for it.

First, I decided to upgrade my Compress Earth.

Sitting down in my tent, I took a deep breath.

"Raise Compress Earth by one rank," I told the System.

Congratulations! You have raised an ability to Rank 5. Please pick an additional effect for your ability from the list below:

- **The Hardness increase for each subsequent rank of this ability will be increased further by an additional 0.5 degrees of Hardness.**
- **The area of earth you can fuse is doubled, and the speed at which the earth merges is increased x2.**
- **You can now use uncommon stones in your fusions. The rarer, denser, or more exotic the stone, the greater will be the effect on the final product.**

These choices were all interesting. The first one would let me fabricate more durable creations, which was useful; however, I had little problem with my current creations breaking. The second option was, again, more of a construction ability that some sort of builder mage or support-caster would choose.

The third option was very interesting. I wasn't sure what qualified as 'uncommon stone' but it sounded like these stones would create more interesting constructions.

I decided to go with the third option which seemed as if it would enable me to do a wider range of interesting things in the future.

Compress Earth (Rank 5): You can fuse dirt and stone together into a more durable, heavier material that can be shaped. You can currently fuse a 16-foot-square section of earth and common stone.

> Your compressed stone has a Hardness rating of 6; your compressed earth has a Hardness rating of 4. The precision of detail with which you can sculpt it is based on your Mind Attribute.

> You can now use uncommon stone in your fusions. The rarer, denser, or more exotic the stone, the greater will be the effect on the final product.

> Cost: 5 Mana per 1-foot square.

> Upgrade this ability to increase the amount you can compress, its durability, weight, and the materials upon which you can use this ability.
> Each upgrade increases your Mind Attribute by 1.

I smiled, remembering that bronze had a Hardness value of around four, so even just compressing dirt could create some impressive stuff. I wanted to increase it further but reminded myself I needed to invest in Perception.

Thirty-five points remained, so I should increase Foresight to Rank Five.

"Increase Foresight to Rank Five," I told the System.

The second rank-up passed, and my eyes began to water so much I could barely read the notification. I dismissed it and tried to block out the quickly growing sense of unease. Then, it started to get even worse. Again, I was stopped by the pain of those needles jabbing into the backs of my eyes, and the terrible ringing rising in my ears.

Oh shit! I had just made a terrible mistake in raising my ability so fast. The notification for the third ability came and again, I dismissed it and moved on.

The pain intensified as my senses were jabbed by more and more needles. The maddening ringing increasing with each second made it hard to think.

The fourth ability notification arrived, but my eyes were closed as the light around me suddenly became blinding. I dismissed it and moved on to the next.

I had fallen back. My hands pressed fruitlessly to my ears, trying to block out the sound as I gritted my teeth to keep from screaming.

> Congratulations! You have raised an ability to Rank 5. Please an additional effect for your ability from the list below:

> - **You can see different possible outcomes based on your actions made within the span of time you can foresee. Choosing to do this will increase the Mana cost by 1.**
> - **You can focus on blocking out all other senses to predict the future a number of minutes hence, equal to half your Spirit Attribute.**
> - **Your dreams will give you prophetic visions of the future to help you make long-term plans.**

I gritted my teeth as I focused on the notification, reading the available options. The choice was pretty straightforward. Only one of these options was applicable in combat, the others only hypothetically useful. I went with the ability to see different possibilities.

My headache worsened.

> **Foresight (Rank 5): You passively see 5 seconds into the future and know what will happen to yourself and the space within 13 feet at all times. This ability is based on your Perception attribute increasing. It will increase the time you can see by one second per rank in Perception above 10.**
>
> **You can see different possible outcomes based on your actions made within the span of time you can foresee.**
>
> **This is a passive ability, costing 2 Mana/sec.**
>
> **Upgrade this ability to increase how far you can see into the future and how far around you can see. Every upgrade to this ability increases your Perception Attribute by 1.**

"I never want to upgrade that Attribute again," I groaned, sitting up and wiping away the tears of pain. I could see better now, and every sound was crystal clear to my ears. I was able to hear the words of my vassals dozens of feet away as if they were right outside my tent.

I sighed and looked at my other abilities.

I had twenty-six available rank points to work with and several abilities still at Rank One, but it was clear which one I needed to increase. My speed was great, especially with the boost able to be activated from my boots, but there were still several times when I'd needed to be faster and hadn't been. I ran my hands along the still-healing burn marks on my chest where I'd had to cauterize wounds incurred by the Nemean lion.

"Increase Heightened Speed by one rank," I said. I'd learned my lesson: don't queue up a bunch of rank-ups all at once!

Heightened Speed (Rank 2): You move faster and can react faster. Your body acts can instantly move at max speed without needing to build up momentum. The speed at which your body can move is increased x2.5.
This is a passive ability, costing 1 Stamina per second and it will cost more Stamina in combat depending on how fast you move.
Upgrade this ability to increase how fast you can move. Every upgrade of this ability increases your Speed Attribute x2.

There was a twisting in my body like snakes crawling under my skin. The muscles on my legs, arms, and back writhed. I gritted my teeth again and waited until the pain was gone. I took a deep breath. "Raise Heightened Speed by one rank," I told the System.

Heightened Speed (Rank 3): You move faster and can react faster. Your body acts can instantly move at max speed without needing to build up momentum. The speed at which your body can move is increased x3.
This is a passive ability, costing 1 Stamina per second and it will cost more Stamina in combat, depending on how fast you move.
Upgrade this ability to increase how fast you can move. Every upgrade of this ability increases your Speed Attribute x2.

Despite having waited, the pain was even greater, feeling my muscles pop and pull and reconnect as they swelled before shrinking again. My skin expanded and retracted. I breathed out as the rank-up finished, the pain ending as abruptly as it had begun.

"Increase Heightened Speed once," I said.

Heightened Speed (Rank 4): You move faster and can react faster. Your body acts can instantly move at max speed without needing to

> build up momentum. The speed at which your body can move is increased x3.5.
>
> This is a passive ability, costing 1 Stamina per second and it will cost more Stamina in combat, depending on how fast you move.
>
> Upgrade this ability to increase how fast you can move. Every upgrade of this ability increases your Speed Attribute x2.

The familiar notification appeared, and the pain returned even greater than before, every new rank more intense than the other. I breathed out and in, focusing on not giving in to the pain. Eventually, relieved that the ordeal had ended, I breathed out again.

"Raise Heightened Speed once more," I told the System.

> Congratulations! You have raised an ability to Rank 5. Please choose an additional effect for your ability from the list below.
>
> - You can run across water and other liquids as if they were solid ground.
>
> - You can briefly multiply your speed x3 at the cost of an equal amount of extra Stamina expenditure.
>
> - You can cause your image to blur at the cost of x10 to your Stamina expenditure for the duration.

I was in so much pain, there was no way to focus on the options, so I skimmed them briefly and chose the only one that wouldn't cost me anything extra. Using my speed was already taxing on my body. I didn't need to add anything else to the cost.

> Heightened Speed (Rank 5): You move faster and can react faster. This ability directly increases your Speed Attribute x10 and increases the speed at which your body can move x4.
>
> You can run across water and other liquids as if they were solid ground.
>
> This is a passive ability, costing 1 Stamina per second and it will cost more Stamina in combat, depending on how fast you move.
>
> Upgrade this ability to increase how fast you can move. Every upgrade of this ability increases your Speed Attribute by 2.

As soon as the notification appeared, it disappeared and was replaced by another one.

> **Congratulations! You have raised one of your Attributes beyond 20, the Mortal limit. Your body will now physiologically change to adjust to this increase to keep your Attribute score from killing you.**

The muscles of my body began to writhe and twist, my heart like a jackhammer trying to punch through my ribcage. My torso expanded and then deflated before expanding again. I spasmed on the ground and kept twitching for ten minutes, even after the changes had passed.

> **Your fast-twitch muscles have been reinforced, and your heart has split in two, giving you two hearts. Please increase your other Attributes beyond 20 to support these changes to your body.**

I lay there until I finally caught my breath. Looking over my notifications, I saw what my choice for my Speed and ability increase had given me. Although unsure how useful running on water would be, at least it was now an option if I needed it. In addition, my Speed Attribute was now twenty-four, including the bonus from my boots.

I sighed in relief as the pain faded completely. I had just spent fourteen rank points on upgrading my skill to Rank 5 and only had twelve points left. I wanted to raise Telekinesis again, but only had enough points to upgrade that skill once. I needed to upgrade Dominion, so it could hopefully work more effectively on Gifted and give me more uses of if it per day.

Also, my Spirit was close to twenty and pushing it past the mortal limit might trigger another of those mutations. In my chest was a fast and rhythmic *thud, thud,* two hearts pumping away. I looked down at my shirt; it seemed oddly tighter and pulled up as if a size too small. "Did I get bigger?" I asked myself, and sure enough, feeling around my torso revealed lean muscles where they hadn't been before.

They weren't thick muscles but thin and honed for fast movement as opposed to heavy lifting. My shirt was definitely a little smaller on me.

Surely, I'd grown at least an inch taller!

I wasn't ready to raise my Attributes again just yet.

Time to take a break. I'd raised Compress Earth, and wanted to make some fortifications for our camp in readiness for the next inevitable assault from the undead. I levitated small boulders and rocks the size of my head and stacked them, fusing them all together with Compress Earth, creating high walls around our camp.

Now, I climbed up the cliff above our camp, drawing the dirt and stone into a watchtower ten feet wide and twenty feet tall. The interior had handholds and footholds forming a ladder, leading to a wide top with a slate-thin roof of stone.

I made the cave bigger, compressing the earth outwards and flattening the floor. This created a forty-feet-deep cave which would give us all some more space. I even made a chimney up through the rock with a fireplace for cooking. I didn't think we'd be here that long, but enjoyed the work and took frequent breaks to let my Mana replenish.

It was sunset by the time I was done, and I collapsed into my tent, almost instantly asleep.

Chapter 6: The Chief

Jamis felt the icy wind blow against his bare skin as the massive Dire Frost Bear charged at him. Neither the snow nor the wind caused him discomfort.

> **Felren the Maneater. Gifted—Beast/Dire Frost Bear. Mortal. Rank: 28.**

The party moved to surround the beast as it fought with its clawed, armored gauntlets.

It roared and grappled with the bear as Mira's arrows struck its side in a rapid volley.

Torvin charged in from the left flank, lance in hand, radiant light surrounding it in a nimbus. The lance struck the bear's side, and it threw back its head and roared in pain.

It tried to breathe a cone of ice at Torvin, but Jamis grabbed the bear's jaw in both hands and began to pull it apart.

The bear clawed at its skin. Its talons left long streaks, but a golden glow suffused it, sealing and healing the wounds as soon as they were made.

With a tear and snap, the jaw broke and the bear dropped down on all fours and then collapsed, its pain too great to continue the fight. It was ultimately felled with a fatal mercy strike to the skull. As it died, it released one last agonized whimper.

> **You have gained 3 rank points to be split amongst all surviving party members.**

"A good fight," Torvin said. "Did anyone gain any abilities from it?"

"Just points for me," Mira said, lithely jumping down from a tree. Her wings extended out as she glided down, making no sound as she landed.

"I got an extra rank point for bringing justice to the family of the slain," Torvin said. "I need to double it again to complete the quest. I didn't get any abilities from it either, just more rank points."

"I gained a Special Attack," Jamis informed them. "It's called Winter's Claws. It lets me apply a moderate amount of frost damage to each unarmed strike for a Mana cost. It fulfils the requirement for my Spirit Attribute."

"Good. Let's get off this mountain. I'm freezing," Helen complained, rubbing her arms.

"I'm doing all right," Felrick said, amused, as he stood in his full fur-padded plate mail.

"We need to find more Gifted beasts to slay and find the Dark God's Champions," Jamis said, flexing the claws of his gauntlets. "I wish Artrix would just tell me where the other champions are."

"If he did that, then their patrons could tell them where we are," Mira reminded him. "I don't know about you, but I don't want the Champion of the God of Assassins to know where I am before I'm ready to face him."

"I suppose so," Jamis grunted in agreement. "So, back to the Lunar Kingdom?"

Everyone in the group nodded, so they quickly skinned the bear and began the long hike down the mountain. They talked a little, enjoying each other's company as they skirted the edges of the Cursed Forest until they came to the Old Road.

They completed the half-day journey from the outskirts of the Cursed Forest back into farmland. At nightfall, they stopped at an inn.

Jamis and the barmaid made eyes at each other. Collectively, the group rolled their eyes, fully aware of what would happen next.

"Just because the women say yes doesn't mean you need to sleep with them," Torvin said. "You've probably conceived half a dozen children with all the taverns you hit the other night."

"You must not remember the night," Jamis said, laughing as he pulled the smiling barmaid into his lap. "I remember you siring a few yourself."

Torvin reddened. "That didn't happen," he protested.

"You were pretty drunk," Mira said. "I do remember you disappearing with a girl a few times."

"And what were you doing?" Torvin asked, trying to deflect some of the attention away from himself.

"Drinking responsibly," Mira said. "One of us needed to be ready in case there was an emergency. Besides, I have no interest in being a parent right now. You two might be able to just abandon your responsibilities but we women have a harder time doing that."

"Why don't you tell the tavern a story?" Felrick asked, taking mercy on the embarrassed Torvin.

They drank into the night, Torvin recounting the story of their adventure to the whole tavern. Everyone from the town came to meet the champions of the gods. They shook their hands and received blessing from Helen as she cleansed various ailments.

***

I was shaken awake and nearly tore out my vassal's throat. I managed to hold myself back before killing him and composed myself, panting. The stress from my battles had obviously affected me more than I'd thought.

I threw my Nemean cloak on and strode out of the cave, hearing the growls and scratching of claws on the wall put up around the cave. Walking up the steps of the wall, I looked out over the hoard of undead. At least a hundred creatures clawed up at me.

Something flashed in my Foresight. I ducked, and my hand snapped out, wrapping around a zombie bat and crushing it. I didn't get any notification for killing it.

"Guess that answers that," I said. "The small ones aren't good for anything."

I stayed on the wall for now, hurling my stone spearheads.

Quin's maul swept the ground, clearing out the smaller ones.

When I'd culled enough of the horde for me to have some space, I jumped down with my club and shield at the ready.

A zombie bear charged me.

I jumped, clearing the bear, also smashing down with my club. My entire weight was behind the blow, smashing into the base of its skull at the spine, severing the connection. I continued fighting, using my Foresight to dodge the most dangerous attacks. I could have stayed on the wall, but needed to learn to fight as much as I needed rank points.

More and more undead animals and beasts came at me, but I kept fighting.

I was dimly aware of my vassals as they watched the battle from the wall, their torches illuminating the area.

I didn't get through the fight without injury.

My cloak prevented my skin from getting pierced, but I felt my ribs crack when something resembling a bull charged and hit me from behind while I was fighting a skeletal giant cat. Exhaustion claimed me, and there were many bloody gashes over my forearms and thighs, but the pain only increased my angry determination to overcome it.

> **Blood and Souls (Repeatable): Kill 160 monsters or humanoids. Current progress: 114/160. When you complete this quest, you will gain 32 rank points.**
> **The next quest will require double the number to be completed but will award double the rank points.**

The fight was finally over, leaving me sagging with exhaustion but I managed to climb back over the wall and fall into bed, asleep again in moments.

I woke up groggily, seeing the sun in the sky outside the cave and I rolled out of bed.

My vassals having already packed everything else up, I sat down to eat and finish my final rank-ups before heading out. I would rank up before eating, just in case doing so messed with my stomach. "Increase Dominion by one rank," I told the System.

> **Dominion (Rank 2): A number of times per day, equal to 10 plus your Spirit Attribute, you can, as a spoken command, force a creature not bound by another creature into your service. You are able to dominate a number of creatures at a time, equal to your Spirit Attribute plus 10. A creature may choose to serve you willingly or may attempt to resist by opposing their Mind Attribute against your Spirit Attribute. You can see the abilities and Attributes of any creature under your Dominion.**
> **You may have a maximum number of creatures under your Dominion equal to your Spirit Attribute x3.**
>
> | Cost: | 1 Mana per creature. |
> | --- | --- |
>
> **Upgrade this ability to increase how many creatures you can dominate per day as well as the multiplier for how many creatures you can have dominated at a time.**
> **Each upgrade increases your Spirit Attribute by 1.**

The fiery burning of my Spirit increasingly surrounded me. It was normally low, but felt incredibly intense this time, like stepping into a bonfire. I gritted my teeth until the pain subsided, breathing in and out.

"Raise Dominion by one rank," I said.

Dominion (Rank 3): A number of times per day, equal to 20 plus your Spirit attribute, you can, as a spoken command, force a creature not bound by another creature into your service. You can dominate a number of creatures at a time, equal to your Spirit attribute plus 15. A creature may choose to serve you willingly, or may attempt to resist by opposing their Mind Attribute against your Spirit Attribute. You can, at will, see the abilities and Attributes of any creature under your Dominion.	
You may have a maximum number of creatures under your Dominion equal to your Spirit Attribute x4.	
Cost:	1 Mana per creature.
Upgrade this ability to increase how many creatures you can dominate per day as well as the multiplier for how many creatures you can have dominated at a time. Each upgrade increases your Spirit Attribute by 1.	

The heat of the fire increased, cold sweat beading all along my body which felt a heat that didn't actually exist. I pushed past the pain and breathed in and out.

"Pain is weakness leaving the body," I grunted out. "One more rank into Dominion."

Dominion (Rank 4): A number of times per day, equal to 40 plus your Spirit attribute, you can, as a spoken command, force a creature not bound by another creature into your service. You can dominate a number of creatures at a time, equal to your Spirit Attribute plus 20. A creature may choose to serve you willingly or may attempt to resist by opposing their Mind Attribute against your Spirit Attribute. You can, at will, see the abilities and Attributes of any creature under your Dominion.
You may have a maximum number of creatures under your Dominion equal to your Spirit Attribute x5.

Cost:	1 Mana per creature.

Upgrade this ability to increase how many creatures you can dominate per day as well as the multiplier for how many creatures you can have dominated at a time.

Each upgrade increases your Spirit Attribute by 1.

I let the fire wash over me and did my best to blank it as I breathed in and out as calmly as I could. The notification came and vanished, to be replaced by another one.

Congratulations! You have raised one of your Attributes beyond 20, the Mortal limit. Your body will now physiologically change to adjust to this increase to keep your Attribute from killing you.

Agony coursed through me, not any specific physical pain, but it pervaded my entire being, a little as though a little demon had broken into my soul and committed arson, my spirit beginning to ravage my being.

Your aura has been reinforced. Your body now counts as magical for the purposes of overcoming damage and you are resistant to any controlling effects of enemy spells. Please increase your other Attributes beyond 20 to support these changes to your body.

I gasped in agony, my mind momentarily going blank with the pain. I came to my senses, realizing I had fallen to the ground and forced myself up.

"Pull up my Attributes," I told the System.

Mordred, Champion of Kelesa. Gifted—Humanoid/Human. Mortal. Rank: 50.			
Available rank points: 6.			
Might:	13	Mind:	13
Speed:	22 (+6) =28	Perception:	13
Toughness:	11	Spirit:	21
Endurance:	10	Power:	10
Maximum Stamina:	71	Maximum Mana:	80
Stamina Regen:	11.2 per second	Mana Regen:	15.6 per second
Abilities:			
Dominion (Rank 4), Telekinesis (Rank 5), Heightened Speed (Rank 5), Foresight (Rank 5), Compress Earth (Rank 5), Bestial Senses (Rank 1).			
Blessings:			
Blessing of War (Mortal).			
Titles:			
Mark of Cain, Bloody Pugilist, Exorcist, Survivor, Feral Barbarian.			

Great, my Might has increased. So, I can raise my attributes without rank points, for now at least. And… I didn't notice before but the bonus to my speed has been ticking up.

I pulled up the description for my boots again, noticing it had been changing as I'd been ranking up.

Boots of Midnight Wind (Artifact, Rank 5): give a +4 bonus to the wearer's Speed Attribute and gain an additional +1 bonus for every 10 ranks you have.
You can double your Speed Attribute for 15 minutes with a cooldown of 55 minutes, with duration and cooldown reduced and increased by 5 minutes every 15 ranks you have, to a max of 1-hour duration and a 5-minute cooldown.
Once every 35 seconds, at the cost of 10 Mana, you can teleport 55 feet to a place you can see. The range is increased by 5 feet, and

> the cooldown is reduced by 5 seconds and increased cost by 1 Mana every 5 ranks to a minimum of a 5-second cooldown and 5-Mana cost.

> Created by the Goddess Kelesa for her champion Mordred, these boots are made from the hide of a black dragon with a mithril alloy for the toe and heel guard.
>
> They are also infused with the power of Kelesa's will. These boots are indestructible except by another deity.

I was pleased with my choice of artifact. It might not have been a magic sword, but I could raise my speed to 44 at a pinch, making me a blur in motion. I perused my abilities and thought back over past fights, considering how I'd be able to handle them now.

All would have been fine except the one with the Nemean lion.

My rank was twice as high as the Nemean lion's had been, but looking back, I still didn't think I could take it on in a direct fight, its armored hide providing an effective counter to my every attack. I'd need some sort of elemental attack or to massively overpower it physically, like Hercules, to take it on in a straight-up fight.

"Maybe it's just a bad matchup between the two of us," I mused.

I ate a quick breakfast of dried venison and roasted bread leaf.

We left the camp I'd made and headed north again.

Jand pointed out the rough direction we'd have to take to get to Bandit King's fort. We hiked for over seven hours, taking a break every couple of hours and for lunch.

We headed deeper into the forest, having to navigate around some lakes and massive cliffs. I kept an eye out for other beasts, but we weren't attacked.

I did manage to find some more cauter fennel, red yarrow, bread leaf, and violet nullifier as well as a new plant.

> Scourge Rose. Type: Poison. Rarity: Uncommon. Grows in places with a fire affinity or where a massive fire has swept the land as the rose bushes feed off the ash.
>
> The thorns of this rose excrete a sap that attacks the blood with a flameless fire, burning the body from the inside out.

The rose bushes spread for a hundred yards, creating a deadly meadow of scarlet blossoms. Their thorns were black and dripped a dark orange sap.

I created some bottles, methodically harvesting the sap by carefully squeezing the thorns. I gave some to my vassals, telling them to be careful when harvesting, explaining what the poison would do to them if they ever were to get it in their blood.

We spent an hour in the meadow, Maria even digging up a small, healthy new bush for me.

I added it to our gear along with nine bottles of the sap, estimating each bottle would coat around a hundred arrows or ten swords, based on the amount it contained.

We kept moving, stopping four hours before sunset to set up camp where I'd discovered a cave near a river.

I used Compress Earth to set up some more walls and expand the cave, carving some rooms with the ability and creating another fireplace and chimney. Looking over my gear, I now had the ability to work with uncommon stone and make much harder material.

I needed to replace my stone spearheads, all dulled by vigorous use.

Quin's maul was also damaged. The steel shaft was fine but the wood of its head had splintered and was barely held together by the iron bands.

My club was also in need of maintenance.

I replaced the stone bindings that held the claws in place, beginning to search for uncommon stones. I wasn't sure exactly what that meant, but felt that I would be able to discern the difference when I spotted one.

I picked up rocks and examined them, not able to identify them all, but I did find some chunks of quartz and onyx which resonated as uncommon to my ability.

I removed the stone bindings of my club and replaced them with bands from the onyx and quartz, creating a smoky, black, glass material. Then, I kept hunting along the riverbed, tossing rocks onto the shore, also smacking my forehead as I realized there was a much faster way to do this. Getting out of the water, I realized that my boots were waterproof but my pants were not. Using telekinesis, I levitated stones out of the water, forty-eight at a time.

I tossed them onto the bank.

Within a few minutes, a very large pile had accrued, and I began to sort them into two distinct, flat, empty sections of ground: one for common rock and the other for uncommon.

Having finally gathered a huge pile of uncommon, I grabbed Quin's maul, removed all the wood from its head and set aside the iron bands which had already almost broken.

Then, I began to create a new head for the maul, compressing earth around the steel rod which acted as its handle. I created a flat side for one section with a convex bulge to one side and a spiraling spike to the other like an antelope horn.

I decorated it with geometric patterns.

The head of the maul now weighed around two hundred pounds, and there was no way I could wield it without Telekinesis. So, I started on my stone spearheads, creating forty-eight of them, each weighing twenty pounds. I could have lifted more, but did not have a surfeit of material and figured there was no need to overdo it.

I returned to camp and stretched out, loosening my muscles. I had not had any proper rest in a while and decided to go to bed early. I soon fell asleep but was abruptly awoken.

"Undead, this early?" I wondered groggily, pulling my cloak around me.

"Goblins, my lord," Maria said fearfully.

"Well, at least that's new," I said.

Standing up, I wandered up the stairs to the top of the wall which overlooked the dimly-lit forest floor. The area was clear for around a hundred feet either side of the river.

A group of approximately fifty humanoids, no taller than four feet were gathered around the outside of the wall, carrying a variety of weapons. None of them looked particularly pretty, but they did all appear effective.

"What do you want?" I asked, not wasting any time.

"You are trespassing on our land," the lead goblin said. "Our chieftain demands you pay him tribute."

"Then please tell him to fuck off," I said.

The goblins stirred and bristled at my words.

"You dare mock our chieftain, human?" the goblin demanded.

I analyzed the goblins but none of them was Gifted. "If he isn't man enough to come here himself, then he's not worthy of respect."

"Who do you think you are, human?" the lead goblin challenged, sneering.

"Dominion," I answered.

Forty-six of the Goblins reached up to their necks and felt at their wrists, yowling as white brands appeared. "Dominion," I said again and the remaining four succumbed to my ability.

---

4 rank points gained.

Whip and Chains (Repeatable): Conquer 40 monsters or humanoids by bringing them under your Dominion. Current progress: 34/40. When you complete this quest, you will gain 8 rank points. The next quest will require double the number to be completed but will award double the rank points.

"I am Mordred, Champion of Kelesa, Goddess of War and Conquest."

The goblins that had been filled with confidence a moment before now cowered beneath me. "We serve you now, Warlord," they groveled.

"You should kill the filthy creatures," Jand muttered, looking down at them from atop the wall.

"They may prove useful," I said, thoughtfully. "But I'll need to make sure the undead don't kill them first."

I spent the next hour creating an outer wall, extending from the cliff to the river in a half circle around the main camp.

"You will stay here for tonight. Tomorrow, you take me to your leader," I commanded.

I went back to bed to get a few hours of sleep before the undead rose and came to attack us. After what seemed like only a minute, my name was being called. I got up to fight.

I left the inner wall and climbed up the stairs of the outer wall and looked over the banks of the river at several hundred milling undead. There were humanoids among the usual bears, wolves, deer, and beasts snarling and clawing at the walls.

While my newly improved maul pulverized undead into gore or bone powder, I also set about hurling spearheads from the wall. Finally, I jumped off, at last able to properly test my new Speed and Foresight. I didn't activate the speed boost from my boots but just used my own natural sprinting prowess, stepping forward with unfathomable stealth, each footfall propelling me forward two yards as my club lashed out in a blur of frenzy.

The skull of a human-sized skeleton flew off at my first strike. I ducked under the swipe of a giant ape-like creature and my maul swept in from behind it, caving in its skull.

I was aware of the goblins in my periphery. They, and a few of my braver human vassals had gathered on the walls to view my battle. I attempted to ignore the distraction of an audience and gave my complete focus to the fight.

In this moment, it was as if I had ceased being human and had transformed into a whirlwind. I ducked, dodged, teleported, and blocked. My club moved rhythmically, methodically as I took off heads or bashed them in, killing undead after undead. I took wounds on my thighs and arms, feeling the familiar rising anger.

Eventually, I altogether lost track of the battle, driven by my now habitual Foresight and by instinct, possessed by the need to kill.

---

32 rank points gained.

I couldn't even register the notification as fervor for the battle consumed me. Kill, dodge, kill, block, kill, teleport. Repeat. Over and over.

My body was moving like a machine programmed to destroy.

I came out of my fury and breathed out heavily, out of Stamina and Mana and the ground was littered with bones and corpses of all shapes, sizes, and creatures. I got up from the ground, reached down, pulled out a broken piece of antler from my thigh and dislodged some teeth that had been embedded in my arm.

Blood and Souls (Repeatable): Kill 320 monsters or humanoids. Current progress: 57/320. When you complete this quest, you will gain 64 rank points.
The next quest will require double the number to be completed but will award double the rank points.

I dismissed the notification to be greeted by another one.

You have completed a hidden objective and earned a title. Objective: Single-handedly defeat over 50 enemies in front of an audience of at least 50 humanoids and impress them with your skill and bravery.

> **Reward. Title: Formidable Gladiator.**
>
> ***Formidable Gladiator: You have inspired those who follow you with both fear and awe. Any allies within 100 feet of you have resistance to fear and mental effects.**

This title was different from most of my others and affected others besides myself. This was to be a first for me. So, I returned to bed, exhausted from my twice-interrupted sleep.

I hated birds, swearing I wouldn't rest until every last one of them was dead and there wasn't another feathered menace left on the planet.

It wasn't even light yet and they were already squawking up a thunderstorm, rudely waking me and preventing me from getting back to sleep.

Grumbling irritably, I got up and took a bowl of stew, digging in and draining the broth. Leaving the inner wall, I surveyed my goblin vassals.

"Which one of you is in charge?" I asked.

"I am!" one said.

"No, me!" another butted in.

Soon, they were all fighting, each proclaiming themselves the leader.

"All right, I'll make this simple. Which one of you is going to be the one I kill when you mess up?" I asked.

Their desperate bids to be the leader ended. Finally, they shoved a medium-heavyset goblin forward and he stood before me, shoulders slumped.

"What are you called?" I asked.

"I am Juruk," the goblin said.

"Where is your chieftain?" I asked.

"That way," he said, pointing to the east.

"Lead the way," I said.

I followed Juruk, all the other goblins following behind me. We broke through the trees into a wide section of plains where the area had been mostly stripped of vegetation and was an ugly brown color. At the center of what was predominately dirt plain, there stood a ramshackle village. As I looked over the area, I realized the fifty goblins under my control weren't even a quarter of the population of this place.

"How many Gifted does your tribe have?" I asked Juruk.

"Only the Chieftain," Juruk said. "No other Gifted allowed. Otherwise, they challenge Chief."

"Can I challenge him?" I asked.

Juruk snorted. "You human."

"I'll take that as a 'no,'" I said. "How good are you at fighting?"

"I'm the best, My Lord," Juruk said, puffing out his chest.

"Great. We'll be attacking in an hour," I ventured.

"I meant, I'm the worst." Juruk amended his statement.

"Then you will be an adequate meat shield," I said, dryly.

I needed to handle some rank-ups before the next fight. This included two remaining rank points and the quest rewards from last night. I had, in total, thirty-nine rank points available.

Retreating into the forest, I sat down against a tree. My only ability still at Rank 1 was Bestial Senses. Thus far, I had chosen not to increase this skill but raising it would be the cheapest way to upgrade my Perception and it might prove more useful at higher ranks.

"Increase Bestial Senses by one rank," I requested.

Bestial Senses (Rank 2): You can activate your senses to smell, hear and see more clearly, picking up the sound of a feather landing or the smell of footsteps on a day-old trail.	
Your hearing, olfaction, and sight are magnified x3 while this ability is active.	
Cost:	3 Stamina per second while ability is active.
Upgrade this ability to increase the magnification of your senses. Each upgrade to this ability increases your Perception Attribute by 1.	

On this occasion, the stabbing needles in my eyes caused by the upgrade appeared to be coated in cyan pepper juice. The accompanying ringing in my ears rose steadily to a deafening, wailing tone. I gritted my teeth, breathing in and out to try and block out the pain.

"Raise Bestial Senses by one rank," I told the System.

Bestial Senses (Rank 3): You can activate your senses to smell, hear and see more clearly, picking up the sound of a feather landing or

the smell of footsteps on a day-old trail. Your hearing, olfaction, and sight are magnified x4 while this ability is active.	
Cost:	3 Stamina per second while ability is active.
Upgrade this ability to increase the magnification of your senses. Each upgrade to this ability increases your Perception Attribute by 1.	

More needles stabbed into my eyes, jabbing into the ocular nerves, spreading the burning pain. The wailing whine rose, and I slammed my head backward, involuntarily hitting the back of my head on the trunk of the tree.

Breathe in, breathe out, I reminded myself, doing all I could to shift focus from the pain.

"Increase Bestial Senses by one rank," I grunted out, sitting back up straight.

Bestial Senses (Rank 4): You can activate your senses to smell, hear and see more clearly, picking up the sound of a feather landing or the smell of footsteps on a day-old trail. Your hearing, olfaction, and sight are magnified x5 while this ability is active.	
Cost:	3 Stamina per second while ability is active.
Upgrade this ability to increase the magnification of your senses. Each upgrade to this ability increases your Perception Attribute by 1.	

The needles changed from being smothered with cyan peppers to ghost pepper level. They stabbed faster. Meanwhile, the ringing became a thunderous, deafening, continuous roar. *Breathe, breathe, breathe!* I repeated the mantra to myself over and again, feeling the pain recede. Cracking the bones in my neck, I steeled myself for the final push.

"Increase Bestial Senses by one rank," I said.

Congratulations! You have raised an ability to Rank 5. Please pick an additional effect for your ability from the list below:
•   You can magnify your vision x 10

• **You gain the ability to turn on infrared vision while this ability is active**
• **The hairs on your arms raise whenever you are being watched by a hidden creature.**

Focusing past the pain in my eyes, I read through my options. They were all interesting, but I wasn't sure which would be the most useful. The ability to magnify my vision seemed as if it would be best for a sniper or archer. The infrared vision was cool and gave me Predator vibes that made it extremely tempting. The ability to sense when I was being watched could be useful but it overlapped too much with Foresight.

It also gave me no additional information beyond that I was being watched.

I chose the second option and went back to blocking out the pain.

Bestial Senses (Rank 5): You can activate your senses to smell, hear and see more clearly, picking up the sound of a feather landing or the smell of footsteps on a day-old trail. Your hearing, olfaction, and sight are magnified x6 while this ability is active.	
You gain the ability to turn on infrared vision while this ability is active.	
Cost:	**3 Stamina per second while ability active.**
Upgrade this ability to increase the magnification of your senses. Each upgrade to this ability increases your Perception Attribute by 1.	

The needles stabbed and jabbed into the backs of my eyes, while the roaring seemed as if it would shatter my eardrums at any second. Finally, the pain receded. I blinked and enjoyed the clarity of vision and crispness of hearing, then activated my Bestial Senses. Initially shielding my ears with my hands, I slowly uncovered them, becoming inundated with the sounds of bugs and birds. I could also make out every goblin conversation as the tribe bickered, squabbled, and fought amongst themselves. I could smell the foul odor of badly managed sewage, also clearly able to see goblins on patrol around the village.

I deactivated the ability and my senses returned to their newly heightened state but without the overwhelming sensory overload of Bestial Senses.

"I'm going to need to practice with that," I said.

I still had twenty-five rank points available, but all my skills were now at Rank Five, except for Dominion. *First Dominion, then I can finally raise Telekinesis*, I promised myself.

"Increase Dominion by one rank," I told the System.

Congratulations! You have raised an ability to Rank 5. Please pick an additional effect for your ability from the list below:
• **You can dominate vast populations at once. This effect multiplies the number of creatures you can dominate at once x2.**
• **The larger your Dominion, the more it grows in power. All Attributes of your vassals are raised by one when in a group of 50 or more. Every 50 vassals increase this bonus by one to a maximum possible Attribute score of 20.**
• **Your Attributes increase by one for every 10 vassals within a 60-foot radius of you.**

These were all interesting but each had its flaws.

The first could be useful, but I dismissed it on the grounds that it seemed like a way to save time. I had yet to even encounter a group of creatures larger than a few dozen.

The second wouldn't do anything for me but could help to make my vassals significantly stronger and resilient by putting all their Attributes at the peak of the Mortal rank.

The last one benefited me but only if I were fighting with my vassals in a group formation or commanding them to do my fighting as if I were a general marshaling troops.

Ultimately, I decided to take the second option. This ability was about acquiring vassals and at that moment, they needed all the help they could get.

> **Dominion (Rank 5):** A number of times per day, equal to 80 plus your Spirit Attribute, you can, as a spoken command, force a creature not bound by another creature into your service. You are able to dominate a number of creatures at a time equal to your Spirit Attribute plus 25.
>
> A creature may choose to serve you willingly or may attempt to resist by opposing their Mind Attribute against your Spirit Attribute. You can, at will, see the abilities and Attributes of any creature under your Dominion. You may have a maximum number of creatures under your Dominion equal to your Spirit Attribute x6.
>
> The larger your Dominion, the more it grows in power.
>
> All Attributes of your vassals are raised by 1 when in a group of 50 or more. Every 50 vassals increases this bonus by 1 to a maximum possible Attribute score of 20.

Cost:	1 Mana per 5 creatures.

> Upgrade this ability to increase how many creatures you can dominate per day, as well as the multiplier for how many creatures you can have dominated at a time. Each upgrade increases your Spirit Attribute by 1.

The burning through my entire being increased. I felt as though I was in a furnace. The sweat erupting all over my body, however, was a cold one. Only through a superhuman effort of will and concentration would I withstand this ordeal.

> **Warning!** You are raising an Attribute beyond 20 while you are still in Mortal rank. Possessing stats significantly higher than 20 while you are still only a Mortal may have unknown repercussions on your spiritual and physical status.

"Good to know," I grunted as the pain faded. "But sadly, I can't quit yet. Increase Telekinesis to Rank Six."

> **Telekinesis (Rank 6):** You can, at will, lift 6 objects or creatures, weighing 330 pounds or less and move them within 150 feet of your body; or up to 96 objects or creatures, weighing 85 pounds or less

and move them within 150 feet of your body. The speed and power of objects are based on your Spirit Attribute.	
You can now crush an enemy with your ability. You deal a moderate amount of damage each second to a creature suspended by your Telekinesis. The damage is increased slightly for every point in Spirit you have above 10.	
Cost:	1 Mana per 10 small objects/sec or 1 Mana per large object/sec.
Upgrade this ability to increase the number of items, their weight, and the range at which you can move them. Every upgrade of this ability increases your Spirit Attribute by 1.	

The burning was intense, making it feel as though someone was using a blowtorch on my insides as the fire bloomed out, spreading farther than my chest toward the rest of my torso and up my neck. My breathing was ragged as I tried to focus through the pain.

I waited until it subsided and braced myself again.

"Increase Telekinesis by one rank," I told the System.

Telekinesis (Rank 7): You can, at will, lift 7 objects or creatures weighing 450 pounds or less and move them within 170 feet of your body; or up to 192 objects or creatures weighing 115 pounds or less and move them within 170 feet of your body. The speed and power of objects are based on your Spirit Attribute.	
You can now crush an enemy with your ability. You deal a moderate amount of damage each second to a creature suspended by your Telekinesis. The damage is increased slightly for every point in Spirit you have above 10.	
Cost:	1 Mana per 10 small objects/sec or 1 Mana per large object/sec.
Upgrade this ability to increase the number of items, their weight, and the range at which you can move them. Every upgrade of this ability increases your Spirit Attribute by 1.	

The scorching in my chest returned, doubling in intensity.

My clothes were now drenched in sweat, and I found myself both burning and shivering. I bit back a scream, the sound dying in my throat.

The pain was gone, and I gasped for breath, having momentarily forgotten to breathe.

I had seven rank points left, not enough to raise Telekinesis again, but I could potentially raise one of my other abilities. I thought about Heightened Speed but dismissed it almost immediately on the grounds that I was already very fast, especially with the bonus from my boots. I decided to go with Compress Earth.

Despite not really being used in combat, it was an ability that I found myself utilizing as much as Telekinesis. It also raised my Mind Attribute which was nowhere near twenty.

"Raise Compress Earth by one rank," I said.

Compress Earth (Rank 6): You can fuse dirt and stone together into a more durable, heavier material that can be shaped. You can currently fuse a 32-foot-square section of earth as well as common and uncommon stone. Your compressed stone has a Hardness rating of 6.5; your compressed earth has a Hardness rating of 4.5. The detail with which you can sculpt is based on your Mind & Perception Attribute.

You can now use uncommon stone in your fusions. The rarer, denser, or more exotic the stone, the greater will be the effect on the final product.

Cost:	5 Mana per 1-foot square.

Upgrade this ability to increase the amount you can compress, its durability, weight, and the materials upon which you can use this ability. Each upgrade increases your Mind Attribute by 1.

Upgrades completed, I stood up. I was sweaty but cleaning myself could come later since I'd likely be covered in blood and sweat anyway before the day was done.

I approached the goblin village with my own goblin vassals following reluctantly behind.

The patrols and goblins milling about noticed us, a clamor arising from the village. They assembled in rough lines. Short but powerful looking bows were drawn on us.

"We should run," Juruk whimpered.

"Keep your cowardice to yourself," I told him, looking over the village defenders. "Is your chief here?"

"Chief big, you'll see him," Juruk assured me.

A volley of arrows was launched at us.

I raised my hand and employed telekinesis to grab approximately half the arrows, proceeding to fling them back toward the archers.

They screamed and cried out as their own arrows rained back down on them.

When I displayed my ability, they scattered.

Whilst not Gifted, their village was designed for this style of fighting. They ducked into holes and trenches around the village, popping out to shoot before disappearing again.

My Foresight was entirely focused on dodging arrows as they buzzed past me or broke against my Nemean cloak, leaving only bruises underneath.

I moved forward, sniping the few goblins I could but there were hundreds of the little shits, and my spearheads were only able to get five or six at a time when they popped up. I rolled to the side, dodging a volley of twelve arrows, and retaliated with an artillery strike of my own.

Juruk and the others hung back, following me from a distance.

They shouted something at me, but I couldn't hear them and didn't have time to go back and listen to what they were saying.

Moving dexterously on the balls of my feet, I rolled, dodged and teleported about the goblins, following them as they trudged through their trenches and tunnels to the center of the village. I didn't think I'd need their help but kept them around in case I required information or a way to carry back loot. I kept moving and reached the center of the village, needing to strafe lithely as the volume of arrows increased. I teleported up into the air using the superior height to send out spearheads down into the trenches, skewering two dozen archers.

Moments before hitting the ground again, my Foresight went into overdrive as a new threat revealed itself. My teleportation was on cooldown, however, and I didn't have time to move as the floor gave out beneath me. Then, I dropped into a massive pit.

Landing in a roll, I sprang back to my feet, club and shield at the ready.

I looked up but had fallen over fifty feet, and couldn't teleport out. I looked down at the wooden wreckage of the floor around me, seeing barred, iron gates made of crude iron.

One of the gates opened and out marched a humanoid figure, seven feet tall.

He wore armor like a Roman gladiator which looked to be of higher quality than any of the armor I'd seen the other goblins wearing.

On his head was a Greek-looking helmet, obscuring his features in shadow.

Mugro the Skull-taker. Gifted—Mortal. Goblin. Rank: 45.

The notification popped up as I surveyed the entry of the newcomer into what I suddenly realized was an arena.

"I take it you are the chief?" I asked.

"I am," Mugro said, his voice deep and growly behind his helmet. "And you are dead."

Smoke began to pour out of the gates, filling the arena and rising thick in the air. It obscured the goblin chief and made me cough, being foul, thick, and black, smelling like burning tires. I ducked as my Foresight showed my head being taken off.

I teleported behind Murgo, slashing out at his back, but he swayed out of the way, surprisingly agile for his size.

My maul swept around.

Mugro bent beneath it and released a concussive wave from his hand, knocking my spearheads off course as I tried to skewer him.

I coughed heavily, the noxious smoke rising even more, growing heavier with every second. Mugro seemed unaffected by the smog; I hadn't heard him cough once.

He plans on suffocating me, I realized. This was similar to how I had considered killing the Nemean lion. *Unfortunately for him, I've got tricks of my own.*

I teleported upwards and took a breath of clear, fresh air, now seeing the goblins had formed a ring around the top of the arena and were peering down, trying to see the fight.

Their eyes widened when they saw me. They cried out, but their voices blended, preventing any words from being made out.

I fell back through the smoke, holding my breath as my eyes stung, but I didn't give up searching for Mugro in the murk.

The crack of wood behind made me spin, blocking with my shield, being tossed practically the length of the arena as the strike slammed into it. I leapt back to my feet, feeling the bruises forming all over my back from when I'd impacted the ground. I heard the pounding of feet and activated Bestial Senses, growing nauseous from the sensory input but I focused only on the sounds of footfalls and breathing from in front of me.

I ducked and dodged around Mugro, who did not even try to block my assault as I swiped at him with the claws of my club. They slashed along his belly but barely broke his skin.

Mugro snarled, kicking out at me.

I sidestepped and brought my own knee up into the back of his.

Mugro swore and stumbled.

I seized the opportunity, my maul swinging in from behind.

He blocked with his forearm but much like me, was unprepared for the force of the strike.

Bone cracked and Mugro howled, the sound not just of pain but of an area-effect attack.

I felt my head spin and froze as my body locked up, stunned by the force of the sound.

The effect only lasted a few seconds, but Mugro was already bearing down on me with a short, serrated blade in his good hand.

I bent it back, sliding across the Nemean pelt, then I grabbed Mugro with my Telekinesis, lifting him and attempting to crush him like a boa constrictor.

He grunted and groaned, but my Mana was draining fast as I held him and he fought against my mental hold. Mugro slumped to the ground, now panting heavily.

I had to teleport upwards, gasping for breath as I took in another fresh burst of air.

Goblins threw trash at me as I appeared, but they all missed as I fell back into the smoke.

Mugro was prepared for me and was swinging at the spot where I'd landed before even touching down fully.

I fell to the ground under his attack, quickly rolling, pulled a dagger from my belt and slashing upwards. I pierced the armor at his waist, right into a man's most sensitive area.

Mugro howled and fell, thrashing on the ground.

I grabbed my club from the ground and was on him in a second, bringing it down on his chest over and over, blood splattering over me.

Blood and Souls (Repeatable): Kill 320 monsters or humanoids. Current progress: 58/320. When you complete this quest, you will gain 64 rank points. The next quest will require double the number to be completed but will award double the rank points.

I kept smashing down, my breath heaving until finally, I got up, ripping the gates off their hinges with my Telekinesis and striding through. I found fires burning and goblins throwing various bits of debris and green-leafed branches into the fire. I slew the goblins and smothered the fires with clouds of dust and dirt created with my maul.

Once all the fires were out, the smoke finally began to thin. I could see clearly once more.

Blood and Souls (Repeatable): Kill 320 monsters or humanoids. Current progress: 89/320. When you complete this quest, you will gain 64 rank points. The next quest will require double the number to be completed but will award double the rank points.

I stepped out into the arena, finding the goblins quiet now as they looked down at me standing over the body of their chief.

Stooping, I began stripping him of his gear.

As I took off his helmet, I noticed he wore a black, silk mask embroidered with silver runes. Removing it, a notification came from the System.

Mask of Winter's Breath. Type: Scarf. Rarity: Rare. While wearing this scarf over your face, you can breathe normally in heavy smoke, poisonous vapors, or underwater.	
Made from the fibers of a lunar silkworm and empowered by a journeyman enchanter.	
Durability:	15/20.

So that's how he did it.

I put the mask in my pocket, not intending to wear it until I'd given it a good wash. I took off the armor on his forearms too but unfortunately, it wasn't the right size for me. Next, I removed the armor from around his waist and legs, but didn't need his shin guards thanks to my boots, leaving those on him. He had a ring on his finger.

When I touched it, another notification popped up.

Ring of Auroch Strength. Type: Jewelry. Rarity: Rare. While wearing this ring, your Might Attribute is increased by +3.	
Made from the horn of an ancient Auroch and empowered by a journeyman enchanter.	
Durability:	19/20.

"Very nice," I said, slipping it on and instantly feeling I could lift more. It was different from the feeling of increasing my stats; there was no pain as my muscle grew and toughened, only a sense that I was stronger than I'd been.

I looked up at the watching goblins above. "Now is the time for all of you to explain why I shouldn't kill you to get progress on my quests for Kelesa."

Chapter 7: Upgrades People

The goblins were nervously silent as I looked up at them. They shuffled from side to side, bereft and unsure what to do now that their leader was dead. Sighing, I ran at the wall, kicking off and running fifteen feet up it before teleporting to land at the rim of the arena.

"That's better," I said. I looked around and found Juruk and my other minions with their weapons dropped and surrounded by goblins. "Congratulations for being officially useless. Why didn't you mention anything about the giant trapdoor?"

"Whole camp trapped," Juruk said. "We goblins. Thought you knew."

I sighed. This was my own fault for assuming they would be competent. I looked at those surrounding them and raised my hand.

"Dominion," I intoned, and they instantly dropped their weapons, reaching to their necks as the brand of my ability appeared there.

8 rank points gained.

Whip and Chains (Repeatable): Conquer 80 monsters or humanoids by bringing them under your Dominion. Current progress: 43/80. When you complete this quest, you will gain 16 rank points. The next quest will require double the number to be completed but will award double the rank points.

I turned to the other goblins and looked them over. "If any of you aren't comfortable taking orders from me, then act now. You won't get a second chance."

Not one of them stepped forward and I snorted in disdain.

"Dominion," I said, bringing another forty-nine goblins under my control.

16 rank points gained.

Whip and Chains (Repeatable): Conquer 160 monsters or humanoids by bringing them under your Dominion. Current

> **progress: 12/160. When you complete this quest, you will gain 32 rank points. The next quest will require double the number to be completed but will award double the rank points.**

I used my ability again, noticing some goblins fleeing but not caring enough to chase them.

> **Whip and Chains (Repeatable): Conquer 160 monsters or humanoids by bringing them under your Dominion. Current progress: 61/160. When you complete this quest, you will gain 32 rank points and the next quest will require double the number to be completed but will award double the rank points.**

I ordered the ones dominated to circle the ones I had not so I could clearly see who I was targeting with my ability.

> **Whip and Chains (Repeatable): Conquer 160 monsters or humanoids by bringing them under your Dominion. Current progress: 110/160. When you complete this quest, you will gain 32 rank points. The next quest will require double the number to be completed but will award double the rank points.**

Only a small group remained for me to dominate but I thought it would be enough to push me past this current quest goal.

> **Whip and Chains (Repeatable): Conquer 160 monsters or humanoids by bringing them under your Dominion. Current progress: 159/160. When you complete this quest, you will gain 32 rank points. The next quest will require double the number to be completed but will award double the rank points.**

There were only a dozen or so goblins left but it was enough as I finished taking control of the last of the tribe.

> **32 rank points gained.**

> **Whip and Chains (Repeatable): Conquer 320 monsters or humanoids by bringing them under your Dominion. Current progress: 14/320. When you complete this quest, you will gain 64 rank points. The next quest will require double the number to be completed but will award double the rank points.**

I smiled darkly to myself, now having seventy-nine free rank points to spend to upgrade my abilities. I looked over my new vassals and wasn't that impressed. The tallest of them was five feet; they were scrawny and wielded poorly-made equipment. I had my doubts about how well they'd do in a battle but for now, they could serve as scouts, guides, and porters.

"Juruk, come forward," I ordered.

Juruk shuffled out of the crowd. "Bring me all the loot your tribe has. And don't try and hide anything or let anyone else keep anything from me."

I didn't trust him to obey me out of any loyalty or honor but my ability would force him to do as I commanded. I was brought a throne to sit on, using it to upgrade a few of my abilities as my tribute was brought forward. I knew what I wanted to upgrade. Whilst Mugro's armor didn't fit me, I had a pretty good idea which ability might be able to change that.

"Raise Compress Earth by one rank," I told the System.

> **Compress Earth (Rank 7): You can fuse dirt and stone into a more durable, heavier material that can be shaped. You can currently fuse a 64-foot-square section of earth and common stone. Your compressed stone has a Hardness rating of 7; your compressed earth has a Hardness rating of 5. The detail with which you can sculpt is based on your Mind & Perception Attribute.**
>
> **You can now use uncommon stone in your fusions. The rarer, denser, or more exotic the stone, the greater will be the effect on the final product.**
>
> | Cost: | 4 Mana per 1-foot square. |
> |---|---|
>
> **Upgrade this ability to increase the amount you can compress, its durability, weight, and the materials upon which you can use this ability. Each upgrade increases your Mind Attribute by 1.**

I felt the approach of a splitting headache and sat back on the throne, focusing on my breathing. When the rank-up was finished and the pain had passed, I sat up straight again.

"Increase Compress Earth by one rank," I told the System.

Compress Earth (Rank 8): You can fuse dirt and stone into a more durable, heavier material that can be shaped. You can currently fuse a 128-foot-square section of earth and common stone. Your compressed stone has a Hardness rating of 7.5; your compressed earth has a Hardness rating of 5.5. The detail with which you can sculpt is based on your Mind & Perception Attribute.	
You can now use uncommon stone in your fusions. The rarer, denser, or more exotic the stone, the greater will be the effect on the final product.	
Cost:	**5 Mana per 1-foot square.**
Upgrade this ability to increase the amount you can compress, its durability, weight, and the materials upon which you can use this ability. Each upgrade increases your Mind Attribute by 1.	

"Put one rank into Compress Earth," I told the System again.

Compress Earth (Rank 9): You can fuse dirt and stone into a more durable, heavier material that can be shaped. You can currently fuse a 256-square-foot section of earth and common stone. Your compressed stone has a Hardness rating of 8; your compressed earth has a Hardness rating of 6. The detail with which you can sculpt is based on your Mind & Perception Attribute.	
You can now use uncommon stone in your fusions. The rarer, denser, or more exotic the stone, the greater will be the effect on the final product.	
Cost:	**5 Mana per 1-foot square.**
Upgrade this ability to increase the amount you can compress, its durability, weight, and the materials upon which you can use this ability. Each upgrade increases your Mind Attribute by 1.	

Once again, my headache came back with a vengeance, but I believed I was getting better at blocking out the pain. Breathing in and out, I opened my eyes as soon as it had passed.

Here goes...! I hope I'm right.

I had theorized that abilities might give an additional effect every five ranks but it could be more. I wouldn't know until I tried. "Raise Compress Earth by one more rank."

Congratulations! You have raised an ability to Rank 10. Please pick an additional effect for your ability from the list below:
• **You can now use non-magical metals in your fusions. The rarer, denser, or more exotic the stone, the greater will be the effect on the final product.**
• **You can now transmute one form of stone to another similar type.**
• **You can now more keenly shape the objects you create with your ability and sculpt finer details.**

Yes! I was right! I fought through the headache to think, really liking the first option since the ability to add metals would greatly increase the strength of my creations. Transmuting stones sounded interesting, but I wasn't after making things out of any particular type of substance. The last option, I was pretty sure I could do on my own with a bit of practice.

So, I went with the first option, completing my upgrade.

Compress Earth (Rank 10): You can fuse dirt and stone into a more durable, heavier material that can be shaped. You can currently fuse a 512-square-foot section of earth, common stone, and metal. Your compressed stone has a Hardness rating of 8.5; your compressed earth has a Hardness rating of 6.5. The detail with which you can sculpt is based on your Mind & Perception Attribute.
You can now use uncommon stone in your fusions. The rarer, denser, or more exotic the stone, the greater will be the effect on the final product.
You can now use non-magical metals in your fusions. The rarer, denser, or more exotic the stone, the greater will be the effect on the final product.

Cost:	10 Mana per 1-foot square

Upgrade this ability to increase the amount you can compress, its durability, weight, and the materials upon which you can use this ability. Each upgrade increases your Mind Attribute by 1.

I had achieved two things for which I had been aiming: discovering if there was an additional effect at Rank 10, and getting my Compress Earth to work with metals. This meant I could adjust the armor I'd got from Mugro as well as the shaft of my maul. The experiment had not been cheap, but it was worth it. Seventy-nine rank points seemed like a lot until you realized I had just spent thirty-four on raising an ability by only four ranks. The cost had gone up again, but I only had to wait a short while for my Mana to recharge.

Taking a break from upgrading my abilities, I looked over the mass of junk the goblins had piled before me. Some of it was literally garbage.

"Why is there a broken coat rack here?" I asked, looking over the trash heap.

"Loot from an old village," Juruk said proudly.

"At least I have a use for the metal now," I sighed.

There were wooden crates, old pots, pans, and even an entire wardrobe with a full mirror on its door, albeit cracked in several places.

I was startled when I caught sight of myself. My facial hair had grown into a straggly beard and my hair hung long and flat. It was my face, however, that was the most startling.

My eyes were brown. They had always been dark but now, they were almost black.

Three angry red lines ran down the side of my face. They were still healing and would leave vicious scars. It had only been a few days, but I already looked different.

My muscle mass was now much leaner and my body more angular.

Turning away from my reflection, I looked back to Juruk. "Most of this is junk. We'll be leaving it behind when we depart. Take anything made of metal or of actual value; not just things you've found or stolen. Make sure you bring the wardrobe door with the mirror," I instructed him. "Have everything packed by tonight. Don't leave behind anything you might need. We will be departing tomorrow morning."

I headed back to camp, thinking over my next upgrades. Both my Perception and Mind Attributes were at seventeen. I didn't have enough points to increase my Mind to twenty, but did have enough to get my Perception to twenty-two. Arriving back at camp, I bathed in the river, allowing the blood, sweat, and dirt to run off. I rubbed mint leaves into the scarf I got from Mugro and headed back into camp. Stripping out of my soaking wet clothes, I set my pelt and new scarf to dry as I lay back to spend the rest of my rank points.

"Increase Foresight by one rank," I told the System.

Foresight (Rank 6): You passively see 11 seconds into the future and know what will happen to yourself and the space within 15 feet at all times. This ability is based on your Perception Attribute. Upgrading it will increase the time you can see by 1 second per rank in Perception above 10.
You can see different possible outcomes based on your actions made within the span of time you can foresee.
This is a passive ability, costing 1 Mana/sec.
Upgrade this ability to increase how far you can see into the future and how far around you can see. Every upgrade to this ability increases your Perception Attribute by 1.

I felt the needles return, stabbing into my eyes with burning fire, hearing a roaring cacophony in my ears. My back arched with the pain as I let out a strained breath and dragged in a lungful of air. When the pain subsided, I breathed out again.

"Increase Foresight by one rank," I said.

Foresight (Rank 7): You passively see 12 seconds into the future and know what will happen to yourself and the space within 17 feet at all times. This ability is based on your Perception Attribute. Upgrading it will increase the time you can see by 1 second per rank in Perception above 10.
You can see different possible outcomes based on your actions made within the span of time you can foresee.
This is a passive ability, costing 1 Mana/sec.

> Upgrade this ability to increase how far you can see into the future and how far around you can see. Every upgrade to this ability increases your Perception Attribute by 1.

The pain redoubled, a terrible scream tearing from my throat before I bit it back, refusing to allow myself to show any weakness. I felt my vision darken as I held back another yelp of agony. The pain faded, and I let myself rest for a moment before continuing.

"Raise Foresight by one rank," I said.

> **Foresight (Rank 8): You passively see 13 seconds into the future and know what will happen to yourself and the space within 19 feet at all times. This ability is based on your Perception Attribute upgrading. It will increase the time you can see by 1 second per rank in Perception above 10.**
>
> **You can see different possible outcomes based on your actions made within the span of time you can foresee.**
>
> **This is a passive ability, costing 1 Mana/sec.**
>
> **Upgrade this ability to increase how far you can see into the future and how far around you can see. Every upgrade to this ability increases your Perception Attribute by 1.**

The pain returned again, greater than ever before, but it was about to get worse.

> **Congratulations! You have raised one of your Attributes beyond 20, the Mortal limit. Your body will now physiologically change to adjust to this increase to keep your Attribute from killing you.**
>
> **Your eyes have mutated to allow you perfect vision, even in complete darkness and your eardrums have mutated to automatically deafen you temporarily when explosions or other loud sounds go off in your proximity, to prevent you from being stunned or permanently deafened.**

Fluid flowed down from my eyes and ears.

I felt my eyes roll and grow white-hot as my eardrums shattered and began reforming. I writhed and flailed on my sleeping bag, the pain now so intense I could not even scream.

Finally, the pain ended, and I gasped for breath. I had raised Perception past twenty, but still wanted to get Foresight to Rank 10 for the additional effect.

"Raise Foresight by one rank," I said.

Foresight (Rank 9): You passively see 14 seconds into the future and know what will happen to yourself and the space within 21 feet of you at all times. This ability is based on your Perception Attribute upgrading. It will increase the time you can see by 1 second rank in Perception above 10.
You can see different possible outcomes based on your actions made within the span of time you can foresee.
This is a passive ability, costing 1 Mana/sec.
Upgrade this ability to increase how far you can see into the future and how far around you can see. Every upgrade to this ability increases your Perception Attribute by 1.

The pain returned again but it was nothing compared to the agony of mutating. I focused on my breathing and was able to push past it.

"Raise Foresight by one more rank," I told the System once the pain had disappeared.

Foresight (Rank 10): You passively see 15 seconds into the future and know what will happen to yourself and the space within 23 feet of you at all times. This ability is based on your Perception attribute upgrading. It will increase the time you can see by 1 second per rank in Perception above 10.
You can see different possible outcomes based on your actions made within the span of time you can foresee.
You can see visions during your sleep that will lead you to objects or creatures that you seek. This is a passive ability, costing 1 Mana/sec.

> **Upgrade this ability to increase how far you can see into the future and how far around you can see. Every upgrade to this ability increases your Perception Attribute by 1.**

Muscles tightened and I sucked in a breath as the pain washed over me. When I had recovered sufficiently, I sighed.

There were five available rank points left, but even if I was up to upgrading another ability, they would all cost more than that. I focused back on my fight against Mugro, reviewing how I'd fought him. I felt the bruises along my body and grimaced. Then, I drank a health potion. The bruises didn't fade immediately but I did feel the pain lessen somewhat.

I had not been able to block Mugro effectively. His Might had been so high that without a roughly equivalent amount, I had just been sent flying. I realized with hindsight that I could probably have blocked his hits if I'd used my Telekinesis instead of my own body. I could lift an object weighing 450 pounds and could likely withstand the same amount of force with my ability. If I manipulated my shield telekinetically, that would leave my other hand free.

I looked at my weapon. My Nemean club had served me well so far and I still had the bones and the rest of the claws from the lion. I took the other leg bones, some quartz and onyx and a few bits of metal from the goblin's scrap heap. I held the claws in place, fastening with the binding of tight compressed uncommon stone and metal, creating three other clubs.

I could wield one in my left hand and use the others telekinetically.

I looked over Murgo's helmet and the single full piece of armor and vambrace. The armor would extend from the wrist all the way up my arm to the pauldron, the vambrace covering my left forearm. He also had a wide, leather belt that covered most of my stomach with dangling leather tassets. Plates of metal were riveted along the leather belt, providing added protection to more vital areas.

The belt would be the easiest to adjust and I quickly made it fit around my own waist.

The other armor wasn't so straightforward. Murgo had been almost two feet taller than me, and his arms and head had been thicker than mine.

By then, my Compress Earth also affected common metal. Placing the ill-fitting armor on my arm, I compressed the steel, shrinking it until it fit near perfectly. I did the same for the vambrace. I hadn't added any more material to the mix so they didn't weigh any more than before, but each square inch would weigh more than steel of the same size and thickness.

I put the Greek-looking helmet on and went over to the mirror of the wardrobe which the goblins had brought over. I adjusted it until it was only a little loose so I could pad it with leather later. It had already grown late, and I decided to get some sleep before anything else could interrupt me. I grabbed some food and ate quickly.

Then, I returned to my tent and took off my newly acquired armor.

I set it to the side with my cloak and weapons, then fell asleep quickly, my battle and upgrades having taken most of my energy.

Chapter 8: Star-fallen

Jamis, Torvin, Mira, Felrick and Helen returned to the capital. They dismounted, and stable hands took their horses back to the stable as they returned to the palace.

Sergeant Heldark looked them over as they returned. "Glad to see you all look the same. Some think scars make them look tougher, but it just shows they didn't go into the fight prepared. With a good healer like Helen, you shouldn't ever even have a sign you've been in battle, apart from the loss of durability to your gear," he said.

"Are we going back to training?" Jamis asked, a little defeated.

"No," Heldark said. "Right now, you need experience. Once you've rested, there will be a new assignment for you. There are reports of a spider nest near one of our lumber operations in the Cursed Forest. Valuable timber, so worth the risk. Lady Kathleen and a few of her bodyguards went to investigate around two months back but we lost contact with both her and the lumber operation. No scouts have returned since."

"Who is Lady Kathleen?" Torvin asked.

"My cousin," Helen said. "She is also the granddaughter of the High Priestess of Luren."

"Indeed," Heldark agreed. "This quest comes straight from the high priestess. She has given you a tracking device to help locate her granddaughter. Your job is to find any survivors, rescue Lady Kathleen if she still lives, and put an end to these spiders."

"How far away is it?" Mira asked.

"Four days into the Cursed Forest but a week from the capital," Heldark said.

The champions all stiffened as they received a notification from the System.

"That might delay us a bit," Helen said as she read it over.

***

I had just sat up in bed, sunlight piercing the covering of my tent when a notification popped into my vision.

> Congratulations! As the Champion of Kelesa, you have been invited to participate in an event to take place in one week's time and which will allow you to interact with some of the other champions. During the event, you will be transported into another realm. You will not suffer permanent death, or other effects such as mind control, domination, or crippling injuries. You can still gain rank points from killing another champion, but they will not lose any rank points they have gathered.
>
> Any participant 'killed' during the event will be teleported back to where they were before the last event and will only lose any materials or equipment gathered during the event. The goal and reward for the event will be revealed when you enter the realm. Do you wish to be entered into the event?

"Yes," I said immediately.

Any opportunity to gain new rank points or gather information on my rivals was welcome. Also, there was basically no risk to this event, which made me slightly suspicious… but not enough to decline the invite.

I felt energized and excited by this new goal, having a time limit now. I needed to gather as many rank points and hopefully new abilities as I could before the event, longing to jump up and rush into the forest and hunt down as many beasts as I could.

I calmed myself, knowing I'd need to use my time wisely; the best way to do that would be to acquire some local knowledge.

I strapped my armor on over my clothes, starting to run out of fully intact garments. I put my cloak on over my armor and slipped two clubs into my belt, then stepped out of the tent and looked at myself in the mirror, seeing my patchy-looking beard. I grabbed one of my rusty daggers and compressed it. The rust disappeared and turned the blade a russet color. I compressed the edge until it was razor fine and stepped closer to the mirror.

Carefully, ran my dagger along my skin, shaving off my beard and nicking myself several times. I rubbed the blood on my cloak and sipped from a healing potion to stop the bleeding. Then I looked myself over again, my face clean shaven, my hair still hanging long.

I'd meant to get it cut just before Kelesa had brought me here.

Not trusting my capacity to cut my own hair, or indeed for any of my vassals to do it, I'd let it be. I tugged my helmet on and went to look for my goblin vassals.

I found Juruk beside a pile of metal bits of junk, animal pelts, and random bits of furniture.

"What are the closest and the most powerful creatures in the area?" I asked.

"There is the spined lion," Juruk said. "We stay out of its territory. The chief didn't want to fight it."

"Could be an interesting fight," I said. "What rank is it?"

"I don't know. The chief never said. He never wanted to enter its territory."

So, it's probably higher than forty, based on his own rank, I reasoned to myself. *I might want to wait on that a while... or maybe not.* "What else?" I pressed him.

"There is the black serpent," Juruk said. "It lives in the swamps, upriver. The chief wouldn't fight it either."

"Is there any creature he *would* fight?" I asked.

"He only fights creatures that come to us," Juruk said. "Like you."

So maybe he isn't the best way to judge the strength of my opponents. "What other creatures? It doesn't matter how powerful they are. I want to know what and where they are."

"There is the forest wyvern," Juruk said. "It dwells in the crags north of here. The spider queen lives with etters near the humans, a day to the south."

Juruk suddenly seemed nervous. "Then, there is the wraith in the old ruins."

"Wraith?" I asked.

"It is cursed to haunt the ruins," Juruk said. "Any creature that enters there never returns. Even Gifted beasts have never made it back."

"Very promising," I said, musing over my options. It seemed the wraith would be the highest-ranked creature if it had been killing Gifted beasts for a while. That left the other targets to start with.

"Which one of them is the closest?" I asked.

"The black serpent," Juruk said, shivering a little as he said its name.

"Great. Show me the way," I said.

"Me?" Juruk asked.

"Yes," I said. "Lead the way to the swamp. Now."

Grudgingly, he stood up and led me along the shore.

We took a narrow trail up the side of the cliff past the waterfall, hiking along the shore of the river for three hours before he stopped and pointed across the river to a swathe of reeds and cattails stretching on for three miles. A scattering of trees growing among the plants and various ponds were visible in the swamp.

"Do you know where its lair is?" I asked.

"No," Juruk said, shaking his head. "This is the end of our territory and as far as I've ever been."

"Go back to camp and wait for me," I said. "We're going to be here longer than I thought."

I ran over the river, my feet never sinking through the water as I crossed the rapids in less than thirty seconds. Standing on the bank, I looked over the swamp, seeking out a black serpent, the name both evocative and also mysteriously vague. I hadn't bothered to ask how big it was but based on my experience so far, all Gifted were typically enormous.

Where would I be if I were a snake? Where might be the most tempting place to hide myself? I moved deeper into the swamp, my head on a swivel as I searched for any movement or hint of something in the water. First, I headed toward the center of the swamp, at the very least, wanting to get a better vantage for the rest of the area.

When absolutely necessary, I ran across the water but generally tried to stay on solid ground. At the center island, I glanced around, bending upon seeing an old snakeskin at least three dozen feet long.

"Holy shit, that's big!" I whispered.

The snakeskin slithered its massive bulk into a hole in the ground.

I sighed. "Well, at least I've got the gear for this."

Pulling my scarf, I dived into the murky water and proceeded tentatively, feeling my way, swimming down as the curved tunnel widened out.

I must have been swimming for ten minutes when I finally broke the surface again.

Water dripped off my pelt, skin, and armor as I moved onto the bank. It was pitch black, but thanks to my Perception Mutation, I could see clearly.

Animal bones rested in the muck, and the cavern was at least a hundred feet tall. A network of roots high above supported the ceiling, and I looked about warily.

Its attack was visible with Foresight and I teleported away, turning around to see… nothing. Not one single thing could my eyes see, but knew the snake had just struck. Again, my Foresight warned me of an attack, and I rolled to the side, still seeing nothing at all.

Activating my Bestial Senses, my nostrils were assaulted by the rank smell of snake scales sliding over mud. I could now see the black serpent, its body glowing a warm purple.

It struck at me again and I rolled under it, my clawed clubs striking upwards. I made contact but my clubs only dug narrow scratches, its tough scales rebuffing all attacks.

> **Allezsia Shadow-fang. Gifted—Mortal. Giant Death Adder.**
> **Rank: 38.**

It lunged forward.

My shield lodged between us. Its fangs bounced off the enchanted steel, reflecting the force of the attack. "Didn't like that, did you?" I taunted. Then I began hurling spearheads at it as my maul and extra clubs swung at it from multiple directions.

The snake hissed and lunged toward me again.

This time, my Foresight let me know I couldn't dodge or block as it was apparently using some sort of ability to cross the distance between us in less than half a second.

Its fangs bit down but couldn't pierce my cloak, so it held me in its jaws with my right arm pinned.

Beating down on its skull with my other club, I was successful in gouging wounds into it, but it shook me and didn't release. A hot liquid seeped down my cloak, dripping onto my skin. I screamed as the poison began eating into my flesh, sending my Telekinesis wild as I threw everything I had at it.

Allezsia wrapped itself around me and began to squeeze.

I gasped and strained as it started crushing me, my club beating on it faster as my other weapons savaged its body.

> **16 rank points gained.**

> **Blood and Souls (Repeatable): Kill 320 monsters or humanoids.**
> **Current progress: 58/320. When you complete this quest, you will**

> **gain 64 rank points. The next quest will require double the number to be completed but will award double the rank points.**

A notification signaled its death, but its viselike grip on me was unwavering. Even in death, it continued to constrict me as its poison attacked my thighs and legs.

I gasped, looking about, then teleported, soon landing on my back, rolling in the mud to coat my legs and ease the burning. I grabbed a health potion from my pocket and drained the contents. The burning in my legs subsided but didn't fully go away.

A notification blinked, and I pulled it up.

> **You have been affected by the enhanced venom ability of a death adder that will stop your heart(s) and destroy your nervous system. Take an antidote or receive treatment before you die. The time until death is 1:30 minutes.**

Shit! I don't have an antidote!

Attempting to subdue rising panic, I searched my backpack, locating my jars of herbs and frantically grabbing the ones containing purity lilies and violet nullifier.

I shoved two of each in my mouth, desperately chewing and swallowing. I waited and felt my stomach churn and boil as heat filled my body, similar to the feeling of increasing an Attribute by three ranks. *That's it. I'm dying.*

Uncontrolled, insane laughter escaped from my lips until the new notification arrived.

> **You have completed a hidden objective and earned a title. Objective: Survive a lethal poison with no outside assistance.**
>
> **Reward. Title: Field Alchemist.**
>
> ***Field Alchemist: You do not acknowledge the dangers of mixing different herbs and liquids inside your body and your very stomach acts as a cauldron. Suffer only half the negative effects of mixing two herbs without processing and gain full benefits from them.**

> You have completed a hidden objective and earned a title. Objective: Be seconds away from death and pull through by your own will and wit.
>
> Reward. Title: Survivor II (requires you to already have Survivor).
>
> * Survivor II: You are resistant to death itself, proving over and again that you have what it takes to continue. Mortal wounds have less impact on you and require damage stages two higher to take effect.

I gasped and looked down at my legs, still raw from the poison. As I drank another potion, my skin healed. The hair along my legs was gone, however, and there were white burn scars around my knees. My lower legs had been protected by tight-fitting boots, and I was again thankful I had chosen them instead of a weapon.

I took out a Nemean claw and approached the cooling body of the death adder, pulling it out straight, using it like a blade and running the claw along its underbelly.

I peeled off the skin and rolled up the bloody hide.

> Death Adder Hide. Type: Material. Rarity: Uncommon. Hardness: 6. This hide was enhanced with extra Toughness, making it extremely durable and unable to be cut by a weapon with less than 6 Hardness.

Taking hold of its skull, I teased out the fangs to examine one. They were some fifteen inches in length.

> Death Adder Fang. Type: Material. Rarity: Uncommon. Hardness: 8. This fang is imbued with the remnants of a powerful poison ability, dealing moderate poison damage when it comes into contact with flesh.
>
> *Death Adder Venom: Causes severe rapid necrosis in flesh, causing organ failure. When injected, requires 1 to 2 drams to be lethal to a moderately-sized human.

I tied the hide to my backpack and put the fangs inside. Then, I dived back into the water, my weapons suspended behind me telekinetically as I felt my way along the tunnel.

Making my way to the surface, I emerged into the noon sun, then ran across the water, jumping the bank of reeds across the river to the other side.

I headed back to camp with my newly-acquired trophies, now having seven days to prepare for the event. I was tired now, but needed to push myself to get as powerful as I could be before it would be time to face the other champions. I dropped the hide off for Jand and the others to start tanning and found Juruk again.

"Take me to the wyvern," I said.

"The wyvern?" he asked, ears twitching with fright. "Don't you want to wait?"

"No," I said. "I've got a time limit, and I want to spend every minute I can getting stronger. Now, lead the way!"

With typical reluctance, Juruk led me out of the camp.

We followed the trail but headed east instead of toward the swamp. After a three-hour hike, he pointed to a ravine, the top of which was lined with trees. The pass continued north toward the mountains, splitting the earth to be joined by other canyons and crags.

"You can return to camp now. I've got this," I told Juruk, surveying my new hunting ground.

Juruk turned and fled.

I moved into the pass, scanning the clifftops and shallow caves for any sign of the wyvern, heading deeper until I heard wings beating. Freezing, I looked around, attempting to pinpoint the sound. They were coming from the top of the cliff, so I started climbing.

My Might was a lot higher thanks to my ring and I quickly pulled myself to the edge of the cliff and looked up. Uprooted trees formed a massive nest, and there, inside of it sat the wyvern, sleeping. It was monstrous, its body the size of a minivan, and its wings easily spanned eighty feet as it lay coiled in on itself.

Yurmir, Prince of the Treetops. Gifted—Draconic/Beast/Wyvern. Mortal. Rank: 54.

It was the strongest creature I'd met so far, and I estimated it to be as difficult to fight as the Nemean lion.

A blazing ball of fire fell from the heavens, striking the sleeping wyvern which snapped awake, letting out a roar of pain and anger. A shadow fell over the ground and the wyvern looked up in time to have its neck clamped down by a beast four times its size.

The force of its landing nearly flung me from the cliffside, barely managing to keep hold of some tree roots. I poked my head back over the cliff to get a look at it.

It had black scales, the edges of which pulsed shades of orange and red.

Its colossal body was the size of a semi-truck, while its eyes were brilliant crimson, and its head boasted a six-horned crown.

> **Exar'kun, the Star-fallen Lord. Gifted—Dragon/Hell Dragon. Veteran. Rank: ???**

The dragon snapped the wyvern's neck and tore into its flesh.

I stayed where I was, motionless, fixated on the sight.

After twenty minutes, the dragon spread its wings and took to the sky again. That was the sight of my first Veteran-ranked creature. The fight against the wyvern would have been difficult and likely to have almost killed me but the hell dragon had slain it in less than thirty seconds with only two attacks.

I'm going to beat that thing, someday, I promised myself.

I waited for five minutes before getting up and approaching the remains of the corpse. The hell dragon had ripped open the wyvern's chest and devoured all its internal organs.

The meat of the wyvern's flanks and neck had been ripped apart but there was still a significant amount of the carcass left untouched.

I began cutting away at its hide, folding it back and skinning all possible parts of it. I also collected loose scales from the ground and spotted a black one, its edges red like burning coal.

> **Hell Dragon Scale. Type: Material. Rarity: Epic. Hardness: 14. The scales of this hell dragon are impervious to any fire and strong enough to withstand the blow of a mountain giant. Requires a weapon of at least Hardness 14 to break it.**

It was both awesome and terrifying. The scales were harder than my Nemean pelt, and to think that the beast was entirely covered in these things.

I've got some way to go before I'm on the level of that thing!

I kept harvesting. Most of the wyvern's wing membrane had been destroyed by the dragon's fire, but I got enough of it to lay it out like a tarpaulin upon which I piled loose scales.

> **Forest Wyvern Scale. Type: Material. Rarity: Rare. Hardness: 9. The scales of this wyvern give it resistance to poisonous and acidic attacks and require a weapon of at least Hardness 9 to break it.**

I set to work on its two back feet. It had three toes and two back claws that were curved like a velociraptor's. It took a great deal of time and cutting to break them free from their hold, but eventually, I acquired the six front and two back talons.

> **Forest Wyvern Front Talons. Type: Material. Rarity: Rare. Hardness: 10. The claws of this wyvern were enhanced by an ability during its life, making them harder and giving them the ability to pierce even material stronger than itself. They can pierce through materials as if they were two Hardnesses lower.**

> **Forest Wyvern Hook Talons. Type: Material. Rarity: Rare. Hardness: 10. The hook claws of this wyvern were enhanced by an ability during its life, making them more effective at tearing flesh. They cause significant bleeding and laceration, preventing the wounds from being easily closed. Requires a weapon with Hardness 10 to break them.**

I continued to carve up the wyvern, finding some sections of its flesh cooked by dragon fire. I tasted some, feeling hungry but clearly not that hungry—so I discarded the flesh as I freed its bones. I would make good use of the longer bones of its wings and legs.

> **Forest Wyvern Bone. Type: Material. Rarity: Uncommon. Hardness: 9.** The bones of this wyvern are enhanced during its life by a high Toughness, making them highly durable. Requires a weapon with Hardness 9 to break it.

After that, I teased out its fangs, being careful as I saw a dark oily liquid coating the teeth. Its four fangs were seven inches long, its other teeth ranging from five to three inches.

> **Forest Wyvern Fangs. Type: Material. Rarity: Rare. Hardness: 10.** The fangs of this wyvern have been enhanced by the remnants of a poison ability, enabling them to deal moderate poison damage that paralyzes targets with low Endurance and Toughness.
>
> ***Forest Wyvern Poison:** the venom of the forest wyvern attacks and destroys the nerves of the body, shutting down the brain's ability to control the body as the poison makes its way through the nervous system. Requires two to three drams to be lethal in a moderately-sized human.

Hmmm, that could have been bad! I don't have good Toughness or Endurance.

My harvesting of the corpse had gone on for several hours.

The sun had already started to set. I had only hunted one Gifted creature today, but I'd gained a decent amount of crafting materials.

So, I began my return hike. My eyes were able to navigate easily, even as darkness fell, and by the time I was back at the camp, it was fully dark. The goblins had set up shacks, lean-tos, and tents in the outer wall and huddled around campfires, roasting animals on spits.

I went inside and took some food from the women, setting down the pack of materials I'd been able to save. I washed off the dirt and grime in the river and returned to my tent.

Despite being tired, I was feeling good about today's work. *Six more days. I need to hunt for new abilities, increase my abilities rank and get as many Attributes as I can above twenty to unlock these mutations.* My ability to see in darkness had been invaluable today and I could feel the benefit of my two hearts to my physical capacity.

I removed my armor and slumped, exhausted, tossing and turning, my mind filled with plans, before eventually falling asleep.

Chapter 9: Berserker

Helen sat down with a silver goblet in her hand.

"I had to practically blackmail the staff to get a decent drink here," she complained.

"You wine drinkers!" Jamis said, chugging back a pewter pitcher filled with a thick, bitter ale. "This, right here, is a proper drink."

"I'm with Helen," Mira said, wincing as she sipped at her own ale. "This stuff is foul."

"Well, it's a border settlement," Felrick said. "They get raided by the myrmidons from the forest so not many skilled crafters want to live here. Those that do are hard people, used to hardship and making do."

"Why do they raid?" Torvin asked. "What is it they're interested in?"

"Women," Helen said darkly.

"And textiles and other manufactured goods," Felrick added. "But yes, they take young women as well as any Gifted children they come across. The women are used to breed more warriors for them, and the children are indoctrinated into their beliefs."

"I don't understand how a race of people can live like that," Mira said.

"It's because of their creator," Helen said, her lip curling. "We are not native to this world. Humans, elves, givarta, kassadrons... We all were brought here as champions over the centuries. But the myrmidons are one of the first six races of this world. They were created by Kelesa, and they will always be drawn to worship and emulate her."

"You don't think they are capable of change?" Jamis asked.

"Maybe individually but as a people, no. Whenever Kelesa chooses a champion, the myrmidons will invariably follow him to bleed the world dry."

"That's enough doom and gloom for one day, thank you," Felrick said. "Let us enjoy what time we have today. Tomorrow, we're entering the Cursed Forest, and we won't see a safe resting place for some time."

"I'm looking forward to fighting some Gifted beasts and getting more rank points," Jamis said, cracking his fists.

"Don't be launching yourself at every Gifted beast and monster you come across!" Helen scolded him. "It's a good way to end up at death's door."

"That's why we have you," Jamis said, toasting her, a big grin on his face. "Now, if you'll excuse me, that girl across the tavern has been eyeing me all night. I'm going to go see if I can make my last stay in town for a while a bit more comfortable."

They shook their heads as they watched the hairy barbican leave to seduce the local woman.

"You said humans aren't native to this world," Mira said. "Why do I see so many of them, then? I thought they were the predominant race in this world."

"They are," Felrick said. "Humans have more children than most races and are compatible with every humanoid species that the gods have brought to this world. Other races usually just get assimilated into them over a few generations."

"Is that why I've seen an asterisk behind some people's description?" Torvin asked.

"Yes," Helen said, nodding. "If Mira and you were to have a child, for example, there would be that same asterisk next to the name of whatever race your child most took after."

"It's not going to happen," Mira told Torvin flatly.

"I'm not the one who suggested that!" Torvin protested as Felrick and Helen laughed at him.

***

I woke and stretched, then strapped on my armor, grabbed breakfast and found Juruk again.

"You're up again," I said. "Take me to the spined lion."

Juruk sighed but on this occasion, did not complain. He led me to a ford across the river and we headed west, the forest thickening until Juruk stopped and pointed ahead.

"Lair ahead. Territory starts here," Juruk said and pointed to scrape marks on the trees.

"Stand by at camp in case I need you to guide me somewhere else," I said, dismissing him.

I stalked forward, scanning for tracks or signs of movement.

Every Gifted I'd ever fought had been territorial, so I was sure the spined lion and I would encounter each other one way or the other. I kept pacing forward before breaking through the line of trees into a wide clearing. I noticed a cave which wasn't set into a cliff face.

Instead, a jagged pile of rocks jutted up and a looming maw led down. There was no eagerness in me to fight another beast in its own lair. Luckily for me, it turned out I wouldn't have to.

A yowl broke out from the cave, echoing about the clearing. A pair of luminous yellow eyes emerged from it as the spined lion stepped out, into the light.

I had been imagining something with a row of spikes along its back or a manticore but what I saw was like a cross between a saber-tooth and a porcupine.

> **Tutaren the Impaler. Gifted—Mortal. Beast/Spined Lion. Rank: 48.**

The thing bared its teeth at me, snarling as its spines bristled on its back. It flicked its tail toward me, and at the same time, dozens of barbs shot at me like arrows.

My shield intercepted them, and they pinged off the enchanted steel.

With stealth, the spined lion ran around me in a circle, soon launching more freshly generated spikes from its tail.

I dodged and interposed my shield as the distance between us closed. Within ten feet, I lunged at the beast, every single spike on it exploding outwards, growing an extra five feet in length. I tried to grab the spikes with my Telekinesis, but they were moving so fast.

Besides, there were so many of them that I lacked the mental ability to keep track of them all. As I twisted my head, they glanced off the dome of my helmet. This was preferable to being skewered through the visor of my helmet or the gap between my shoulders and neck.

I was, however, unable to prevent six spikes from puncturing my left bicep.

Another was sticking out of my thigh just above the knee.

Whilst this was clearly sub-optimal, this was without a doubt the most favorable outcome out of the possible futures of which I'd been able to catch a glimpse.

Most of them pictured me lying in a pool of my own blood.

My maul swept in, but the cat disappeared in a flash, zipping along the ground and whirling to face me again, its spikes visibly regrowing by inches in a split second.

I ripped the spikes out of my body and crouched down, taking cover behind my shield as I was bombarded by another volley of spikes.

I hurled a volley of spearheads but the lion didn't even dodge them, merely flattening its spikes and not even flinching as my spearheads bounced off them.

Then, the beast nimbly dodged my maul and again hurtled across the ground.

Activating my boots, I rolled under its pounce, continuing rolling as a volley of spikes launched at me from midair. I teleported to the side of my foe, slashing down with my clubs on its head. I didn't cut into it, but both my weapons connected with meaty thuds; Tutaren staggered back for a second before hissing and expanding out again.

A second time, I ducked down behind my shield as it exploded with spikes and I let loose a roar for the first time in the fight, wrestling with the urge to flee.

Pushing forward, I slashed down with my club.

Tutaren twisted and grabbed my weapon with its jaws, ripping it out of my hand.

I rested for a second, the beast using the opportunity to whip its tail under my cloak. Thorny javelins peppered my back, jutting out like a pincushion.

I screamed in pain and teleported away, reaching behind me to pull out the spines.

In a flash, Tutaren pounced at me.

I dropped and managed to roll under it but it used an ability, its spikes shooting out and pushing it back, midair. Suddenly, there it was, on top of me.

I was only marginally faster than this thing. Whatever skills and abilities it had, speed was obviously one of them. To my horror, it went for my throat.

I shoved my right arm in its mouth, causing its saber teeth to grind against my armor. I felt it start to bend, the lion beginning to crush and penetrate what I believed was my unbreachable defense. I scrambled under it, the weight of it shoving the spikes deeper. I felt myself gasp in shock and pain as they pierced what I was sure were vital organs.

My hand reached out, grabbed one of its spikes and jammed it deep into its right eye.

Tutaren released me as it stumbled backwards, yowling in pain and pawing at its face.

I didn't let up even as blood streamed down my back. Instead, stepping forward, I wrapped my cloak around the beast and held on as tightly as I could. I felt its spikes discharge but my cloak was tough enough to withstand the barrage and I held on.

Grabbing one of the lion's own spikes, I stabbed into the fur under its chest.

We rolled on the ground, and it managed to get a paw around me and run its claws across my back, shredding my skin, causing even more blood to spurt from my back.

My vision was red and blurry by this time and not just due to the loss of blood. Deep anger was welling inside me. I used it to help me survive.

Again, the lion thrashed, slamming me against trees and onto the ground.

I stubbornly held on and stabbed relentlessly into its chest, my enhanced dagger and my arm coated in our mingling blood.

---

24 rank points gained.

Blood and Souls (Repeatable): Kill 320 monsters or humanoids. Current progress: 59/320. When you complete this quest, you will gain 64 rank points. The next quest will require double the number to be completed but will award double the rank points.

I finally let go and dropped to the ground.

You have suffered a massive internal injury to vital organs and still have foreign objects inside you. The time until death is 52 seconds.

I snarled, refusing to accept death. I felt the spikes and ripped them out with Telekinesis as I poured cauter fennel over my back. As it came in contact with my blood, it seemed to ignite. I kept pouring, emptying the jar, downing the health potion.

You have suffered a massive internal injury to vital organs and still have foreign objects inside you. The bleeding has slowed. Time until death is 95 seconds.

Grim laughter spilled from my throat and soon transformed into a blood-filled cough. I had stopped the external bleeding, but the health potion had only slowed the internal bleeding. I went through my other herbs and picked up another I had gathered.

> **Scourge Rose. Type: Poison. Rarity: Uncommon. Grows in places with a fire affinity or where a massive fire has swept the land. The rose bushes feed off the ash. The thorns of this rose excrete a sap that attacks the blood with a flameless fire, burning the body from the inside out.**

It wasn't a cure, but I was dying and had nothing to lose. Hoping my Field Alchemist title lived up to its description, I dumped a bit of the sap into a health potion with a pinch of the remaining cauter fennel and a bit of raw red yarrow, violet nullifier, and purity lilies.

Chugging back the mixture and chewing as vigorously as I could, I fell back and prepared for death.

"Fuck you, Dad!" I said as I stared up into the blue sky.

The blue sky faded to be replaced by a dark expanse.

I couldn't tell whether I'd closed my eyes in my last moments or gone blind. Pain wracked my body, and I curled up on myself, my stomach burning, and my veins beginning to throb as fire traveled down them, followed by an icy chill. It was ten times worse than the last time I had combined some random herbs. Simultaneously, I felt the burning, searing agony with the icy pain of the freezing liquid nitrogen coursing through me.

The two forces battled it out as I thrashed on the ground, unable to focus on anything through the agony. I fought to stay alive but could feel my grip on life loosening.

I wanted to growl in anger and rage but did not have the strength to even whimper. I was dangling over a precipice, a black abyss beneath me. In my mind, I felt the hunger of death below me, and there, at least I found the strength to rage against my fate.

"You said I'd never be anything!" I screamed into the darkness, although at what or at whom I screamed I could not be sure. "I am the champion of a god!"

The darkness laughed back at me.

"I am more than you ever were!" I shouted into the blackness. "More than you could ever have been!"

I felt a sudden strength as if something was shoving me up from the depths. It wasn't much, but my body was suddenly driven by a new force, pushing back the darkness, scrambling and scratching for every last inch of life I had left. The agony began to ease slowly. It wasn't the sudden release from pain like the jolt of a rank-up but a gradual release, more akin to a glacier melting. When I could finally sit up, it was late in the evening.

You have completed a hidden objective and earned a title. Objective: Kill a Gifted beast with a primitive weapon of bone while in a state of rage and severely injured.
Reward. Title: Berserker (Requires you to have the titles, Mark of Cain, Feral Barbarian, and Survivor II).
*Berserker: You have overcome pain, suffering, and even the brink of death by the force of your anger alone. Whenever you are filled with anger and enmity, your body becomes less receptive to pain, letting you push through life-threatening injuries more easily.

"I'm not sure if that's a good thing," I said, reading over the title. "This seems like a good way to get myself killed." I stopped talking, realizing I'd already been doing a good job of that already. As I dismissed the notification, another one popped up.

You have completed a hidden objective and earned a title. Objective: Consume several herbs as well as at least one poison and survive the combination.
Reward. Title: Field Alchemist II (Requires you to have Field Alchemist).
*Field Alchemist II: You do not care for the dangers of mixing different herbs, liquids, and even poisons inside your body and your very stomach acts as your cauldron. Suffer only a quarter of the negative effects of mixing different unprocessed herbs and gain full benefits from them.

The title was basically the same as my last one, merely including an added description for poison and no longer limiting me to the combination of two herbs.

Considering I had only just attained the first title that day, it probably said something about me and how I threw myself unflinchingly into life-and-death situations.

"Without risk, there is no reward," I said quietly, standing.

I looked at the body of Tutaren but there wasn't much use I could see for it. Its spines were highly effective, but my spearheads were probably more suitable for my needs. I picked one that was four feet long but could bend it only slightly. Gathering up several bunches and tying them with paracord just in case I found a use for them, I looked again over the body of the spined lion, ending up collecting its saber-tooth fangs.

Spined Lion Fang. Type: Material. Rarity: Uncommon. Hardness: 9.
The tooth of a Gifted Spined Lion: This material can only be broken
by a weapon of Hardness 9 or higher.

I headed back to camp, stopping when I reached the river to soak the dried, merged lion and human blood out of my skin, clothes, and cloak, also washing my armor clean. Bone weary, I eventually made it back to camp. Having once again narrowly survived death, I collapsed into my tent without even eating.

I was still on a time limit, however, and forced myself to sit up and concentrate. I only had a few abilities I could raise, so looked them over. I still wanted to raise Telekinesis, but Compress Earth would also let me increase my Mind Attribute and get me closer to a mutation for that stat. I decided to compromise and raise Telekinesis by one and Compress Earth by two, since even if I put all my points into Compress Earth it wouldn't get it over twenty. "Raise Telekinesis by one rank," I told the System at last.

Telekinesis (Rank 8): You can, at will, lift 8 objects or creatures
weighing 610 pounds or less and move them within 190 feet of your
body; or up to 384 objects or creatures weighing 150 pounds or less
and move them within 190 feet of your body. The speed and power
of objects are based on your Spirit Attribute.

> **You can now crush an enemy with your ability. You deal a moderate amount of damage each second to a creature suspended by your Telekinesis. The damage is increased slightly for every point in Spirit you have above 10.**
>
> **Cost: 1 Mana per 10 small objects/sec; or 1 Mana per large object/sec.**
>
> **Upgrade this ability to increase the number of items, their weight, and the range at which you can move them. Every upgrade of this ability increases your Spirit Attribute by 1.**

I felt the burning as my Spirit, already over twenty, went even higher. The raging inferno burned, spreading from my center out through my chest, stomach, shoulders, and neck and reaching ever further along my body. After the agony of pushing past death, this was nothing. I focused only on my breathing as the rank-up increased my Spirit, the pain vanishing.

Breathing out, I quickly reviewed the increase in my ability before dismissing the notification. "Raise Compress Earth by one rank."

> **Compress Earth (Rank 11): You can fuse dirt and stone into a more durable, heavier material that can be shaped. You can currently fuse a 1,024-square-foot section of earth, common stone, and metal. Your compressed stone has a Hardness rating of 9; your compressed earth has a Hardness rating of 7. The detail with which you can sculpt is based on your Mind & Perception Attribute.**
>
> **You can now use uncommon stone in your fusions. The rarer, denser or more exotic the stone, the greater the effect on the final product.**
>
> **You can now use non-magical metals in your fusions. The rarer, denser or more exotic the stone, the greater the effect on the final product.**
>
> **Cost: 10 Mana per square foot.**
>
> **Upgrade this ability to increase the amount you can compress, its durability and weight, and the materials upon which you can use this ability. Each upgrade increases your Mind Attribute by 1.**

A throbbing headache stabbed into my brain as if nails were being driven into my skull. Despite finding it extremely difficult to focus on my breathing, I had an epiphany, thinking about everything that made me angry. Thoughts of my parents, the foster system, and people I'd known throughout my life flitted through my mind.

The stabbing in my head faded into the background, still there, but the pulsing in my veins suppressed it as a feeling of wrath rose in me.

I focused on the anger, channeling the emotion, breathing in and out. The pain ended and I barely even noticed except for the notification flashing behind my eyelids.

"Increase Compress Earth once," I said, the words coming out as a snarl.

Compress Earth (Rank 12): You can fuse dirt and stone into a more durable, heavier material that can be shaped. You can currently fuse a 2,048-square-foot section of earth, common stone, and metal. Your compressed stone has a Hardness rating of 9.5; your compressed earth has a Hardness rating of 7.5. The detail with which you can sculpt is based on your Mind & Perception Attribute.
You can now use uncommon stone in your fusions. The rarer, denser, or more exotic the stone, the greater will be the effect on the final product.
You can now use non-magical metals in your fusions. The rarer, denser, or more exotic the stone, the greater the effect on the final product.
Cost: 10 Mana per square foot.
Upgrade this ability to increase the amount you can compress, its durability, weight, and the materials upon which you can use this ability. Each upgrade increases your Mind Attribute by 1.

The pain returned. I could dimly feel how much more it had increased but it was an annoying throb in my head instead of an all-consuming pain, no longer as it was before. I let my hate and resentment simmer, my breathing now ragged from emotion instead of pain.

"Raise Compress Earth, again," I said, my voice hard and sour.

Compress Earth (Rank 13): You can fuse dirt and stone into a more durable, heavier material that can be shaped. You can currently fuse a 4,096 square-foot section of earth, common stone, and metal. Your compressed stone has a Hardness rating of 10; your compressed

earth has a **Hardness** rating of **8**. The detail with which you can sculpt is based on your **Mind & Perception Attribute**.
You can now use uncommon stone in your fusions. The rarer, denser, or more exotic the stone, the greater the effect on the final product.
You can now use non-magical metals in your fusions, The rarer, denser, or more exotic the stone, the greater the effect on the final product.
Cost: 10 Mana per square foot.
Upgrade this ability to increase the amount you can compress, its durability, weight, and the materials upon which you can use this ability. Each upgrade increases your **Mind Attribute** by 1.

The pain came again but in my state of meditative anger, was barely palpable. Once it was done, I stood, needing to cool off despite my weariness. I took a bowl from the fire and walked to the edge of the river. I dipped my bare feet into the water as I slowly ate the heavy stew. When I was done, I felt better physically and mentally. I returned to the inner wall, dropped my bowl off at the wash basin and returned to my tent.

Chapter 10: Antidote

Mira was at the front of the party. She had two perception abilities which served her in her role as scout as she led the group under the trees of the Cursed Forest. Jamis was behind her with Helen in the middle, followed by Torvin and Felrick. The forest's terrain was too rough for regular horses, so they had been forced to go on foot.

"How many Gifted monsters are in this forest?" Torvin asked.

"It's thick with them," Felrick said. "The System doesn't usually spawn Gifted beasts and monsters in areas with high population. Usually, it does it in wilderness areas like this."

"Keep in mind," Helen added, "that Gifted pass on their abilities to their offspring, so when the System spawns a Gifted animal and it starts breeding, there will be even more Gifted as a consequence."

"How is the place not overrun with hordes of Gifted then?" Jamis asked, looking about.

"Well, for one, they like to kill each other," Felrick said. "Also, beasts and animals aren't like us. Usually, only a quarter of their offspring are born with their abilities, instead of every child like humanoids."

"And we tend to keep our abilities within families, to keep chaos from spreading," Helen said, looking pointedly at Jamis.

Jamis laughed. "I can't help it if the ladies like me."

"But you can help where you unsheathe your sword," Torvin said with a slightly mischievous smile. "You're going to have a bastard in every town if you keep this up."

"Well, I won't be doing that for a while," Jamis said, looking around. "I'm guessing the locals aren't romantically inclined."

"Don't be so sure," Helen said. "I'm sure some goblin women would find you very attractive."

The party laughed at Jamis' expense as it kept moving deeper into the forest.

***

I awoke a little before dawn and rolled my shoulders. With five days left to prepare, I armed myself and ate a quick breakfast before heading to the shore of the river.

I started to compress new spearheads until I had 380 of them.

Then I headed into the goblin section of the camp.

This time, Juruk was waiting for me. I looked at his weapon and saw he had one of the spines of the lion, using it as a spear; the spines were just about the right size for short spears or javelins for the goblins.

"Hand me that," I said.

Juruk reluctantly handed it over.

Taking a handful of sand from the ground, I held it next to the point of the spear.

"Compress Earth," I said, creating a long spear point with razor-sharp edges and tip and handing it back to Juruk.

"There, that should work a little bit better now," I said.

Juruk took the weapon with reverence.

I suppressed a smile as he held it like a sacred artifact.

"Where to now, Warlord?" he asked me, no longer seeming reluctant to serve as my guide.

"I want to take a look at that spider nest and those etter things you were talking about," I informed him. "By the way, what exactly are these etters?"

"Spider herders," he said. "They are a type of bestial humanoid, like four-legged spiders. They breed the big spiders, as big as goblins or even bigger. They eat them and drink their venom like milk."

"They sound very pleasant. Well, lead the way."

Juruk led the way down the river until we came to a cliff. He pointed to a cascading waterfall, beneath which was what looked like a sawmill. There was also a walled encampment with cabins and a few other buildings built within thick sturdy walls. The only problem with the encampment was it was covered in spiderwebs.

"Spiders built a nest nearby. They grew quickly and overwhelmed the humans," Juruk said. "This is the outskirts of their territory. The main nest is deeper within."

"I'll leave you here, then," I said. "If I need you again, I'll find you back at camp. Go tell the other goblins I said to forage and hunt for food. I've killed the black serpent and spined lion, and the forest wyvern is dead, so you can hunt and search their territories now."

"You killed the wyvern?" Juruk asked, impressed.

"Well, no, a dragon beat me to that," I said, impassively.

"The Star-fallen?" Juruk asked, his voice filled with awe and horror.

"I think that was part of its name, yes," I said. "You know of it?"

"They say it is the most powerful Gifted in the forest," Juruk said. "Rumor says it's close to Hero rank."

"Well, it's gone for now. I'll have to deal with it another day," I said.

I descended the cliff by a narrow trail and landed on the roof of the sawmill, venturing to the edge and looking down. It was only thirty or so feet to the ground.

From there, I jumped, landing on the hard, compact dirt and looking around. I didn't see any movement, but spiders were good at hiding; those wretched things could be anywhere.

Turning around, I saw the doorway was covered in seemingly impenetrable webs. The windows were broken open, however, so I climbed through. There was a thick network of webbing everywhere here too. Weapons and broken arrows also littered the ground where I guessed some people had made a last stand. A massive circular sawblade sat in the track where it probably would have cut timber. Seeing nothing of use, I exited out of the window and took a brief look around. There was nothing of real note in the work camp.

I moved farther south just as Juruk had suggested, finding the intricate webbing becoming gradually denser until the tree trunks were blanketed in the stuff, as was the forest floor. The webs spread themselves so thickly amongst the trees that it appeared to be night rather than early morning. No way would I have been able to see without my eye mutation.

My weapons levitated alongside me as I advanced under the trees, not exactly sure how to find the densest part of the nest but continuing moving roughly south. After hiking for ten minutes, there came a skittering sound, hundreds of spiders scuttling toward me from the trees. They ranged in size from that of a chihuahua to a clenched fist. Strange two-legged figures, which I assumed to be the etters, emerged out onto the tree limbs carrying javelins.

I hurled my spearheads and spiders began falling off the tree trunks. I was killing them too slowly, however, and they were getting far too close for comfort. I focused on my spearheads, each one starting to gyrate in a circular motion. When the spearheads were linked together as one, I realized I had fashioned a makeshift flying grinder.

I retreated slowly. By now, hundreds of spiders had turned into thousands. They started dropping from the trees around me. Only my Foresight kept me from one landing on the back of my neck. My clubs moved in a blur as I batted the hairy critters from the air and ripped them apart. More and more came for me and soon, I was unable to fight them all.

---

64 rank points gained.

That small notification provided enough of a distraction to cost me.

A spiderling snuck beneath my cloak, a tiny pair of fangs biting into my back.

I smashed that creature to pieces, but could already feel the poison working its way through my system, my limbs slowing; I had to get out of there now or I'd never make it.

Activating my boot's speed boost, I teleported eighty feet and after that, ran like hell, my body a blur as I did so, dodging falling spiders. My spearheads flew behind me, spinning in a circle, catching anything that tried to follow me in the shredding maelstrom.

Sunlight was warming my head and the backs of my shoulders, yet still I kept running, not daring to stop until I reached the banks of the river where I collapsed. I cut my boot's speed boost, feeling the backlash as my body caught up with the strain it had been placed under.

My heart faltered but I chugged back a health potion, digging through my other herbs. I grabbed a bulb of a violet nullifier, chewing and swallowing, feeling the numbing paralysis of the poison retreating. I finally fell back, my chest heaving as I let my body rest.

After five minutes, my heart stopped trying to break its way out of my chest.

Blood and Souls (Repeatable): Kill 640 monsters or humanoids. Current progress: 107/640. When you complete this quest, you will gain 128 rank points. The next quest will require double the number to be completed but will award double the rank points.

As I looked over the notification, a grim smile formed on my lips. I'd just found the perfect place to grind for rank points.

Based on what I'd seen, even the fist-sized spiders counted for progress and there were thousands of them! If I could wipe out this spider nest, I'd soon have more rank points than I could even use. So, I needed to prepare, and if my last fight had taught me anything, it was that I could be overwhelmed by sheer numbers. My ability to spin spearheads had been effective, but I needed more and for that, I needed to increase Telekinesis.

"Raise Telekinesis by one rank," I told the System as I sat down to focus on my anger and breathing.

Telekinesis (Rank 9): You can, at will, lift 9 objects or creatures weighing 790 pounds or less and move them within 210 feet of your body; or up to 768 objects or creatures weighing 190 pounds or less and move them within 210 feet of your body. The speed and power of objects are based on your Spirit Attribute.
You can now crush an enemy with your ability. You deal a moderate amount of damage each second to a creature suspended by your Telekinesis. The damage is increased slightly for every point in Spirit you have above 10.
Cost: 1 Mana per 10 small objects/sec or 1 Mana per large object/sec.
Upgrade this ability to increase the number of items, their weight, and the range at which you can move them. Every upgrade of this ability increases your Spirit Attribute by 1.

The burning of my Spirit intensified and I struggled to contain the pain at first, but the fiery agony helped to focus my anger and the pain dulled as my Berserker Title activated. I breathed in and out, my thoughts focusing on nothing but my hate and my breath. The pain disappeared, and I turned my focus outwards again.

Congratulations! You have increased your ability to Rank 10. Please select an additional effect from the options below:
• **The weight of large objects you can lift is doubled.**
• **The weight of small objects you can lift is doubled.**

> • **You can hurl objects faster with your Telekinesis. Each object moves an extra 30 feet per second. (Base rate 10 feet per second x rank of Spirit).**

I looked over my three options, for once, wanting every single outcome. There were no boring or useless ones here; I mostly used small objects so the second option was better than the first but lifting house-size boulders would be quite impressive. I looked at them objectively and realized I had to pick the third, an ability I almost entirely used for combat.

I could move things swiftly with the power of my Telekinesis. The System provided a useful formula to show how fast I could currently move things.

If my mental math was right, I could currently move objects at a rate of 260 feet per second, nearly as high as many compound bows back on my world.

If it were possible to increase the speed, I could potentially reach bullet-level velocity with my spearheads. I selected my preferred option, analyzing the changes.

Telekinesis (Rank 10): You can, at will, lift 10 objects or creatures weighing 990 pounds or less and move them within 230 feet of your body; or up to 1,536 objects or creatures weighing 235 pounds or less and move them within 230 feet of your body. The speed and power of objects are based on your Spirit Attribute.
You can now crush an enemy with your ability. You deal a severe amount of damage each second to a creature suspended by your Telekinesis. The damage is increased slightly for every point in Spirit you have above 10.
You can hurl objects faster with your Telekinesis. Each object moves an extra 30 feet per second. (Base rate 10 feet per second x rank of Spirit, current rate 290 feet/sec).
Cost: 1 Mana per 10 small objects/sec or 1 Mana per large object/sec.
Upgrade this ability to increase the number of items, their weight, and the range at which you can move them. Every upgrade of this ability increases your Spirit Attribute by 1.

The inevitable fire spread down to my knees and elbows and to the base of my skull. By now, however, I was numb to it. My anger had an all-consuming fire of its own. The pain passed but my own fire did not. As I opened my eyes, it felt as if my ire had grown even more intense. I had always had issues with anger but now, at Berserker level, it seemed to amplify to a rage I had only felt a few times in my life.

"Increase Compress Earth by one rank," I ground out.

Compress Earth (Rank 14): You can fuse dirt and stone into more durable, heavier material that can be shaped. You can currently fuse an 8,192 square-foot section of earth, common stone, and metal. Your compressed stone has a Hardness rating of 10.5; your compressed earth has a Hardness rating of 8.5. The detail with which you can sculpt is based on your Mind & Perception Attribute.

You can now use uncommon stone in your fusions. The rarer, denser, or more exotic the stone, the greater the effect on the final product.

You can now use non-magical metals in your fusions, The rarer, denser, or more exotic the stone, the greater the effect on the final product.

Cost: 10 Mana per square foot.

Upgrade this ability to increase the amount you can compress, its durability, weight, and the materials upon which you can use this ability. Each upgrade increases your Mind Attribute by 1.

I felt nails being driven into my brain as my Mind Attribute increased, albeit a distant pain as my Attribute went above twenty.

Congratulations! You have raised one of your Attributes beyond 20, the Mortal limit. Your body will now physiologically change to adjust to this increase to keep your Attribute from killing you.

Your brain is now encased in an impact-resistant gel, making it harder for you to be knocked unconscious. Your cerebral cortex is beginning to convert from flesh to a more durable, biological crystal that will store memories in perfect condition with no degradation and allow for faster thought and mental processing.

Reading through the notification, my hate helped me to focus past the pain. It wasn't a spectacular mutation and was easily applicable like the one with my eyes, but it would come in handy. In addition, my Foresight was straining to have to focus on what was currently happening. Clearer and faster thought would help me to focus.

I still had thirty-two rank points available, and I wanted to raise Compress Earth to Rank 15 before I focused on my other abilities.

"Increase Compress Earth by one more rank," I mandated.

Congratulations! You have raised an ability to Rank 15. Please pick an additional effect for your ability from the list below:
• By compressing only units of the same type, you have a 25 percent chance of turning the material into a higher-grade, rarer version of the same material.
• You can compress different metals together and form the alloy they make when properly smelted.
• You can now use rare and magical stone in your fusions. The levels of rarity, density, or individual powers of the stone will affect the final product.

The abilities here were all similar but I had already known which I wanted before even seeing it. I picked the third option, going back to focusing on my breathing and my resentment.

Compress Earth (Rank 15): You can fuse dirt and stone into a more durable, heavier material that can be shaped. You can currently fuse a 16,384 square-foot section of earth, common stone, and metal. Your compressed stone has a Hardness rating of 11; your compressed earth has a Hardness rating of 8.5. The detail with which you can sculpt is based on your Mind & Perception attributes.
You can now use uncommon stone in your fusions. The rarer, denser, or more exotic the stone, the greater will be the effect on the final product.
You can now use non-magical metals in your fusions, The rarer, denser, or more exotic the stone, the greater the effect on the final product.

> **You can now use rare and magical stone in your fusions. The levels of rarity, density, or individual powers of the stone will affect the final product.**
>
> **Cost: 15 Mana per square foot.**
>
> **Upgrade this ability to increase the amount you can compress, its durability, weight, and the materials upon which you can use this ability. Each upgrade increases your Mind Attribute by 1.**

The stabbing pain in my head intensified. I retreated into my breathing exercise, while still cocooned by my animosity. The pain disappeared as my Attribute finished increasing. I could really notice the difference, able to visualize things more clearly and faster. I could also think about more than one thing at a time. Annoyingly, the cost for my ability had gone up another five Mana. I expected it would keep up that pattern every five ranks.

I sighed. *Well, I suppose the System has to make effects balanced.*

I still had seventeen available rank points and decided to invest in Telekinesis again to prepare for destroying the nest.

"Raise Telekinesis by one rank," I said, returning to my meditation.

> **Telekinesis (Rank 11): You can, at will, lift 11 objects or creatures weighing 1,210 pounds or less and move them within 250 feet of your body; or up to 3,072 objects or creatures weighing 285 pounds or less and move them within 250 feet of your body. The speed and power of objects are based on your Spirit Attribute.**
>
> **You can now crush an enemy with your ability. You deal a severe amount of damage each second to a creature suspended by your Telekinesis. The damage is increased slightly for every point in Spirit you have above 10.**
>
> **You can hurl objects faster with your Telekinesis. Each object moves an extra 40 feet per second. (Base rate, 10 feet per second x rank of Spirit, current rate, 310 feet/sec).**
>
> **Cost: 1 Mana per 10 small objects/sec or 1 Mana per large object/sec.**
>
> **Upgrade this ability to increase the number of items, their weight, and the range at which you can move them. Every upgrade of this ability increases your Spirit Attribute by 1.**

The fiery pain extended up along my chin and past my elbows and knees.

It grew ever hotter, as if my soul was trying to melt its way out of my body. I ignored it, secure in my bastion of resentment and hostility.

> **Warning! You are raising an Attribute beyond 20 while you are still in Mortal rank. Having stats significantly higher than twenty while you are still only a Mortal may have unknown repercussions on your spiritual and physical status.**

I dismissed the warning, allowing the fire within me to burn like a crucible, refining my Spirit. The pain ended abruptly, and I stood as my Spirit ranked up.

"Pull up my stats," I told the System.

Mordred, Champion of Kelesa. Gifted—Humanoid/Human. Mortal. Rank: 50.			
Available rank points: 6.			
Might:	13 (+3) = 16	**Mind:**	22
Speed:	22 (+7) =29	**Perception:**	23
Toughness:	11	**Spirit:**	28
Endurance:	11	**Power:**	10
Maximum Stamina:	75	**Maximum Mana:**	115
Stamina Regen:	15 per second	**Mana Regen:**	22.2 per second
Abilities:			
Dominion (Rank 5), Telekinesis (Rank 11), Heightened Speed (Rank 5), Foresight (Rank 10), Compress Earth (Rank 15), Bestial Senses (Rank 5).			
Blessings:			
Blessing of War (Mortal).			
Titles:			

> **Mark of Cain, Bloody Pugilist, Exorcist, Survivor II, Feral Barbarian, Field Alchemist II, Berserker.**

I was specializing in my mental stats but that was currently only because of a lack of options, missing a lot of abilities for my other Attributes. I could have raised my Attributes directly, but wasn't willing to waste them on just stats. Pulling up the description of my boots, I reviewed the changes to them that had occurred since I'd last checked.

> **Boots of Midnight Wind (Artifact, Rank 5): Gives a +7 bonus to the wearer's Speed Attribute and gains an additional +1 bonus for every 10 ranks you possess.**
>
> **You can double your Speed Attribute for 25 minutes with a cooldown of 45 minutes. Duration and cooldown are reduced and increased by 5 minutes every 15 ranks you have a maximum of 1 hour duration and a 5-minute cooldown.**
>
> **Once every 5 seconds, at the cost of 15 Mana, you can teleport 85 feet to a place you can see. The range increases by 5 feet, and the cooldown is reduced by 5 seconds and increased cost by 1 Mana every 5 ranks to a minimum of a 5-second cooldown and maximum 15-Mana cost.**
>
> **Created by the Goddess Kelesa for her champion Mordred, these boots are made from the hide of a black dragon with a mithril alloy for the toe and heel guard and infused with the power of Kelesa's will. These boots are indestructible except by the hand of another deity.**

Cooldown and Mana cost for my teleport had reached their minimum and maximum. I could flit around the battlefield easily and my range with it was also getting impressive, enabling me to reach my opponents almost instantly, or to find space if I needed it.

I wasn't ready for my fight yet, needing to prepare for the possibility of being poisoned again. I searched for herbs in the forest on the other side of the river.

I found five patches of cauter fennel and restocked my jars. There was even enough for an extra jar. I kept searching. After another three hours, I found a bush with strange, crystal bulbs growing on it. I was unable to identify if they were fruit or flower but could see they were filled with a clear liquid.

> **Diamond Orb Bush. Type: Miscellaneous. Rarity: Epic. The shells of these berries are hard as glass but filled with a clear, sticky juice that hardens quickly after exposure to air. It then turns into a clear resin with a Hardness rating of 14, making it highly valued as an adhesive by crafters.**

It wasn't what I was looking for, but I made note of it. It wasn't clear how well I could transport it but if the plant was an epic rarity, I wanted to transplant it and take it with me. I kept searching in order to find a few patches of red yarrow which I harvested and put in the jars. Again, I kept searching, running low on purity lily and violet and didn't want to run out at a crucial moment. I either needed more of them or a different herb to replace them, so I continued foraging.

I found a plant with white bioluminescent petals hanging along its underside. It was in several patches growing in the shade under a massive, fallen tree.

> **Ghost Blossom. Type: Medicinal. Rarity: Uncommon. The petals of this flower help to soothe nightmares, remove fevers, and reduce the effects of curses.**

Interesting but still not what I needed. I harvested the petals into a jar. I kept looking and wound up along the river again as my search carried me in a circular direction. Searching along the banks, I found four large bushy plants with glossy semi-transparent leaves.

> **Emerald Jewelweed. Type: Medicinal. Rarity: Uncommon. The leaves of this plant, when pureed and mixed with water, will remove rashes and skin conditions when applied and allowed to set.**

I was not sure if they were useful, but I plucked the leaves off all the plants and stored them in jars to dry for later use. I found a very small patch of Violet Nullifier. I continued to search, and finally found what I was looking for. I feasted my eyes on a plant with long, flowing tendrils that reached toward the surface and a long stem with dark purple berries hanging above the water.

> **Viper Bane. Type: Medicinal. Rarity: Rare. The berries of this plant are a powerful antidote for almost all poisons. A berry added to a small cup of water and boiled or blended into the mixture will cure a large human of almost any poison with which they are afflicted.**

I gathered forty-three berries and made a small potion bottle for each, then mashed and mixed them with water, shaking the concoction until the liquid was a consistent shade of purple. I placed the bottles in my backpack and sat down.

Activating Compress Earth, I focused on using uncommon stones to create a stronger product as I began compressing more spearheads.

Only when I had amassed almost two thousand, each weighing almost a hundred pounds, did I stop. I could make them heavier, but didn't need to, having already compressed every stone around me in a hundred-foot radius, in the process ripping gaping holes in the ground.

Now, ready to exterminate the nest, I moved toward the lair with about five hours left in the day; I would use all of them to the best of my abilities.

Chapter 11: Beast Slayer

I re-entered the etters' territory.

This time, they didn't wait for me to come in deeper but rushed down their trees to assault me immediately.

My spearheads spun in tight circle formations, shredding through groups of small spiders while I used a few individual weapons to snipe the creatures.

Webbing spat down on me from the trees above.

I pushed in deeper, allowing the spiders to surround me.

In a flash, I teleported away, my spearheads plunging in from all directions on the place where I had been a split second before.

Gore and spider parts fountained and splattered on trees and the ground as they rushed me in a mad desire to kill. I spun with my weapons, my shield brushing aside wolf-sized spiders that tried to leap on me from behind. My maul and levitating clubs focused on the bigger spiders while I teleported up into the trees.

Bridges made of spider silk had been constructed and the etters turned their spider heads toward me in surprise.

Their arms hung low, almost to their knees, and they had massive pot bellies. They jabbed at me with spears of wood tipped with spider fangs, lashed to the shafts with webs.

I shoved etters off the branches, ripping into flesh and caving in exo-skeletons with my clubs. Black ichor sprayed me with each palpable hit. A spiderling landed on my shoulder and buried its fangs into my neck. Needless to say, it was dead in an instant.

I continued fighting. Feeling the poison start to take effect, I teleported away and downed an antidote.

---

128 rank points gained.

The notification arrived, but this time, I did not let it distract me.

I wasn't nearly done yet, pushing deeper into their territory.

Their swarm was growing more numerous and the spiders bigger. Another spider, this time the size of a rottweiler, sank its fangs into my thigh. Six more jumped me, giving the one spider enough time to inject its venom into my flesh.

Teleporting away again, I downed a potion.

This poison was acting much faster than that of the spiderling, my body already starting to numb, leaving me feeling distinctly woozy. I kept fighting, a hot, joyous rage building inside me. I laughed and screamed, tearing into the spiders, javelins bouncing off my cloak and armor. I was badly bruised, but barely felt it through my rage.

A dozen etters, riding spiders the size of ponies, charged me.

Their long lances leveled at my position, I teleported onto one of their backs, the claws of my club passing right through its skull. The spiders fell back as every assault on me failed.

The trees were growing taller, and I could no longer teleport into their branches as I attempted to penetrate deeper into their territory.

A clay pot smashed down beside me, a green mist pouring out. I coughed and gasped, feeling my lungs start to dissolve as I inhaled it. I teleported away, but another pot dropped down. Since the etters couldn't pin me down with area effects, they had instead decided to try area-of-effect attacks; these were more successful as I had needed to take time to down an antidote and a health potion, the caustic gas eating into my lungs and throat.

"Is that all you have?" I shouted at the etters above, driving them into hiding by launching salvos of spearheads at them.

They fell back, chittering.

I continued my progress through the trees, dodging spider-fang arrows and javelins and the dropped pots of poisonous gases.

As I pushed forward, the incensed spiders began dropping like rain.

They were coming down so thick there was no way to escape them.

My shield hovered over me like an umbrella, but spiders still crawled up my legs and cloak. Some died on impact but most only took an injury and charged me, leaping to join the maddened swarm. My spearheads buzzed around me but even my upgraded skill could barely hold back the tide of their fangs and skittering limbs.

I fell back again, the swarm pursuing me. I'd been bitten a dozen times already by the spiderlings, but hadn't yet had the opportunity to drink a health potion. I kept fighting, gradually retreating as the spiderlings hurled themselves into the shredder.

> **256 rank points gained.**

The notification came and I made the decision to retreat. I had already gained more rank points today than I could feasibly use, and I was exhausted from thirty minutes of constant fighting. My Stamina and Mana were dangerously low too, so I beat a determined retreat.

The swarm slowed as I culled their numbers. Eventually, they all broke off as I left the web-covered trees and received the update for my quest.

> **Blood and Souls (Repeatable): Kill 2560 monsters or humanoids. Current progress: 2,467/2560. When you complete this quest, you will gain 512 rank points. The next quest will require double the number to be completed but will award double the rank points.**

I was close to finishing this quest.

As tempted as I was to rush back in and fight again, I needed to rest, downing an antidote and healing potion. Soon, the bite marks from the last push to bring me down began to disappear. As I dismissed the notification, a new one popped up.

> **You have completed a hidden objective and earned a title. Objective: Kill at least a thousand beasts in one battle.**
>
> **Reward. Title: Beast Slayer.**
>
> ***Beast Slayer: You deal a minor amount of extra damage against beasts.**

I dismissed the notification, and it was immediately replaced by another.

> **You have completed a hidden objective and earned a title. Objective: Kill at least 2000 beasts in one battle.**
>
> **Reward. Title: Beast Slayer II (Requires Beast Slayer status).**
>
> ***Beast Slayer II: You deal a moderate amount of extra damage against beasts.**

Wonder what would have happened if I'd kept fighting?
Well, I guess I'll see what happens when I get to three thousand.

I hiked back to camp, a storm of spearheads floating behind me. When I arrived, I dunked myself in the river to wash off spider ichor, poison, bits of webbing, and my own blood.

Sitting myself down to eat, it occurred to me just how hungry I was. Would an increase in my physical stats require me to up my calorific intake? I finished off three bowls of soup and seven cooked bread leaves. Stuffed, I stripped out of my armor, threw myself on my sleeping bag and fell asleep almost immediately.

***

Jamis held the basilisk down. His eyes closed as he strained to keep its jaws shut.

Helen slowly unpetrified Torvin as Felrick hacked into the basilisk with his sword and Mira shot arrows into its side. The basilisk bucked, Jamis being slammed into the roof of the cave. A stalagmite pierced his shoulder and made him lose his grip.

The basilisk whirled and met Jamis' open eyes.

Jamis' veins bulged but he pushed past the petrifying gaze and let out a roar that shook the cave. The hair on his body thickened and lengthened as a massive bear took his place.

Jamis swiped down in his bear form, the air fogging around his claws as he unleashed a physical attack, augmented by freezing cold. Patches of ice formed along the scales of the basilisk, and it let out an unearthly hiss. Its jaws opened wide to reveal rows of teeth, and it lunged forward, clamping down on the shoulder of Jamis.

Nidrog. Gifted—Mortal. Beast/Basilisk. Rank: 54.

Mira's arrows sank into the serpent, but its flesh pushed them back out and re-sealed itself.

Felrick stabbed into it beneath its jaw.

Blood spurted out and he jumped back, but some of the caustic blood splattered across him, sizzling on his armor and eating through his clothes and flesh.

Torvin jumped back into the fight as Helen freed him from his petrification. He leaped into the air. A golden horse appeared under him, and his spear was transformed into a lance of the same hue. He charged and plunged the lance through the chest of the basilisk.

It screamed with pain, releasing its hold on Jamis.

Helen healed the acid burns on Felrick, and the stalactite popped out of Jamis' shoulder as her magic excised it and sealed his wounds. Jamis' bear paws grabbed the jaws of the basilisk, forcing them wide as he tried to break them.

Torvin wheeled around on his horse, riding away before turning about again and rushing forward. Gaining speed, his lance plunged up through the roof of the basilisk's mouth, all the way into its brain. With a final shudder, the basilisk collapsed.

"That was intense," Jamis said as he returned to his human form, his chest heaving for air.

"I wasn't even in the fight the whole time and my Mana pool is gone," added Torvin.

"Same here. Keeping all of you in the fight is draining in the extreme," Helen said.

"That's because all of your abilities only use Mana," Mira said, handing Helen a waterskin. "I have a balanced build for my abilities between Stamina and Mana."

"I don't even know whether there are any healing abilities that use Stamina," Helen said, taking the waterskin and chugging from it.

"Then get some offensive and defensive abilities," Felrick said. "We aren't always by each other's side, and nor is there any guarantee we'll be together during this event."

"I was hoping we'd be able to find your cousin beforehand," Jamis said. "But after the two fights we've had today, I don't think we'll make it before the event starts."

"Is she even still alive?" Torvin asked, looking at Helen.

Helen held up the amulet they were following. "It wouldn't work if she were dead. She must still be alive. For now."

"Should we not go to the event, so we can rescue her?" Jamis asked.

"No," Felrick said firmly, surprising the group. "I don't mean to be over cautious, but we are champions, so our first duty is to our gods. These events are a chance to grow stronger, so we can try to make it to the top and stop the Champions of Chaos."

"Felrick's right," Helen said. "One life—even my cousin's—won't be worth the devastation the Champions of Chaos will unleash if we let them get too powerful."

"Then we should make camp here," Mira said.

"Next to that thing's corpse?" Helen asked, wrinkling her nose.

"This cave is easily defensible and is the safest place we'll find today," Mira said.

"It's not so bad," offered Jamis, looking around. "We won't even have to set up our tents."

Chapter 12: Etter Queen

It was a little after midnight when Jand shook me awake.

"My lord, we have spiders approaching the camp," he whispered.

I threw on my armor, my Telekinesis buckling it in place as I wrapped my cloak around me. I levitated my weapons, grabbed two clubs and ran to the outer wall. Looking out, I heard a skittering as spiders swarmed up the shore toward our camp. Not waiting for them, I jumped down and unleashed a barrage with my spearheads. I charged into the swarm, my weapons swinging low as I targeted the larger spiders.

512 rank points gained.

My mace flew out, smashing into the head of a hairy spider the size of a wolf and dodging as a pony-sized horse tried to pounce on me from behind.

As it passed overhead, I lashed out, the claws of my Nemean club ripping open its underbelly. I teleported to the wall as a massive spider tried to maneuver around me and get inside; appearing on its back, I savaged it with my clubs.

Twitching, it fell off the wall.

Launching myself into the fight, the same savage joy resounded in me from the night before. A laugh tore out of my chest as I splattered myself with black spider ichor.

The spiders flowed like a tide out of the woods, trying to go around me, but my spearheads spun on the castle walls like the blades of a blender, pureeing any spider or spiderling foolish enough to try and scale them. Goblins now swarmed over the wall, carrying the spikes from the spined lion. They seemed to have more of them than I had brought back with me.

Must have looted the battlefield where we fought.

Without pausing, I ignored everything else but the creatures around me.

The goblins began bombarding the spiders, targeting the larger Arachnida and leaving the small ones to me, only stabbing at them when they tried to scale the wall.

A massive warhorse spider charged me, its fangs ready to stab.

I strafed, but it shoved its abdomen forward.

A projectile of sticky web shot out, hitting my right arm, knocking me off my feet and fastening my arm to the ground. I rolled to the side as fangs lunged for me, then I swung the club in my left hand, smashing the eyes on the right side of the horse-sized spider's face. I reared back and sent a spearhead through its head. I cut through the silk holding me in place with my other club, rolling out of the way of a tide of the endless spiderlings.

"I wish I had a fireball," I said to myself, hurling a spinning ring of spearheads at the swarm, grinding them into a mess of chitin and ichor.

I heard a scream and turned to see the spiders had formed a circle; they were coming down the cliff and into the inner ring of the camp. I heard a roar, my head whipping around from the distraction to see a horrifying monster headed my way.

A tarantula the size of a bulldozer was moving in my direction, one with orange fur, striped black and a dozen etters riding on its back, wielding bows.

Giant Tiger Tarantula. Ungifted—Mortal. War Beast/Tiger Tarantula.

*A War Beast's physical Attributes will naturally rise above 20 and they suffer no ill effects from not being the appropriate rank.

I dismissed the notification and focused on the tarantula. My vassals were about to be overwhelmed and I couldn't be in two places at once. I needed a distraction.

"Dominion," I said. I felt something—not the tarantula—push against my ability. My Spirit, however, was one of my highest Attributes and I shoved back. Eventually, through a supreme force of will, I managed to break the resolve of the beast. White brands of chains formed around its neck and each of its legs as my influence formed a grip.

"Attack," I ordered.

The tarantula reared, throwing the etters off its back as it whirled around and began tearing into the swarm around it. Momentarily distracted, the spider stopped focusing on me and I turned to give attention to my vassals.

The goblins were doing well, holding both the inner and outer walls, but I could already see my human vassals, wrapped in silk, being hauled away.

Teleporting into camp, my limbs were ablur as I lashed out with both my clubs. A whirlwind of spearheads spun around me as I obliterated every spider in the camp. They we attempting to carry away my remaining four human vassals.

I scoured the cliff above us with my spearheads as blood and chitin rained down.

The spiders above fled from my assault, and I teleported back onto the field outside the walls before rushing toward my newly-acquired vassal, sweeping swept away the etters and spiders swarming it.

I laid into their clubs, my maul sweeping around as my spearheads tore into their ranks.

The tarantula darted forward, its fangs ripping in half spiders the size of ponies.

I was no longer being pushed toward the wall. We pressed forward.

The spiders and etters started to flee before me.

I kept hunting them down, refusing to let them just attack me and retreat.

Our battle continued through the forest to the edge of the cliff over the lumber camp. Barely a tenth of their original number remained, and I used my maul like a golf club to dispatch the survivors off the edge of the clifftop.

Heaving and gasping for air, I stood among the corpses, my own blood and spider ichor dripping down my back, chest, arms, and legs.

Blood and Souls (Repeatable): Kill 5,120 monsters or humanoids. Current progress: 3,683/5,120. When you complete this quest, you will gain 1024 rank points. The next quest will require double the number to be completed but will award double the rank points.

I dismissed the notification and another popped up to replace it.

You have completed a hidden objective and earned a title. Objective: Kill at least 3000 beasts in one battle.

Reward. Title: Beast Slayer III (Requires Beast Slayer II).

*Beast Slayer III: You deal a severe amount of extra damage against beasts.

So, it was 3000. I dismissed the notification.

> You have completed a hidden objective and earned a title. Objective: Defend a position with a group of chaotic humanoids who follow you as their leader, against a force three times your size.
>
> Reward. Title: War Chief.
>
> *War Chief: Those you lead into the battle deal a minor amount of extra damage.

I downed an antidote and healing potion, looking over my new war beast as I proffered a healing potion to it as well. The creature reared back, opened its cavernous mouth and allowed me to pour the potion down its gullet. I had to use three more to close all its wounds.

We returned to camp, where I surveyed the devastation outside the walls. Goblins were eagerly scavenging the battlefield, harvesting spider parts and fangs, and collecting the spine javelins. I was surprised at how effective the goblins had been but then I considered the ability I had chosen for Dominion at Rank Five.

> Dominion (Rank 5): A number of times per day, equal to 80 plus your Spirit Attribute, you can, as a spoken command, force a creature not bound by another creature into your service. You can dominate a number of creatures at a time equal to your Spirit Attribute plus 25. A creature may choose to serve you willingly or may attempt to resist by opposing their Mind Attribute against your Spirit Attribute.
>
> You can, at will, see the abilities and Attributes of any creature under your Dominion. You may have a maximum number of creatures under your Dominion equal to your Spirit Attribute x6.
>
> The larger your Dominion, the more it grows in power. All Attributes of your vassals are raised by 1 when they are in a group of 50 or more. Every 50 vassals increase this bonus by 1 to a maximum possible Attribute score of 20.
>
> Cost: 1 Mana per 5 creatures.
>
> Upgrade this ability to increase how many creatures you can dominate per day as well as the multiplier for how many creatures you can dominate at a time. Each upgrade increases your Spirit Attribute by 1.

I had over three hundred vassals, giving them a plus six to all their Attributes.

Some probably had a higher Toughness and Endurance level than I did right then, I thought, finding that a little funny. My vassals were missing but I could feel a vague sense they were still alive.

I intended to get them back since no one takes what's mine. But first, I needed to catch my breath, eat, and fortify myself for the fight to come.

By my estimate, the entire spider nest was almost completely eradicated, but I still hadn't faced the creature I'd originally come to fight. Their queen, mother, or whatever she was called was still alive and somewhere in the nest.

She hadn't shown herself yet, but I had a feeling any creature able to control over six thousand spiders and etters was not an easy opponent.

I found some leftover soup and heated it as my goblins got busy cutting free my four remaining vassals. It was Jand and Maria and two of the others, whose names I had forgotten.

"I'm going to get the others back," I told Jand and Maria. "I need new clothes. Take some from my tent and use the hides we've been getting to start working on new garments for me."

I turned to the goblins, a little less dismissive of them now. "Good work on defending the camp. Start working on recovering weapons from the etters and making new bows and arrows. I also want you to work on making new armor for yourselves."

My orders given, I approached the tarantula. Apparently unsqueamish about cannibalism, the beast was busy feasting on the remains of some spiders.

I grabbed the thick hair on its abdomen, slinging myself onto its back.

It got up and scuttled toward the spiders' nest. I wasn't sure how fast it could move but it was fast. We were currently traveling at around sixty or seventy miles per hour, but how long could it maintain such a speed? It scuttled down the cliff of the lumber camp and charged through the forest of the spider's territory. I had mentally commanded it to take me to the nest and was allowing it to navigate since it obviously knew the way.

The trees grew wider and thicker, all light strangled out by the thicket of leaves and webs.

The arachnid stopped and I looked up to see a circular arboretum around a wide central tree. Webbing strung from the trees to the center and was woven thick, resembling a giant white trampoline. The tarantula climbed up the tree, onto the web and stopped.

I looked around. More webbing hung above us like clotheslines with cocoons of various sizes hanging from them, the remains of what had to be thousands of creatures inside them.

How long has this nest existed?

The tarantula was stirring uneasily, shifting its weight under me.

Moments later, the reason became apparent as a slight tremor went through the webbing, causing my mount to sway and shake.

Four massive spiders approached us, one even larger than the tarantula whilst the other three were only around half its size.

Their bodies were covered in glossy black chitin with blue spots resembling a star-filled sky. Looking them over, I received a notification for each one.

> **Mother, the Etter Queen. Gifted—Mortal. Beast/Etter Queen. Rank: 54.**

> **Female Etter. Gifted—Mortal. Beast/Etter Female. Rank 14.**

> **Female Etter. Gifted—Mortal. Beast/Etter Female. Rank 16.**

> **Female Etter. Gifted—Mortal. Beast/Etter Female. Rank 13.**

I could already tell this fight, if it didn't kill me outright, would take a huge toll.

Female etters came charging at me in a flanking maneuver, while at their center, the queen surged forward.

I swung my maul down to meet Mother, the spike leading the sweep as it swung down with enough force to shatter a tree. It struck her back and bounced off, only a small crack visible.

She lunged forward and I teleported off the tarantula's back and landed on hers.

I slid off her smooth carapace, battering her shell with my clubs but making no further progress through her armor. *She's as heavily armored as the Nemean lion.*

She sprayed a net of webbing at me which I barely managed to evade by rolling. As a small mercy, the ground was soft and springy as I danced between the Etter Queen's legs, dodging a stinger from her abdomen and another spray of webbing. She snapped at me with her fangs, ripping a hole in the webbed flooring as I teleported behind her again.

The tarantula faced off against the three etter females. Despite not being Gifted, he was doing well but they were nipping at him from all directions like wolves.

I spun my maul, striking one in the middle of its back. It broke through its armor surprisingly easily, not even half as hard as their mother's carapace.

The tarantula took advantage of its pain and lunging forward, ripped off its head.

---

4 rank points gained (split between contributing members).

I rolled out of the way as the Etter Queen snapped at my position again; she was as durable as rock but nowhere close to my speed. I rolled under her belly and lashed out at her legs, feeling a spray of black ichor and hearing a piercing scream.

She's not completely armored. There are vulnerabilities; she has gaps along her legs, so she can bend her joints.

Jumping back to my feet, I rushed back in, dodging in and out and teleporting as required. I felt I was beginning to make an impact on the Etter Queen.

My tarantula was also now enjoying greater success.

Giant Tiger Tarantula. Gifted—Mortal. War Beast/Tiger Tarantula. Rank: 4.

Its newly-acquired abilities seemed to be reaping rewards, particularly since it only had to focus its attack on two opponents.

I used to good effect the Nemean claws on my club to repeatedly stab the Queen, inflicting deep gouges on her joints, and I noticed a wobbliness in her legs.

She stopped trying to bite me, grotesquely raising her abdomen. She began spraying the area with nets of the sticky web. I rolled and dodged, but she was able to fire at a ridiculous speed and one of my legs got trapped. She noted my vulnerability, charging at me.

I was unable to teleport, so resorted to something desperate, beginning to slash at the webs underneath me, cutting a wide hole in the floor.

The Etter Queen landed on me, and the floor gave way as we both began to fall. She had inadvertently saved me as I dangled by my foot.

She hung from a strand of web some three hundred feet up; I lashed at the silken cord and severed it. After she plummeted down, I heard a crack. She wasn't dead yet and staggering to her feet, she began making her way toward the central tree, her carapace slowly regrowing.

I had to act fast.

"To the brave go the spoils," I said and cut loose my foot, calling my maul to my side.

I plummeted downwards and hurled my maul ahead of me, faster than the speed of gravity and guided by my Telekinesis.

The Etter Queen looked up but couldn't move fast enough, the maul bursting through her in the pedicel where her carapace had cracked. She wailed and curled in on herself.

I didn't stay around to see her die, having other pressing matters to attend to. I spotted a strand of webbing, teleported and grabbed it. In the process, I was unable to control my momentum and found myself swinging wildly and very rapidly.

The trunk of the tree was fast approaching and I braced for impact. *Bam!*

I hit the tree and fell, rolling on the ground and feeling where the bones had cracked and broken in my chest and left arm.

Staggering to my feet, I stumbled toward the thrashing Etter Queen, seeing the female etters scrambling down the tree too; no doubt they were trying to protect their mother.

I bowled forward, faster now, the anger of battle temporarily nullifying the pain as I ducked a thrashing limb. I ripped the maul out with my mind and Mother howled again. She was dying but wasn't out of the fight yet.

She stumbled to her feet and we both faced each other again. She lunged at me.

I tried to dodge but stumbled. Her fangs gnashed down on me.

One fang was stopped by my cloak but the other slid under my arm and into my chest. I felt it penetrate one of my hearts. I feverishly lashed out with the maul, her poison coursing through me.

Finally, she dropped and I dragged myself off her.

27 rank points gained.

My vision already swimming, I weakly reached for an antidote, sensing the female etters approaching. One was tackled by the tarantula but the other, still limping from where she had been wounded in the battle, charged at me.

I downed the antidote and felt it slowly take effect. In a blur, I chewed a purity lily and a violet nullifier, chasing them down with a healing potion.

"Dominion," I said as I felt encroaching darkness. Then, everything went black.

As I hung from the edge of the cliff, I felt the jaws of death reach up for me.

Straining against the call from the abyss, I was digging deep down inside me, finding rage and resentment… emotions I needed to channel if I were to survive.

"Not today!" I promised the darkness. "I won't be weak. I'll never submit myself to you."

I strained but felt my fingers loosen, believing that laughter was audible in the darkness, a strange, hateful, malevolent sound.

The hate gave me new strength as if something was pushing me upwards. I scrambled up the cliff edge, having once again denied death.

Chapter 13: Ultimate Survivor

My eyes snapped open, and as my awareness came back, so too did the burning in my gut.

Sitting up, I vomited the entire contents of my stomach and thankfully, the burning disappeared. Looking around, there seemed to be only one remaining female etter, she and the tarantula eyeing each other but not attacking. There was a connection now between me and the female etter.

> **Blood and Souls (Repeatable): Kill 5,120 monsters or humanoids. Current progress: 3,684/5,120. When you complete this quest, you will gain 1024 rank points. The next quest will require double the number to be completed but will award double the rank points.**

Now that I was lucid, the notifications were popping up.

> **Whip and Chains (Repeatable): Conquer 320 monsters or humanoids by bringing them under your Dominion. Current progress: 14/320. When you complete this quest, you will gain 64 rank points. The next quest will require double the number to be completed but will award double the rank points.**

So, I was able to dominate her after all. I hadn't been able to tell if it was successful while I was blacked out. I dismissed the quest notification.

> **You have completed a hidden objective and earned a title.**
> **Objective: Suffer multiple mortal wounds and debilitating effects and pull through by your own will and wit.**
>
> **Reward. Title: Survivor III (Requires you to already have Survivor II).**
>
> *** Survivor III: You are resistant to death itself, proving over and again that you have what it takes to continue. Mortal wounds are less effective on you and require damage 3 stages higher to occur.**

"Almost dying sucks," I said looking over the notification. "And I keep almost dying even though this says I'm getting harder to kill."

You have completed a hidden objective and earned a title. Objective: Survive deadly poison injected directly into your vital organs.
Reward. Title: Venom Resistant.
*Venom Resistant: Poison damage deals one less damage stage against you, meaning deadlier poisons will be required to kill you.

"Time to head back to camp," I told my new vassals and climbed back onto the tarantula. "I can't keep referring to you as the tarantula."

I looked over the two giant spiders. "I'm naming you Tigris," I said to the female etter. "And you, Euphrates," I said to the tiger tarantula. The names made me smile, knowing that I was the only one on this planet who would get the reference.

"Before we leave, I need to grab my vassals," I said, turning to Tigris. "Bring me any living creatures you still have as well as any loot."

What is loot? Tigris asked. She didn't speak but I heard her words.

"You can talk?" I asked, surprised.

I can speak through the bonds you put on me, Tigris said.

"Loot is anything made by people, often of metal, or anything magical or rare, like a highly durable animal skin," I explained.

While I was waiting, I went to the body of the queen and cut out her fangs, each of them around fifteen inches long and still dripping poison.

Etter Queen Fang. Type: Material. Rarity: Rare. Hardness: 10.
The fangs of an etter queen will forever naturally excrete her poison; usable in both poison and weapon crafting.
*Etter Poison: Destroys blood vessels and causes heart failure soon after being ingested; requires only one dram to be lethal to a moderately-sized human.

I heard scuttling and watched as two dozen spiders, the size of wolves, began dropping things at my feet. They lay a dozen cocoons around me and I sliced them open, finding my vassals as well as three other people.

Still opening them up, there were a few deer, a goblin, a bear, and a skunk.

"I totally forgot I had that," I said, looking at the skunk briefly before turning to the three new people. "Who are these?" I asked, analyzing the new people.

> **Kathleen Moontouched. Gifted—Humanoid/Moon Elf. Mortal.**
> **Rank: 5.**

> **Sylas Windwalker.**

> **Utrid Blessed-Blade.**

Kathleen had long silver hair, six-inch-long pointed ears and a slender frame with a white and silver outfit bearing sections of chainmail.

The other was a half-elf, I guessed, and a human. One was lean, the other broad and heavy. Both wore armor, the first attired in leather, the other in half-plate.

They came to burn the nest, Mother captured them. She wanted to breed the female, Tigris explained.

For my own sanity, I decided not to ask what they planned to breed her with.

"Dominion," I said. Brands of chains appeared around their necks and wrists.

I analyzed Tigris again, pulling up all her Attributes.

Tigris (Vassal). Gifted—Mortal. Beast/Etter Female. Rank: 13.			
Might:	15	**Spirit:**	17
Speed:	12	**Perception:**	14
Toughness:	16	**Mind:**	6
Endurance:	15	**Power:**	9
Abilities: Control Spiderkin (Rank 10).			
Titles: Royal Spider, Weaver III.			

> **Control Spiderkin (Rank 10): Can passively take control of a spider**
> **within 25600 feet with a Mind Attribute of 2 or lower, or one that**
> **willingly submits to you. Can control up to 2560 spiders at a time,**
> **multiplied by a quarter of your Spirit Attribute.**

Spiders within your area of influence are immune to fear effects and mind control.
Spiders within your area of influence grow twice as fast and need half the amount of food in order to survive.
Cost: 2 Mana per 500 spiders/sec.
Upgrade this ability to determine the range and number of spiders you can control. Each rank in this ability increases your Spirit Attribute by 1.

Steel Silk (Rank 2): Your silk is stronger and harder to cut. A single strand of your silk can support 40 pounds and has a Hardness score of 4.
Cost: 1 Stamina and 1 Mana per 20-foot strand.
Every upgrade of this skill increases the tensile strength and durability of your silk. You gain an additional point in Endurance for each upgrade.

Hardened Carapace (Rank 1): Your carapace is toughened and has more resistance to slashing and piercing attacks. Your carapace has a Hardness score of 6.
Cost: 1 Stamina/sec.
Every upgrade of this ability increases your Damage Resistance and your Hardness score by 2 and increases your Toughness Attribute by 1.

Specialized in controlling spiders? That's not particularly useful to me but that steel silk could be useful.

I pulled up Euphrates' abilities.

Giant Alpha Tiger Tarantula (Vassal). War Beast. Gifted—Mortal. Rank: ??			
Might:	30	Spirit:	4
Speed:	17	Mind:	3
Toughness:	18	Perception:	9
Endurance:	15	Power:	6

Abilities: Monstrous Brawn (Rank 1), Hardened Spikes (Rank 1), Razor Hair (Rank 1), Blitz Charge (Rank 1).

Titles: War Beast.

Monstrous Brawn (Rank 1): You can lift and carry up to twice your weight, which increases your Might score by 2.

Cost: 1 Stamina per second.

Every upgrade of this skill increases your Might score by 2 and the amount you are capable of carrying.

Hardened Spikes (Rank 1): The tips of your legs and fangs are hardened with armor-piercing qualities. You penetrate any armor with a Hardness score of 6 or lower and your attacks pierce through armor more easily.

Cost: This ability is passive and has no cost.

Every upgrade to this ability increases your Toughness by 1 and the amount of Hardness you ignore by 0.5 to a maximum of ignoring Hardness 10.

Razor Hair (Rank 1): You can, at will, turn the hair on parts of your body razor sharp. Your body hair is harder, providing flexible armor. Your hair has a Hardness score of 4 and can deal moderate slashing damage.

Cost: 2 Stamina per second, while active.

Every upgrade to this skill increases the hardness of your hair and the damage dealt by your hair by a small amount. Each rank-up increases your Toughness Attribute by 1.

Blitz Charge (Rank 1): You double your speed in a straight line for 7 seconds and the damage to your next attack during that timeframe is doubled.

Cost: 3 Stamina per second.

Upgrade this ability to increase the duration you can run and the damage your next attack will deal. Each rank-up increases your Speed Attribute by 1.

Euphrates was built like a tank and could easily be the battering arm of my budding army. I looked at the pile of loot brought for me. Most was junk, but there were weapons and bits of armor in the mix. I had it wrapped in bundles with spider silk and draped over Euphrates' back. I slung my new vassals on board and rode back to camp.

The goblins were scurrying inside the walls until they saw me.

I unloaded my new, semi-conscious vassals and instructed my existing underlings to attend to them. Then, I laid out the loot. There were polearms, swords, numerous axes, pieces of ruined leather, scale, and chainmail.

I pulled out the teeth and talons from the wyvern and the fangs from the saber-tooth, fixing the saber fangs to the end of one of the wyvern's wing bones, making two long spears.

Taking another one of the wing bones, I studded it with the wyvern's teeth, creating a sort of fanged, serrated sword. Then, I fixed the talons of the wyvern to its leg bone, creating another spiked club. I took the halberds and added onyx and quartz to them, increasing their weight and durability. When I was done, I held the two Nemean clubs in my hands.

The other weapons I levitated around me: one wyvern club; a fang sword; two fang spears; and five halberds. I took the swords and compressed one, making its blade as thin as cereal-box cardboard, then took the other four swords and compressed them together.

From several leather belts, I started to fashion a bandolier for my potions and flattened it out. When completed, it would hold fifteen potions across the front of my chest.

I left camp and returned to the mill in the lumber camp, hacking away at the machinery holding the saw blade in place. I compressed the metal pieces into heavy ingots, levitating out of the building the sawblade which was at least six feet in diameter.

Moving it back to camp, I began compressing stone and earth into it, thickening the blade and increasing its hardness. Then I used the goblin's spine javelins to make spearheads for all of them, ensuring they were not too heavy to wield.

I had Tigris spool out yards and yards of silk thread, winding it into a spool for later use, also making shears capable of cutting the thread for my vassals to use for crafting.

With my equipment taken care of, two tasks remained before I was as ready as I could be for the event. I wanted to push up my abilities and to fight the last Gifted, and according to Juruk, that Gifted was also the most powerful. I'd only ever fought one wraith-like creature before, only defeating it by forcing it to step into direct sunlight.

I doubted I'd be able to do that with this creature.

I also remembered it could only be damaged by magical weapons or light magic of which I had neither but my Spirit mutation said my body counted as a magical weapon.

I'd need to fight it and only had one physical Attribute I could rank up.

It would be reckless and probably life-threatening but that was par for the course for me.

In fighting it, I'd upgrade my Telekinesis to Rank Fifteen and my Heightened Speed to Rank Ten. It had been sitting at Rank Five for far too long and I'd discovered some creatures to be sometimes even faster than me. "Increase Heightened Speed by one rank," I said.

Heightened Speed (Rank 6): You move faster and can react faster. Your body acts can instantly move at max speed without needing to build up momentum. The speed at which your body can move is increased x4.5.
You can run across water and other liquids as if they were solid ground.
This is a passive ability, costing 1 Stamina per second and it will cost more Stamina in combat, depending on how fast you move.
Upgrade this ability to increase how fast you can move. Every upgrade of this ability increases your Speed Attribute x2.

I felt my muscles writhe like snakes under my skin, expanding and retracting faster and faster. I focused on my breathing and my hate, allowing it to flow through my lungs in hot, slow breaths. The pain ended and I exhaled deeply.

"Raise Heightened Speed by one rank," I instructed the System.

Heightened Speed (Rank 7): You move faster and can react faster. Your body acts can instantly move at max speed without needing to build up momentum. The speed at which your body can move is increased x5.
You can run across water and other liquids as if they were solid ground.

This is a passive ability, costing 1 Stamina per second and it will cost more Stamina in combat, depending on how fast you move.
Upgrade this ability to increase how fast you can move. Every upgrade of this ability increases your Speed Attribute x2.

My skin writhed and undulated, and my muscles coiled in on each other like springs. I retreated behind my walls of hate to shield myself from the pain, waiting out the physical agony of my muscles changing, adapting, and growing. The pain ended and I cracked my neck, snapping my head from side to side.

"Raise Heightened Speed by one rank," I said.

Heightened Speed (Rank 8): You move faster and can react faster. Your body acts can instantly move at max speed without needing to build up momentum. The speed at which your body can move is increased x5.5.
You can run across water and other liquids as if they were solid ground.
This is a passive ability, costing 1 Stamina per second and will cost more Stamina in combat, depending on how fast you move.
Upgrade this ability to increase how fast you can move. Every upgrade of this ability increases your Speed Attribute x2.

The skin on my body rippled again as new muscles grew, retracted and wove themselves into my existing muscle fibers. I could feel usually imperceptible changes in my body. I clung to my anger, numb to everything as I raised my ability and attribute levels.

The pain ended and the rank-up was done.

Warning! You are raising an Attribute beyond 20 while you are still in Mortal rank. Having stats significantly higher than 20 while you are still only a Mortal may have unknown repercussions on your spiritual and physical status.

I dismissed the notification.

"Raise Heighted Speed by one rank," I said and closed my eyes again.

> **Heightened Speed (Rank 9): You move faster and can react faster. Your body acts can instantly move at max speed without needing to build up momentum. The speed at which your body can move is increased x6.**
>
> **You can run across water and other liquids as if they were solid ground.**
>
> **This is a passive ability, costing 1 Stamina per second and will cost more Stamina in combat, depending on how fast you move.**
>
> **Upgrade this ability to increase how fast you can move. Every upgrade of this ability increases your Speed Attribute x2.**

I breathed in and out. My thoughts turned inwards as emotions tumbled through my mind in a twisted version of meditation. My muscles bulged and shrank, sending agony pulsing through my body. Sweat poured out of my skin, but I was largely insensitive to it.

The pain ended and I let out a sigh.

> **Warning! You are raising an Attribute beyond 20 while you are still in Mortal rank. Having stats significantly higher than 20 while you are still only a Mortal may have unknown repercussions on your spiritual and physical status.**

I dismissed the notification with irritation.

"Raise Heightened Speed by one more rank," I said.

> **Congratulations! You have raised an ability to Rank 10. Please pick an additional effect for your ability from the list below:**
>
> - **Your body replenishes itself faster, revitalizing your blood, skin, and muscle fibers more quickly. This allows you to heal and regenerate cells at twice the previous speed. It also enables you to subsist on half the needed time for sleep.**
>
> - **Your metabolism is accelerated, letting you process more quickly both the beneficial and negative effects from herbs, poisons, potions, and illnesses. Your body will purify, heal, and process materials x2 faster. (Does not affect your need to eat food).**

> - **You can speed up and slow down your heart(s) at will and manually vent your body's heat to reduce the high temperatures caused by moving at high speeds.**

I looked over my options, finding them all good in their own ways.

The first one would sharpen my readiness for fights and help me to stay in top condition; on the other hand, I had health potions. The second option would let me deal with the effects of eating multiple herbs or of being poisoned, both of which were happening to me on a regular basis these days. The third option would help with the crash I suffered after battle, especially when using the speed boost on my boots.

I went with the second option, having been forced to chew herbs too many times just to stay alive. Because of this, I could not discount it.

Anything that could help on that front would probably save my life.

Heightened Speed (Rank 10): You move faster and can react faster. Your body acts can instantly move at max speed without needing to build up momentum. The speed at which your body can move by is increased x6.5.
You can run across water and other liquids as if they were solid ground.
Your metabolism is accelerated, letting you process more quickly both the beneficial and negative effects from herbs, poisons, potions, and illnesses. **Your body will purify, heal, and process materials x2 faster. (Does not affect your need to eat food).**
This is a passive ability, costing 1 Stamina per second and will cost more Stamina in combat, depending on how fast you move.
Upgrade this ability to increase how fast you can move. Every upgrade of this ability increases your Speed Attribute x2.

My muscles writhed and my skin strained over my bones to what felt almost like ripping point in certain places. I began to understand what the System was saying but could not stop now. I needed to be stronger, retreating into my fortress of anger, the pain beating itself against my walls.

> **Warning! You are raising an Attribute beyond 20 while you are still in Mortal rank. Having stats significantly higher than 20 while you are still only a Mortal may have unknown repercussions on your spiritual and physical status.**

I dismissed it again, my irritation growing. "Only warn me about raising my Attributes every five ranks," I told the System.

My skin was tight and felt thin, as if wearing a shirt a size too small that might rip along the seams. There was nothing I could do about it now. I had a feeling it had to do with me having a low Toughness Attribute compared with my Speed.

> **Telekinesis (Rank 12): You can, at will, lift 12 objects or creatures weighing 1,210 pounds or less and move them within 270 feet of your body; or up to 1,536 objects or creatures weighing 340 pounds or less and move them within 270 feet of your body. The speed and power of objects are based on your Spirit Attribute.**
>
> **You can now crush an enemy with your ability. You deal a severe amount of damage each second to a creature suspended by your Telekinesis. The damage is increased slightly for every point in Spirit you have above 10.**
>
> **You can hurl objects more rapidly with your Telekinesis. Each object moves an extra 50 feet per second (base rate 10 feet per second x rank of Spirit).**
>
> **Cost: 1 Mana per 10 small objects/sec or 1 Mana per large object/sec.**
>
> **Upgrade this ability to increase the number of items, their weight, and the range at which you can move them. Every upgrade of this ability increases your Spirit Attribute by 1.**

A raging fire spread from my center through my body, stopping midway down my forearms and past my knees before traveling up to my nose. I felt the fire around me as I sat in my mental fortress, replaying every painful moment from my life. I had to cling to the anger to stop myself from feeling the pain. The fire around me disappeared as my Spirit finished its rank-up.

"Raise Telekinesis by one rank," I said.

> **Telekinesis (Rank 13):** You can, at will, lift 13 objects or creatures, weighing 1,450 pounds or less and move them within 290 feet of your body; or up to 3,072 objects or creatures weighing 395 pounds or less and move them within 290 feet of your body. The speed and power of objects are based on your Spirit Attribute.
>
> You can now crush an enemy with your ability. You deal a severe amount of damage each second to a creature suspended by your Telekinesis. The damage is increased slightly for every point in Spirit you have above 10.
>
> You can hurl objects more rapidly with your Telekinesis. Each object moves an extra 60 feet per second (base rate 10 feet per second x rank of Spirit).
>
> Cost: 1 Mana per 10 small objects/sec or 1 Mana per large object/sec.
>
> Upgrade this ability to increase the number of items, their weight, and the range at which you can move them. Every upgrade of this ability increases your Spirit Attribute by 1.

The fire progressed to my wrists and ankles and past my nose to my eyes. Even in my fortress, the pain began to beat itself against me. My Berserker title was only able to suppress so much of my pain, forcing me to endure the discomfort but I'd already experienced far worse in my week of being in this world. Finally, the pain was shut off and I emitted a sigh of relief before readying myself to continue.

"Increase Telekinesis by one rank," I said.

> **Telekinesis (Rank 14):** You can, at will, lift 14 objects or creatures, weighing 1,690 pounds or less and move them within 310 feet of your body; or up to 6,144 objects or creatures weighing 455 pounds or less and move them within 310 feet of your body. The speed and power of objects are based on your Spirit Attribute.
>
> You can now crush an enemy with your ability. You deal a severe amount of damage each second to a creature suspended by your Telekinesis. The damage is increased slightly for every point in Spirit you have above 10.

> You can hurl objects more rapidly with your Telekinesis. Each object moves an extra 70 feet per second (base rate 10 feet per second x rank of Spirit).

> Cost: 1 Mana per 10 small objects/sec or 1 Mana per large object/sec.

> Upgrade this ability to increase the number of items, their weight, and the range at which you can move them. Every upgrade of this ability increases your Spirit Attribute by 1.

The fire extended over my hands and feet, now covering my head. Every inch of my body was lit from within by the blaze as it purified my soul, turning it into something beyond human limits. Firmly stationed in my fortress, I gritted my teeth, unwilling to let the burning pain stop me. The pain ended and I cracked my neck to ease the tension.

"Raise Telekinesis by one more rank," I told the System.

> Congratulations! You have raised an ability to Rank 15. Please pick an additional effect for your ability from the list below:
> - Your Telekinesis can now interact with items or creatures of energy and magic as well as physical objects.
> - Your Telekinesis can now create barriers of your choosing to slow everything passing through the area.
> - The damage dealt to objects wielded by your Telekinesis increases by a minor amount.

As soon as I read the first option, I knew I needed it. I read the others and the second was useful. I really wanted the third, but I'd need a way in the future to interact with incorporeal creatures. It was also highly likely that I would find a beneficial use for spells. So, it was a choice I needed to make. I was disappointed I wouldn't be able to increase my abilities damage but I didn't really need it.

> Telekinesis (Rank 15): You can, at will, lift 15 objects or creatures weighing 1,970 pounds or less and move them within 330 feet of your body; or up to 12,288 objects or creatures weighing 520 pounds or less and move them within 330 feet of your body. The speed and power of objects are based on your Spirit Attribute.

You can now crush an enemy with your ability. You deal a severe amount of damage each second to a creature suspended by your Telekinesis. The damage is increased slightly for every point in Spirit you have above 10.
You can hurl objects more rapidly with your Telekinesis. Each object moves an extra 80 feet per second (base rate 10 feet per second x rank of Spirit).
Your Telekinesis can now interact with items or creatures of energy and magic as well as physical objects.
Cost: 1 Mana per 10 small objects/sec or 1 Mana per large object/sec.
Upgrade this ability to increase the number of items, their weight, and the range at which you can move them. Every upgrade of this ability increases your Spirit Attribute by 1.

My entire body was filled with fire and now it could only grow hotter instead of spreading. The heat increased and I almost cracked a tooth from gritting my teeth so hard. I couldn't hold back all the pain and strained to hold my anger in place as the torture all but overwhelmed me. Just when I felt I would break, the pain ended, and I gasped for air.

"Pull up my Attributes," I said, opening my eyes and wiping sweat from my brow.

Mordred, Champion of Kelesa. Gifted—Humanoid/Human. Mortal. Rank: 60.			
Available rank points: 840.			
Might:	13 (+3) = 16	Mind:	22
Speed:	32 (+8) =40	Perception:	23
Toughness:	11	Spirit:	32
Endurance:	11	Power:	10
Maximum Stamina:	89	Maximum Mana:	97
Stamina Regen:	20.8 per second	Mana Regen:	26.8 per second

Abilities:
Dominion (Rank 5), Telekinesis (Rank 15), Heightened Speed (Rank 10), Foresight (Rank 10), Compress Earth (Rank 15), Bestial Senses (Rank 5).

Blessings:
Blessing of War (Mortal).

Titles:
Mark of Cain, Bloody Pugilist, Exorcist, Survivor III, Feral Barbarian, Field Alchemist II, Berserker, Beast Slayer III, War Chief, Venom Resistant.

I looked over my Attributes, not pleased with how imbalanced they were. I understood the System's warning about the danger of raising those stats so high. My skin felt too tight, my heartbeat was too fast, and a fire was trying to burn its way out of my chest. For all the pain, however, I knew I was unable to stop and needed the power. My foes had, in theory, been more potent than me in every battle, and I needed to surpass them all if I were to win.

I went and found Juruk.

"Tell me more about the wraith. I plan on fighting it tomorrow," I said.

"You can't fight it in the daytime," Juruk said.

"Why not?" I asked, but already had an idea.

"It doesn't appear until the sun has set," Juruk said. "Some have braved its lair in the day, but even then, sometimes they don't return. No one has ever seen it in the daylight."

"Then we leave after sunset," I said. "I'll meet you here. Be ready to guide me."

I ate dinner and went to bed to rest before my last attempt to gain a new ability.

Chapter 14: Spirit of Vengeance

Mira stopped before the ruins of a stone tower.

"This seems like a good place for us to hole up and wait for the event," she said.

"You don't want to press on?" Jamis asked.

"We don't know what the challenge will entail," Felrick said. "If we get separated or one of us gets killed in there, the System said we'd be returned to where we were before. I wouldn't want to be alone and vulnerable out in the woods if that happened to me."

"I suppose," Jamis grunted reluctantly. "Should we hunt for more Gifted beasts and push our abilities and rank up?"

"This is a marathon, not a sprint," Helen said. "The path to power is slow and gradual. It will probably take a century or two before we reach the final ranks to godhood."

"We're going to live for centuries?" Torvin asked.

"Once you reach Hero rank, your lifespan shoots up and you become something more than flesh and blood," Helen said with a wistful tone.

"What happens at Veteran rank then?" Mira asked.

"Your body and soul get fully reinforced," Felrick said. "Think of it as the rank where raw iron gets smelted into ingots so it can later be forged into a sword."

"How strong do you think the other champions will be?" Jamis asked, turning the conversation back on topic.

"We're all in our early twenties," Helen said. "I don't imagine there will be many above Rank Thirty and possibly a few rare outliers at Rank Forty who've had stronger Gifted carry them through dangerous zones and dungeons."

"Why haven't we done that?" Torvin asked.

"It kills the number of titles you get," Felrick said. "And you get noticeably fewer abilities. The system rewards risk and doesn't like people playing it safe. There are obscure titles that almost no one has heard of or learned to unlock that have powerful effects, especially when paired with certain abilities."

"Also, the System sometimes changes the requirements to get titles so no one is ever sure how to unlock them," Helen added.

"My Monster Brawler title is pretty good," Jamis said, smashing a stone with the claws of his gauntlet.

"We'll get more, soon," Helen said. "The Cursed Forest is the perfect place to encounter lots of danger to earn powerful titles and abilities."

***

My eyes snapped open as I woke from a dark dream, the details of which I couldn't recall. Faintly, I remembered a dark, malevolent, hungry force that had tried to consume me. My hearts pounded, drenching me in a cold sweat as I tried to recall the nameless dread conjured by my fear, but the memory of the dream's images escaped me.

The sun was just setting so I wrapped my cloak around me and strapped on my armor but left my gauntlets off. It was feasible they'd interfere with my body by counting as a magical weapon, and I didn't want to risk it. I ate a light breakfast and found Juruk waiting for me, wearing bits of leather and with a spider carapace fashioned into a suit of armor.

"Take me to the wraith," I ordered.

Juruk led me north again. We went farther than before, and it wasn't until noon that we reached our destination.

A tower stood alone, no tree growing around it for two hundred feet.

It was surrounded by rubble and thorny weeds. The tower looked as though it was falling apart but blocks of stone hung motionless in the air.

Mist seeped from the stones, blanketing the whole area in a layer of flowing fog.

Juruk hung back fearfully and pointed at the tower and its impossible architecture.

"There is its lair, my lord," he said.

I looked the area over and couldn't see the wraith, but this was absolutely the place I would expect to find one.

"You're free to go, Juruk. I may not see you or the others for a while. Wait in the camp, forage, hunt for food and improve your gear until I return," I instructed him.

I had brought all my weapons with me and set them down. I wouldn't be able to use them in this fight but would need them for the event. I had a little over twenty-four hours left, but I did not plan on returning to camp until after the Event.

Juruk fled back to camp, and I proceeded, weaponless, to the tower. The remains of a stairway led upwards, and I climbed, teleporting over the missing sections of the ruined, hovering tower. "It's like when a building blows up in Minecraft," I said to myself as I looked over the stones. "Only super creepy."

I kept moving. The stairway spiraled widely around the tower which had to be at least seventy feet in circumference. There were the remains of floors, scattered with stones and bones jutting out of the mist. I reached the top of the tower, the most intact part of the structure. I looked around but still could see nothing.

"Well?" I asked. "Aren't you going to say hello?"

"Why do I not sense fear from you?" a voice said.

I turned around but still saw nothing.

"Going for the voiceless presence?" I asked. "A bit clichéd, don't you think?"

"All others who come, reek of fear… but not you. Why is that?"

"Fear is for the weak," I said.

"Then before the sun rises, you shall know true fear," the voice said.

I turned to see an apparition rising from the ground. Its body was pitch black but outlined in a pale, silvery light. It carried a ghostly longsword and two red eyes burned in its sockets. It rushed at me, and as it did, I twisted to evade the strike of its sword.

Karnen. Cursed in Death. Gifted—Mortal. Undead/Spirit of Vengeance. Rank: 74.

"It has been long since I have tasted the spirit of man," Karnen said, his voice filled with hunger and longing. "And your power shall taste sweet."

"Then you shouldn't play with your food," I said. In a blur, I lunged at the entity, surprising him as my fists connected in a rapid combination.

I pressed myself close into his 'body' like a boxer. Karnen was not a physical being, but nevertheless, the blade of the undead Spirit of Vengeance twisted and slashed at me.

I dodged but was unable to escape the blow entirely; it grazed my forearm, sending searing pain lancing into the fire that burned inside me. I snarled in anger, the pain dissipating into the background. I kicked out, making Karnen slide but he did not stumble.

His form smoothly glided across the ground.

"You are much stronger than any trespasser I have slain before," Karnen said, approvingly. "Perhaps killing you shall finally restore some of my family's honor."

"That's what got you cursed?" I took the time to catch my breath, genuinely curious.

"I was betrayed!" Karnen said, a madness seeming to light the flames that served as his eyes. "The one I loved the most cast me aside and revealed my secrets to her order. I cannot rest until I have avenged her betrayal!"

"It's your own fault," I said, shaking my head.

"What!" Karnen howled, lunging at me as he brought his sword down in a two-handed grip.

I dodged his enraged strike, my fist colliding with his face.

"You got what you deserved! You made the stupid mistake of putting your trust in someone besides yourself. You exposed yourself to weakness," I said as I stepped backwards, narrowly avoiding his sword as it slid past my stomach.

"I loved her!" Karnen cried, his voice filled with a pain that I recognized.

"That was the mistake you made," I repeated, stepping past his guard and throwing another combo of blurring fists into his ethereal form. His body rippled with silver light with each punch.

Karnen fell back, disappearing from sight. He reappeared behind me.

My Foresight warned me of the strike coming for my neck. I ducked and gyrated back with a kick and a spinning back-fist.

Karnen staggered backwards.

Whenever I made contact, it was not like feeling a true physically present body, more akin to pushing against a wind tunnel and overcoming dense resistance.

Karnen released the two-handed grip on his blade. "I'll admit you are more skilled than you appeared, but I am not some beast of the woods, boy! I am ancient and hold otherworldly powers you cannot contend with."

"Bring it!" I said, slightly breathless but unimpressed.

The blank, black visage of Karnen disappeared, replaced by the deathly face of a rotting skull. I felt something attack my mind, commanding me to cower, flee, surrender or beg for my life. The burning fire inside me rose like a tide, making me feel like a slumbering beast awoken from hibernation. I set about the business of ripping to shreds this incorporeal force.

Karnen persisted and silver claws appeared on his fingers which he thrust toward me, a deep, withering cold emanating from his claws.

I felt my body stiffen and start to shudder as my limbs grew weak. I snarled and rushed at him, surprising both of us as I tackled him.

We fell through a hole in the floor, suddenly finding ourselves resuming our conflict on the level below. My fingers began finding firmer purchase on his body as if he were becoming more physical or I was becoming more spiritual.

"What are you?" Karnen growled, clawing at me.

His fingers for the first time made solid contact with my helmet and ripped it from my head. "How are you able to touch me like this?"

"Guess your otherworldly powers are a bit worldlier than you'd like," I said, repeatedly slamming my fist into his torso, my arm moving like a bolt in a rapid-fire machine gun.

Karnen sprang from his knees and lunged at me.

I went flying, barely managing to grab the edge of the floor before I fell two hundred feet to the ground, pulling myself up and rolling to the side as his sword struck again.

He continued to strike.

I produced a scissor kick, snatching his legs from under him, and we continued to grapple as one writhing mass, hitting the stairs and again tumbling to the floor below.

I sprang to my feet, twisting as his sword slashed past my chest. Then, his hand clamped down on my arm, sending a bone-chilling shudder through my body.

The cold withered my flesh, but the fire that had been growing with each increase in my Spirit flared up, spilling out.

Karnen yanked back his hand, screaming as the blue fire burned along it.

I felt my own body suddenly growing hot as the cold was pushed out of me, blue flames exploding from my hands. I pounced on him again and we fell through a hole in the floor. I pummeled him, my fists spouting blue fire which spread over his body and began to consume him.

"I will not end like this!" Karnen howled as the wind began to whip at us.

I grabbed the edge of a massive stone block as the gust almost hurled me from the tower.

Karnen howled, his voice a maddening force amplified by the wind. He appeared unable to move as he channeled the windstorm in an attempt to knock me from the tower.

His sword rose up, taken by the wind; it came flying straight at me.

I let go of the stone with one hand, and taking hold of the sword with my Telekinesis, hurled it back at Karnen.

The sword pierced his chest, a scream tearing from his form. The stones around him scattered and I went temporarily deaf as my eardrums steeled themselves to protect me from the piercing noise. After a while, my hearing returned. I stood and ripped the sword out. It hovered by my hand, grasped only by the force of my will.

Karnen snarled in rage, his eyes shooting sparks that showered about his face. He held out his hand and another spectral sword appeared.

"You're a tricky one, I'll give you that, mortal!" he snarled.

"We're both mortal," I said. "I'm just not made of wind like you."

Karnen sprang forward in a duelist's lunge.

I beat back his sword as it twisted about, my fingers operating dexterously, like those of a puppeteer. I leapt forward, catching his sword and pushing it down.

Then, I felt my fist smashing into his face though it felt less like pushing against the wind and more like hitting something physical.

Karnen slid backwards, his sword breaking my hold and slashing across my chest.

An explosion of heat flowed out as an icy cold stabbed into me, not physically but like an attack on my very soul. Even a Berserker couldn't withstand this pain. It seemed to penetrate deep inside my very being, forcing me to scream in pain and anger.

"Yes!" Karnen cackled madly. "All of you will die! I will not die until I avenge myself!"

"What do you know of vengeance?" I charged into him, shouldering him.

Together, we burst through the wall.

The wind had kicked up a storm and rain was falling all around us. We struck a ledge. I took the sword I had claimed and stabbed down again and again.

Karnen refused to let my attacks go unanswered. His own sword ran me through, the cold eating into me even as I tore bits of smoke and wind from his diminishing frame. He grew paler and dimmer under my onslaught, each attack making him less real and tangible.

His pitch-black hue had faded to gray, the surrounding silver light dim like the moon behind a cloud.

I was pale, filled with the sword's soul-piercing pain.

"You have bested me in battle, mortal," Karnen said, his grinning skull-like visage clear now as the mask of darkness peeled away. "But I shall not end here."

Karnen disappeared into the mist as I slashed into him again. The mist flowed into the sword, piercing my chest.

Then, the sword vanished, and I felt something icy cold settle in me.

> **37 rank points gained.**

> **Blood and Souls (Repeatable): Kill 5,120 monsters or humanoids. Current progress: 3,685/5,120. When you complete this quest, you will gain 1024 rank points. The next quest will require double the number to be completed but will award double the rank points.**

I felt a burning through my body that struggled against the icy weight. I dismissed the notification, seeing more prompts pop up in the corner of my vision.

> **You have absorbed a Spirit of Vengeance which has bonded to your Spirit Attribute. It will fuel and guide your soul's mutation when you pass the Veteran limit for your Spirit Attribute. (Warning: this entity is still sentient, and its effects will be greater on you).**

I could feel Karnen inside me, like a storm somehow trapped inside a bottle threatening to escape at any moment. His cold raged against the fire of my soul, two immovable forces, neither making any progress against the other.

> **Ability gained. Phantom Form (Rank 1): Your spirit has grown in strength, now equaling that of your body, making you as much a creature of the ethereal world as that of flesh and blood. You can transform into an incorporeal state for up to 0.5 seconds, becoming**

immune to most types of damage but still vulnerable to certain forms. After using this ability, there is a cooldown of 15 seconds before you can use it again. While in this form, all the physical damage you deal is converted to Soul Damage.

Cost: 15 Mana per use.

Upgrade this ability to increase the time you can remain incorporeal and reduce the cooldown time. Each upgrade to this ability increases your Spirit Attribute by 1.

I dismissed the notification.

Warning! You have taken damage to your soul and will be vulnerable to Soul Damage and attacks until you repair the damage to your spiritual self.

Figures. It also explained the pain I was experiencing, despite the lack of wounds to my body. My flesh was withered in places and frostbitten but no bloody mortal wounds marred it this time. I dismissed the notification and was given another.

You have completed a hidden objective and earned a title. Objective: defeat an incorporeal undead with the energy of your soul and a weapon made of Spirit. Reward: Keytaro's Guardian.

*Keytaro's Guardian: You have stepped into and interacted with the Ethereal Realm. When subjected to a Soul Attack, your Spirit will manifest an avatar to defend yourself.

Who or what is Keytaro?

No helpful prompt came from the System, so I dismissed the thought for another day.

Disappointingly, I had acquired a third Spirit-based ability. Equally annoying was that it looked especially powerful and useful which meant I had to upgrade it. I stood and carefully descended the tower. Once on the ground, I gathered my weapons and found a spot to compress the earth into a dais. I lay down with my hand clasped over my stomach.

"Increase Phantom Form by one rank," I told the System.

> **Phantom Form (Rank 2):** Your spirit has grown in strength, now equaling that of your body, making you as much a creature of the ethereal world as that of flesh and blood. You can transform into an incorporeal state for up to 1 second, becoming immune to most types of damage but still vulnerable to certain forms. After using this ability, there is a cooldown of 14 seconds before you can use it again. While in this form, all the physical damage you deal is converted to soul damage.
>
> **Cost: 15 Mana per use.**
>
> Upgrade this ability to increase the time you can remain incorporeal and reduce the cooldown time. Each upgrade to this ability increases your Spirit Attribute by 1.

It was agony.

Before, I had felt as though I was leaking fire. Now, it spewed forth like a volcano erupting. The streams of lava ran along my veins, lighting me up from inside and out.

Smoke billowed from my clothes as the fire took hold.

I thrashed on the dais, stripping off my armor and clothes. I writhed naked on the stone, battling the pain, unable to focus enough to get angry.

Suddenly, the cold weight of Karnen began to fight against the heat.

His arctic chill suppressed some of the burn and I felt emotion coming off him, leaching into my own feelings. I latched onto his hatred and made it into my own.

Soon, relief flooded through me. It was easier to focus and rebuild my walls as the searing heat and lava pounded against my fortress.

Endure this, human! a voice demanded from inside me. *Show me your hatred, your anger!*

A new heat was rising in me, an old familiar heat that had been with me my whole life. My anger fought against my pain. Moments later, it was gone as my ability finished ranking up.

I lay there for five minutes before summoning the strength and courage to continue. This time, I made sure I was in the right frame of mind although my thoughts still seethed hot with anger. "Raise Phantom Form one rank," I snarled.

> **Phantom Form (Rank 3):** Your spirit has grown in strength, now equaling that of your body, making you as much a creature of the ethereal world as that of flesh and blood. You can transform into an incorporeal state for up to 1.5 seconds, becoming immune to most types of damage but vulnerable to certain forms. After using this ability, there is a cooldown of 13 seconds before you can use it again. While in this form, all the physical damage you deal is converted to soul damage.
>
> Upgrade this ability to increase the time you can remain incorporeal and reduce the cooldown time.
>
> Each upgrade to this ability increases your Spirit Attribute by 1.

The firestorm of rose up again, but my walls were ready. I waited it out, knowing I wasn't alone in my bastion; someone or something else was with me, their cold fury reinforcing my walls. It was Karnen. He was somehow close enough to touch and too far away to communicate. I felt flashes of emotions and snippets of thoughts from him as he helped maintain my barriers. The pain disappeared and I lay for ten minutes, chest heaving, until my body and mind were ready to continue.

"Increase Phantom Form by one rank," I said, my voice hoarse with exhaustion and fury.

> **Phantom Form (Rank 4):** Your spirit has grown in strength, now equaling that of your body, making you as much a creature of the ethereal world as that of flesh and blood. You can transform into an incorporeal state for up to 2 seconds, becoming immune to most types of damage but still vulnerable to certain types. After using this ability, there is a cooldown of 12 seconds before you can use it again. While in this form, all the physical damage you deal is converted to soul damage.
>
> Cost: 15 Mana per use.
>
> Upgrade this ability to increase the time you can remain incorporeal and reduce the cooldown time. Each upgrade to this ability increases your Spirit Attribute by 1.

The fire raised a hell storm that spilled out of my body from the cracks in my soul.

Smoke and steam rose from me and made me thankful for the rain. Karnen and I hunkered in the bastion of anger created by my title and the force of my will.

The pain ended, and I lay for what could have been half an hour or five minutes. Finally, I was ready to continue. The immense heat within me burned.

"Raise Phantom Form by one rank," I growled, now curling up in anticipation of the pain.

Congratulations! You have raised an ability to Rank 5. Please pick an additional effect for your ability from the list below:
• **You can see into the Ethereal Realm while this ability is active.**
• **You can bypass magical wards and locks.**
• **You lose your vulnerability to Light Magic and silver weapons.**

I didn't see any application for the first ability and even if there had been one, its duration was way too short to make it useful. The second one could have proved useful, but I had yet to encounter either of those and there were probably other ways around them.

The third one wasn't flashy, but I intended to use this ability defensively.

It wouldn't do to try and dodge an attack only to become vulnerable to a damage type and instantly get my ticket punched. Picking option three, I retreated into my wrathful meditation to outlast the pain.

Phantom Form (Rank 5): Your spirit has grown in strength, now equaling that of your body, making you as much a creature of the ethereal world as that of flesh and blood. You can transform into an incorporeal state for up to 2.5 seconds, becoming immune to most types of damage but still vulnerable to certain forms. After using this ability, there is a cooldown of 11 seconds before you can use it again. While in this form, all the physical damage you deal is converted to soul damage.
You lose your vulnerability to Light Magic and silver weapons.
Cost: 15 Mana per use.

> Upgrade this ability to increase the time you can remain incorporeal and reduce the cooldown time. Each upgrade to this ability increases your Spirit Attribute by 1.

The fire scorched my body as my soul became refined. My Spirit had now increased in excess of all of my other Attributes including my Speed.

The inferno raged on, and I writhed, gritting my teeth and clinging to my anger as I rode out the rank-up. It seemed as if it was taking longer but that might just have been a perception thing as I endured the agony. Finally, it subsided and I lay there, gasping.

I began to shiver, the cold and rain finally getting to me. I compressed the stone around me, repairing the floor above to make a roof. I wrung out my clothes and hung them to dry, quickly drying off my body. It was hot to the touch as if I had the mother of all fevers.

I drank a health potion, and my frost-bitten flesh began to repair itself. It was slower with the withered flesh taking three potions to fully regenerate. I tried sleeping but could only toss and turn, the anticipation and strain of my Spirit keeping me from resting.

The sun rose. I completed some stretches and practiced moving and attacking with my clubs as well as fighting with my weapons telekinetically. I explored the tower, but there was nothing of interest apart from a single flower, a spectral, white-petaled rose.

> Spirit-Rose. Type: Unknown. Rarity: Epic. The flower of this plant brims with energy. Its purpose and use have been lost to time and very few are ever found as they only grow in places touched on by the Ethereal Realm.

I'll leave the rose for now and dig it up after the Event.
I kept waiting, and around noon, received a notification from the System.

> The first Event of this cycle will take place in 5 hours. Please make sure you are prepared and have all your required equipment with you. Only items with which you are physically in contact will be taken with you to the event.

I strapped my weapons onto my back and hooked them on the belt at my waist, my spearheads the hardest. I had over a thousand of them, and they were too heavy to carry.

I rolled out my sleeping bag, piled the weapons onto it and tied up the large bundle. I'd put my foot on the sack and hopefully, that would count as physical contact. I propped the giant sawblade and my maul together, clasping a hand on each of them.

Hours passed. A new notification came.

> **This is your 1-minute warning! The countdown will begin at the 10-second mark. Prepare yourself, Champion! The Event will test you and the foundation you have so far built for yourself. Only the worthy will prevail.**

I put my foot on the sack with a hand on my maul and the saw blade, feeling the eager anticipation for exploration and battle.

Seconds ticked by and the long-awaited notification arrived.

> **10**
> **9**
> **8**
> **7**
> **6**
> **5**
> **4**
> **3**
> **2**
> **1**
> **Initializing Event**

Chapter 15: Visitor of Death

I blinked and my surroundings had changed from blackened stone and mist to mossy stone walls and a carpet of grass. The walls stretched up fifty feet and were topped by blue crystal spikes with electricity buzzing and arcing between them.

> **You have entered the Realm of the Labyrinth. At the center is the boss.**
>
> There are treasure chests and mini bosses scattered throughout the maze, along with roaming dungeon beasts possessing abilities similar to Gifted.
>
> There are 103 other champions in the Labyrinth with you.
>
> You can team up or take each other out to help increase your odds of getting to the final 10 and ultimately the prime spots of first, second, and third place.
>
> Victory will be determined by several parameters: the number of mini bosses slain by you or your party; reaching the center of the maze first; and killing the final boss. When the boss is slain, the event will last another 10 minutes before returning you to the Prime Realm. The Event will end in 5 days, regardless of whether or not the boss has been slain. Any loot you acquire will be taken with you at the end of the Event but will be lost if you are killed before the boss is slain.

I blinked away the notification after reading it.

Then I opened my sleeping bag, levitating my spearheads above my head like a flock of birds. After this, I rolled my bedroll back up to tie it to the top of my backpack, moving forward at a jog, my eyes scanning the area around me all the time. This was a competition and to win, I needed to both navigate a maze and kill as many mini bosses as I could.

I ran down a side passage, my Mind mutation letting me perfectly recall the path I had taken. I twisted, turned and came to a dead end, about to turn around when I saw a shimmer in the wall; it was there for less than half a second. Stepping forward, I touched the wall which felt solid, but pushing hard against it, my hand passed through. Beyond a veil-like curtain was a small room containing a copper-bound chest sitting atop a stone plinth.

It could be a trap. I extended my Foresight but it didn't show me anything happening, so I lifted its lid. A single ring, set with a sharp obsidian, rested on a pillow in the chest.

I picked up the silver band.

> **Duelist's Ring. Type: Jewelry. Rarity: Rare. Wearing this ring, you deal a minor amount of damage while wielding only a one-handed weapon. Passively gives you a bonus that makes your feet more easily slide along the ground. It magnetically connects you to the ground, making you hard to knock over.**
>
> **Made from Sainted Silver and set with the heart of an earth elemental, this ring is the weapon of someone who prefers to master one type of weapon and perfect their fighting style with it.**

It was not particularly useful to me, but its passive was all right. It wasn't as though I was drowning in options, so I equipped it, turning and retracing my steps.

Although concerned that the maze would change on me, I couldn't detect any alteration in the path taken. So, I simply kept searching, constantly on the lookout for illusions and hidden chests of loot, but running into a dozen dead ends. In short, no treasure turned up.

While backtracking, there came a sound in front of me and I stopped but couldn't hear anything. I activated Bestial Senses, inhaling a whiff of the air. There was something ahead, something up on the wall. I moved forward, acting unaware. Meanwhile, I had activated infrared vision to see what the thing was. Near the top of the wall sat a lizard-like creature, and in my vision, its body was a warm violet color. I turned off infrared and it disappeared.

> **Guresen. Adult Dungeon Creature. Mortal. Beast/Guresen. Power Level: 25.**

Even if they were cold-blooded, these lizards were still warmer than their environment. I wasn't sure what their power level was, but it was likely to be analogous to rank. The creature was called a Guresen, something that had never appeared in any examples of Earth mythology; consequently, I knew nothing about it.

I hurled my sawblade at it, and the enormous disc was sent spinning ferociously upwards.

The Guresen tried to dodge the blade. It failed to do so and was sliced in half.

> **Blood and Souls (Repeatable): Kill 5,120 monsters or humanoids. Current progress: 3,685/5,120. When you complete this quest, you will gain 1024 rank points. The next quest will require double the number to be completed but will award double the rank points.**

The creature slowly turned visible as it manipulated whatever effect it used to hide itself. Along with its spikes along a whip-like tail, it had thick scales, while its eyes and head were like a chameleon's with sticky little gecko hands for scaling the stone walls.

I chopped off the barbs from its tail.

> **Guresen Tail Spike. Type: Material. Rarity: Uncommon. Hardness: 8. The tail spikes of the Guresen have a natural paralytic poison in them, making them prized by hunters and bounty hunters for taking in targets alive. Can only be broken by a weapon of Hardness 8 or higher.**
>
> ***Guresen Poison: The venom of the Guresen travels to the nervous system and begins to suppress it. The poison does not kill those afflicted by it since Guresen like their prey fresh and will drag their meals back to their lair before eating them.**

Shoving the five, six-inch-long spikes in my pack, I kept running.

It was a drain on my Stamina, but I kept Bestial Senses active with infrared vision up all the time, scanning for more Guresen. I had to stop every five minutes to let my Stamina recharge, my breath escaping me. I was running so fast that it was barely possible to stop in time, even as Bestial Senses bombarded me with sounds and scents.

As a Guresen jumped down on me from the wall above, I ducked, whirling and slamming my clubs into it, raking its side.

My maul swung with its pointed end, penetrating the creature's brain.

There was barely any delay before another Guresen pounced on me, lunging in from behind. The padding of feet sounded above as more and more were drawn to my location.

My sawblade carved up a Guresen-infested wall, blood and gore raining down.

I jumped up, and pushing off the wall, kicked off the next gecko-like creature. I used my maul, clubs and saber fang spears to inflict further carnage on the Guresen swarm. One creature, I skewered, leaving it pinned and clawing at the ground.

My clubs flew back into my hands and a spined tail whipped through the air.

In a flash, I drew my sword and severed the tip of its tail.

My sawblade spun back toward me, cutting a path through anything in its way.

I twisted to the side, letting it pass as a rain of spearheads fell around me, spraying blood from the invisible monsters. The battle had lasted less than a minute, leaving me drenched in blood and gore.

Blood and Souls (Repeatable): Kill 5,120 monsters or humanoids. Current progress: 3,691/5,120. When you complete this quest, you will gain 1024 rank points. The next quest will require double the number to be completed but will award double the rank points.

Wiping off blood and guts, a numbness spread across my lower body and when I looked down, there was a tail spike sticking out of my leg. I fell back against the wall, levitating an antidote from my bandolier to my lips, then swallowing it, my body going stiff.

A burning in my stomach spread through me and I soon regained control of my body.

I got to my feet and collected as many of the tail spikes as I could find, continuing to run and to search as more and more Guresen pounced on me.

By now, there were so many and it was so overwhelming that I could not even be bothered to stop and kill them all, simply running past them as I searched the maze.

They were as strong as a Gifted, but I didn't get any rank points from them. Furthermore, they weren't in numbers great enough to help my quest.

I had tried to dominate them, but my Dominion just slid ineffectually off their minds.

> **Blood and Souls (Repeatable): Kill 5,120 monsters or humanoids. Current progress: 3,712/5,120. When you complete this quest, you will gain 1024 rank points. The next quest will require double the number to be completed but will award double the rank points.**

Turning the corner of the maze, I came to a massive, circular chamber with a tree growing in its center and a gate leading into the chamber.

A bridge had formed from the massive tree's roots which crossed a chasm of water, the waterfall plummeting hundreds of feet before disappearing into a white mist.

A grinding sound behind made me snap my head around. Bars slid out of the wall, blocking the way out. I'd played enough games to recognize a boss battle and scanned the area looking for the mini boss, locating it up in the branches.

The creature glowed a bright violet in my infrared vision.

> **Guresen Pack Lord. Dungeon Mini Boss. Mortal. Beast/Guresen. Power Level: 50.**

It seemed to sense my attention and jumped down. Raising its head, it let out an ear-piercing shriek. My eardrums sealed briefly.

Then, I attacked with a club in one hand and a spear in the other.

Its tail snapped forward. I ducked and then quickly lunged forward with the spear.

The Guresen twisted and the spear slid along its scales; this was when I saw that it was roughly three times the size of any of the other Guresen, and I estimated its body to weigh as much as a car.

It spat something at me.

I rolled out of the way as the grass sizzled where its projectile saliva had fallen.

"Come on!" I taunted it. "I've been killing your pack for hours now. I was hoping at least *you'd* be a bit of a challenge."

I didn't know if it could understand me, but it shrieked in rage and rushed at me, its tail snapping around to stab at me from the side.

The spikes shot out in a wide arc, breaking apart midair into a storm of needles.

There were too many for me to evade so I decided to rush at the needles. At the very last second, I activated Phantom Form and the needles passed through harmlessly. Seconds later, my body resumed its form, and I continued my assault on the chief Guresen.

My clubs smashed down and ripped off scales, but its hide was tough and resistant even against the Nemean claws. It whirled about, teeth snapping on my armored limb as I jumped back. It shook my arm like a dog with a rat.

My shoulder palpably dislocated as it thrashed me about. I turned incorporeal again whilst attempting to use my sawblade on the creature which disappeared in another cloud of smoke.

I lunged forward.

Its tail snapped forward too, in the manner of a scorpion.

It wasn't possible to attack it from a distance since like me, it was too good at countering ranged, heavy attacks. I ducked and spun, preparing myself for a risky move that I thought might have a shot if the lizard's ability had certain restrictions.

I jumped over the tail, my sawblade slicing forward to attempt to bisect it.

There was another flash of smoke and the Guresen vanished, the sawblade passing through the smoke. Suddenly, the creature appeared behind me, stabbing urgently at me with its tail, and I bent double as it passed overhead. This time, I grabbed on and pulled a dagger from my belt, clinging on like a sloth as I stabbed into its thrashing tail with which it slammed me into the ground. Rabidly, it tried chasing its tail, but its teeth snapped just out of reach.

Bright arterial blood spurted repeatedly as I stabbed into the meat and bone of the tail.

Then I grunted in pain, thudding into the stone.

The Guresen jumped around in an attempt to dislodge me.

I tried slicing it in half with my sawblade, but at that moment, we both vanished into smoke; in a split second, we had reappeared ten feet away.

Its tail thrashed with a life of its own and it was like wrestling an eel. The spines shot out and regrew like the spined lion's. One shot into my gut, the numbing starting immediately as the paralysis began to take effect.

This time, it was accompanied by a searing pain that raced toward my heart.

My dagger finally dug through the bone.

The Guresen's tail came free and fell to the ground.

After I'd rolled away, I swiftly sprang to my feet, spear in hand, bracing it against the ground. The Guresen lunged at me desperately, its maw wide open, and it impaled itself on the spear. I slumped backwards, my body aching all over as my ribs were cracked and my bones bruised. The paralysis took effect, and I became unable to move.

> **Blood and Souls (Repeatable): Kill 5,120 monsters or humanoids. Current progress: 3,713/5,120. When you complete this quest, you will gain 1024 rank points. The next quest will require double the number to be completed but will award double the rank points.**

Darkness crept in from the corners of my vision and I could hear faint laughter from afar. I couldn't grit my teeth or struggle against death. As the poisons spread through my body, my thoughts grew foggy, and it became harder and harder to think.

> **You have been affected by multiple poisons and are suffering from the conditions: Paralyzed, Heart(s) Failure, and Neurological Damage. Remove the poison before you die. The time until death is 5:30 minutes.**

With straining will, I overcame the fuzziness and manipulated the potions on my bandolier. I poured an antidote and healing potion into my mouth. Much of the concoctions spilled as I lost control and dropped them. I couldn't swallow and had to let it slide down my throat as I held my breath. I felt the burning and jerked with a spasm. It was a few minutes before I willed my twitching fingers into submission. Eventually, control slowly returned to my body.

> **You have completed a hidden objective and earned a title. Objective: Survive at least two deadly poisons being injected directly into your system.**
> **Reward: Venom Resistant II (Requires Venom Resistant).**

> ***Venom Resistant II: Your body is becoming increasingly resistant to poison, the more you are subjected to it. Poison damage deals 2 fewer damage stages against you, making it so deadlier poisons will be required to kill you.**

Sitting up, I pulled out the remainder of the spike embedded in my stomach and splashed some healing potion on the wound. I then drank the remainder of the restorative liquid.

I'm really tired of almost dying from poison.

An icon flashed in the corner of my vision and I quickly brought it up.

Bosses Slain by You:	1
Total number of Bosses Slain:	1
Total Contestants Remaining	102

So, I'm the first. This was satisfying, even if yet another close call. In fact, without my Venom Resistant title, I might be dead already.

Poison was no joke, and I needed a way to slow down its impact more effectively. I now had Venom Resistant II, but was there a way to get to Venom Resistant III on my own?

I gathered all my weapons, laying down the wyvern fang spears, the etter and the death adder fang daggers.

I went over to the body of the Guresen pack lord and cut out its tail spikes.

> **Guresen Tail Spike. Type: Material. Rarity: Rare. Hardness 9.5. The tail spikes of a Guresen Pack Lord have multiple types of poisons in them. These will paralyze the target as well as cause severe poison damage, making them prized by alchemists and assassins. Can only be broken by a weapon of hardness 9.5 or higher.**
>
> ***Guresen Pack Lord Poison: The venom of the Guresen pack leader is different from the rest of its pack. They are responsible for defending their territory, so their poison develops lethal qualities in addition to causing paralysis.**

> The poison ruptures blood vessels in the heart, causing internal bleeding as well as damaging brain cells which leads to neurological failure.

I set down one of the spikes with my other weapons, thinking of my plan; it was risky but not as much as the other things I'd done. Compressing a bowl from some dirt and stone, I poured a health potion into it, then dropped in a violet nullifier, purity lily, viper bane, and scourge rose sap, preparing my antidote.

Summoning my nerve, I grabbed all the weapons and tail-spiked them with their points facing toward me. I took a breath and stabbed them all into my gut.

The pain was intense, but I'd had worse. Clenching my teeth and grabbing the stone bowl, I chugged back its contents, yanking out the weapon and splashing a healing potion on the wound. It refused to close. I packed it with cauter fennel.

A gasp of pain escaped my lips as it flashed with fire and cauterized the wound. I fell back, my vision growing dim, a grim smile playing on my lips.

To have survived all this only to die by my own hand!

"On my terms, and no one else's," I whispered, the darkness pulling at me.

Once again, I hung from the edge of the cliff, but this time, it felt as if I had a rope. Laughter echoed about me, but I pulled up, clawing my way out from death's grasp.

I reached the edge of the cliff and pulled myself up. Light stabbed into my eyes, and I sat up, gasping for breath as my hearts restarted.

> You have completed a hidden objective and earned a title.
> Objective: Survive at least 3 deadly poisons being ingested directly into your system.
>
> Reward: Venom Resistant III. (Requires Venom Resistant II).
>
> *Venom Resistant III: Your body is becoming increasingly resistant to poison, the more you are subjected to it. Poison damage deals 3 fewer damage stages against you, making it so deadlier poisons will be required to kill you.

The notification disappeared as soon as I read it and another one popped up.

| You have completed a hidden objective and earned a title. |
| Objective: Consume several herbs, at least two of which are extremely rare, as well as at least 3 poisons and survive the combination. |
| Reward. Title: Field Alchemist III. (Requires you to have Field Alchemist II). |
| *Field Alchemist III: You disregard all caution for the dangers of mixing different herbs, liquids, and even poisons inside your body and your stomach acts as your cauldron. Suffer only a tenth of the negative effects of mixing different herbs without processing and gain twice the benefits from them. |

I smiled grimly and dismissed the notification, but another one popped up and I opened it.

| You have completed a hidden objective and earned a title. |
| Objective: Earn the interest of a Spirit of the Void. You have survived multiple near-death experiences, catching glimpses of the void each time, and have earned the attention of one of its denizens. |
| Reward. Title: Visitor of Death. (This is a unique title). |
| *Visitor of Death: A spirit of the void has taken a liking to you. |

"That cannot be good," I said, re-reading the message which was way too vague and mysterious. I couldn't quite remember what I'd seen each time, but flashes of deep, hungry darkness flashed through my memory, bringing a shudder.

Anything dwelling in that place couldn't be friendly and should be avoided at all costs.

I looked around and saw the gates to the boss arena were open, a chest sitting on a pedestal under an enormous tree. I approached the silver chest but unable to detect any traps with my Foresight, I opened the lid. A leather satchel sat on the cushion.

Picking it up, I read the description the System gave me.

Storage Pouch Type II. (Uncommon). Made from the hide of a Gifted beast and enchanted with special magic to create pocket dimensions, it can hold items in a volume of 5000 square feet. Items are not preserved and will rot and degrade over time.			
Weight:	**5 lbs.**	**Durability:**	**20/20**

This had some use; I was a lot happier with this than the ring. The opening of the satchel could stretch about three-and-a-half feet wide.

I stuffed my backpack inside it, as well as the sack of Guresen spikes.

Feeling much lighter, I looked about.

I'd been searching the maze for around eight hours and could keep going, but I needed a place to rest and had yet to identify anything resembling a haven.

I grabbed the thick bark of the tree and climbed up to its lower branches. Finding a good spot, I opened my storage pouch. My spearheads flew inside, and I proceeded to store all my weapons except my saw blade. After this, I lay down on the ground, my brand-new hide cloak providing cushioning. I slowly drifted off, jerking awake now and then until finally able to relax enough to fall asleep completely.

***

Jamis and Helen struggled against a two-headed serpent as they trudged through knee-deep water. They had appeared in the maze near each other but didn't even know if the rest of their party was there. Jamis was acting as the tank and melee fighter, keeping the monsters off Helen. Meanwhile, she provided ranged support and healing using one ranged spell attack.

The fangs of one of the heads sank into Jamis' shoulder.

Helen blasted it with two beams of silver light, and the head released its grip, now blind in one eye, its face smoking. Jamis beat its other head into a pulp with his clawed fists.

The snake fell dead, and Helen quickly healed Jamis by casting a purity spell on him, removing the poison. They both felt the drain in their Stamina and Mana, but they pressed on, eager to find a way out of the swamp and onto dry *terra firma* on which to rest.

"Do you think the others are all right?" Jamis asked.

"They're all competent fighters," Helen said. "Even if they aren't with the rest of our party, they will find other champions happy to have people like them on their side."

"What if they run into one of the Champions of Chaos?" Jamis asked, perturbed.

"It would be bad," Helen agreed. "But remember, the Champions of Chaos are few. The gods of order exist in the hundreds, each with their own champion. There are only fifteen Champions of Chaos. If all the events only have around a hundred contestants, then there will only be two or three per contest."

"What do we do if we run into one?" Jamis asked.

"We kill them," Helen said. "Even if it means one of us dies and gets removed from the event, it's better we lose one than let one of them win."

"Agreed," Jamis said, cracking his knuckles. "I'd kind of like to test myself against one of them, anyway."

Chapter 16: Safe Zone

Mira stalked through the maze, her bow drawn as she scanned for threats. Hearing the battle ahead, she drew close and saw a man in golden plate with a longsword blazing with fire. He was fighting a humanoid creature, twelve feet tall, with two sets of arms. The giant towered six feet over the broad-shouldered man. Another creature moved above the man too, its hands pressing against his flanks as it swung above him to drop down from behind.

Mira drew her bow and fired.

The creature howled, putting a hand to its eye.

Fast as the wind, she fired again and again, shooting into its three other hands.

It lost its hold on the wall and dropped down, falling on the other creature.

The man in plate took advantage and stepped forward, plunging his blade into the creature's neck. Then, he decapitated the other.

He turned around and on seeing Mira, saluted her with his sword.

"I thank you for your assistance." He removed his helmet, revealing dark hair and green eyes. He bowed to Mira and peered at something over her head.

"I am Lancelot, Champion of Orella, Goddess of Duty and Trust," he said, bowing to her.

"I can read your name and title on your description," Mira said.

Lancelot flashed her a bright smile. "Ah, but it is still polite to introduce yourself."

"I am Mira, Champion of Jastrin, God of Hawks and Archery," she said, slinging her bow across her back.

"I wasn't brought here with the rest of my party. Do you have your own group or do you prefer to go alone?" Lancelot asked.

"I don't know where the rest of my party is," said Mira.

"Then would you do me the honor of being my companion for this event?" Lancelot asked, bowing, and extending a hand.

Mira smiled and took his hand. "I'd like that very much."

***

My eyes opened and I almost rolled off the branch of the tree. Grabbing its bark, I carefully sat up, cracking the bones in my neck and back. I wasn't well rested, but was good enough to continue. As I climbed down the tree, jumping ten feet to the ground, my eyes cast toward the opposite end of the boss arena, then began running toward it. Once inside, I stopped abruptly. This part of the maze looked very different from the part I'd previously been in.

After some twenty feet, the floor disappeared into a vast chasm enshrouded with white clouds. At the bottom, thirty feet ahead, was a platform.

Beyond that was another level that shifted up and down. I ran and jumped the first distance, then looking at the moving platform, I teleported onto it and looked forward, up and down. A tunnel opened to my left and right. Once level with the top tunnel, I stepped in.

Thick vines grew along the walls and ceiling, moss coating the stones of the floor. I continued my progress and thirty feet in, my Foresight went wild, presenting me with an image of my burning body. Behind me, I caught a glimpse of a bowling orange blaze moving toward me very quickly.

I sprinted forward, reached the end of the tunnel and jumped out into space, the fire passing below me. I grabbed a vine and swung onto another, crossing the chasm into another passage which split into two branches. I took the right turn and kept moving. The passageway came to another platforming section with several levels, floating in midair but somehow also connecting.

Teleporting onto a stable platform, I needed to keep moving, either by jumping or teleporting again to dodge fire and spike traps that proliferated through the passages of the maze.

Crossing a tunnel with various spike pits, I heard a chittering and turned to see a beetle the size of a large dog. It had a pair of horns on its head and a large snapping mandible, its shell a glossy dark red. It glowed malevolently as its thorax lit up.

Suddenly, as if on fire, it hurled itself at me, mandibles wide open.

> **Blast Beetle. Dungeon Creature. Mortal, Beast/Beetle. Power Level: 15.**

I sidestepped and crushed the beetle with a smack from my maul. Orange goo and carapace shell spattered across the ground.

Blood and Souls (Repeatable): Kill 5,120 monsters or humanoids. Current progress: 3,714/5,120. When you complete this quest, you will gain 1024 rank points. The next quest will require double the number to be completed but will award double the rank points.

I could see nothing to collect from it and moved on, hearing more chittering; behind me, a swarm of the things was coming down the passage toward me. They weren't as numerous as the spider hoard, but I was not interested in a protracted battle against a swarm of creatures as powerful as Rank 15 Gifted.

I kept running, beetles crawling out of cracks, harrying me down the passages. I was backtracking, desperately renavigating the maze by trial and error. At this incredible speed, I left my pursuers in the dust and had the opportunity to quickly map the area.

There weren't just the blast beetles to worry about; there were also Guresen in this part of the maze. Might I even run into a blast beetle mini-boss?

It had only been three hours since I'd entered the maze again, but my speed and ability to teleport made light work of even that amount of platforming. Making rapid progress, I found another hidden chamber behind a curtain of vines.

A bronze chest sat there, and I approached cautiously, by now even more wary of traps.

I opened it up to reveal an amulet embedded with a bright red gemstone. I picked it up and read its description.

Necklace of the Fire Adept. Type: Jewelry. Rarity: Rare. Provides a moderate increase to the damage of fire-based spells and abilities and reduces fire damage taken by one stage.

Not totally useful since I had no fire abilities but I'd been subjected to various fire attacks. I put the amulet on and continued to search the maze, having reached a vast chasm with a broken bridge. Sections of it floated in space, others missing, and yet others wobbled precariously, moving up and down on currents of air.

Jumping from one stone to the other, I almost fell once but teleported to a stable section and regained my balance. Crossing the death trap of a bridge, I reached the other side and looked upon what had to be another boss arena, this one circular in design. The moss of the last arena in which I'd fought had been replaced by a surface of coarse sand, while the area above was designed like the seating of a Roman colosseum.

There were two passages leading out of it, equal distances from each other. The gates to these passages were decorated with spikes. Similar, but much longer spikes jutted out all around the rim of the arena, offering to impale anyone who got too close to the wall.

Between me and the other passages was a massive ram with curled horns, its hide and skin metallic, its eyes blazing with fire and smoke rising from its nostrils.

> **Chatalen Ram Herd Leader. Dungeon Mini-Boss. Mortal.**
> **Monster/Chatalen Ram. Power Level: 60.**

I stepped into the arena, but the gates did not immediately close. I waited as the dungeon boss remained motionless, standing in the center of the arena, watching me. I looked on as another figure stepped out of the passage to the left, wearing full plate armor and carrying a longsword and shield. Another figure, that of a woman, stepped up behind him, carrying a recurve bow.

As soon as the two stepped into the arena, the gates shut, locking us in. ram reared up, snorting, and kicking up sand.

I attempted to take a careful look at the two others, but they were too far away to analyze at that moment. So, I turned my attention to the mini-boss that was pawing at the ground.

I stepped forward, charging at me, and I waited for it to get closer.

Every step propelled the ram into the air, a bullet train hurtling toward me.

When it was almost on me, I sidestepped, my maul hitting the beast mid-airborne stride and sending the top-heavy monster staggering in a struggle to stay on its feet.

The two other champions approached, briefly gaining my attention.

Felecia, Champion of Seshera, Goddess of Fertility & Abundance.
Gifted Mortal. Humanoid/Dusk Fey. Rank: 25.

Hornar, Champion of Amadra, Goddess of Shieldmakers and
Defense. Gifted Mortal. Humanoid/Kassadron. Rank: 27.

I turned my attention back to the boss, now rocking unsteadily on its hooves.

An arrow whizzed past my head as I jerked it to the side. My Foresight had given me a warning, but nevertheless, the arrow had almost clipped my carotid artery. I turned my attention back to the two other champions who were ignoring the boss and charging me.

"Figures," I grumbled.

The ram snorted, blasting out of its nostrils a cone of fire on my position, scorching an area of forty feet all around. I activated Phantom Form and teleported behind the two champions.

The ram seemed now completely focused on me. It charged.

Clearly assuming it was heading for them, the two champions fired salvos at the fiend.

Hornar braced his feet and activated an ability. His shield glowed with static power as he held his ground.

Felecia kept firing at the ram. Her quiver constantly replenished arrows as she fired, but the arrows simply bounced off its metallic fur and hide.

"You don't seem very good at this," I said.

Hornar whipped his head around, but the ram was almost on him. He could not move, or he'd be trampled. The ram struck his shield and bounced off.

I was surprised that Hornar was able to withstand the hit at his rank.

He was stockily built, thick and heavy, way more than anyone I'd seen. I guessed it might be a difference due to our races.

"You're the Warlord," Hornar said, moving to interpose himself between me and Felecia.

"That's what people keep telling me," I said with a shrug. "The Warlord seems a bit dramatic though."

"You have been chosen by Kelesa to wreak death and destruction on her behalf," Felecia said. "It's not a compliment. You are everything that embodies a warlord, someone who exists only to cause death and gain power."

I teleported away as she fired on me.

The ram dug furrows into the ground with his horn at spots I'd been occupying moments beforehand. I was not yet sure how I'd defeat it, but I wanted to see if I could get any useful information out of these two first.

"So, if they call me the Warlord, what do they call you?" I asked.

"We won't be talking to each other for much longer, so I wouldn't be worried about it," Hornar said, lunging forward, his feet blasting up sand as he shot across the distance.

I knocked away his blade with my club and bent to the side. "Don't cut yourself so short! You might even be able to last a few minutes against me!" I said with a grin.

Felecia raised her bow and fired an arrow straight up; it fell as a storm of arrows around me. "We won't be the ones dying here." She rolled to the side, her body multiplying into dozens of forms, all drawing bows and pointing them toward me.

"I was wondering what sorts of abilities the champion of a goddess of fertility would have," I said, activating Phantom Form and passing through her arrows. "Because lying on your back and getting knocked up doesn't strike me as a particularly useful power. Well, not for you at least,"

Next, I teleported away, appearing next to Hornar and elbowing him playfully in the ribs. "Am I right, Hornar?"

Hornar and Felecia turned red; whether this was with anger, embarrassment or both, I could not tell.

Hornar rushed at me and I smiled, sidestepping and letting the ram hit him full force as it tried *literally* ramming me from behind. Hornar was tossed across the arena and after rolling ignominiously across the sand, slowly staggered to his feet.

"You should probably use your shield next time," I said.

"Stop messing around and fight," Felecia snarled, firing arrow after arrow at me.

My shield flew in between us and intercepted the assault.

"If you insist," I said with a shrug, letting my smile fall away.

I teleported behind Hornar, and my club slashed across the back of his neck.

He crumpled to his knees, gasping and I ripped the claws out, blood fountaining into the air.

> **13 rank points gained.**

"Kelesa has made whoever you once were into a monster," Felecia said, circling me and trying to kite me with a barrage of arrows.

"Someone else made me a monster long before Kelesa ever came along," I responded.

"Who?" Felecia asked scornfully.

"My father," I replied, my voice dripping with hatred. I lunged forward as I teleported again the second it was off cooldown. I grabbed her bow, pulling it to the side and buried my club into her chest, punching through her leather armor and ripping out the claws. Blood sprayed out over me, and she fell to the ground, gasping for life and coughing blood.

> **12 rank points gained.**

I turned to face the Chatalen ram, teleporting above it. It jerked its head upwards in an attempt to impale me but could not because I landed on its back, seizing both curled horns.

The ram started bucking, angered by me holding on with every bit of strength my Might of 16 gave me. The mini-boss was going absolutely ballistic, charging in random directions, stopping, and trying to fling me off, or kicking out with its hind legs at impossible angles.

Still I held on, not just to maintain control but also because being flung off now would result in shattering almost every bone in my body. So, I clung on with my legs, my knuckles white as I yanked its horns, slowly guiding it closer and closer to the wall. Its steel wool cut through my pants and into my skin, leaving nasty cuts. I focused on my anger to push away the pain.

At the very last second, it charged left and I yanked its head, steering us sharply left whereupon the spikes along the wall punched right through its hide. I jumped off as the ram extricated its agonized self, molten metal pouring out of its chest from multiple wounds.

Clearly in a great deal of pain, it bellowed angrily and charged at me again.

I grabbed my spear from the air and stepped to the side, then rammed the weapon deep into the wound in its chest. My speed gave me the time to take aim and avoid its charge.

It bellowed again. A blast of fire immolated where I had stood a nanosecond beforehand.

Now, I teleported beside it, kicking into the spear shaft, driving it deeper into its chest.

The ram bellowed again, this time more in anguished pain than anger. It slowly fell to its knees and eventually crumpled, molten metal pouring onto the sand underneath it.

Stepping forward, I drove another spear through its eye to end its suffering.

Blood and Souls (Repeatable): Kill 5,120 monsters or humanoids. Current progress: 3,717/5,120. When you complete this quest, you will gain 1024 rank points. The next quest will require double the number to be completed but will award double the rank points.

I dismissed the minor notification to my quest update and another one popped into my vision.

Bosses slain by you:	2
Total number of bosses slain:	7
Total contestants remaining:	93

Seeing more prompts, I closed the tracker for the event and pulled up the next message.

You have completed several hidden objectives and earned multiple titles. Objective: Stay on the back of a wild monster or Gifted beast for over 3 minutes.

Reward. Title: Rodeo Rider > Rodeo Rider III.

*Rodeo Rider III: You have ridden a beast that bucked like a wild storm and through sheer grit and determination, never lost your grip. Your Might Attribute is doubled when trying to maintain your grip on your mount.

While the title was situational, it was interesting to learn you could earn multiple titles in a series at a time. I saw one last prompt and pulled it up.

> **You have completed a hidden objective and earned a title.**
> **Objective: Withstand an attack from a horned and hooved quadruped, defeating it with melee weapons without being hit by it once.**
>
> **Reward. Title: Matador.**
>
> ***Matador: You proved your bravery in the arena, standing before the charge and showing your skill. Damage against creatures that are charging you is increased by 1 stage while they are moving, and you remain motionless.**

This title was interesting. It would reward me for standing before charging creatures and hitting them instead of dodging away. I wasn't sure if I should take the risk for the increased damage, but the System seemed to reward risky behavior, judging by the number of titles I'd got.

Was this number normal for everyone else or did I have more or less than average?

I didn't know. There was no one I could ask, since all these champions were seemingly more hellbent on killing me than on pursuing their own glory.

I looked about to the center of the arena and walked over to the silver chest. After checking for traps, I opened the lid and looked at a steel helm, curled ram horns on its side. It resembled the images you'd see on the cover of some fantasy book or game on Vikings.

I picked it up and read the description for it.

> **Juggernaut Helm (Epic Helm): At the cost of 30 Mana, you double your size for 30 seconds. Your physical stats are increased by 30 for the duration and all your damage is increased by a minor amount. You suffer backlash at the end of this as your body recovers from the rapid increase and decrease in your attributes. Durability: 40/40.**

The helmet was fantastic, its magical properties meaning it was an upgrade on my current one. It was also a perfect 'ultimate' to bring to any battle, although I knew from the experience of my boots that the backlash to rapidly increasing your stats had a nasty effect.

I still put on the helm; it did not fully cover my face like my old gladiator helm but left everything under my chin exposed. I put the old helmet in my storage pouch and kept exploring the maze for more mini-bosses and the route to the maze's center.

I took the door not used by the two champions, figuring it would lead deeper into the maze. It changed slightly again, and I watched as walls slammed together and slowly pulled apart, showing the safe zone sixty feet beyond. I ran through, my immense speed enabling me to clear it with seconds to spare. I kept moving to dodge crushing traps and sped through timed corridors.

In the next corridor, I spotted a Chatalen ram; only a quarter of the size of the mini-boss, it snorted and charged at me and I waited, holding my ground.

I struck just as it arrived in front of me, stepping to the side and letting it plow into the earth as life left its body. It was impaled on my spear by a combination of all the damage increases from my titles together with its own momentum.

Blood and Souls (Repeatable): Kill 5,120 monsters or humanoids. Current progress: 3,718/5,120. When you complete this quest, you will gain 1024 rank points. The next quest will require double the number to be completed but will award double the rank points.

I kept moving, seeing no more Guresen but continuing to have brief skirmishes with blast beetles and Chatalen rams. I found no loot chests in this section of the maze as I sped through it. Finally, slowing as I approached, I arrived at another chamber with dozens of people milling around the area, sitting down or talking in groups.

Stepping into the area, a message from the System greeted me.

You have entered one of the Safe Zones of the event. The ability to analyze other champions has been removed while in the zone. Any attempt to attack another champion while in the Safe Zone will result in immediate expulsion from the area. This is meant to help

Dismissing the notification, I moved fully into the area.

People had set up tents, some sleeping while others were trading items. There were only around thirty people in the Safe Zone; presumably, this meant that the champions were likely to be split between the other Safe Zones in the event.

Most people were gathered in front of a gate with a strange lock.

"What's going on?" I asked someone at the back of the crowd.

"It's the gate to the rest of the labyrinth," the man replied, wearing a combination of leather and plate armor and carrying a long spear. "We're trying to figure out the puzzle to unlock it."

"How long have you been at it so far?" I asked.

"My group and I got here twenty minutes ago after defeating the mini-boss in our maze section. We've only five people in our party, so let me know if you're interested in joining us when we're through the gate. I saw you came alone, so guess you're looking for a party."

"Yeah," agreed a woman with a staff made of bronze set with a blue crystal. "I came in alone, and I've been lucky. I found some other champions early on to help me through the maze."

"Thanks, but I'm fine," I said.

"You're sure?" the man asked doubtfully. "I can see by your scars you haven't had a proper healer in a while. There is strength in numbers, you know."

"Relying on others will make you weak," I replied. "I'm fine on my own."

"Don't come back crying later, then!" he said with a shrug and went back to watching the people at the front of the group who were trying out different combinations as they argued about the solution to the puzzle.

People traded materials, food, and magical items they couldn't really use. I just waited in the line that formed as people took turns trying to figure out the solution in a range of ways.

I got bored and went to a corner to lie down to get some rest while I could.

Chapter 17: Storm Soul

Torvin charged through the gap as the walls closed around him. His spectral speed proved to be just enough as he and his companion reached the other side. They fell. Torvin leapt to his feet and helped his new party member keep their balance.

"Thanks," Olton said, shouldering his massive two-handed warhammer.

"Not a problem," Torvin answered. "You helped me through the last trap."

"I'm glad you have that mount," Olton said. "These corridors are a nightmare! How many people are expected to be fast enough to move through them?"

"I'm guessing it's to challenge parties to work together and find different solutions to make sure only the worthy reach the end," Torvin said.

"I just hope we find a place to rest soon," Olton said, rolling his massive shoulders.

"Come on," Torvin replied, smiling as he moved forward. "We haven't even fought a mini-boss yet."

***

I woke up and cracked the bones in my neck, then looked around to see almost everyone had gone to sleep, with the exception of a small, dedicated group still working on the gate. I sighed and walked over, getting a better look at it now that the crowd had dispersed. It was a combination lock with five dials, each with ten different runic symbols. Every time they got a wrong combination, a trap went off and the person trying would have to dodge or get healed, which was why I guessed people had lost their enthusiasm.

"Mind if I give it a shot?" I asked the man who was nervously scrutinizing the lock.

"Sure," he said with a relieved look, stepping aside.

I put my hands on the lock, but didn't move a single dial.

Instead, I looked through my Foresight into the future, reviewing my potential choices. I kept going through the combinations, watching as my body was subjected to shooting spikes, spear traps, fire blasts, and swinging blades.

"Are you going to do anything?" someone asked behind me, clearly annoyed.

"Shhh! I'm concentrating!"

"Abilities don't work on the door. We already tried that," someone else offered with a sigh.

"I'm not using it on the door," I replied and returned my focus to the lock.

I had heard there were over a thousand combinations in a five-digit lock. I'd lost track of how many I had tried but eventually, I hit upon the right one.

Finally, I turned the dials and the runes lit up.

The doors groaned and creaked open extremely slowly.

"How did you do that?" a girl asked, looking at me with awe.

"Magic," I said with a slight smile and stepped through the gap in the gates. "I'll see those of you who survive at the final boss, I guess."

"Wait!" someone yelled.

I turned back to them.

"Are you looking for a party?" he asked eagerly.

I sighed. "You guys really don't want to party up with me."

"Why?" he asked.

"Step through the gate and find out," I said.

Ildred, Champion of Kashila, Goddess of Grain and Harvest. Gifted Mortal. Humanoid/human. Rank: 21.

He stepped through the gate and looked at me. His eyes went distant as he read a notification and then they widened. He jumped back through the gate.

"He's a Champion of Chaos!" he shouted.

I had to smile at how frightened he was.

"Really?" a warrior in heavy plate with a two-handed axe asked eagerly. "Then let's take him now, together!"

Ildred shook his head emphatically. "I'm not going out there! You didn't see his rank. He's over 60!"

"That's as powerful as a mini-boss," the axe wielder argued. "If we all rush him, then we can kick him from the event and earn his rank points."

"That's right, Ildred," I said. "Listen to your friend here. If you all come at me at once into this tight narrow corridor, you can definitely overwhelm me. He certainly isn't trying to lower the numbers for his competition."

Ildred's face was filled with doubt and suspicion. "If you're so eager to fight him, then why don't you lead the charge?"

"Come on, man!" said the axe wielder. "We're all on the same side here."

"We're really not," I said, shaking my head. "This is a competition, both this event and the game between the gods. There are only ten winners for this event and one winner for the big game."

"Shut up!" the axe wielder snapped at me.

"Or what?" I scoffed.

"Or I'll make you," he blustered.

"You were already planning on fighting me!" I was now really starting to enjoy myself. "Try to keep up with your own plan!"

"I'm ready to kill this fucker. Who's with me?" he asked, planting his feet for the charge.

Twelve other champions faced me as they lined up beside and behind him. With a cry, they rushed through the gate, unleashing a salvo of abilities on my position.

I jumped up, kicking off the wall and gaining height as they came at me. I dodged bolts of lightning, fire, and light as well as snaring plants and shattering rocks all around me. At one point, I had to turn incorporeal to avoid half a dozen otherwise inescapable area effect attacks. The light and fire still hurt but the pain was muted, and I was out of the area in seconds. As the last group entered, I backflipped and landed at the end of the corridor.

"My turn," I said with a vicious smile.

My sawblade dropped from behind them at the beginning of the corridor and bisected a female archer. It rotated ninety degrees, now horizontal to the ground and began spinning down the corridor. I strode forward, ducking an incoming spear.

As I opened my storage pouch, a storm of spearheads flew out.

The corridor turned into a meat grinder. While I was outnumbered, it didn't really matter if my opponents didn't have room to maneuver. Sandwiched between the spinning disk of death, me and my spearheads, every last champion who had entered lay dead on the ground. The whole thing had taken no more than ten seconds.

Their blood soaked into the moss and grass of the maze.

125 rank points gained.

A new group of people stood in the gateway to the corridor, taking in the scene of carnage with horror-stricken faces.

"Let this be a lesson to all of you!" I declared. "This isn't a game for the weak. If you aren't on my level, then don't even bother stepping out of the safe zone. You simply cannot compete against me; and if you try... well, they say a picture is worth a thousand words."

I gestured to the butchered bodies.

Most of their items had disappeared and I didn't stick around to loot them. Despite my words, I knew from experience that a much weaker creature could still kill a Gifted of a higher rank if they were clever or lucky.

I began scouting the maze again, racing down halls and tunnels.

The monsters in this section included Chatalen rams, Guresen, and blast beetles as well as a new mob type. This part of the maze was a water level, and I knew from my past life that many people hated water levels, but I'd always liked them, the alien world that could be found just below the surface always intriguing me. This level of the maze required you to dive and swim through passages of water filled with the usual traps as well as powerful jet currents and poisonous urchins, not to forget they were also filled with a type of carnivorous fish.

Fire-belly Piranha Swarm. Dungeon Creature. Mortal. Beast (Swarm)/Piranha. Power Level: 28.

I sped through the swarm as they ripped into vulnerable sections of flesh. My weapons killed dozens, but every swarm was composed of at least a hundred piranha.

I found it was best to simply swim, take the damage and heal when I got through the section. I did collect two dozen of the fish.

Finding a dry dead end, I gathered some kindling from a spear trap and started a fire.

The fish were surprisingly tasty, possessing a naturally spicy flavor. Their juices were also highly flammable, making me wonder if the fire-belly part of their name meant more than just their red underside.

Now full, I kept exploring the maze, finding an underwater chest in a dead end. I threw it open and grabbed what was inside. Then, I turned around and swam upwards. When at the surface, I scanned for any creatures waiting to ambush me. Thanks to the scarf from the goblin chief, I could stay underwater indefinitely as it filtered in air for me to breathe.

A swarm of fire-bellies was almost upon me, their red undercarriages glowing in the water.

I pulled myself onto shore out of their reach and looked down at what I had grabbed.

Far-Seeing Mirror. Type: Utility. Rarity: Rare. This mirror will show you any person or place you have seen before as long as both of you are in the same realm.			
Made from moon silver and the scale of a phantom koi, this was created by a master crafter and empowered by a master enchanter.			
Hardness:	**10.**	**Durability:**	**20/20.**

This was one of the most interesting items I had come across. There were doubtless countless uses for it but none coming to me right now. So, I put it in my storage pouch and kept exploring, making what I considered to be good progress. However, I had yet to encounter another champion. I didn't know how quickly they explored but I was moving fast, with around three-and-a-half days left to reach the center of the maze. Not prepared to slow down to search for loot, I sharply focused on penetrating deeper into the maze in my quest for the next mini-boss. I swam down a deep chasm before finally emerging into a massive underwater cavern.

Stalagmites and stalactites rose and fell from the tunnel behind me, closing my route to escape as I entered the boss arena, seeing movement from the floor of the cavern.

At first glance, I had taken it to be a massive rock, illuminated with red lights. Suddenly, a bright red orb rose from the base of the cave and I got a good look at the mini-boss within, analyzing its name.

> **Fire-Lure Angler Lord. Dungeon Mini-Boss. Mortal. Beast/Angler Fish. Rank: 62.**

It was only a few ranks lower than me. More importantly, we were in an environment much more suited to its abilities. It came closer. Its nightmarish teeth opened wide as its lure rose up.

I felt something pushing at my mind, as if it was trying to subvert my thoughts and draw me closer to the glowing orb of light. My Mind and Spirit were high, so I pushed aside the mental intrusion and fired my spearheads at the mini-boss.

A shockwave went through the water, knocking all my projectiles off course.

The angler swam toward me, its mouth still gaping.

I darted forward, spear in one hand and club in the other. I pushed with my feet and found out that Heightened Speed worked as effectively underwater as on dry land. I darted into the mouth of the fish, succeeding in avoiding its teeth and once inside, forced them shut.

Its tongue tried to push me deeper inside.

I stabbed up with the spear, jabbing and stabbing, right into its brain.

Caustic blood rained down on me, but still I stabbed upwards, deeper. The red torrent continued to cascade over me and I felt my skin burn and blister.

The angler opened its jaws and spat me out, my spear still stuck in its brain.

I dodged a follow-up attack as it tried to rip me in half. I grabbed the stalk of its lure and swung back into the huge eyeball on the left side of its face.

It thrashed about, swimming toward a wall in an attempt to bash me against it.

So, I let go and tumbled through the water as the force of the current caught me.

The angler was slowly losing strength and I observed how its movements were becoming labored. It was, however, not out of the fight just yet. Its lure let out a burst of light.

Unable to see, I activated Bestial Senses, accomplishing this by focusing on feeling my way and 'hearing' through the water.

The fish-monster was almost on me.

Its scales brush underneath me and I kicked away, lashing out with my club. The claws on the weapon dug into the flesh of the beast, enabling me to cling on to its flank, holding on tightly as I was yanked along. Pulling the other club out of my belt, I stabbed its claws through the scales and flesh, beginning crawling along its body toward the head, using the club's spikes like crampons on a cliff face.

Simultaneously, using Telekinesis, I sent a volley of my spearheads flying toward the giant fish. Once again, it sent a shockwave through the water and I barely held on, making very slow progress toward the head. The spider-fang dagger sat in the belt on my waist, so I reached for it, then for a viper-fang dagger strapped along my leg.

I drove them both through the right eye of the leviathan.

Blinded, poisoned, and with a spear in its brain, its battle was over.

I swam away and waited.

The angler boss thrashed around, ramming itself into the walls and floor before it finally flopped belly-up and lifeless in the water.

Blood and Souls (Repeatable): Kill 5,120 monsters or humanoids. Current progress: 3,719/5,120. When you complete this quest, you will gain 1024 rank points. The next quest will require double the number to be completed but will award double the rank points.

Bosses Slain by you:	3
Total number of Bosses Slain:	9
Total Contestants Remaining:	79

A silver chest rose from the sand. I swam down and opened it to find a pair of leather boots sitting at the top. Had I not been under water, I would have released an underwhelmed sigh.

Swashbuckler's Boots. Type: Footwear. Rarity: Rare. Hardness: 11. You have perfect balance even on moving surfaces and your movement is increased by 3 feet per step. Durability: 15/15.

Created by a journeyman leatherworker from the leather of a deep ocean lion and infused with magical powers by a journeyman enchanter.

The boots were good… great even… if I hadn't already had a much better artifact set. I put the boots in my storage pouch.

I might trade them later for something better or find another use for them.

Retrieving my spear and daggers from the corpse of the boss, I swam a little further and emerged into a dark tunnel, moving down it until I came into a section of the maze which appeared to be stylized like a marsh.

Reeds and cattails lined the paths which were strewn with thick patches of mud. I was exhausted and desperately needed a rest but I did not trust this section. I kept moving, scouting for a good place to hole up. I jumped over sections of mud, which turned out to be fortuitous since one suddenly erupted and a strange creature emerged.

> **Minor Magma Elemental. Dungeon Creature. Mortal.**
> **Elemental/Magma. Power Level: 30.**

My maul smashed down, splattering the creature across the walls.

After a few seconds, the mess seemed to ooze together and reform itself into a vaguely discernible humanoid shape.

Each time it rematerialized, I smashed it more vigorously than the last. It was gradually getting smaller after each beating. Eventually, it was gone completely.

> **Blood and Souls (Repeatable): Kill 5,120 monsters or humanoids.**
> **Current progress: 3,720/5,120. When you complete this quest, you**
> **will gain 1024 rank points. The next quest will require double the**
> **number to be completed but will award double the rank points.**

Dismissing the notification, I looked over the remains of the elemental, able to feel the metal and uncommon stone in the cooled magma. I compressed all the elements into a rock the size of my fist and tossed it into my storage pouch, then kept moving through the marsh. I still ran into the occasional monster from the other zones. Apparently, each new section would introduce a new mob in addition to all the monsters I'd been fighting in the other zones.

I kept moving, 'filling my boots' fighting the magma elementals. They were a new challenge, and their entire body could be used by one of my abilities. I had killed over fifty by the time I found a spot to rest, calculating I'd collected several hundred pounds worth of material from the magma elementals. Fortunately, my storage pouch was based on size and not weight.

There was a swamp with a series of trees sprouting from the muck and mire. Here, I could identify swarms of fire-belly piranha swimming in the water. I ran across the surface, avoiding the carnivorous fish completely, climbing into one of the trees and finding a branch to lie on.

I figured I was halfway through this section of the maze and resolved to only sleep for a few hours, my recent exertions having taken a toll. With the exception of speed, my physical attributes were all dangerously low by now, and I tied myself to a branch so I wouldn't roll off into the water and get eaten by the piranha.

Despite how uncomfortable I was, I quickly fell asleep, exhausted.

I felt a jarring pain pulsate through me, straining to open my eyes. It was dark now, but the area around was flooded with light. Blue lights floated and settled on my skin, the buzzing shock passing through my body. I tried to sit up and swat the lights away but my muscles only twitched. Panic-stricken, I quickly realized I could only move my eyes.

I looked around as much as possible and tried to figure out what was happening.

Will-o-wisp. Gifted Mortal. Elemental Spirit/Will-o-wisp. Rank: 2.

The creatures were all over my skin and body, drawing something out of me. It was hot and painful but my body would not even let me scream.

Warning! You are under the influence of a paralysis ability, with a duration of 10 seconds per application.

Warning! Your soul is under assault and your Mana is being drained. When your Mana reaches zero, the attackers will begin to feed off your soul itself. This may result in permanent damage or even death.

I struggled against the rising heat inside my chest which felt as if this same heat was simultaneously being pulled out of me and devoured. I screamed internally, an explosion of heat rising from me as if my soul had detached itself from my body. I looked down at myself on the branch, seeing I was made of silver light.

My new form was naked and weaponless, but I could move so struck out at one of the wisps, my hand clamping down on it and squeezing. It was like grabbing a burning fire but my rage at being attacked dulled the pain and I crushed the wisp in my hand.

> **1 rank point gained.**

The other wisps rose up and swarmed over my new body, leaving my physical form still paralyzed in the tree. I lashed out at them, fists ablur. I was not as fast as I had been physically, but it was close. I grabbed, crushed, punched, and dodged, all without having to touch the ground. As I floated through the air, three dozen wisps amassed themselves into a swarm and attacked.

> **5 rank points gained.**

I crushed a wisp in my hand, its body disappearing in a burst of electricity.

> **1 rank point gained.**

I fell through the air under the swarm, then shot back up into their midst, a blur of arms and legs. I could feel my Bloody Pugilist title still active, even in this spectral form. More and more wisps died at my onslaught as they stabbed into me with electric arcs of lightning that ripped through my spirit self.

> **1 rank point gained.**

I struck out, hitting a wisp whose light was flickering faintly. It exploded into a burst of electric sparks.

> **1 rank point gained.**

My leg swept through the swarm in a vicious kick, killing multiple wisps at once. As I did so, I felt a lightning shock to my skin.

4 rank points gained.

My fists flashed forward in a rapid machine gun rhythm, pinpointing multiple wisps. I felt them dissolve into a shower of sparks.

6 rank points gained.

I tried levitating my weapons but did not seem to have access to my abilities in this form. Again, I rushed at the diminished swarm, a spinning hurricane of fists, elbows, knees and feet as I pummeled my way through.

10 rank points gained.

Only four of the wisps remained. They tried to flee, but I chased them down, catching and crushing each one. After they had ambushed me in my sleep, I was ruthlessly unwilling to let any escape.

4 rank points gained.

Blood and Souls (Repeatable): Kill 5,120 monsters or humanoids. Current progress: 3,753/5,120. When you complete this quest, you will gain 1024 rank points. The next quest will require double the number to be completed but will award double the rank points.

I dismissed the quest notification as I noticed others on my screen.

You have completed several hidden objectives and earned multiple titles. Objective: defeat at least 5 enemies assaulting your spirit as a spiritual avatar.
Reward. Title: Keytaro's Guardian III. (Requires Keytaro's Guardian and Keytaro's Guardian II).
*Keytaro's Guardian III: You have stepped into and interacted with the Ethereal Realm in both physical and spiritual forms, learning to fight and survive in this realm. When subjected to a Soul

> **Attack, your Spirit will manifest an avatar to defend yourself. Your Spirit can now manifest armor and weapons with which to defend yourself.**

So, this is what it means to manifest an avatar. I looked down at my form, finding it was naked, but my body was smooth at my crotch, like a doll's, with a distinct absence of genitalia. I guessed spirits did not have genders or must have other methods of procreating. I focused on my body and armor which were almost identical to those of my physical being. Equipment appeared, including a pair of clubs in my hands. My form was fading even as I experimented with it.

The eyes in my physical form opened once more. I read…

> **Warning! You have taken damage to your soul and will be vulnerable to Soul Damage and attacks until you repair the damage to your spiritual self.**

I couldn't tell whether I had taken more Soul Damage, or the System was just giving me a timely reminder. One more prompt was waiting for me and I dismissed the warning, pulling up the latest notification.

> **Storm Soul (Rank 1): Your soul is energy, and as such, you can absorb lightning to gain a permanent increase in your power. For every bolt of natural lightning by which you are struck, you gain a +5 to your maximum Mana. Increases your damage with lightning abilities by 5 percent.**
>
> **Cost: an extra 1 Mana to lightning spells. No other cost.**
>
> **Upgrade this ability to increase how much max Mana and lightning damage you gain. Each upgrade increases your Power Attribute by 1.**

"Yes!" I said. Despite the burning pain from almost being killed in my sleep, I was now exhilarated. The ability itself seemed of little use but it was the last one I needed to finish upgrading all my mental stats. From my status, there were eight stats, each divided between mental-based attributes. Half of them increased my maximum Mana and Mana regen rate. The other four, related to the body, increased my maximum Stamina and Stamina regen rate.

I had 920 Rank Points to spend and I intended to upgrade this ability as much as I could to get my Power Attribute over 20 and get this ability to at least Rank 15. I climbed out of the tree and ran to the next corridor, sitting crosslegged, trying to prepare my emotional state for ranking up.

"Raise Storm Soul by one rank," I told the System.

Storm Soul (Rank 2): Your soul is energy and as such, you can absorb lightning to gain a permanent increase in your power. For every bolt of natural lightning by which you are struck, you gain a +8 to your maximum Mana. Increases your damage with lightning abilities by 6 percent.
Cost: An extra 1 Mana to lightning spells. No other cost.
Upgrade this ability to increase how much max Mana and lightning damage you gain. Each upgrade increases your Power Attribute by 1.

I felt a tingling, buzzing sensation reverberate down my spine. The pain had yet to arrive. My Power had been low at 10, and going up to an 11 was barely any change at all.

"Increase Storm Soul by one rank," I said.

Storm Soul (Rank 3): Your soul is energy and as such, you can absorb lightning to gain a permanent increase in your power. For every bolt of natural lightning by which you are struck, you gain a +11 to your maximum Mana. Increases your damage with lightning abilities by 7 percent.
Cost: An extra 1 Mana to lightning spells. No other cost.
Upgrade this ability to increase how much max Mana and lightning damage you gain. Each upgrade increases your Power Attribute by 1.

The tingling increased slightly, the shuddering, buzzing sensation extending up my spine to my neck. Simmering anger made me only passively aware of the pain. I had to strain through my ire to identify that anything at all was happening behind the numbing sensation.

"Raise Storm Soul once more," I said.

> **Storm Soul (Rank 4): Your soul is energy and as such, you can absorb lightning to gain a permanent increase in your power. For every bolt of natural lightning by which you are struck, you gain a +14 to your maximum Mana. Increases your damage with lightning abilities by 8 percent.**
>
> **Cost: An extra 1 Mana to lightning spells. No other cost.**
>
> **Upgrade this ability to increase how much max Mana and lightning damage you gain. Each upgrade increases your Power Attribute by 1.**

The tingling went down to my tailbone and up my neck to the base of my skull, where it increased to an electric buzz as if I had grabbed the bare wires of an outlet. It was then joined by a pinching pain, like fire ants biting into my nervous system.

> **Congratulations! You have increased your ability to Rank 5. Please select an additional effect to the ability from the list below:**
>
> - **You can sense when a storm is coming and where it will arrive within one day and 5 miles of your location.**
> - **Being hit with lightning, natural or otherwise, is sustenance. When struck by a bolt of lightning, you will be given the benefits of a full meal and a long rest.**
> - **Damage from lightning-based attacks or abilities will restore a minor amount of Mana in proportion to the damage received.**

I read over my options and selected the third, the only one related to combat; the others were way too boring and useless for my tastes.

> **Storm Soul (Rank 5): Your soul is energy and as such, you can absorb lightning to gain a permanent increase in your power. For every bolt of natural lightning by which you are struck, you gain a +17 to your maximum Mana. Increases your damage with lightning abilities by 9 percent.**

> Damage from lightning-based attacks or abilities will restore a minor amount of Mana in proportion to the damage received.
>
> Cost: An extra 1 Mana to lightning spells. No other cost.
>
> Upgrade this ability to increase how much max Mana and increase in lightning damage you gain. Each upgrade increases your Power Attribute by 1.

"Increase Storm Soul by one rank," I said.

> **Storm Soul (Rank 6):** Your soul is energy and as such, you can absorb lightning to gain a permanent increase in your power. For every bolt of natural lightning by which you are struck, you gain a +20 to your maximum Mana. Increases your damage with lightning abilities by 10 percent.
>
> Damage from lightning-based attacks or abilities will restore a minor amount of Mana in proportion to the damage received.
>
> Cost: An extra 1 Mana to lightning spells. No other cost.
>
> Upgrade this ability to increase how much max Mana and increase in lightning damage you gain. Each upgrade increases your Power Attribute by 1.

The tingling increased as the ants multiplied, the pain in my spine magnifying to an almost unbearable level. I retreated behind my mental walls, the pain traveling up to my skull and delving into my anger and hate. Then, it passed.

"Raise Storm Soul by one," I said, immediately retreating into Wrathful Meditation.

> **Storm Soul (Rank 7):** Your soul is energy and as such, you can absorb lightning to gain a permanent increase in your power. For every bolt of natural lightning by which you are struck, you gain a +23 to your maximum Mana. Increases your damage with lightning abilities by 11 percent.
>
> Damage from lightning-based attacks or abilities will restore a minor amount of Mana in proportion to the damage received.
>
> Cost: An extra 1 Mana to lightning spells. No other cost.

> **Upgrade this ability to increase how much max Mana and lightning damage you gain. Each upgrade increases your Power Attribute by 1.**

The pain in my spine increased, making me experience a growing discomfort in my stomach and two sharp points of pain in the center of my chest and the top of my head.

The tingling was now the thrumming of a power line.

With venomous mandibles, the army of ants nibbled deep into my nervous system. Finally, the pain stopped bombarding my mental fortress and I was able to open my eyes again.

"Raise Storm Soul by one rank," I said.

> **Storm Soul (Rank 8): Your soul is energy and as such, you can absorb lightning to gain a permanent increase in your power. For every bolt of natural lightning by which you are struck, you gain a +26 to your maximum Mana. Increases your damage with lightning abilities by 12 percent.**
>
> **Damage from lightning-based attacks or abilities will restore a minor amount of Mana in proportion to the damage received.**
>
> **Cost: an extra 1 Mana to lightning spells. No other cost.**
>
> **Upgrade this ability to increase how much max Mana and increase in lightning damage you gain. Each upgrade increases your Power Attribute by 1.**

My spine thrummed with agony, and the points of pain grew in intensity and number. New pain appeared between my eyes, in my throat, in my gut, and most annoyingly in my groin, my loins feeling as if they were on fire. I endured the pain for as long as the rank-up took.

"Increase Storm Soul by one rank," I told the System, my voice thick with both anger and the remnants of pain.

> **Storm Soul (Rank 9): Your soul is energy and as such, you can absorb lightning to gain a permanent increase in your power. For every bolt of natural lightning by which you are struck, you gain a +29 to your maximum Mana. Increases your damage with lightning abilities by 13 percent.**

> **Damage from lightning-based attacks or abilities will restore a minor amount of Mana in proportion to the damage received.**
>
> **Cost: an extra 1 Mana to lightning spells. No other cost.**
>
> **Upgrade this ability to increase how much max Mana and increase in lightning damage you gain. Each upgrade increases your Power Attribute by 1.**

The pain increased all along my spine and various other points in my body. I felt like Marv from 'Home Alone, Part Two,' the part when he grabbed the sink and got electrocuted. With that rather dark but happy memory in my mind, I was able to withstand the pain, gritting my teeth until it disappeared as the rank-up ended.

"Rank up Storm Soul once more," I said.

> **Congratulations! You have increased your ability to Rank 10. Please select an additional effect from the list below:**
>
> - **Electrical effects are drawn toward you when cast or manifested within 50 feet of your person.**
> - **You know where any storm is occurring within one league of your location.**
> - **You can trap lightning into temporary crystals.**

These abilities were more interesting. The first could be used to help draw lightning toward me to gain more Mana. The second was not as useful but could be employed for farming Mana.

The third was really tempting. I did not know if I could merge these crystals with Compress Earth, but I would love to try.

Ultimately, I went with the first option, needing to absorb every bolt of lightning I could to make this pain worth it. Hopefully, the distance at which they would be drawn toward me would increase as I further upgraded the skill.

> **Storm Soul (Rank 10): Your soul is energy and as such, you can absorb lightning to gain a permanent increase in your power. You are a lightning magnet, drawing natural and artificial electricity toward your person. For every bolt of natural lightning by which**

you are struck, you gain a +32 to your maximum Mana. Increases
your damage with lightning abilities by 14 percent.

Damage from lightning-based attacks or abilities will restore a
moderate amount of Mana in proportion to the damage received.

Electrical effects are drawn toward you when cast or manifested
within 50 feet of your person. Cost: An extra 1 Mana to lightning
spells. No other cost.

Upgrade this ability to increase how much max Mana and
increase in lightning damage you gain. Each upgrade increases your
Power Attribute by 1.

The pain in my spine and along my body seemed to explode, making me
bite back a scream. Even a Berserker was not built to withstand this level of
pain. I gritted my teeth, and with tears rolling down my face, I waited until
it had passed.

I rolled my shoulders and cracked my neck, feeling my body tense from
the pain. One more rank-up and my Power Attribute would be 21, and I
would get the designated mutation.

"Raise Storm Soul by one rank," I said.

Storm Soul (Rank 11): Your soul is energy and as such, you can
absorb lightning to gain a permanent increase in your power. You
are a lightning magnet, drawing natural and artificial electricity
toward your person. For every bolt of natural lightning by which
you are struck, you gain a +35 to your maximum Mana. Increases
your damage with lightning abilities by 15 percent.

Damage from lightning-based attacks or abilities will restore a
moderate amount of Mana in proportion to the damage received.

Electrical effects are drawn toward you when cast or manifested
within 70 feet of your person. Cost: An extra 1 Mana to lightning
spells. No other cost.

Upgrade this ability to increase how much max Mana and
increase in lightning damage you gain. Each upgrade increases your
Power Attribute by one.

I blacked out from the pain for a second before it all came rushing back.

> **Congratulations! You have raised one of your attributes above 20, the Mortal limit. Your body is adjusting to keep these changes from killing you.**
>
> **Your body has grown crystal along your spine with major gem receptacles in your chakras. These crystals will transfer Mana to the gem receptacles in your chakras to store your Mana and let it be used more easily. Spells cast will now use less Mana.**

I felt my spine crack and pop as the changes were made to it, a debilitating pain correspondingly growing in my brain, quickly migrating to behind my eyes, my throat, heart, stomach, and groin. As my companions pinned me down, I rolled on the ground and then, at last, the pain ended abruptly and I let out a sigh of relief.

> **Congratulations! You have raised all your Mental Attributes beyond Rank 20 and may now raise them higher, without risking self-inflicted death.**

That was surprising. I no longer felt the burning from inside my body from my Spirit Attribute. My body began to cool. My maximum Mana had shot up. Apparently, Power was the main attribute for determining my maximum Mana and I guessed that Spirit was responsible for the Mana regen rate. I could now put more into all my mental attributes.

This was good because those were pretty much the only abilities I had.

There was another blinking notification, so I dismissed the one in view, pulling up the next.

> **You have created a new hidden title based on your actions. By using your anger and hate to ignore devastating and debilitating pain, you have ranked up all physical and mental attributes without the use of pain relievers.**
>
> **Reward. Title: Wrathful Meditation (Requires Berserker).**
>
> ***Wrathful Meditation: Your conscious mind retracts into your anger and hatred as it distances itself from body and soul, allowing you to completely disconnect from all pain.**

This was an incredible title, but I could immediately see its dangers. Pain was a biological reaction to damage. If you couldn't feel pain, it would be easy to overextend and even kill yourself. Still, this ability would let me rank up much faster.

"Increase Storm Soul by four ranks," I told the System, retreating into my anger.

I felt my thoughts disconnect, everything instinct now. As I sat there, I could feel nothing, not the wind on my skin or the hard stone under me. It was as though I was floating in a void, and only the incoming notifications showed any changes were happening.

Storm Soul (Rank 12): Your soul is energy and as such, you can absorb lightning to gain a permanent increase in your power. You are a lightning magnet, drawing natural and artificial electricity toward your person. For every bolt of natural lightning by which you are struck, you gain a +38 to your maximum Mana. Increases your damage with lightning abilities by 16 percent.

Damage from lightning-based attacks or abilities will restore a moderate amount of Mana in proportion to the damage received.

Electrical effects are drawn toward you when cast or manifested within 90 feet of your person.

Cost: An extra 1 Mana to lightning spells. No other cost.

Upgrade this ability to increase how much max Mana and lightning damage you gain. Each upgrade increases your Power Attribute by one.

I waited for the next detail to appear.

Storm Soul (Rank 13): Your soul is energy and as such, you can absorb lightning to gain a permanent increase in your power. You are a lightning magnet, drawing natural and artificial electricity toward your person. For every bolt of natural lightning by which you are struck, you gain a +41 to your maximum Mana. Increases your damage with lightning abilities by 17 percent.

Damage from lightning-based attacks or abilities will restore a moderate amount of Mana in proportion to the damage received.

Electrical effects are drawn toward you when cast or manifested within 110 feet of your person.
Cost: An extra 1 Mana to lightning spells. No other cost.
Upgrade this ability to increase how much max Mana you gain and the increase in lightning damage. Each upgrade increases your Power Attribute by one.

I was able to identify the set rate at which my abilities would increase. The distance lightning would be drawn to me increased by twenty feet for every rank. The percentage increase to damage with lightning went up by one, my Mana maximum going up by three for each rank.

Storm Soul (Rank 14): Your soul is energy and as such, you can absorb lightning to gain a permanent increase in your power. You are a lightning magnet, drawing natural and artificial electricity toward your person. For every bolt of natural lightning by which you are struck, you gain a +44 to your maximum Mana. Increases your damage with lightning abilities by 18 percent.
Damage from lightning-based attacks or abilities will restore a moderate amount of Mana in proportion to the damage received.
Electrical effects are drawn toward you when cast or manifested within 130 feet of your person.
Cost: an extra 1 Mana to lightning spells. No other cost.
Upgrade this ability to increase how much max Mana and lightning damage you gain. Each upgrade increases your Power Attribute by 1.

I read the confirmation of my analysis and dismissed the notification. This next prompt was the one I'd been waiting for:

Congratulations! You have increased your ability to Rank 15. Please select an additional effect from the list below:
• **You can trap lightning into temporary crystals**
• **When struck by natural lightning, you become immune to all damage for 5 seconds**
• **Your lightning abilities and spells inflict increased damage against items and structures.**

These choices were good, even offering me one of the same as last time, one I had been very tempted to take. The second could be crucial to surviving this ability.

If I got struck by a bolt of lightning, the chances were high of being wiped out for a while. Then again, it was only temporary. I had not reached this far by relying on safety nets.

The third option would make future abilities into siege weapons.

It sounded fun, but I earned no progress toward my rank points by destroying buildings.

Perhaps unsurprisingly, I decided to risk it and chose the first option. Even if it couldn't combine with Compress Earth, I imagined these crystals would have other uses too.

Storm Soul (Rank 15): Your soul is energy and as such, you can absorb lightning to gain a permanent increase in your power. You are a lightning magnet, drawing natural and artificial electricity toward your person. You are capable of manipulating it into physical form. For every bolt of natural lightning by which you are struck, you gain a +47 to your maximum Mana. Increases your damage with lightning abilities by 19 percent.

Damage from lightning-based attacks or abilities will restore a major amount of Mana in proportion to the damage received.

Electrical effects are drawn toward you when cast or manifested within 150 feet of your person.

You can trap lightning into temporary crystals.

Cost: An extra 1 Mana to lightning spells. No other cost.

Upgrade this ability to increase how much max Mana and lightning damage you gain. Each upgrade increases your Power Attribute by one.

I had the ability, but could not imagine a way to use it. Pausing to think about it, I realized it only mentioned trapping lightning into crystals, not that I could produce lightning.

Until I acquired a lightning-based ability, the effect I had chosen could not be used.

It wasn't that much of a loss. So far, nothing about this ability could be used except the increase it gave to my attributes.

"Raise Storm Soul by five more points," I told the System, determined to max out this ability before using it. Plus, I wanted as much Mana as I could get, since it was the resource I used the most for my abilities.

Storm Soul (Rank 16): Your soul is energy and as such, you can absorb lightning to gain a permanent increase in your power. You are a lightning magnet, drawing natural and artificial electricity toward your person. You are capable of manipulating it into physical form. For every bolt of natural lightning by which you are struck, you gain a +50 to your maximum Mana. Increases your damage with lightning abilities by 20 percent.
Damage from lightning-based attacks or abilities will restore a major amount of Mana in proportion to the damage received.
Electrical effects are drawn toward you when cast or manifested within 170 feet of your person.
You can trap lightning into temporary crystals.
Cost: An extra 1 Mana to lightning spells. No other cost.
Upgrade this ability to increase how much max Mana and lightning damage you gain. Each upgrade increases your Power Attribute by one.

I read the description and dismissed it.

The abilities were still advancing as normal except that being hit by lightning abilities would not restore. Even more Mana now made it somewhat of a counter to lightning mages.

Storm Soul (Rank 17): Your soul is energy and as such, you can absorb lightning to gain a permanent increase in your power. You are a lightning magnet, drawing natural and artificial electricity toward your person. You are capable of manipulating it into physical form. For every bolt of natural lightning by which you are struck, you gain a +53 to your maximum Mana. Increases your damage with lightning abilities by 21 percent.
Damage from lightning-based attacks or abilities will restore a major amount of Mana in proportion to the damage received.

Electrical effects are drawn toward you when cast or manifested within 190 feet of your person.
You can trap lightning into temporary crystals.
Cost: An extra 1 Mana to lightning spells. No other cost.
Upgrade this ability to increase how much max Mana and lightning damage you gain. Each upgrade increases your Power Attribute by one.

There were no other changes. I dismissed the message, safe in the numbing void.

Storm Soul (Rank 18): Your soul is energy and as such you can absorb lightning to gain a permanent increase in your power. You are a lightning magnet, drawing natural and artificial electricity toward your person. You are capable of manipulating it into physical form. For every bolt of natural lightning by which you are struck, you gain a +56 to your maximum Mana. Increases your damage with lightning abilities by 22 percent.
Damage from lightning-based attacks or abilities will restore a major amount of Mana in proportion to the damage received.
Electrical effects are drawn toward you when cast or manifested within 210 feet of your person.
You can trap lightning into temporary crystals.
Cost: An extra 1 Mana to lightning spells. No other cost.
Upgrade this ability to increase how much max Mana and lightning damage you gain. Each upgrade increases your Power Attribute by one.

Again, there were no unexpected changes.

Storm Soul (Rank 19): Your soul is energy and as such, you can absorb lightning to gain a permanent increase in your power. You are a lightning magnet, drawing natural and artificial electricity toward your person. You are capable of manipulating it into physical form. For every bolt of natural lightning by which you are struck, you gain a +59 to your maximum Mana. Increases your damage with lightning abilities by 23 percent.

Damage from lightning-based attacks or abilities will restore a major amount of Mana in proportion to the damage received.
Electrical effects are drawn toward you when cast or manifested within 230 feet of your person.
You can trap lightning into temporary crystals.
Cost: An extra 1 Mana to lightning spells. No other cost.
Upgrade this ability to increase how much max Mana and lightning damage you gain. Each upgrade increases your Power Attribute by one.

I dismissed the notification as soon as I got it and eagerly awaited the next prompt.

Congratulations! You have increased your ability to Rank 20. Please select an additional effect from the list below:
•   **You can travel from one bolt of natural lightning to the other.**
•   **You take one fewer damage stage from lightning, both natural and created.**
•   **You can grab and manipulate raw lightning without it dissipating.**

Again, all these choices sounded interesting. I loved the sound of the first one and pictured myself flying through a storm, leaping from one bolt of lightning to another. However, it was too situational, so I set it aside. The second one was hardly flashy but would be incredibly useful for surviving my ability. The third one was strange; it had the same problem as my previous choice, letting me manipulate lightning, but I still had no way to produce it.

I went with the sensible choice and selected option two. First, I needed to survive this ability and gain lightning abilities before worrying about doing flashy stuff with it.

Storm Soul (Rank 20, max. rank): Your soul is energy and as such, you can absorb lightning to gain a permanent increase in your power. You are a lightning magnet, drawing natural and artificial electricity toward your person. You are capable of manipulating it

into physical form. For every bolt of natural lightning by which you are struck, you gain a +65 to your maximum Mana. Increases your damage with lightning abilities by 25 percent.
Damage from lightning-based attacks or abilities will restore a severe amount of Mana in proportion to the damage received.
Electrical effects are drawn toward you when cast or manifested within 250 feet of your person.
You can trap lightning into lasting crystals.
You take one fewer damage stage from lightning, both natural and created.
Final rank bonus: Storms will be drawn to your location, veering off course when they come within 7 leagues of your location. They will remain over you until they naturally disperse.
Cost: An extra 1 Mana to lightning spells. No other cost.
Upgrade this ability to increase how much max Mana and lightning damage you gain. Each upgrade increases your Power Attribute by one.

I read over my ability, including the final rank bonus.

It was exciting to have earned a random extra effect as a reward for maxing out an ability, so I wanted to raise all my other abilities to Rank 20 as soon as possible. But for now, quelling that particular thought, I refocused on the task at hand as if in a race with the other champions and needing to reach the center of the labyrinth.

"Pull up my attributes," I said.

Mordred, Champion of Kelesa. Gifted Humanoid/Human. Mortal. Rank 85.			
Available rank points: 710.			
Might:	13 (+3) = 16	Mind:	22
Speed:	32 (+10) = 42	Perception:	23
Toughness:	11	Spirit:	36
Endurance:	11	Power:	30
Maximum Stamina:	91	Maximum Mana:	141

Stamina Regen:	21.2 per second	Mana Regen:	32.4 per second
Abilities:			
Dominion (Rank 5), Telekinesis (Rank 15), Heightened Speed (Rank 10), Foresight (Rank 10), Compress Earth (Rank 15), Bestial Senses (Rank 5), Phantom Form (Rank 5), Storm Soul (Rank 20).			
Blessings:			
Blessing of War (Mortal).			
Titles:			
Mark of Cain, Bloody Pugilist, Exorcist, Survivor III, Feral Barbarian, Field Alchemist II, Berserker, Beast Slayer III, War Chief, Venom Resistant, Visitor of Death.			

Reviewing my changes, I was satisfied for now, springing to my feet and running into the labyrinth.

Chapter 18: Uneasy Allies

Felrick stood beside the four other warriors. He had been alone in the maze for the past few days and had to navigate around mini-bosses.

He had found this group when he'd seen them entering a mini-boss arena. He had joined forces with them, and now, here they were, fighting the massive four-armed troll.

> **Mountain Troll Lord. Dungeon Mini-Boss. Mortal.**
> **Monster/Mountain Troll. Power Level: 55.**

Their leader wore armor made of woven bands of bronze and carried a massive greatsword, its edge made of blue light. The weapon sheared effortlessly through the troll's flesh, the monster regenerating quickly. The warrior, however, did not just possess a powerful artifact blade but was clearly a master swordsman.

He ducked and dodged two of the troll's fists, blocking the third on the flat of his blade.

Despite his skill, the blow threw him backwards.

The troll-lord jumped into the air and raising all its hands, brought them heavily down onto the prone champion.

Felrick stepped up, standing over the fallen champion.

A dome appeared above them, and the troll hit it, bending it inwards, the structure seeming to then recoil, flinging the troll backwards.

While it was on the back foot, the other three champions charged in from all sides.

Felrick helped the man to his feet, the two nodding in tacit, mutual appreciation and rushing to help their companions. Felrick moved close to the boss, issuing a challenge.

The troll's slimy head jerked toward Felrick. It laid into him with its fists which pounded on his shield. Felrick activated one of his abilities and stood his ground.

The maddened troll pounded on him, seeming almost oblivious to the opening up of its flesh by the other warriors.

Their leader with the greatsword jumped into the air, a pair of wings appearing along his back. He hit the ground like a meteor, then with one swift, smooth motion, he neatly removed the troll's head. The rest of the beast then crumpled to the ground.

Felrick joined the group as five silver chests appeared, one for each of them. He stood by one as they all pulled out the rewards of their battle. Tugging the white cape around his shoulders, Felrick then went to join the other champions.

"Thank you for your timely assistance," said their leader, extending a hand to Felrick.

"You're welcome, my lord," Felrick said, shaking his hand.

"Please...! We are all equals here, brother," the blond-haired warrior said, laughing. "Just call me Arthur. I'm not sure if we have met before."

"We have but it was brief," said Felrick. "I was one of Princess Helen's bodyguards when she was visiting Camelot. It is good to see you again, Prince Arthur."

***

I charged through the marsh, battling the magma elementals and collecting their remains when they cooled. I only fought the other beasts when I felt cornered. Unfortunately, despite their metallic appearance, it turns out that Chatalen rams were not, in fact, made of metal.

I did skin a few to make sure.

> **Chatalen Ram Hide. Type: Material. Rarity: Uncommon. Hardness: 9. The skin of a Chatalen ram is a tough leather with high piercing and slashing resistance as well as high fire resistance. Can also be useful in crafting.**

I threw the not-metal hides into my storage pouch and continued to ignore the rest of the rams. My Nemean hide cloak was superior to any other material I'd come across, being immune to damage from anything except artifacts and Nemean weapons.

It was important for me to keep moving, only stopping to fight the occasional monster that got in my way. I came to a stop upon hearing the battle ahead.

I approached warily and spotted an intersection.

A young woman with light-gray skin and white hair was cornered by a gang of over a dozen, her lower face obscured with a fanged, half-skull mask made of gold.

> **Ammerila, Champion of Salrilla, Goddess of Assassins & Murder.**
> **Gifted Mortal. Humanoid/Dusk Elf. Rank: 42.**

I was surprised. She was the strongest champion besides myself that I'd met so far. How were the others still so weak? It was unfathomable since I'd shot up in power in just one week, with no assistance or guidance from anyone. Based on their gear, these people had access to civilization to help them. Maybe that was what made them weak, a reliance on civilization instead of being forged in the fire of the wilderness and its monsters.

I scanned the others, seeing there were champions of all sorts, but not one was above Rank 30.

The woman was holding them back but she would soon be overwhelmed.

I made my choice and stepped forward, my spear inadvertently lancing a dawdling archer through the neck, and she collapsed to the ground.

> **12 rank points gained.**

Someone noticed me and half the group turned to face me, their eyes widening as they took in my impressive weaponry including the hundreds of spearheads floating behind me.

"I despise it when weaker creatures gang up on the powerful," I said. "If you really wanted to prove your strength, you should have taken her on individually!"

"What?Are you her protector?" mocked a man with full plate, shield and mace. "You're a Champion of Chaos! You never team up; it's not in your nature."

"What isn't in my nature is to let the weak tear down the strong," I said. "This is a competition to prove which of us is the strongest."

"Well, let me just say you're not stronger than all of us," said a man clothed in leather and cloth. He held a black staff blazing with fire as he pointed it toward me.

"Prove it," I said and teleported into the middle of them.

They scattered as I lashed out with my weapons. This area was not a narrow corridor where I could easily target them.

Ammerila threw something on the ground, becoming obscured by enveloping smoke.

I dodged a spear, my shield interposing itself between me and a volley of fireballs. I didn't want to use Phantom Form and give away all my tricks, so let my sawblade and maul keep my enemy scattered while my spearheads shot toward small groups of them.

13 rank points gained.

They were dying but not solely at my hand. A black shadow stepped out from behind a woman with a staff. It appeared to be healing her companions from the damage my sawblade had dealt, and blood spurted out of the woman's mouth as the assassin slayed her.

The champions were in a panic, most trying to focus on me as the most visible target. I responded by swathing through large numbers of them.

Meanwhile, Ammerila slipped from the shadows and quietly threw her daggers, taking out several.

10 rank points gained.

My maul crushed a warrior in heavy plate. As he tried to block, it shattered his shield and pancaked him against the wall.

12 rank points gained.

Five champions remained from the group. They turned and ran.

Ammerila appeared before them, her daggers ripping out the throats of the leading two. She then threw the knives which quickly dispatched two more.

The last of the feckless warriors was cut precisely in half by my sawblade.

The battle was done, at least for now.

13 rank points gained.

I looked over at the assassin.

Ammerila wore tightfitting armor over clothes that were a mix of blacks and dark grays. Her armor matched, providing stark contrast to the haphazard mash of different, random pieces of armor and animal hide in which I was attired. She eyed me warily, and I took a step back.

> **Blood and Souls (Repeatable): Kill 5,120 monsters or humanoids. Current progress: 3,758/5,120. When you complete this quest, you will gain 1024 rank points. The next quest will require double the number to be completed but will award double the rank points.**

"Are we fighting now?" I asked.

"I don't know," she said, her voice soft but clear. "Are we?"

"Up to you," I said, ready to turn incorporeal if she disappeared from sight.

"There are still many other champions," she said. "And there is the rest of the labyrinth to consider."

"I'm not worried about the others," I said. "What are you suggesting?"

"That we team up to make it to the final ten. I don't have anything against you or your goddess and it will increase our chances if we work together to reach the end."

"Lets fight a mini-boss together before we decide on anything," I said.

"Agreed," Ammerila said, nodding.

We set off together, both ensuring we maintained a careful distance and with the other in our peripheral vision. Five other corridors had converged on this location and we took the one that seemed to be leading deeper into the labyrinth.

We reached a set of doors and opened them, entering the next boss arena. We stepped apart and scanned the arena for the boss, able to see nothing. The area was constructed from black stone, obsidian spikes which hung from the ceiling. Molten lava flowed down the inverted pillars and disappeared into the ground, illuminating the area in a red light.

Out of the center of the arena, the ground glowed red hot.

The stone was bubbling, and a gargantuan figure rose from the ground. Its hands reached upwards and it seemed to be pulling itself out of the earth.

> **Magma Knight. Dungeon Mini-Boss. Mortal. Elemental/Magma. Rank: 65.**

I moved to the right while Ammerila stepped left.

The knight stepped forward, molten droplets falling off its form and bubbling on the ground. Sections of its body cooled and turned hard like armor.

Instead of hands, long, clawed blades appeared.

My sawblade and maul swung at the entity from two directions. The maul cracked the stone plates of its armor and the sawblade sent sparks flying as it ground against the hardened magma.

Ammerila appeared behind the boss, her daggers flashing, striking the Magma Knight. She performed a backflip and landed fifteen feet away.

This is too much! She's obviously showboating for my benefit.

The elemental seemed to possess neither weak points nor vital organs. This battle was going to be about overwhelming damage.

I reached out my hand and using my Telekinesis, grasped its body, then lifted it into the air and slowly crushed it.

Ammerila leapt forward while I was holding it immobilized.

Its power palpably strained against my Spirit and would soon break free unless I compressed it. Its armor plates cracked every second, making a terrible noise.

Ammerila stabbed and dodged as jets of magma shot out like spouts of blood, her hands and blades a blur.

The Magma Knight broke free and turned, making swipes at Ammerila who slid under its claws and disappeared into shadow.

I charged forward, my maul striking down on its armor plates.

There was a tectonic shift on the surface of the entity, plentiful magma again spurting from the gaps in its armor, newly breached by my maul.

The boss was not yet done, however, more arms growing from its sides and whips of magma flowing from it as octopus-like appendages. It lashed out at me with the whips, while its clawed hands blocked Ammerila's daggers. It was moving faster now, as if losing its mass increased its speed. The whips were as fast as lightning and coiled with a sinister life of their own.

I was able to dodge one but another wrapped around my arm. Even through the armor, the burning heat was scorching my skin.

I focused on my anger, letting the pain dull and charging the Magma Knight.

Instead of repelling my attack, the entity only pulled me closer to it, my clubs tearing into its frame. I dodged as much of the molten stone and metal as I could, but could not avoid all of it. The pain was unbearable, and I quickly had to change from Berserker to Wrathful Meditation in order to keep fighting. I was numb and a cursory glance at my arm revealed the damage my exposed body was being forced to endure.

Horrific burn marks had appeared on my skin and muscle tissue.

Regardless, I kept fighting, my battle now akin to operating a video game character, immune to the pain. Everything seemed to be happening to someone else as I gave my body the commands to duck, dodge, attack and block.

Ammerila joined the attack from the other side and the two of us ripped into the creature.

The lava whip around my arm dropped as the tentacle gripping it was ripped off. I was able to quickly down a health potion and splash three more over the burns to my left arm and thighs. Luckily, I was mostly just cooked instead of incinerated.

With some relief, I could see the wounds starting to close.

The Magma Knight was weakened, and I hurled my weapons at it, my sawblade bisecting it and my maul smashing it to pieces.

I waited to drop Wrathful Meditation until my wounds were just pink marks on my skin. When I had fully returned to my senses, I noticed my body was still hot.

Dry skin flaked off me like snow, and Ammerila was panting heavily. She was able to focus on damage only, however, and did not look as if she had taken any hits. She glanced over at me.

By now, my wounds were all closed, due in no small measure to Field Alchemist III. My potions were even more effective because of an amplification of the effects of the herbs.

Both of us turned our attention back to the Magma Knight and attacked again.

After a furious onslaught of attacks from me, coupled with tactical, pinpoint strikes from Ammerila, the boss finally fell.

> **Blood and Souls (Repeatable): Kill 5,120 monsters or humanoids. Current progress: 3,759/5,120. When you complete this quest, you will gain 1024 rank points. The next quest will require double the number to be completed but will award double the rank points.**

I dismissed the quest update, seeing more notifications waiting for me to view.

Bosses slain by you:	4
Total number of bosses slain:	11
Total contestants remaining:	65

You have completed multiple hidden objectives and earned several titles. Objective: survive multiple lethal burn wounds.
Reward. Title: Fireproof I and Fireproof II.
***Fireproof II: Damage from heat and fire is reduced by two stages.**

I dismissed the new title and looked around.

Ammerila was drinking a red potion, healing any damage she might have taken.

Two silver chests had risen out of the stone. I went over to one and opened the lid, finding only that a square of thick cloth—like a washcloth—sat in it.

Cleansing Cloth. Type: Utility. Rarity: Rare. Hardness: 6. At the cost of 5 Mana, all dirt, sweat, blood, gore, and grime is removed from a creature or a single item.	
Created by a master weaver from Asgard linen and enchanted by a journeyman necromancer.	
Durability:	**10/10.**

The cloth was not that useful although I supposed it would make it easier to clean myself. The most interesting thing about it was the material, Asgard linen, another reference to earth mythology. I kept coming across these. The only question was, had the name originated in my world or this one? I shoved the cloth into my storage pouch and turned to Ammerila.

"You ready to continue?" I asked.

"You want to keep fighting together?"

"Sure," I said with a shrug. "Why not."

We continued through the gates of the boss arena into the next section of the maze. There were no other doors, only a straight path deeper into the labyrinth. I had to slow down slightly but Ammerila was very fast. I guessed she had a Speed ability of her own.

The monsters in this area were changed, the fire-belly piranha glowing even brighter. When I got close to the water, they leaped out of it toward me and exploded.

The Chatalen rams had smoke billowing from their nostrils and blasted fireballs at us, while the Guresen tail spikes were wreathed in flames. As for the blast beetles, they assailed us, now with the tips of their stag beetle horns glowing ember hot.

We kept fighting our way through until we came to another large clearing; as soon as we entered it, we were ready to fight another mini-boss but received a notification.

> You have entered one of the Safe Zones of the event. The ability to analyze other champions has been removed while in the zone. Any attempt to attack another champion while in the Safe Zone will result in immediate expulsion from the Safe Zone. This is meant to help you interact without knowing each other's allegiances. In short, to encourage cooperation between all the champions.

We took the opportunity to relax, so we sat down. I rolled my shoulders and pulled some piranha and Guresen meat out of my storage pouch.

Then I created a small fire with some wood I had collected and built it up with coal.

"So," I said, deciding to strike up a conversation. "Are you from this world?"

"No," Ammerila said, skewering some fish on an arrow. "My world is much more technologically advanced than this. I was an enforcer to a crime lord in the slums."

"Must have been tough," I said, starting to grill Chatalen ram ribs and some Guresen flanks.

"It made me strong and taught me how to survive," she said with a shrug. "I didn't have anything to leave behind and was tired of taking orders from others. What about you?"

"My home world is more advanced, but I didn't do anything as exciting as working for a crime boss. I worked in construction," I said.

"Then why did you choose this?" Ammerila asked, gesturing loosely to indicate our environment.

"Because I wanted to be someone greater," I said. "I didn't want to end up like my father."

"Who was your father?" Ammerila asked.

"He's the man who made me what I am," I said. "I'd rather not talk about him. Let's just say I didn't leave anything or anyone behind when I came here, either."

We grilled the meat and ate.

Ammerila rolled over and started to take a nap, but we could not rest for long with the imposed time limit on us. I took the time to upgrade my abilities further. Moving away from the lightly sleeping Ammerila, I sat down, my back to the wall.

I had several abilities I could rank up, but I needed to consider what would best keep me alive. Compress Earth and Telekinesis were the closest to Rank 20 but only one was a direct combat skill. Foresight was my main way to avoid damage and it was only Rank 10. Phantom Form was only Rank 5 and could be upgraded significantly. I was still not willing to reveal that trick in front of Ammerila, since it might be necessary to it use against her at some point.

I decided to focus on my Spirit Attribute for now. I would get Telekinesis to Rank 20 and get its max rank bonus, and I'd raise Phantom Form to at least Rank 10.

I settled into my Wrathful Meditation and made sure I was ready for the pain of the rank-ups. "Raise Telekinesis by five ranks," I told the System.

Telekinesis (Rank 16): You can, at will, lift 16 objects or creatures weighing 2,270 pounds or less and move them within 350 feet of your body; or up to 24,576 objects or creatures weighing 590 pounds or less and move them within 350 feet of your body. The speed and power of objects are based on your Spirit Attribute.

You can now crush an enemy with your ability. You deal a severe amount of damage each second to a creature suspended by your Telekinesis. The damage is increased slightly for every point in Spirit you have above 10.
You can hurl objects more rapidly with your Telekinesis. Each object moves an extra 90 feet per second (base rate 10 feet per second x rank of Spirit).
Your Telekinesis can now interact with items or creatures of energy and magic as well as physical objects.
Cost: 1 Mana per 10 small objects per sec or 1 Mana per large object per sec.
Upgrade this ability to increase the number of items, their weight, and the range at which you can move them. Every upgrade of this ability increases your Spirit Attribute by 1.

I looked over the changes, noting the increase. The number of large objects only went up by one while the number of small objects doubled each rank.

The weights seemed to increase slightly each rank, but I wasn't sure of the exact number.

Telekinesis (Rank 17): You can, at will, lift 17 objects or creatures weighing 2,590 pounds or less and move them within 370 feet of your body; or up to 49,152 objects or creatures weighing 665 pounds or less and move them within 370 feet of your body. The speed and power of objects are based on your Spirit Attribute.
You can now crush an enemy with your ability. You deal a severe amount of damage each second to a creature suspended by your Telekinesis. The damage is increased slightly for every point in Spirit you have above 10.
You can hurl objects more rapidly with your Telekinesis. Each object moves an extra 100 feet per second (base rate 10 feet per second x rank of Spirit).
Your Telekinesis can now interact with items or creatures of energy and magic as well as physical objects.
Cost: 1 Mana per 10 small objects/sec or 1 Mana per large object/sec.

> Upgrade this ability to increase the number of items, their weight, and the range at which you can move them. Every upgrade of this ability increases your Spirit Attribute by 1.

Apparently, larger objects got an additional twenty-pound increase. I could already lift objects over a ton, and I expected it would be about two tons by the time this skill was maxed out.

> **Telekinesis (Rank 18):** You can, at will, lift 18 objects or creatures weighing 2,930 pounds or less and move them within 390 feet of your body; or up to 98,304 objects or creatures weighing 745 pounds or less and move them within 390 feet of your body. The speed and power of objects are based on your Spirit Attribute.
>
> You can now crush an enemy with your ability. You deal a severe amount of damage each second to a creature suspended by your Telekinesis. The damage is increased slightly for every point in Spirit you have above 10.
>
> You can hurl objects more rapidly with your Telekinesis. Each object moves an extra 110 feet per second (base rate 10 feet per second x rank of Spirit).
>
> Your Telekinesis can now interact with items or creatures of energy and magic as well as physical objects.
>
> Cost: 1 Mana per 10 small objects/sec or 1 Mana per large object/sec
>
> Upgrade this ability to increase the number of items, their weight, and the range at which you can move them. Every upgrade of this ability increases your Spirit Attribute by 1.

The speed increase to my ability was a steady extra 10 feet per rank. There was no change to my effects to interact with energy or magic and to crush creatures. That last skill had gone up, but it only did so every five ranks. I did not know exactly what severe damage was, but so far it was the highest damage I'd seen something do.

> **Telekinesis (Rank 19):** You can, at will, lift 19 objects or creatures weighing 3,290 pounds or less and move them within 410 feet of your body; or up to 196,608 objects or creatures weighing 830 pounds or

less and move them within 410 feet of your body. The speed and power of objects are based on your Spirit Attribute.

You can now crush an enemy with your ability. You deal a severe amount of damage each second to a creature suspended by your Telekinesis. The damage is increased slightly for every point in Spirit you have above 10.

You can hurl objects more rapidly with your Telekinesis. Each object moves an extra 120 feet per second. (Base rate 10 feet per second x rank of Spirit).

Your Telekinesis can now interact with items or creatures of energy and magic as well as physical objects.

Cost: 1 Mana per 10 small objects/sec or 1 Mana per large object/sec.

Upgrade this ability to increase the number of items, their weight, and the range at which you can move them. Every upgrade of this ability increases your Spirit Attribute by 1.

No unexpected changes. I eagerly awaited the next prompt.

Congratulations! You have raised an ability to Rank 20. Please select an additional effect for your ability from the list below:

- The weight for objects you can levitate is doubled.
- The range at which you can levitate objects is doubled.
- You can form a blade of pure telekinetic force.

The first choice would let me fling elephants around; useful but I had yet to encounter many things that I could not lift, already having the capacity to raise almost two tons. The same thing was true for the second option. Yes, having increased range would have been useful, but first and foremost, I was a warrior and enjoyed getting involved up close in hand-to-hand combat. The idea of being a sniper or mage, hanging back in the shadows, was anathema to me.

The third option was the most interesting; I could levitate so many objects, but did not have that many possessions. I was not particularly interested in carrying a quarter of a million spearheads around. This option would enable me to more effectively weaponize my telekinetic ability. If for some reason I was unable to access my spearheads, I would never be out of objects to manipulate with Telekinesis. I selected the third option.

Telekinesis (Rank 20, max rank): You can, at will, lift 20 objects or creatures weighing 4,000 pounds or less and move them within 450 feet of your body; or up to 400,000 objects or creatures weighing 950 pounds or less and move them within 450 feet of your body. The speed and power of objects are based on your Spirit Attribute.
You can now crush an enemy with your ability. You deal a severe amount of damage each second to a creature suspended by your Telekinesis. The damage is increased slightly for every point in Spirit you have above 10.
You can hurl objects more rapidly with your Telekinesis. Each object moves an extra 150 feet per second (base rate 10 feet per second x rank of Spirit).
Your Telekinesis can now interact with items or creatures of energy and magic as well as physical objects.
You can form a blade of pure Telekinetic force. (The size of the blade determines the number of objects it counts as. A grain of sand, for example, equals one small object, an arrowhead-sized object equals ten small objects, and a sword-sized blade counts as a hundred objects).
Final rank bonus: You can combine the weight you can lift into one object, lifting one object weighing 20 tons.
Cost: 5 Mana per 10 small objects/sec or 10 Mana per large object/sec.
Upgrade this ability to increase the number of items, their weight, and the range at which you can move them.
Every upgrade of this ability increases your Spirit Attribute by 1.

The max rank of Telekinesis was impressive, each category having gone up more than usual. It would seem the System did not like odd numbers and preferred neat order to abilities.

I could now levitate objects weighing two tons; or if I chose to, almost half a million objects weighing almost half a ton.

With my final rank bonus, I could lift one object weighing twenty tons, more than a passenger plane back on my world. The ability to create blades from telekinetic force had a more detailed description. Even with the cost for making the blades, there was no shortage in the number of objects I could levitate. Speaking of cost, the Mana cost for my ability had gone up, but I had plenty of Mana and with my Spirit so high, my Mana regen rate was incredible.

I was not done yet. I wanted to upgrade Phantom Form to Rank 10 before continuing with the Event. "Increase Phantom Form by five ranks," I said.

Now that I had Wrathful Meditation, there wasn't the need to read every notification, so I dismissed the next four, waiting until the important one popped up.

Congratulations! You have raised an ability to Rank 10. Please select an additional effect for your ability from the list below:
• Your spirit damage is increased by one stage while in this form.
• You lose your vulnerability to Psychic and Soul damage while in this form.
• Your form can move x2 as fast as your physical form.

The first option was tempting but this was not an ability required for combat. Having an option for creatures resistant to physical damage was something I currently lacked, however.

The second choice was in line with the previous decision I had made.

What is the point of a defensive ability if you become vulnerable to certain types of damage? After all, it only takes 'one shot'? The third one was not necessary.

Maybe other people would find it useful, but I was already very fast.

I decided to double down on my last choice and picked the second option.

Phantom Form (Rank 10): Your spirit has grown in strength now equaling that of your body, making you as much a creature of the ethereal world as that of flesh and blood. You can turn incorporeal for up to 5 seconds, becoming immune to most forms of damage but still vulnerable to certain types. After using this ability, there is a

cooldown of 6 seconds before you can use it again. While in this form, all the physical damage you deal is converted to Soul Damage.
You lose your vulnerability to Radiant Damage and Silver Weapons while in this form.
You lose your vulnerability to Psychic and Soul Damage while in this form.
Cost: 15 Mana per use.
Upgrade this ability to increase the time you can remain incorporeal and reduce the cooldown time. Each upgrade to this ability increases your Spirit Attribute by 1.

My rank-ups done, I got to my feet and went to the gate. It led deeper into the dungeon.

Ammerila got up and joined me. "You ready?" she asked.

"More than ready." My body felt the heat from the strength of my spirit.

Chapter 19: The Fire Knight

Jamis and Helen stood alongside their four champion allies over the body of the mud elemental lord. Wiping sludge off her face, Helen looked down in disgust. In its last moments, the elemental had exploded, showering them all in muck.

"This is disgusting," she said. "It's been nothing but horrible swamp creatures and mud elementals for the past four days."

"It can't be much longer to the center now," Jamis said, wiping the mud off his own body.

"Do you think it will be some other sort of mud monster?" Helen asked as she healed the injuries of Jamis and the others, bringing them all to perfect health.

"If it stays on theme," said Larent, a bow-wielding champion.

"Time for loot," Jamis said, opening his silver chest and pulling out a broad belt. "Excellent. It increases my Might and Toughness!"

"Lucky!" said Helen, raising a black metal staff. "This one increases the damage of fire abilities by one stage and increases their range by a quarter."

"The System does not seem to care if you can use the item or not," said Relia, a champion in mages robes. She had an icy aura and held up a thick, metal breastplate.

"Hopefully, the final rewards are a little more tailored to the victors," Helen said.

They all continued deeper into the labyrinth on their quest to reach the center.

***

Ammerila and I stepped past the gate, entering a new section of terrain. I was not sure if we were still in the labyrinth because this place did not look at all like a maze. It was too open, having massive pillars like the mines of Moria in The Fellowship of the Ring.

These weren't ruined but fully intact and made of glossy, black obsidian.

The hall stretched into the distance, appearing to go on for at least a mile, eventually vanishing in a heat haze. It was some two hundred feet wide too, with curtains of lava formed on the walls on either side, making it sweltering hot.

We hurried forward, and I could feel the presence of the boss ahead of us. Soon, I could see past the heat haze to a massive dais with four other halls and somehow, it felt as if this way would lead us to the boss. I activated Bestial Senses and heard the sound of running feet ahead.

Ammerila looked about, apparently hearing it too.

I teleported forward to the dais, seeing two small groups of champions charging down two of the other halls, obviously heading for the center of the labyrinth.

I still couldn't see the boss and looked around for where it could be hiding on the dais.

Something dropped from the ceiling, a clang of metal on stone echoing out through the chamber and halls. A figure in spiked, plate armor and black billowing robes landed from the ceiling. Orange light shone out from the bars of its visor, and it carried a massive greatsword which glowed red hot as it rose from a crouch to stand thirteen feet tall.

Maroloth—the Knight of Fire. Gifted Mortal. Elemental Lord. Rank: 85.

Blindingly quickly, the huge sword swung at me and I Managed to sidestep, my boots making my speed a pretty rapid 42. I lunged at the Knight of Fire, my claws skidding off its armor and I spun about as Maroloth tried to backhand me.

In the next moment, Ammerila was by my side, having arrived seemingly out of midair. Then, she drove her daggers into Maroloth's back, a ring of fire exploding out of him.

Ammerila escaped the flames.

I did not. Fire engulfed my form and only my Berserker title kept me from screaming and rolling on the ground. My maul struck down from above.

Maroloth raised his greatsword in defense and slid across the floor at the force of the blow. "Sword of the Primal Fire!" he bellowed.

This surprised me somewhat. As he was an elemental, I didn't think he was capable of speech.

His molten sword burst with flames, and he slammed it down across the ground. A line of lava formed, quickly transforming to stone that fell as steaming rocks into the chasm below.

"You have evaded my first strike, Warlord!" Maroloth said. "You shall not evade the next."

"Try me," I said.

The other champions were fast approaching.

Suddenly, Ammerila was among them, obviously leaving me to handle the boss while she assassinated the others.

"Ring of the Encircling Flame!" Maroloth had spoken again and had activated another ability. He swung horizontally at me, his sword rising then slashing down again.

A ring of fire rose around the edge of the dais. Soon, it was over a hundred feet tall, its flames making me sweat even from some distance.

Despite his immense size, Maroloth was surprisingly fleet in his movement.

I did not possess the physical power to punch through his armor... even if I had, I doubted he had vital organs to target.

The fire was extremely close, now only fifteen feet away.

I was already having difficulty dodging Maroloth's greatsword and I took a look at the other champions fighting Ammerila; making sure no one was looking my way, I activated Phantom Form and sped through the fire, feeling it flickering at my spirit, but the pain was negligible.

On the outside ring of the fire, I turned to face Maroloth. This boss had a plethora of abilities. So far, I'd been able to avoid or counter them, but it was highly dangerous for me to assume I could keep doing that indefinitely. I'd have to end this quickly.

I lack the might to give my weapons enough power to damage his armor but I might have a way to change that.

I activated the effect of my new helmet for the first time.

My size swelled, and in milliseconds, I had doubled in size. I probably should have tested if this affected my clothes before trying it! Fortunately, it turned out that it did: my weapons, clothes and armor all grew with me, and I had grown an inch in height since coming to this world due to increases to my Speed 'stretching me out'. My normal height here was a little over six feet, but with this effect active, I now stood at over twelve feet tall. Stone cracked beneath my feet as I charged forward. My clubs, now five feet long, swung down from two directions.

Maroloth blocked one with his greatsword but the other struck across his helm.

Molten metal and fire splashed out across my arm but luckily, the temporary size increase had also upgraded all my physical stats by thirty for the duration of the current combat situation. In addition, my Toughness let me shed the fire off my skin.

I struck the elemental repeatedly with my maul, pounding the boss into the ground. My Speed increased even further, now standing at around sixty and being multiplied further by my Heightened Speed. My hands and weapons moved faster than my Perception could really keep track of. I laid into Maroloth with everything I had.

Molten metal seeped out of his armor like blood as Maroloth lay at my feet. His armor was breached and broken. Whatever force had animated his body, it now seemed to have left him.

You have gained 22 rank points. These are to be split between surviving party members.

The final boss of the event has been slain. Please finalize all actions and if close enough, try to reach the center of the labyrinth.
The opportunity to do so will end in 9 minutes and 55 seconds.

You have completed multiple hidden objectives and earned several titles. Objective: Survive multiple lethal burn wounds.

Reward. Title: Fireproof II and Fireproof III (requires Fireproof I).

*Fireproof III: Damage from heat and fire is reduced by 3 stages.

I dismissed the notification as something pulled on my waist and entered my chest.

You have absorbed an Iron Heart which has bonded to your Endurance Attribute and will fuel and guide your soul's mutation when you pass the Mortal limit for your Endurance Attribute.

Ability gained. Magma Heart(s) (Rank 1): Fire burns through your veins, fed by the fuel of battle and death. Every kill you make

restores 1 Stamina and 1 Mana as your blood begins to burn for fuel.
This is a passive ability, costing no Stamina and no Mana.
Upgrade this ability to increase how much Stamina and Mana you regenerate per kill. Each upgrade increases your Endurance & Power Attribute by 1.

Apparently, even though she had barely participated, Ammerila got half the reward for defeating the boss. Having gained a new ability, however, I was not too sore about it. I'd already absorbed the Iron Heart from defeating the Nemean lion.

So, the ability to absorb can extend into my storage pouch? Good to know. This ability was different to all my others in that it increased two different attributes, even though it was only bound to my Endurance Attribute.

I felt myself shrink back to normal size. A weakness then overcame me. Barely summoning the strength to get to my feet, I looked around and noticed that every other champion was dead. *Wait. Every champion? Where is…?* I foresaw the attack but was too sluggish to evade it, my mind still in a daze from the crash of losing all that strength.

A pain blossomed in my back. I looked down to see a dagger jutting through my stomach.

You have suffered lethal damage that will result in death in 2 minutes. Lethal poison has been injected directly into your system. Survivor III reduced damage from Mortal wound to Lethal, Venom Resistant III reduced damage from Mortal wound to Lethal. Heal your wounds before you die. Time until death is 2:45 minutes.

"You never should have trusted me," Ammerila said, her voice calm but infused with a tangible, dark joy. "It's like you said: 'there is only one victor in this game'."

I activated Phantom Form and whirled about my clubs' claws which raked into her chest and passed through her.

Her face contorted in a writhing blend of agony, surprise and fear.

I lunged forward again but she flipped backwards, creating space between us.

"Who said I trusted you?" I asked, returning to physical form.

I was in a much worse condition than she was, covered in savage burns, with two wounds going through multiple organs in my stomach. Poison coursed through my system too. I activated Wrathful Meditation and the pain vanished. I teleported beside her and ripped a gash through the leather of her armor, opening the muscle of her thigh.

She disappeared into shadow, reappearing a distance away.

I popped open a health potion and downed it, soon feeling my wounds start to close.

My Foresight showed me getting stabbed in the back again. If I hadn't just suffered the backlash of my helm's ability, I wouldn't have been hit the first time. I went incorporeal, activating Phantom Form and the daggers passed through me. I turned, but she had already disappeared. I began creating blades of force with Telekinesis, surrounding my body in a tornado of the blades. The air distorted around me, the blades creating a shimmering heat haze.

Ammerila appeared behind me, jerking back from the wall of blades, glaring at me. I could see her narrowed eyes through her golden skull mask but not her lower face.

"Did you really think it would be that easy, assassin?" I challenged.

"Honestly, yes," Ammerila retorted. "You're just a construction worker. I've been killing people since I was ten. I doubt you have the temperament to last in this world."

"That's where you're wrong," I said with a savage grin. "You killed at ten. I tried to kill my own father when I was seven, chosen for my temperament and because I wasn't set into the patterns of my old life. You've already been forged by another world, the one that's making me."

I launched my blades at Ammerila and she rolled away, disappearing into the shadows.

The blades still spun around me, and I watched with my Foresight and Bestial Senses to see where she would appear next. I could hear her in the shadows, fifty feet to my right. I teleported next to her and swung at her. The skin along my arms, taut ever since I'd raised it to almost twice every other physical stat, ripped open along my joints. The strain from the battle and dramatic increase in size was too much for my low Toughness Attribute to keep up with. I didn't feel the pain, thanks to Wrathful Meditation, but I was dangerously close to killing myself.

Ammerila dodged my strike and moved backwards, keeping a wary eye on me.

I created blades of force behind her and sent them toward her back.

Somehow, she sensed them and rolled out of the way, disappearing into the shadows again.

5 minutes left until event ends.

"You're really making me work for this," Ammerila said, her voice seeming to come from all directions.

"I'm not the sort to just lie down and let others take what's mine," I said. "I did that enough in my past life."

"You talk as if that part of you is gone," Ammerila said. "But it's clear from the way you talk that you still haven't let it go."

My shield failed to intercept a dagger that flew from the darkness, passing through my defense and continuing its journey toward my back. I sidestepped, the dagger disappearing in a puff of mist.

"Why should I?" I asked.

"Because it makes you weak," she said, appearing above me and bringing down her daggers.

My blades flew upwards.

She disappeared and then suddenly manifested behind me.

I turned incorporeal, kicking at her, and she cried out as I dealt Soul Damage to her.

"You are the expert on being weak," I taunted. "How are you so pathetic? Even your best attack wasn't enough to take me down."

"That ability deals Mortal physical and poison damage," Ammerila said. "I have no idea how you survived that."

"I've had worse," I said.

"Yes, so I see by your scars. Only weak Gifted have scars; they can't afford a proper healer." Her voice appeared behind me, but I could smell her in the shadows ahead.

"Who taught you that?" I asked. "The same people who trained you to be so weak? Look at my rank, then look at yours and we can see whose methods are superior."

"You must have had a higher-ranked Gifted carry you through multiple dungeons."

I laughed. "Is that where you got your strength? No wonder you're so pathetic! As I said before, relying on others makes you weak."

---

30 seconds left until event ends.

"It's now or never, assassin," I jibed, but inwardly, I was thankful for the timeout. My body was ready to collapse from the backlash, and I was barely staying on my feet.

"I'll get you next time, Warlord! You won't see me coming!" Ammerila promised.

5
4
3
2
1
0

"We'll see," I said, and the world flashed white and disappeared.

***

Ammerila stood in the tower of the Order of Assassins as she had done before the event. About to take a step, she vanished again, transported by an undeniable force. She looked about at the blood-red pillars and black marble floor, then knelt.

"What do you require of me, my Goddess?" she asked.

"Do not pursue the Warlord," said Salrilla, Goddess of Assassins and Murder. She looked out of a window into a pitch-black sky, her pale skin made prominent by her black and red dress. Her fangs extended over her lips, and she turned her crimson eyes on her champion.

"He is the most powerful champion in the entire Event," Ammerila said. "He practically slew the final boss, single-handed!"

"He *did* slay it single-handed," Salrilla corrected her. "The System may count your single attack as contribution, but I do not. He is not a good match-up for you. You were not even able to ultimately defeat him when he was at his weakest."

"So, I'm just supposed to let him grow in power and surpass me?" Ammerila asked.

"You are to continue with your own goals and training," Salrilla said. "Do not concern yourself with the Warlord and risk yourself by going after him. Only one of Kelesa's champions has ever won and that was ages ago. The champions of the Gods of Law will band together to defeat the Warlord as they have done in ages past."

"I am concerned that Mordred is different," Ammerila said. "Do you know how he has become so strong? I thought perhaps he was power-leveled, but he seemed to scorn the idea."

"It is mostly luck. His reliance on it is the very reason I'm sure that you won't have to worry about him for long," Salrilla said. "Now go and continue your training… and remember, leave the Warlord for the other champions to deal with."

Chapter 20: Every Hit Makes Me Stronger

> **Congratulations! You placed first in your Instance of the Event. As one of the final ten and by placing first, you have been granted a golden chest.**

A golden chest materialized on the ground in front of me. I was at the base of the tower where I had been before, the sun just starting to rise, and the mist and rain were gone.

I bent down, opened the latch and glanced inside.

A set of pauldrons with guards extending along the collarbone to form a gorget sat in the chest, a line of golden spines jutting out from them, made of a glossy black metal, gold-trimmed and etched with glowing red runes. The straps were of dark green leather that looked as if it had been taken from some sort of crocodile. I picked it up and the System offered me a prompt.

> **Pauldrons of Ares (Artifact, Rank 4): One of the 4 pieces of the armor of Ares. This was earned with the blood of the 4 nations he conquered during the quests of Kelesa. She crafted them with the aid of the System. These pauldrons are part of a larger set that gains more power the more pieces of the armor the wearer possesses. Made from black mithril, celestial gold and the leather of a deep ocean dragon, they are enchanted by Kelesa herself. Can only be worn by the Champion of Kelesa.**
>
> **Stygian Blessing: like the hero Achilles, your skin is made almost unbreakable. Its hardness is increased by 10. Every 20 ranks, the hardness bonus increases x2.**
>
> **(2 pieces) Battle-Hardened Warriors: Your aura extends to your allies. They receive a hardness bonus to their skin, equal to a quarter of yours. They are also immune to the negative effects of your auras from this set and your abilities.**

(3 pieces) Battle Glory: When you kill an enemy, your allies within 100 feet are heartened, increasing their damage stages by one each for the next 5 seconds.	
(4 pieces) Authority of the Warlord: You can telepathically speak to any of your vassals within your Aura.	
Weight:	10 lbs.

This piece would solve my armor problem. I pulled off my cloak and the armor on my right arm to make room for my newest gear, buckling on the straps and feeling my skin toughen. I drank a potion which healed the ripped skin and lingering wounds from my battle.

Suddenly, I realized I had forgotten to drop Wrathful Meditation.

The pain came back, but I clenched my teeth and bore it. Now mostly healed, it was just the remnants of how my body had been feeling. I pulled a dagger and stabbed into my arm; the blade was razor sharp and hardened by my Compressed Earth.

It scratched the surface, shaving the hairs of my arm without piercing my skin.

Quest gained. Heir of Ares: You have been given the Pauldrons of Ares as a reward for achieving the highest score in the first event of this cycle. Find the other 3 pieces of the armor of Ares to complete the set.
Helm of Ares: Location unknown.
Pteruges of Ares: Location unknown.
Maninca of Ares: Location unknown.
Reward. Title: Spirit of Ares.

I wrapped myself in the Nemean cloak. There was no reason to take chances and I'd grown used to wearing the garment. Although I was exhausted after the battle, there was one last thing to take care of before heading back to my camp. Sitting down, I pulled up my latest ability. I hadn't had much time to look over it before the fight had started with Ammerila.

Magma Heart(s) (Rank 1): Fire burns through your veins, fed by the fuel of battle and death. Every kill you make restores 1 Stamina and 1 Mana as your blood begins burning for fuel.
This is a passive ability, costing no Stamina and no Mana.
Upgrade this ability to increase how much Stamina and Mana you regen per kill. Each upgrade increases your Endurance & Power Attribute by 1.

Finally, I had another physical attribute to raise, though I wasn't sure exactly what the Endurance aspect really meant, just guessing that it would have something to do with either by how much or how fast my Stamina regenerated. All mental stats increased Mana and regen to maximum, although I had noticed Power and Spirit delivering greater impacts than Perception and Mind, so I theorized the physical stats would be the same.

Until I could find someone familiar with the System, I had to learn by trial and error, and there was only one way to do that!

"Raise Magma Hearts to Rank 10," I told the System, settling back into Wrathful Meditation.

Magma Heart(s) (Rank 2): Fire burns through your veins, fed by the fuel of battle and death. Every kill you make restores 1.2 Stamina and 1.2 Mana as your blood begins to burn for fuel.
This is a passive ability, costing no Stamina and no Mana.
Upgrade this ability to increase how much Stamina and Mana you regen per kill. Each upgrade increases your Endurance & Power Attribute by 1.

The quantity of Stamina and Mana I regenerated was small. If it only went up by 0.2 per rank-up, by the time I got to Rank 20, I'd only regen around four Stamina and Mana per kill.

This was disappointing and would be mostly useless unless I was in huge battles against weaker creatures such as when fighting the spider horde.

Magma Heart(s) (Rank 3): Fire burns through your veins, fed by the fuel of battle and death. Every kill you make restores 1.4 Stamina and 1.4 Mana as your blood begins to burn for fuel.
This is a passive ability, costing no Stamina and no Mana.

> **Upgrade this ability to increase how much Stamina and Mana you regen per kill. Each upgrade increases your Endurance & Power Attribute by 1.**

The increase to the amount of Stamina and Mana regened per kill did not rise exponentially. This ability seemed weaker than my others. I had noticed that about most of my new abilities. Compress Earth was good, Bestial Senses had its uses and Storm Soul had lots of potential, but they were nothing compared to my first four abilities. Was that because they had been given to me directly by Kelesa and the System? So far, this ability was sub-optimal too but hopefully, I'd get an effect from it to make it worth ranking up besides the increase to my Endurance.

> **Congratulations! You have raised an ability to Rank 5. Please select an additional effect for your ability from the list below:**
>
> - **Your fiery hearts burn, allowing you to endure the coldest of environments and survive harsh exposure without ill effect. Frost Damage dealt to you is reduced by 1 stage. You can now survive without shelter for twice the length of time, normally without ill effects.**
>
> - **You gain an adrenalin rush, increasing your Stamina regeneration by 60 per second for the next 10 seconds, but you suffer a massive backlash afterwards.**
>
> - **You can expend an eruption of Stamina and Mana to deal double damage for the next 7 seconds. Eruption cost is equal to 7/8 of max Stamina and Mana.**

These were some good options, but most brought severe costs in one way or the other. The only one that did not was the most boring one. I wasn't worried about Frost Damage, having yet to encounter it and even if I did, I was pretty sure there would be a way to earn more titles that would help me resist frost. So, there was no need to waste an ability choice on it here.

The second option would give me a second wind but afterwards, I'd be even worse off. The last one was a way to finish a fight, but its cost was enormous in Stamina and Mana. If that cost were somehow reduced as I ranked up, it could be worth it.

I decided to risk it and chose the third option.

Magma Heart(s) (Rank 5): Fire burns through your veins, fed by the fuel of battle and death. Every kill you make restores 1.8 Stamina and 1.8 Mana as your blood begins to burn for fuel.
You can expend an eruption of Stamina and Mana to deal double damage for the next 7 seconds.
Eruption cost is equal to 7/8 of max Stamina and Mana.
This is a passive ability, costing no Stamina and no Mana.
Upgrade this ability to increase how much Stamina and Mana you regen per kill. Each upgrade increases your Endurance & Power Attribute by 1.

There were no new changes but the next rank-up notification would be the moment of truth.

Magma Heart(s) (Rank 6): Fire burns through your veins, fed by the fuel of battle and death. Every kill you make restores 2 Stamina and 2 Mana as your blood begins to burn for fuel.
You can expend an eruption of Stamina and Mana to deal double damage for the next 7 seconds. Eruption cost is equal to 3/4 of max Stamina and Mana.
This is a passive ability, costing no Stamina and no Mana.
Upgrade this ability to increase how much Stamina and Mana you regen per kill. Each upgrade increases your Endurance & Power Attribute by 1.

Yes!

It only went down by a fraction but if it remained on this trajectory, it would only be around a sixteenth of my maximum Stamina and Mana available when I reached max rank for the ability.

What I really needed was an effect that would make this ability useful in one-on-one fights, instead of only being effective in massive battles against hundreds of weak enemies. I skipped to the important pop-up, dismissing the next three notifications without even reading them.

Congratulations! You have raised an ability to Rank 10. Please select an additional effect for your ability from the list below:
• You have awoken the fires of the earth within you, drawing forth its energy to fuel you. Mana and Stamina regeneration are increased by 1 each per second.
• Your fiery hearts burn, allowing you to endure the coldest of environments and survive harsh exposure without ill effect. Frost Damage dealt to you is reduced by 2 stages. You can survive without shelter for quadruple the amount of time, normally without ill effects.
• No longer is death the only thing fueling you. Now, it is now also pain. Whenever you draw blood from your opponent, it counts as a kill for the purpose of this ability.

The first choice seemed as if it doubled down on the main effect of this ability but would help to increase it even further. It was not what I needed even if it would make each kill restore more.

The second one was just an upgraded version of one of my earlier choices.

The third option was exactly what I needed to make this ability useful in most fights... Maybe not every fight, since creatures like elementals did not have blood, but this would help me to regen resources in one-on-one fights.

Magma Heart(s) (Rank 10): Fire burns through your veins, fed by the fuel of battle and death and pain. Every kill you make restores 2.8 Stamina and 2.8 Mana as your blood begins to burn for fuel.
You can expend an eruption of Stamina and Mana to deal double damage for the next 11 seconds. Eruption cost is equal to 7/16 of max Stamina and Mana.
No longer is death the only thing fueling you. Now, it is also pain. Whenever you draw blood from your opponent, it counts as a kill for the purpose of this ability.
This is a passive ability, costing no Stamina and no Mana.
Upgrade this ability to increase how much Stamina and Mana you regen per kill. Each upgrade increases your Endurance & Power Attribute by 1.

> **Congratulations! You have raised one of your attributes beyond the Mortal limit of 20. Your body will now physiologically change to adjust to this increase to keep your attribute from killing you.**
>
> **Your hearts have begun the process of shifting from flesh to an organic metal and will slowly alter the nature and composition of your blood. The process will be complete by the time you reach the next rank stage. Your blood is now mixed with a type of mercury that will energize your body and clot faster to prevent death from blood loss.**

This mutation was similar to the one for my Mind, both reducing the balance in my body of flesh and blood with other materials. But just how human would I be at the end of all this?

Not at all human! You're fighting to become a god. The status is about as far from human as you can get. I almost snorted with laughter at the realization.

I could have gone back to camp at that point, but now that I'd got my ability to Rank 10, I wanted to take it all the way! I had two artifacts that increased in power, based on my overall rank. If I increased this ability all the way to 20, then my skin's hardness would increase by another two points. "Raise Magma Hearts to Rank 20," I said, still just about in a state of Wrathful Meditation.

I skipped the next four notifications until I got to the one for my next additional effect. I was hoping to improve this ability even further and make it a true part of my combat style.

> **Congratulations! You have raised an ability to Rank 15. Please pick an additional effect for your ability from the list below:**
>
> - **Your blood is caustic and flammable and will deal damage to any creature on which it splashes.**
>
> - **You regen double the Stamina and Mana per second.**
>
> - **Your inner fire has grown, giving you resistance immunity to exposure and reducing Frost Damage by 3 stages.**

The question I had about these options was, *Do I gain extra effects or double down on the purpose of this ability?* The first option was tempting, giving me serious Alien vibes and I loved the idea of copying some of that classic movie monster's abilities. There was, however, a significant con attached: to use this effect, I had to get damaged.

Yes, I know I get damaged all the time, but with my new armor, getting cut would hopefully be happening a lot less to me. The third option was again a repeat of a previous effect.

I was still not going to pick it although the immunity to exposure was a good upgrade.

I decided to pick the second option, making the weak addition to Stamina and Mana, in reality, more effective.

Magma Heart(s) (Rank 15): Fire burns through your veins, fed by the fuel of battle and death. Every kill you make restores 7.6 Stamina and 7.6 Mana as your blood begins to burn for fuel.
You can expend an eruption of Stamina and Mana to deal double damage for the next 16 seconds. Eruption cost is equal to 1/8 of max Stamina and Mana.
No longer is death the only thing that fuels you. Now, it is also pain. Whenever you draw blood from your opponent, it counts as 2 kills for the purpose of this ability.
This is a passive ability, costing no Stamina and no Mana.
Upgrade this ability to increase how much Stamina and Mana you regen per kill. Each upgrade increases your Endurance & Power Attribute by 1.

The choice I'd just made was immediately justified upon noticing that the effect selected for Rank 10 would now count for two kills when I drew blood; therefore, I'd now regen 14.5 Stamina for every wound made, and that figure would only increase over time.

I dismissed the next three notifications, only stopping upon noticing something strange.

Close to my final effect for the ability, I was feeling no pain but looking down at my chest, there was a glow under my skin and past my bones. *That cannot be good.*

I dismissed the notification, needing to get this over with.

The final choice for my ability had come and I was glad to get it done and figure out what the hell was happening inside my chest.

Congratulations! You have raised an ability to Rank 20. Please select an additional effect for your ability from the list below:
• You do not suffer the negative effects for bottoming out on your Stamina.
• You regen double the Stamina and Mana for every kill you make.
• Your inner fire has grown, giving you resistance immunity to exposure and all Frost Damage except Divine stage is reduced to minor Frost Damage. Divine stage Frost Damage is reduced to Severe Frost Damage.

I sighed internally. The third choice was again on my list. It felt as if the System was telling me something, so I grudgingly picked it over the other two flashier choices.

Magma Heart(s) (Rank 20, max rank): Fire burns through your veins, fed by the fuel of battle and death. Every kill you make restores 10 Stamina and 10 Mana as your blood begins to burn for fuel.
You can expend an eruption of Stamina and Mana to deal double damage for the next twenty seconds. Eruption cost is equal to 1/16 of max Stamina and Mana.
No longer is death the only thing fueling you. Now, it is also pain. Whenever you draw blood from your opponent, it counts as 3 kills for the purpose of this ability.
Your inner fire has grown, giving you resistance immunity to exposure and all Frost Damage except Divine stage is reduced to minor Frost Damage. Divine stage Frost Damage is reduced to Severe Frost Damage.
Final rank bonus: Your inner body is filled with fire, making you one with the flame. You do not suffer the effects of overheating or heatstroke and can go for twice the amount of time without water.
This is a passive ability, costing no Stamina and no Mana.

> **Upgrade this ability to increase how much Stamina and Mana you regen per kill. Each upgrade increases your Endurance & Power Attribute by 1.**

The rank-up was done. I carefully turned off Wrathful Meditation and looked down at the red-orange glow in my chest. I guessed this was where the magma in my hearts was going about its business.

> **Warning! You have increased your Power Attribute to 50, the limit for Veteran rank, while you are still Mortal ranked. Increasing your Power beyond 50 will likely cause lethal, permanent damage to you. For your own safety, do not raise your Power Attribute again until after you have raised all other attributes past 20.**

That was close. If I hadn't had an initial low Power Attribute, I could have just accidentally raised Power over 50 and potentially killed myself. It was also disappointing because my Spirit was 46. I clearly still had to wait on raising to max several Spirit abilities. I needed an ability for Might and Toughness before finally being able to leave the Mortal rank and enter Veteran.

At least I knew the limit; I should really find out what all the ranks were and how high each of my attributes would have to be to access them.

"Pull up my attributes," I told the System, deciding to look up my stats now and see what I was working with.

Mordred, Champion of Kelesa. Gifted Humanoid/Human. Mortal. Rank: 115.			
Available rank points: 560.			
Might:	13 (+3) = 16	Mind:	22
Speed:	32 (+13) = 45	Perception:	23
Toughness:	11	Spirit:	46
Endurance:	31	Power:	50
Maximum Stamina:	112	Maximum Mana:	191

Stamina Regen:	26.8 per second	Mana Regen:	40.4 per second
Abilities:			
Dominion (Rank 5), Telekinesis (Rank 20), Heightened Speed (Rank 10), Foresight (Rank 10), Compress Earth (Rank 15), Bestial Senses (Rank 5), Phantom Form (Rank 10), Storm Soul (Rank 20), Magma Heart(s) (Rank 20).			
Blessings:			
Blessing of War (Mortal).			
Titles:			
Mark of Cain, Bloody Pugilist, Exorcist, Survivor III, Feral Barbarian, Field Alchemist III, Berserker, Beast Slayer III, War Chief, Venom Resistant III, Keytaro's Guardian III, Wrathful Meditation, Fireproof III, Visitor of Death.			

If desired, I could get my Perception to 50 and increase my Mind to 27, the only abilities and attributes I could raise without risking killing myself. I was already worried about the possibility of picking up another ability for Power which would automatically push me to 51.

And then, who knew what would happen?

I stood up, cracking the bones in my neck. It was time to head back to camp.

Chapter 21: Sight and Stone

Helen, Jamis, Torvin, Mira and Felrick all appeared back in the cave. They were battered, covered in blood and grit, but smiles adorned each of their faces.

"I take it the event was a success?" Felrick asked.

"Yes," said Helen. "We defeated the final boss just before the time limit. A lot of champions got eliminated in the fight, but we pulled through in the end."

"We had an hour left in our event," Mira said. "That Rain Knight was a tough opponent.

"Rain Knight?" Felrick asked. "The final boss was an Iron Knight. Not a Rain Knight."

"We fought a Mire Knight," Jamis said. "Looks like every instance of the event had a different final boss, then."

Five gold chests rose from the ground. The party looked at each other as they read their messages from the System.

"Looks like I placed second in the Event," Jamis said, proudly.

"Good job!" Felrick said. "I only placed ninth. I was on my own for most of the Event and couldn't fight the mini-bosses."

"Don't feel bad," Torvin said. "Those things were nasty. It's not as if anyone could have fought them by themselves."

***

I ran through the woods, my Stamina barely decreasing as my regen was now easily able to keep up with my expenditure. I was a blur in the forest, leaping over logs and rocks as I pounded down animal trails. Finally, I reached the waterfall, looking down at the camp below the cliffs. Carnage littered the ground as the goblins were in a pitched battle with what I could only describe as a feathered and spiked velociraptor. The goblins were barely holding the wall. Bodies were piled high outside it and not just velociraptors but other beasts as well.

I sped down the trail to save my vassals before they were all wiped out. I rushed onto the field of battle, jumped into the air and came down on the back of a velociraptor.

My clubs smashed into the back of its skull.

---

1 rank point gained.

The velociraptor had been a Gifted beast. I analyzed the rest.

Spined Knight Raptor. Gifted Mortal. Beast/Drake. Rank: 2.

Looking over the rest of the raptors, I saw they were all Gifted. In common with the wolf pack I'd fought, every single one had only acquired one rank point.

An enormous raptor lay on the battlefield, its body porcupined with javelins. Apparently, the goblins had been able to kill it. The more I looked around, however, the more I became aware of the heavy casualty rate suffered by the goblin horde.

Around half their number lay dead on the ground outside of the wall.

I raised my hand as the raptors swarmed the wall.

"Dominion," I called out, although I doubted anyone but me could hear me over the screams, howls, and shouting. I couldn't Dominate the entire pack of raptors, but felt my vastly superior Spirit crush down on the weaker Gifted. Soon, collared chain brands appeared on their necks.

"Stand down," I commanded them.

Even though they couldn't hear me, my will rippled across the pack and the seventy-one raptors froze, cowering at my command. Other members of their pack continued the assault on the wall but with their numbers cut in half, they were far less effective.

"Dominion," I said again.

Only around a dozen of the raptors had been unaffected by my ability. They too now froze as my ability took hold of them.

I approached and noticed the veins in my arms glowing an orange-red hue.

The goblins looked at me, most shrinking back in fear. But a familiar one stood up, raising his spear in tribute.

"The Warlord has returned!" Juruk shouted.

The rest of the goblins were silent for a moment. Suddenly, as one, they raised their weapons, shaking and smacking them against crude shields.

"Warlord!" they shouted over and over.

"Good to see I was missed." I looked down at the raptors now under my control and then back to the goblins.

Juruk. Gifted Mortal Humanoid/Goblin. Rank: 5.

Juruk was the highest ranked among them although every surviving goblin had at least one or two ranks. There were only around a hundred goblins left.

"What happened?" I asked Juruk, surveying the carnage.

"They attacked us, yesterday," Juruk said. "We drove them off, but then, they returned with their leader." He pointed to the body of the massive raptor which had to be the size of a warlord.

"We lost almost half the tribe, slaying it. When it was dead, they all went berserk and attacked the walls like you saw," Juruk explained.

"I see," I said, looking over the fallen. "Deal with your dead in whatever manner is customary to your people. Loot the battlefield, skin their dead. These raptors are your mounts, so you'll be able to keep up with me. Make saddles for them and carry any stuff you plan on bringing."

"As the Warlord commands," he said, bowing. "Because you told us to make weapons and armor, we were prepared for when the beast attacked. We shall be even stronger now."

"I'm sure you will," I said and watched him as he left. "Pull up Juruk's attributes," I told the System.

Juruk (Vassal). Gifted Humanoid/Human. Mortal. Rank 5.			
Available rank points: 0			
Might:	7	**Mind:**	8
Speed:	13	**Perception:**	13
Toughness:	7	**Spirit:**	11
Endurance:	8	**Power:**	8
Maximum Stamina:	42	**Maximum Mana:**	48
Stamina Regen:	8.6 per second	**Mana Regen:**	10.2 per second
Abilities:			
Feral Rage (Rank 1), Greater Size (Rank 1), Savage Blow (Rank 1), Fell Step (Rank 1) Hunter's Sight (Rank 1).			

Titles:
Swarm Leader, Rising Star.

*Swarm Leader: You deal 1 more stage of damage when leading 10 or more of your own species in combat and reduce their damage taken by one stage.

*Rising Star: You deal 1 more damage stage to those of a higher rank than yourself.

Juruk had acquired a lot of abilities from that fight. I could have looked them up, but wasn't that interested. They were all rank 1 and I didn't plan on bringing him into my fights to rank him up. If he wanted to get stronger, he could go off fighting on his own.

For now, he and the rest of my vassals were stronger and less likely to die the next time I had to leave them alone for a week.

Entering the camp, I saw the goblins had constructed hide tents for themselves. There were three cages for the three people I'd rescued from the vassals. Jand was watching over them, passing them waterskins. He looked relieved when he saw me, running over to me.

"Warlord, you're back," he said.

"Just call me Mordred," I said. "This whole warlord thing is a little too pretentious for my liking."

"Yes, Mordred," Jand said. "The people you rescued awoke and tried to leave, but the goblins surrounded and imprisoned them."

"Sensible of them," I said.

"Sir," Jand hissed, pointing to one of the cages. "She's the daughter of a duke of the kingdom. Imprisoning her could bring a whole army down on us."

"Well, I have a feeling I'll be fighting them one way or another," I said with a shrug. I walked over to the cages and cut open the rope securing the cages. The human, half-elf and elf all got up. The daughter of the duke looked incandescent.

"I demand you release us immediately! "she said with some force.

"No," I said calmly, taking out my Cleansing Cloth and spending 15 Mana to wipe the blood and sweat off my body. I felt my every pore cleansed as the cloth scoured every bit of dirt, grime, and dead skin cells from my body.

"What do you mean, 'no'?" Kathleen asked, her voice now definitely a shout.

"Slap her," I commanded the slim, half-elf bodyguard.

In a blink, his hand struck across her face. He looked down at it in horror. The brand around his neck was now perfectly visible as it shone bright white on his skin.

"I am Mordred, Champion of Kelesa," I told Kathleen.

She held back tears. Her cheek was red from the force of the slap.

"You are now my vassal and will do whatever I say."

"So, I'm one of your concubines, now?" Kathleen snarled, her spirit unbroken.

"I'm not interested in you," I told her flatly. "I'm interested in what you know. I'm a stranger to your world and need a local to help me understand how things are done."

"And you think I'll help you?" Kathleen asked me, defiantly.

"I don't think you have a choice," I said. "I command you to answer all my questions both promptly and honestly. You will also tell me when you believe I am making a tactical mistake and assist me in whatever way you think would benefit me."

The brands around her neck glowed white as my command was imposed upon her. She grimaced in pain, her bodyguards glaring at me.

I looked back at them, flatly unimpressed by their silent show of defiance.

"This should go without saying but you are all forbidden from attacking me or any of my vassals except in self-defense, also from trying to betray me, giving away our position or seeking to harm me in other ways," I told them.

"Follow me," I told Kathleen. "The rest of you, wait here."

I entered the main camp and sat down, gesturing for Kathleen to do likewise. Ostentatiously unhappy, she sat and looked at me.

"I recently participated in an Event run by the System and encountered many other champions," I told her. "They were all weak and low-ranked, and I want to know why."

Kathleen looked above me, no doubt reading the description there. "What rank are you?" she asked. All I get is three question marks for your rank."

"I just reached one hundred," I said.

I had given her a direct order not to betray me, and it wasn't exactly a secret, so I did not feel uncomfortable telling her.

"Gifted operate in parties. Usually, one will specialize in healing, one in withstanding attacks and the others on inflicting damage."

"Standard healer, tank and dps... I understand that," I said. "But why are they so weak?"

"I'm not sure what you mean by weak, but when you slay a Gifted beast, you only get rank points equal to half their rank. If you fight a beast in a group, those halves of the rank points are further split among anyone who contributed."

"So, it massively slows down their growth and makes them weak," I said.

"They are stronger together as a group than an individual twice their rank," Kathleen said. "There is a reason there are only fifteen Gods of Chaos and over seven hundred Gods of Order."

"Yes, I'm familiar with them trying to group up and kill me," I said, slightly amused. "If they hadn't been so weak, it might have actually worked. Fighting them was like fighting children."

"Children?" Kathleen asked with apparent skepticism.

"Yes. I can tell they're better with weapons, but they aren't good at fighting. It's as if they've never properly tested themselves before."

"And you've been properly tested?" Kathleen asked.

I pulled back my cloak, revealing the scars across my body. "Every time I fight, I put my life on the line, throwing myself into the crucible willingly. They fear getting burned by the flames, whereas I have no fear. They fight as if there is someone there waiting to step in and hold their hand when they get in too deep."

"A champion's patron deity will give them trainers to help them establish themselves and build their foundation." It was as if Kathleen was reciting a history lesson, off pat, as opposed to speaking with a reliance on first-hand knowledge and experience. "The people she put you with should have helped to train you to fight and explain how our world works."

"Kelesa shoved me through a portal into an old crypt and I was in a life-or-death fight within two hours of arriving," I said. "I haven't even spoken with her or received any contact from her since."

"Why would she do that?" Kathleen asked, seeming empathetically horrified and confused.

"I think I'm an experiment," I said with a shrug. "A way to try things out differently in the hope of getting different results."

"That makes some sense," Kathleen admitted. "Kelesa has only ever had one champion who won the game of the gods."

"I intend to make it two," I said. "What is the fastest way to gain abilities?"

"You need to fight Gifted beasts of your own rank, or higher," she said. "You're mortal right now, so it's fine, but when you ascend to Veteran rank, you only get a quarter of the rank points from kills gained from Mortal-ranked creatures, instead of half. Added to that, the chance of getting an ability is greatly reduced. That only goes up as you increase your rank above mortal."

"Do you get more rank points from killing higher-ranked creatures?" I asked.

"Yes," Kathleen nodded. "And it is believed the abilities you get are also stronger."

"What exactly are the ranks?" I asked. "And what is the required attribute to get to them?"

"As you probably know, Mortal rank ends at Rank 20," she began. "Veteran rank is next. Its max attribute is 50. After Veteran is Hero, its attribute limit 125. Exarch is after that, its max attribute 250. Then it is Hierophant with an attribute limit of 350, and Demigod is the highest rank attainable on this world. Its max rank is 499. After that, it's God status at 500."

"I knew the last one," I mused. "How do your people get new attributes? Do you just come into the forest and hunt down beasts?"

"Some do," Kathleen said. "But the most common way is to seek out a temple and get a quest from one of the gods to slay a beast. The quest usually rewards rank points as well, so it makes it more profitable than just hunting beasts or rogue Gifted."

I sat back, mulling over her words. "What do you know of the Bandit King?"

"The Bandit King?" Kathleen asked, surprised. "He's an outcast noble from Drancia on the other side of the Cursed Forest. He's taken over a ruined fortress along the river Ulrus and has been shaking down merchants and travelers using the river for the past thirty years."

"Why hasn't he been taken out, then?" I asked.

"Because he's powerful Gifted on the cusp of Hero rank, and the forest is contested land." Kathleen explained. "Bounty hunters and Gifted slayers have gone after him, but he's dealt with them all. If regular kingdom forces went after him though, it could be seen as one kingdom staking claim to the forest – and result in war between our kingdoms."

"Well, we're going to go and meet him," I said, standing up and cracking the bones in my neck.

"Why?" Kathleen asked. She now seemed very nervous.

"Because he seems like a powerful opponent and you just told me the best way to gain powerful abilities was to fight Gifted above my rank," I said, turning and leaving her behind as I went into my tent. While I couldn't raise my physical stats, I could max out Compress Earth and raise my Perception to close to 50.

"Increase Foresight to Rank 20," I told the System as I settled into Wrathful Meditation.

I could now see a solid thirteen seconds ahead. It was increasing by one second with every increase in my Perception Attribute, but I had a feeling I'd eventually get capped out. I skipped the next four notifications until I got to the prompt after hitting Rank 14. Every rank increased the range I could foresee by two feet. Usually, I'd only focus on the area directly around me.

The strain from so many possible futures was extremely taxing on my brain. I estimated that to ease the burden of seeing all potential outcomes at once, I'd probably need to increase my Mind Attribute.

Congratulations! You have raised an ability to Rank 15. Please select an additional effect for your ability from the list below:
• **Your Foresight now gives you the ability to look back in time. While sleeping, you have a chance to see a vision of the distant past.**
• **Your Foresight now lets you see random events a few hours into the future.**
• **You can share this ability with one creature. Once given, this ability cannot be shared further with another creature until the death of the initial donor.**

These ability choices were weird. The first was interesting, but it didn't carry any guaranteed benefit. The same was true for the second choice. The third would let me donate the positive effects of my ability to one other creature. While I still believed in working alone, it could be good to give to a lieutenant to help them better defend themselves.

I chose option three as the best of a bad bunch.

Foresight (Rank 15): You passively see 17 seconds into the future and know what will happen to yourself and the space within 33 feet of you at all times. This ability is based on an enhancement of your Perception Attribute. It will increase the time you can see by one second per rank in Perception above 10.
You can see different possible outcomes based on your actions made within the timespan.
You can see visions during sleep that will lead you to objects or creatures you seek.
You can share this ability with one creature. Once given, this ability cannot be shared further with another creature until the death of the initial donor.
This is a passive ability, costing 1 Mana/sec.
Upgrade this ability to increase how far you can see into the future as well as the physical span of your Foresight. Every upgrade to this ability increases your Perception Attribute by 1.

Ranking up this ability increased the timeframe and physical span of the Foresight, one of my most powerful abilities but also one of the most subtle and esoteric. Most of its effects were, at best, passive, and at worst, not in my control. I skipped the four notifications between Ranks 15 and 20. Then, the pop-up for the extra effect appeared.

Congratulations! You have raised an ability to Rank 20. Please select an additional effect for your ability from the list below:
• You have learned to cast out your sight to see even further. The span of your prediction is now doubled.
• You have learned to strain your mind to see even further. The timeframe of your Foresight is now doubled.

> • **Just as you have learned to master the threads of fate through time, so have you also learned to disguise yours. The capacity of others with similar abilities to foresee your own action through time is blocked.**

These effects are all good! The first would probably help me detect hidden attackers more quickly. Thinking about it, this was not *that* useful in reality. I would mostly use the ability to predict the actions of those I fought in melee combat and to avoid being backstabbed. The second choice would double the time I could foresee; this would be insanely powerful, but I could barely keep track of all possible futures as it was. The third option did not enhance or give me anything particularly impressive, but I was instantly drawn to it. This was one of my most powerful abilities and I did not want anyone to be able to use something like it on me.

Selecting the third option, I got ready to reach the max rank effect of my Foresight.

Foresight (Rank 20, max rank): You passively see 22 seconds into the future and know what will happen to yourself and the space within 45 feet of you at all times. This ability is based on your Perception Attribute. Upgrading it will increase the time you can see by one second per rank in Perception above 10.
You can see different possible outcomes based on your actions made within the timespan.
You can see visions during sleep that will lead you to objects or creatures you seek.
You can share this ability with one creature. Once given, this ability cannot be shared further with another creature until the death of the initial donor.
Just as you have learned to master the threads of fate through time, so too have you also learned to disguise yours. The capacity for others with similar abilities to foresee your own action through time is blocked.
Final rank bonus: You can focus on one creature and see the threads of fate around them and how these could be intertwined with your own destiny.
This is a passive ability, costing 1 Mana/sec.

> **Upgrade this ability to increase how far you can see into the future as well as the physical span of your Foresight. Every upgrade to this ability increases your Perception Attribute by 1.**

With one of my first abilities unlocked, it was time to look at the two others I could currently upgrade. Compress Earth was at Rank 15 whilst Bestial Senses was still at Rank 5. I wanted to see the final rank bonus for Compress Earth, so decided to max that out first, before dealing with Bestial Senses. "Raise Compress Earth by five ranks," I told the System.

I could fuse a massive area of stone, but the Mana cost was too much for me to affect that large an area. Thanks to Storm Soul, I had a chance of doing that in the future, but I had yet to even see a storm.

I was excited by the idea that I had the ability to use basic dirt to one day create walls harder than diamond; there was no need to worry about structural integrity when the building was all one piece of almost unbreakable stone. I skipped the next four notifications. The time had come to choose my last effect for Compress Earth, and I had a feeling I already knew my choice.

> **Congratulations! You have raised one of your abilities to Rank 20. Please select an additional effect from the list below:**
>
> - **By fusing together materials of the same type, you have a 10 percent chance of creating a divine version of the material.**
> - **You can invert the process to make something lighter and more fragile as opposed to denser and harder.**
> - **You can now use rare and magical metal in your fusions. The rarity, density or level of magic power of the metal will affect the final product.**

I was momentarily rapt in thought, only imagining the effects of something made of divine steel or obsidian. Only having a 10 percent chance of success, however, was not attractive. The second ability was the opposite of what I wanted, and I dismissed it without another thought. With little more consideration, I chose the third option; it was just what I wanted.

Compress Earth (Rank 20, max rank): You can fuse dirt and stone and shape it into more durable, heavier material. You can currently fuse a 525,000-square-foot section of earth, stone, and metal. Your compressed stone has a hardness rating of 15; your compressed earth has a hardness rating of 12. The detail with which you can sculpt is based on your Mind & Perception Attribute.

You can now use uncommon stone in your fusions. The rarity, density, or exotic nature of the stone will affect the final product.

You can now use non-magical metals in your fusions. The rarity, density, or exotic nature of the metal will affect the final product.

You can now use rare and magical stone in your fusions. The rarity, density, or magical powers of the stone will affect the final product.

You can now use rare and magical metal in your fusions. The rarity, density, or magical powers of the metal will affect the final product.

Final rank bonus: You can now affect magical and enchanted objects made of stone or metal.

Cost: 20 Mana per square foot.

Upgrade this ability to increase the amount you can compress, its durability, weight, and the materials on which you can use this ability. Each upgrade increases your Mind Attribute by 1.

The max rank was awesome. The area of effect had been bumped up slightly to even it out, but the best part was the hardness for the compressed stone had jumped up two whole points to a hardness rating of 15. The final effect was interesting. It would be useful to have the ability to affect the magical items I got as loot, to shape them and possibly repair them.

I decided to wait before upgrading Bestial Senses; there were a few things I wanted to do before we left the next morning, and I could always upgrade it tomorrow. Getting up, I headed off to find something I had promised myself I'd collect before leaving the camp.

It took me a while, but eventually, I found the bush again.

Diamond Orb Bush. Type: Miscellaneous. Rarity: Epic. Shells of these berries are as hard as glass but filled with a clear, sticky juice that hardens quickly after exposure to air. It turns into a clear resin

> **with a hardness rating of 14, making it highly valued as an adhesive by crafters.**

I didn't dig around the bush. Instead, I compressed the earth around it in a wide area, lifted out the shrub and placed it into large pot. I levitated it alongside me back to camp.

Back at the camp, I set down the huge pot, the goblins and my other vassals gathering around with chattering curiosity.

"A diamond orb bush?" Kathleen asked as she examined it. "I've heard of them. The Crafter's Guild supposedly has one they keep well-guarded."

"Well, now I have one too," I said. "You can use it, but don't over-take from the bush, and under no circumstances are you to damage it," I said to the collective assembly. "We leave first thing tomorrow." I went to my tent for the night.

Before going to sleep, I took out my new magical items and my journal, examining closely all of their inscriptions, drawing sketches of the runes and next to each, writing down the effects of each item's enchantments. With enough examples, I was hoping to find commonalities between the runes and their effects with a view to ultimately creating my own Rosetta stone.

Eventually, I put away my journal and items, lying down to get some much-needed sleep.

Chapter 22: Dangling Chains

Maria examined the worn forest road. "We're close. We're now only two days from the lumber camp," she said, getting up and leading the party forward.

"Why didn't we take this road in the first place?" Jamis asked.

"It would have added another day and a half to our journey," Helen said. "These roads were constructed over a thousand years ago." She smacked her staff on the stone. "They are practically unbreakable, but don't necessarily follow routes that are useful to the rest of us."

"Earth abilities do that when you max them out," Felrick said, nodding. "One of the local border nobility is well-known for the earth abilities in their family; they have similar powers."

"Now, I wish we had a horse," Torvin said.

"Horses are a bad idea in the forest," Felrick said, shaking his head. "Too many predators looking for an easy meal."

"I could try to convince some bears to let us ride them," Jamis offered.

"We'll keep that in mind," Maria said. "But right now, we're close... So, let's do some hard marching and worry about more exotic modes of transport later."

***

I woke up and stretched, putting on my new armor. I no longer wore the single pauldron and chainmail guard for my right arm, and I kept the single steel bracer for my left hand to help against bludgeoning damage. Even with the Pauldron of Ares making my skin as hard as steel, it was still essentially as flexible as normal skin.

The goblins roused themselves quickly and began saddling the raptors.

These makeshift saddles were made from bits of bone and leather from the raptors themselves as well as from other beasts. Saddlebags were slung over the backs of the raptors and the goblins cautiously mounted their rides, swaying precariously.

It was going to take a while before they were fully comfortable with their new means of transportation, but they were more afraid of me than of the raptors or of falling off.

I marched alongside my human vassals who were riding the spiders at my instruction. I levitated the bush as we proceeded, traveling much lighter than previously, thanks to my storage pouch. I had even Managed to fit into it the massive mirror, all the tents and equipment as well as a collection of bones and leather hides.

My vassals had made me leather armor out of the skin of the black adder. As I no longer needed it, I told Jand to wear it. The humans were also better equipped with crude leather armor and goblin weapons. As I led my unusual, somewhat raggle-taggle band of warriors through the trees, I was happy we were making good time. Obviously, I led from the front. Then, it was Euphrates who Managed to make a clearer trail for everyone else to follow.

"Couldn't you have made a saddle for this?" Kathleen asked as she uncomfortably held onto Euphrates' fur.

"I don't need one," I said. "If you need one, you can work on it tonight when we stop to rest."

As we pressed on, the goblins became slightly more confident in riding. This made them more effective as scouts.

Soon, it was midday and we stopped for lunch, building a fire. Maria and the other women began heating up some stew to serve. Meanwhile, the goblins began digging into their own rations. It was already clear that food was going to be an issue for us. I was becoming increasingly concerned over how we would make rations last for the whole party over an undefined period, resolving that the best solution was for me to simply hunt and kill more food. At least the goblins were not particular about what they ate.

I found some more red yarrow and cauter fennel, jarred them and added them to my storage pouch. After this, I consumed a revitalizing bowl of stew and left the group. Since I had some time, I wanted to finish my upgrades and get Bestial Senses to Rank 20.

Sitting down, I focused on my anger, entering into Wrathful Mediation.

"Raise Bestial Senses to Rank 20," I told the System.

Bestial Senses (Rank 6): You can activate your senses to smell, hear and see more clearly, for example by picking up the sound of a feather landing, or the smell of footsteps on a day-old trail. Your hearing, olfaction and sight are magnified by x7 while this ability is active.

> You gain the ability to turn on infrared vision while this ability is
> active.
>
> Cost: 5 Stamina per second while ability is active.
>
> Upgrade this ability to increase the magnification of your senses.
> Each upgrade of this ability increases your Perception Attribute by
> 1.

The main reason for me seldom using this ability was because of sensory overload, the sudden rush of smells, sounds, and the blinding influx of colors and light like a flashbang going off in my head. The magnification of my senses went up only by one per rank. I was not exactly sure how that was measured, but I hoped the sensory overload wouldn't kill me on the next use.

I dismissed the next notification without even looking at it, doing the same with the two after that. There was little difference between ranks.

> Congratulations! You have raised an ability to Rank 10. Please select
> an additional effect for your ability from the list below:
>
> - You are a master tracker. The magnification of
>   your sense of smell is doubled.
>
> - You are attuned equally to both the physical and
>   spiritual worlds. You are now able to smell and pinpoint
>   the presence of obvious and hidden magic within 40 feet of
>   you (this is a passive effect that is always active).
>
> - Your sense of touch is so fine that you can even
>   feel the disruption in the air when a creature moves within
>   30 feet of you.

I dismissed the first option. It wasn't bad, but the second was better. This one would have been helpful in the trial to locate loot chests. The third option was cool but unnecessary. My Foresight pretty much already had that area covered.

Going with my gut, I picked the second option.

> Bestial Senses (Rank 10): You can activate your senses to smell, hear
> and see more clearly, for example by picking up the sound of a
> feather landing, or the smell of footsteps on a day-old trail. Your

hearing, olfaction and sight are magnified by x11 while this ability is active.
You gain the ability to turn on infrared vision while this ability is active.
You are attuned equally to both the physical and spiritual worlds. You are now able to smell and pinpoint the presence of obvious and hidden magic within 40 feet of you (this is a passive effect that is always active).
Cost: 2 Stamina per second (passive), 5 Stamina per second while ability is active.
Upgrade this ability to increase the magnification of your senses. Each upgrade of this ability increases your Perception Attribute by 1.

Looking over the full description, I dismissed it and checked to see if there would be any new changes at the next rank-up.

Bestial Senses (Rank 11): You can activate your senses to smell, hear and see more clearly, for example by picking up the sound of a feather landing, or the smell of footsteps on a day-old trail. Your hearing, olfaction and sight are magnified by x12 while this ability is active.
You gain the ability to turn on infrared vision while this ability is active.
You are attuned equally to both the physical and spiritual worlds. You are now able to smell and pinpoint the presence of obvious and hidden magic within 45 feet of you (this is a passive effect that is always active).
Cost: 2 Stamina per second (passive), 5 Stamina per second while ability active.
Upgrade this ability to increase the magnification of your senses. Each upgrade of this ability increases your Perception Attribute by 1.

The range at which I could smell magic had increased by five feet. Other than that, the ability progressed as normal. The only sense not magnified by my ability was taste, for which I was grateful. I didn't see a need for it. The ability to taste everything within fifty feet did not seem like a pleasant or necessary experience to go through every time I activated the ability.

What other senses did I need? *The ability to see colors on other visual spectrums, normally undetectable to the human eye?* I didn't see a need for that, but there could be ways that abilities could create illusions or stealth effects that this effect could negate.

Like last time, I skipped the next three effects, waiting for the inevitable pop-up.

Congratulations! You have raised an ability to Rank 15. Please select an additional effect for your ability from the list below:
• **Like a spider in its web, you can feel vibrations through the ground for 40 feet around you.**
• **You have eagle-like vision. The magnification for your vision is doubled.**
• **Your eyes can easily penetrate minor obstructions in the air. Your vision is not hindered by smoke, fog, or magical darkness while this ability is active.**

The first option was really tempting, but then again, it had significant crossover with my Foresight, so wasn't really needed. The second option wasn't necessary either because I wasn't signing up to NASA to look at the stars. The third option had numerous possible uses in combat to help avoid effects caused by other abilities.

I picked the third option and dismissed the notification.

Bestial Senses (Rank 15): You can activate your senses to smell, hear and see more clearly, for example by picking up the sound of a feather landing, or the smell of footsteps on a day-old trail. Your hearing, olfaction and sight are magnified by x16 while this ability is active.
You gain the ability to turn on infrared vision while this ability is active.
You are attuned equally to both the physical and spiritual worlds. You are now able to smell and pinpoint the presence of obvious and hidden magic within 65 feet of you. (This is a passive effect that is always active).

Your eyes can easily penetrate minor obstructions in the air. Your vision is not hindered by smoke, fog, or magical darkness while this ability is active.
Cost: 2 Stamina per second (passive), 8 Stamina per second while ability active.
Upgrade this ability to increase the magnification of your senses. Each upgrade of this ability increases your Perception Attribute by 1.

Despite how many rank points I had gained recently, upgrading my abilities was expensive. I was now down to a little under 300 points. Upgrading another ability to Rank 20 would practically empty my bank of rank points. Each ability cost a total of 209 points to level up from Rank 1 to Rank 20. For the purposes of the game, the abilities, in themselves, were not even that important. The key was ensuring you raised all attributes to 500.

It just so happened that the cheapest way to do that was by increasing your abilities rather than by directly increasing your attributes. I dismissed the next four notifications, then got to the pop-up. I was almost done with this ability. One choice and one more rank to go.

Congratulations! You have raised an ability to Rank 20. Please select an additional effect for your ability from the list below:
• Your sense of hearing is as sharp as a bat's, allowing you to get a visual image of up to within 60 feet of your surroundings by using echo location.
• Your ability to pierce the magical veil has increased. You can now see into the Ethereal Realm when you activate this ability.
• Your ability to 'read' creatures has grown immensely. You can tell a creature's emotional state by their smell and body language as if they were speaking a second language to you.

The first option would be useful to some, but I wasn't trying to be a daredevil here, so I put it to one side. The second option was interesting. I had interacted with incorporeal creatures only twice since arriving on this world, but I knew they were tough and inextricably linked with the Ethereal Realm. The third option would let me see the emotional state of my enemies in combat.

Whilst potentially interesting, this was effectively already covered by my Foresight.

I selected the second option.

Bestial Senses (Rank 20, max rank): You can activate your senses to smell, hear and see more clearly, for example by picking up the sound of a feather landing, or the smell of footsteps on a day-old trail. Your hearing, olfaction and sight are magnified by x20 while this ability is active.
You gain the ability to turn on infrared vision while this ability is active.
You are attuned equally to both the physical and spiritual worlds. You are now able to smell and pinpoint the presence of obvious and hidden magic within 100 feet of you. (This is a passive effect that is always active).
Your eyes can easily penetrate minor obstructions in the air. Your vision is not hindered by smoke, fog, or magical darkness while this ability is active.
Your ability to pierce the magical veil has increased. You can now see into the Ethereal Realm when you activate this ability.
Final rank bonus: Your opponent's weak points are highlighted to your vision while this ability is active.
Cost: 2 Stamina per second (passive); 8 Stamina per second while ability active.
Upgrade this ability to increase the magnification of your senses. Each upgrade to this ability increases your Perception Attribute by 1.

My final rank bonus gave me video game powers. I would certainly find an effective use for this during combat.

"What are my current attributes?" I asked the System.

Mordred, Champion of Kelesa. Gifted Humanoid/Human. Mortal. Rank: 145.

Available rank points: 285.			
Might:	13 (+3) = 16	Mind:	27
Speed:	32 (+16) = 48	Perception:	47
Toughness:	11	Spirit:	46
Endurance:	31	Power:	50
Maximum Stamina:	117	Maximum Mana:	220
Stamina Regen:	30.4 per second	Mana Regen:	46.2 per second
Abilities:			
Dominion (Rank 5), Telekinesis (Rank 20), Heightened Speed (Rank 10), Foresight (Rank 20), Compress Earth (Rank 20), Bestial Senses (Rank 20), Phantom Form (Rank 10), Storm Soul (Rank 20), Magma Heart(s) (Rank 20).			
Blessings:			
Blessing of War (Mortal).			
Titles:			
Mark of Cain, Bloody Pugilist, Exorcist, Survivor III, Feral Barbarian, Field Alchemist III, Berserker, Beast Slayer III, War Chief, Venom Resistant III, Keytaro's Guardian III, Wrathful Meditation, Fireproof III, Visitor of Death.			

I stood up and signaled to the others that break was over.

We kept moving, traveling for another four hours. We proceeded down a trail, the river to our left and a cliff to our right.

Suddenly, arrows cascaded at us from the cliffs. My Foresight showed me fallen goblins, pierced by arrows, also images of arrows bouncing off my skin.

"Take cover!" I ordered, turning up to the clifftops.

Dozens of small humanoids appeared on the cliffs, firing short bows down on us.

I lifted my hand and with Telekinesis, caught the arrows midflight and flung them back in the direction from which they had come.

Several of the figures fell off the cliff with arrows in their necks or chest. Others scuttled backwards. The cliff was a hundred feet tall. I teleported to the top of it but the figures were already gone, vanished into the thick underbrush.

I knelt down and inspected one of the figures, a goblin in hide armor.

These goblins had a lighter green skin than the ones under my dominion and were taller but willowier than my short stocky goblins. I wasn't sure if they were some sub-species or if goblins maybe just developed differently, based on their environment or diet.

Activating my upgraded Bestial Senses, I breathed in the smell of blood and sweat, moving forward rapidly, following the crack of twigs. I pursued the goblins as they fell back through the woods, moving with stealth and speed.

It was doubtful that anyone could have tracked them as fast as I did without an ability of their own. I followed them almost half a mile from the river until we came to a walled fortification.

This goblin village was very different from the last; there were no ramshackle huts here. Instead, the goblins had converted some stone ruins into a fortress.

It looked like something similar to when I'd used my Compress Earth to fuse stones back together. At the center of the ruins, a tower rose into the air, reminding me of pictures of Rapunzel's tower, the circular building spiraling impossibly upwards toward what looked like a crow's nest at its zenith. A wooden balcony extended all around the top, while the roof wattle glinted as if its shingles were made of metal. Goblins stood atop the wall, while the ones I had chased dragged wounded members inside their fort.

I stepped out of the tree-line, a cry of alarm immediately going up from the goblins who drew their bows and fired. Deciding to put on a bit of show, I stood motionless and allowed the arrows to bounce off me, on one occasion needing to move my head a little to keep an arrow from going through my eye. Thanks to my Foresight, I knew which hit would cause damage, so I didn't waste any energy on dodging their pathetic strikes. The System was not perfect or infallible, but my ability enabled me to dodge most of their arrows.

A woman stepped up onto the wall, raising her hand and uttering a single word.

My Foresight behaved in a curious and unprecedented fashion as if I could tell something was about to happen, but was unable to identify the details of it. I tried to react and lifted a dozen spearheads into the air, feeling myself growing tired and weak.

Sinking to my knees, I felt whatever magic or ability the woman possessed seep over me.

***

I stood in a ring of warriors, a giant standing in front of me.

We fought with ferocity, blood spilling from both of us. Beyond that, I was unable to focus on or recall any details from the battle.

Raising his sword, the giant lunged forward and plunged it through my chest.

Darkness claimed me as twisted laughter echoed all around.

***

I jerked awake. My hands were bound, and I was gagged and hanging from the top of the tower, still attired in my boots and pauldrons, but my weapons and cloak were missing. I cursed myself for being so reckless; why did I give the enemy a chance to attack? I should have simply destroyed them all on first encountering them.

The chains rattled and I rose until I was looking at the shoes of a tall woman in a dark blue robe that hung all the way down to her ankles.

She had long, scarlet hair and her skin was like porcelain.

She was beautiful but wore a cruel smile. "So, who are you, Mordred? It's rare to see any other humans so deep in the forest."

I couldn't answer, didn't even try, just glaring at her.

I hung two hundred feet above the ground, not really in a position for polite conversation.

"Your items are curious," she said. "I tried having you stripped, but we couldn't remove your pauldrons or boots… nor can I identify them, which is very strange."

Instead of speaking, I went through my available abilities. Compress Earth was out since I needed to be able to speak to activate it. Most of my other abilities were mentally activated, so I could use my Telekinesis. I tried to grab the woman with it, but… nothing.

In that moment, it became apparent that none of my abilities were working. Foresight was off. I felt slower, meaning Heightened Speed was also out of commission. Looking up, I saw runes etched into the Manacles restraining me.

"Those are Sorcerer's Manacles. They negate all Gifted abilities," the woman explained. "Got them off a bounty hunter who was trying to capture me." She leaned forward, yanking the gag out of my mouth. "Now let's see about getting some answers out of you!"

I said nothing and felt the cold wind on my skin, swinging gently in the cruel harness.

"Not talking, then?" said the woman. "Perhaps after my goblins bring your friends back, you'll be more talkative."

I broke my silence. "Are any of your goblins Gifted?"

"Gods, no!" she laughed. "If they were, they wouldn't serve me!"

"Then, you've sent them to their deaths," I said with a smile.

"And what do you mean by that?" she asked.

She bent down in front of me, her chin resting on her knees.

I focused on her. To my surprise, a System notification came into view. Whatever these Manacles were, apparently, they weren't powerful enough to block out the System.

Morgaine Feysworn. Gifted Mortal. Humanoid/Human. Rank: 115.

"I mean that my army is coming," I said. "I doubt you'll be able to sleep them all. Good luck."

***

Arthur and Lancelot spun around the armored troll, striking it from behind in the back of its knees. Lancelot made contact, but the troll Managed to deflect Excalibur off his armored greave. Sparks flew as the sword dug into the metal. The Troll Knight bellowed and backhanded Arthur with his left while his right swung a warhammer at Lancelot.

Lancelot ducked, his longsword blazing with fire as he sliced up between the joint in the troll's bracers. The smell of burning flesh filled the air.

Arthur stepped in and slashed down with his two-handed sword.

"Bypassing Strike!" he said, activating the special attack. Excalibur passed through the troll's armor as if it wasn't there and bit into flesh. It let out a blinding flash of light and the troll fell backwards, clutching its eyes.

Sir Kay stepped up, a spear raised above his head.

"Iron Cascade," Kay said.

Spears fell from the sky above the troll, piercing its armor and pinning it to the ground.

Lancelot stepped forward and decapitated the troll with his flaming sword.

The three knights took a moment to the catch their breath.

"I get the next one on my own," Arthur said. "I need to duel three more creatures single-handed to complete my quest for Viviane."

"Fine," Kay said. "But I get the metal from the trolls. I need to forge more spears for my quest for Xander."

"I'm good," Lancelot said with a shrug. "Can't really complete any of my quests here."

The three champions continued through the dungeon; the tunnel opened into another chamber and Arthur stepped forward as the armored troll knight lumbered into view.

> **Troll Knight. Dungeon Creature. Mortal. Giant/Troll. Power Level: 100.**

"I challenge you, beast!" Arthur said as he stepped forward, saluting the troll with his blade.

The troll saluted back, the two clashing.

Arthur ducked and weaved. He seemed to glide across the ground as if his feet had sprouted wings. His stance was perfect, every stroke of Excalibur masterful. Finally, when he had broken through the troll's guard, he activated his two ultimate abilities.

"Heroic Blade, Bypassing Strike!" he shouted. Excalibur seemed to shine brighter than the sun as he brought it down, severing the troll's head from its shoulders in one strike. The troll's armor provided no resistance against the effects of the artifact sword and the hardness-bypassing ability, not to mention the divine attack-boosting ability.

The blood dripped off Excalibur, leaving no stain.

The knights continued their mission, and Arthur repeated the duel twice more.

> **20 rank points gained.**

> **Blood and Sand (Repeatable): Duel 80 monsters or humanoids in single combat. Current progress: 0/80. When you complete this quest, you will gain 40 rank points. The next quest will require double the number to be completed but will award double the rank points.**

"Wait one second while I rank up Holy Aura," Arthur said.

"Come on!" both Lancelot and Kay groaned in unison.

"You do this every time. We've beaten this dungeon tons of times. Just wait till we're done," complained Kay.

"Plus, I'm going to start hiding your rank-up serums," Lancelot said. "I'm tired of fighting the dungeon boss with you high on painkillers."

"Fine!" Arthur reluctantly agreed. "At least let me check my attributes."

"They won't have changed since you last looked," Kay said but did not naysay him further.

"Pull up my attributes," Arthur mandated.

Arthur, Crown Prince of Camelot. Champion of Viviane. Gifted Mortal. Humanoid/Human. Rank: 137.			
Available rank points: 2.			
Might: 48		Mind: 21	
Speed: 48		Perception: 23	
Toughness: 33		Spirit: 16	
Endurance: 33		Power: 20	
Maximum Stamina: 195		Maximum Mana: 100	
Stamina Regen: 39 per second		Mana Regen: 19.2 per second	
Abilities:			
Heroic Blade (Rank 22), Bypassing Strike (Rank 20), Gryphon's Flight (Rank 20), Unparalleled Body (Rank 15), Inner Wellspring (Rank 20), Holy Aura (Rank 10), Discerning Sight (Rank 10), Restoring Spirit (Rank 8), Waters of Avalon (Rank 10), Rending Blade (Rank 1), Mirage Steps (Rank 1).			
Blessings:			
Blessing of the Duelist (Mortal).			
Titles:			

> **Knight of Camelot, Heir of Camelot, Swordmaster II, Protector I, Iron Resolve, Pain Resistance, Resilient Form, Stunning Physique.**

"All right. I'm done," Arthur said. "Let's finish this dungeon to get its reset timer started."

"Finally!" Lancelot said. "You need to learn from Guinevere. When she's in a dungeon, she's all business right 'til the end. Probably why she's a higher rank than you."

"You know it's because her father has access to more dungeons," Arthur said grumpily.

"Doesn't change the fact she's a higher rank than you," Kay teased. "Bet that has to sting: Your betrothed at least 50 ranks higher than you!"

"I'm not worried," Arthur said. "I'm a champion, she's not. Soon, I will surpass her."

Chapter 23: Superhuman

Jamis looked around at the webbed trees. He kicked aside a dead spider and followed Mira as she led the party deeper into the spider's territory, seeing hundreds of dead spiders littering the ground. He nearly tripped as he kicked through the bodies and leaves, and bending down, he ripped a stone out of the earth and hefted it carefully.

"Look at this," he said, calling over the others.

"What is it?" Helen asked.

"Looks like a spearhead," Jamis said.

Felrick grabbed and nearly dropped it, taking it in both hands. "It has to weigh at least fifty pounds."

"Fifty pounds?" Mira asked. "But it's so small; what's it made of?"

"Nothing I've seen before," Helen said. "Do you think it's related to whatever killed all these spiders?"

"I think that's a safe bet," said Torvin.

They continued their journey and arrived in a clearing under a massive net of webbing. Bodies thinly littered the ground. An enormous spider corpse lay on the forest floor, flies buzzing ironically around it.

"That's huge," Torvin said, circling the body. "What is it?"

"It's an etter queen," Helen said. "Etters are a type of humanoid, but occasionally, one will spin a cocoon and evolve into one of these. They can breed thousands of spiders the size of hares that grow to the size of wolves and bears. I've never heard of one that was allowed to live long enough to get to this size, though."

"Where is your cousin?" Felrick asked.

Helen closed her eyes and frowned. "I just received a new quest," she said when she opened her eyes.

The eyes of the others became opaque glass as they received notifications of their own.

An End to Chaos (Repeatable): A Champion of Chaos has risen up in the ancient forest and is growing rapidly in strength. Destroy him before he becomes a threat to the civilized lands.
Progress: 0/1.

"Whichever champion did this, their party will undoubtedly outnumber us," Helen said. "We need to return to the Capital and tell my mother. It's time to raise an army."

"What about your cousin?" Mira asked.

"If Kathleen still lives, then she is a captive of this Champion of Chaos," Helen said. "We will try to rescue her, but the good of the kingdom comes first."

***

I hung in the breeze as Morgaine looked down on me with derision.

"What army?" she asked.

"An army of goblins, each with the Gift and stronger than any one of your minions," I said. "I saw how long it took you to cast whatever sleep magic you had on me. You'll be overrun by nightfall."

"Not if I kill you first!" Morgaine spat the words as she put a knife to my neck.

"Try it," I said, pushing my neck into the blade.

Morgaine frowned and looked down as the blade pressed into my skin and drew not a drop of blood. "How are you doing that? Your abilities shouldn't be able to protect you."

"Maybe you've got some defective Manacles?" I suggested.

She frowned and stood. "I'll handle your little army and come back and find out your secret soon enough."

She left and I remained hanging. Despite the bravado in my words, I had little faith in my vassals. They had not been told to come after me, so they would be exactly where I'd left them. I could rely on myself alone to break loose and get out of this mess. I kicked my legs back and then forward, building up a swinging, pendular momentum with an ever-widening arc.

Soon, my legs were kicking off the tower and I Managed to get one foot on the edge of the rim.

I stopped swinging, pulled myself forward and Managed to hook my other leg over the edge. I inched forward slowly until the back of my knees hit the ledge.

Next, I put the soles of my feet flat and pushed up, shoving up my hips until they were above the ledge rim. I dropped down and rolled to my feet, still chained, but my situation was looking better. It was possible to unhook my Manacles from the chain, looking around.

I was at the top of the tower, on a wide balcony which fully wrapped itself around the outside of the edifice. A door led into the tower, and I tried it, finding it unlocked.

I stepped into a surprisingly luxurious bedroom, the walls covered in bright tapestries and a four-poster queen-size canopy bed. It was covered in thick furs and blankets, set against the wall. Next to the bed was a desk stacked with papers, a quill and a pen. Alongside that stood a wardrobe with a mirror on its door. The room also contained a copper bathtub, a spiral staircase and a small table with a singular chair which sat in the center of the room.

Rummaging in the drawers of the desk did not reveal any keys or my stuff. I checked the wardrobe too but there were only clothes in there. Down the stairs, I came to another door and tested the door handle. It was unlocked. Opening the door, there was a click and I narrowly avoided a spray of electricity but the jolt of a few volts still made me stagger.

By now, I was getting more than a little pissed. To my surprise, however, my pain started to dissipate. *What does this mean? Is the effect of Berserker still active despite the fact I'm bound by Manacles? Are titles separate from abilities?*

I continued down into some sort of laboratory where shelves lined the walls, laden with books, scrolls, potions and jars containing preserved and living creatures.

And there it was, my stuff sitting all spread out on a table.

My hands still Manacled, I eventually completed the awkward task of putting on my rings. Setting my helmet on my head and wrapping myself in my cloak, I then grabbed one of my clubs. Using two weapons was completely impractical at that time, and even one was awkward with my hands cuffed. Crossing to the other side of the room, I began to descend the staircase.

There were doors opening into storage rooms, also to a kitchen, a pantry and what looked like a torture chamber.

Finally reaching the ground floor, I tried the door here too, but it was locked; it was also heavy, and the lock looked too hard to break without access to my abilities.

Moving into the shadows at the side, I waited for at least half an hour before the door opened, Morgaine stepping through.

I lunged at her.

A transparent barrier popped up and she screamed.

I appeared out of the darkness, teleporting behind her. I was unable to teleport when physically connected to something like the chain, but the Manacles didn't block the enchantments of my items. My club swung down.

In one deft motion she seemed to spin and raise her hand.

A barrier appeared, the force of which flung me back a dozen yards. I skidded along the ground but kept my feet. Life and death battles had been honing my reflexes and my Speed Attribute was close to Veteran rank. Even without the effects of Heightened Speed, I was fast. I charged back toward Morgaine.

She uttered an incantation and a staff appeared in her hand.

I needed to go all out. Morgaine obviously had access to her abilities. I did not. What I did have, however, were my artifacts, attributes, and magic items. I activated the Juggernaut ability from my helmet. My body swelled and doubled in size.

Morgaine's eyes widened and a bolt of ice shot from her staff.

Activating the Speed Boost from my boots, I dodged to the side while maintaining my momentum. I hit her magical force field, only this time, I didn't bounce off. Instead, the barrier cast Morgaine a few steps backwards, making her lose balance.

I used my shoulder to ram repeatedly into the obviously weakening force field, and Morgaine staggered again, falling on her ass. The barrier popped, and then I was on her, swinging my club.

She was surprisingly agile, rolling to the side and using her staff as a lever to help her vault to her feet.

My foot swept out and she barely blocked my kick.

Now, I launched my club toward her head.

Dozens of copies of her appeared all around me, each identical and moving in their own way.

My club swung through where I had last seen Morgaine but when I struck her, the duplicate popped and disappeared. Closing my eyes, I used my high Perception Attribute and heard the scuff of feet on stone. Turning, I launched myself at her location, ripping through three cloned images that stood in my way; I was on her again.

She blocked my first strike with the club, but the force of the attack flung her back into the wall. Undeterred, she continued her spell chanting and extended her arm in my direction.

"Dispel!" she shouted.

The Juggernaut effect was fading, and I was shrinking, a weariness coming over me. My speed boost was still effective, however, and I charged forward, jumping into the air, my leading foot enabling me to perform a flying kick.

Her eyes widened.

My foot collided with her chest, and she slammed into the wall and slumped down.

I fell to the ground as the backlash from the Juggernaut enchantment washed over me.

Now entering Wrathful Meditation, I lost all feeling. Hauling myself to my feet, I crawled over to Morgaine and padded her down, Managing to locate the keys on her belt and beginning to try them on my Manacles. On the sixth key, the lock popped open.

I put them on her wrists and stood up.

"Dominion," I said, looking down on her as the brands appeared on her neck and wrists.

You have completed a hidden objective and earned a title. Objective: Defeat a Gifted of a higher rank than you without access to any of your abilities.
Reward. Title: Superhuman (must be race, human).
*Superhuman: When in combat, your physical attributes are boosted by 5 percent.

Whip and Chains (Repeatable): Conquer 320 monsters or humanoids by bringing them under your Dominion. Current progress: 15/320. When you complete this quest, you will gain 64 rank points. The next quest will require double the number to be completed but will award double the rank points.

I exited Wrathful Meditation and passed out, unconscious for at least a few minutes—though exactly how long, I was unsure—and on regaining my senses, I got up and looked around carefully to see if anything had snuck up on me while I'd been helpless. There wasn't a single goblin, or any other creature except for the still unconscious Morgaine.

So, I started running, taking off toward where I had left my vassals.

Leaping over the wall, I hurried back to the river where I found the two factions locked in battle. My forces were doing all right, but Morgaine's goblins had now equaled their number, showering arrows on my army from the ridge.

"Dominion," I said.

Around half of the archers on the ridge were brought under my control.

"Dominion!" Now, I was taking control of the other half.

The archers on the ridge stopped firing, their hands grasping desperately around their necks as the brand appeared. The goblins fighting my forces panicked. They had a spear wall but had been barely able to withstand the raptor riders who circled and darted in from the flanks to attack.

Whip and Chains (Repeatable): Conquer 320 monsters or humanoids by bringing them under your Dominion. Current progress: 126/320. When you complete this quest, you will gain 64 rank points. The next quest will require double the number to be completed but will award double the rank points.

I felt close to the limit on how many vassals I could have, so stood back and let my forces rip the remaining goblins to pieces. Stepping down, I surveyed my remaining vassals.

It looked as though all the humans had survived by staying back. Kathleen and her companions had defended them. The spiders had been avoided but Euphrates and Tigris had devastated around a quarter of their numbers. Several of my raptors and goblins had died. Despite this, I had made a net gain with my new vassals.

"Bring everyone up the ridge and follow me," I told Jand and Juruk.

Turning around, I left them and returned to the tower, seeing Morgaine motionless on the ground. I nudged her with my boot and her eyes suddenly blinked open.

She leapt to her feet. Her hands darted out, but the tables had been turned and now her abilities were blocked.

"Take these off of me," she demanded.

"Sure," I said, shrugging. "Don't attack me or any of my vassals."

I unlocked the Manacles, and she immediately raised her hands to unleash a spell, then dropped to her knees as the brand around her neck flashed white-hot.

"What did you do me?" she hissed.

"I am Mordred, Champion of Kelesa, Goddess of War and Conquest," I said, my voice hard and flat. "You serve me now. You will do as I command. You will not seek to betray me. You will act in what you believe is my best interest and not seek to undermine or cause discord among my other vassals."

Her brand flashed again as she heard my orders and the color drained from her face. "You've enslaved me?" she asked, her voice faint and full of fear.

"It's one way of looking at it," I said with a shrug. "Pack what you want to take with us; we leave first thing tomorrow morning."

I entered the tower and explored the rooms more thoroughly. Looking at the books, I discovered something: I couldn't read this world's language. Come to think of it, I didn't know how to even speak it. I guessed it was some sort of system effect, although why it had chosen to allow me to speak the language but not read it I did not know. I looked through the potions, but they appeared to be for experiments and not the kind you could drink.

I left the tower and went to the gates where my minions were filing inside. I used Compress Earth on the walls to harden them and used the earth outside to create a trench outside the walls. It was tight but everyone fitted within the walls. So, I found a spot to rest and waited. This was a new area and new undead would inevitably appear tonight for me to fight.

I woke up from my nap when a horn blew.

My eyes snapped open, and I nearly threw Juruk off the wall.

"What was that?" I asked, looking at him.

"The alarm, Warlord," Juruk said proudly, holding a war hand in both hands.

"You're standing five feet away from me, just tap me on the shoulder next time. Blow that thing in my ear like that again and I'll toss you over the wall," I said grumpily and stood, cracking the bones in my neck.

Zombies and skeletons filled the ditch, clawing at the walls of the fort. As I raised my hands, stone spearheads and blades of Telekinesis went hurtling into the horde. I spent twenty minutes wiping up the remains of the undead before returning to lie down and rest.

> **Blood and Souls (Repeatable): Kill 5,120 monsters or humanoids. Current progress: 4,364/5,120. When you complete this quest, you will gain 1024 rank points. The next quest will require double the number to be completed but will award double the rank points.**

I felt no cold or discomfort from lying on the ground. *The perks of being immune to exposure!* I drifted off to sleep again.

***

Prince Arthur rode up alongside his father as they tracked the stag through the forest.

"Aura of Discretion," King Arthur said, activating an ability to give them privacy. "I've been hearing reports of you and some of the noblewomen of the court."

"I've just gone on some walks," said the prince, rolling his eyes. "I made sure we stayed in public places with witnesses."

"Good," King Arthur said. "We can't risk your marriage to Lady Guinevere."

"Guinevere trusts me, Father. And anyway, I haven't done anything!"

"But you must be seen to toe the line," King Arthur said dryly. "I was young once, remember. Merlin controls access to some of the most powerful dungeons in the country and we need access to them."

"He's your brother, so why don't you just ask him?" said the younger.

"You know why, son. My brother's desire for power has always been his defining trait, and he won't give up access to those dungeons without a heavy cost. The only way to pay that price is for you to marry Guinevere. As his son-in-law, he won't be able to restrict your access to those dungeons."

"I don't like using Guinevere like this," said young Arthur, sighing.

"It is her place in society," King Arthur said. "It's good that you have feelings for her, but your loyalty is to Camelot first. The sooner you marry her the better, for her sake as well."

"What do you mean?" Arthur asked.

"I received an anonymous tip. There is at least one assassin close to Guinevere."

"But why assassinate her?" asked the prince.

"To weaken you and thus me," King Arthur said. "If you don't marry Guinevere, I will have to give my brother considerable concessions and even more political power to gain access to those dungeons. The best way to stop the marriage is to remove one of the players."

"Where is Guinevere now? We should bring her to the capital to keep her safe."

"Her father has her running diplomatic missions for him before she marries you, trying to get as many political and economic favors as he can. She is currently heading to the ancient forest at Lunara and should be there in a week or so," King Arthur said.

"Should we send to have her brought back?" Prince Arthur asked.

"Could you get her to listen to you?"

"No, and until we get married, she doesn't have to listen to me," the prince admitted.

"Then we do nothing for now," declared the king. "Guinevere is Veteran rank, so unless she chooses to attract trouble, she should be fine... for now."

Chapter 24: Troll Hide

"We should take the time to get more ranks," Jamis said as they traveled back through the Cursed Forest.

"Do we have time?" Mira asked.

"The Chaos Champion is gaining in strength," Helen said. "Jamis is right, we need to make sure we're prepared for them and their party."

"I thought the chaos spawn were too power hungry to operate in parties," Jamis said.

"They don't think of their companions as equals," Felrick answered. "Their companions are usually just followers of their god who are tasked to serve their champion. The chaos spawn views them as expendable and usually, so does their god."

"They will let their champion take on as many of the ranking points as possible," Helen said. "It makes the champion especially strong, but the party's overall strength is weakened."

"How do we find some monsters to slay?" Torvin asked.

"As much as I would like to encourage us to gain strength, we should alert your mother," Felrick said to Helen. "The presence of a champion here is a matter of concern for the entire kingdom."

Helen sighed. "You're right, we should inform my mother. After that, we can focus on our own development."

***

The ruins of a castle stood on a hill. As I approached it, from out of crude wooden and sod houses emerged a group of warriors forming a ring around me. A huge giant stepped out from them and vague details of a ferocious battle flashed before my eyes. The giant's sword plunged through my chest, and I felt myself falling into the blackness. The hungry claws of death reached for me, a malicious laugh echoing all around.

***

I awoke, startled, my hearts racing as I composed myself after the nightmare.

… Only it wasn't a nightmare, was it? At least, not wholly. It was more like a vision, or perhaps a premonition. I remembered my upgraded Foresight ability. Sometimes, that ability was strange and disturbing and I didn't even know what to do with the information. Was it warning me away from something? Foresight showed me a future; could I change it or was it locked in? Was it my destiny to die at the hands of this mysterious giant?

I guessed he was the Bandit King. This realization would not, however, sway me from my goal. I was not afraid of death, unafraid to face the giant and spit in the face of fate.

Getting to my feet, I took a stroll around the camp, finding Maria and the other women already making breakfast. I ate quickly and went up to the top floor of the tower to discover Morgaine packing all her things.

"Are you ready?" I asked.

"No," she snapped. "How can I be ready? I don't have a way to carry my belongings since you stole all my minions."

I sighed, beginning to shove all her stuff into my storage pouch. "I guess I'll help, then," I said. "Go down and get ready for marching."

"I'm a lady. Ladies don't march. Don't you know that?"

"Well, you do march now," I said, unsympathetically, throwing her books, potions, and other stuff into my satchel and walking through the door.

The goblins had assembled into a semblance of ranks. I gave a nod to Juruk, and the raptor riders rode out, followed by columns of goblin archers. Jumping from the top of the wall, I cleared the trench as we set off back into the woods again.

We traveled along the road, the raptors ranging out ahead, scouting the area to prevent any more ambushes. I walked easily, my stride propelled by my boots. I had to stop occasionally, to keep from leaving everyone behind.

The goblin scouts had orders to report back to me any more sightings of Gifted beasts or monsters. So far, they had found nothing for me to fight.

We reached a river, the source of which seemed similar in size to that of the Mississippi. Assessing the fast-flowing water, I realized there was no good way for anyone besides me to get across. I led everyone up the riverbank as we looked for a better crossing point.

"Where exactly is this Bandit King?" I asked Jand and Juruk.

"He's on the other side of the river," interjected Morgaine, panting. Juruk and Jand simply shrugged.

"Why do you know where he is?" I asked.

"Because I make it my business to know things," said Morgaine primly. "He's also Veteran rank, rumored to be approaching Hero rank. Why are you going there?"

"To face him," I said. "He seems like a worthy challenge."

Morgaine laughed. "Well, it looks rather like I won't be your vassal for very long, after all. He will cut you down in moments. Bounty hunters, wannabe heroes and Gift hunters have been trying to take him down for nearly two decades."

"It wouldn't be a proper challenge if it were something people believed I had a shot at," I said with a shrug.

"Do you not care for your own life?" Kathleen asked as she caught up with us.

"Even if I knew for certain that fighting him would result in his sword plunging through my hearts, I'd still face him," I said.

"Why though?" Morgaine asked.

"Because fear is what held back my father and I'd rather die than become anything like him," I said with finality, walking forward, signaling for everyone to follow.

We took lunch on the shore, where I saw a ship pass by. We were hidden by the forest and leaves, but I watched the barge with intense curiosity. It occurred to me that this was the first sign of civilization I'd seen.

"Is that a merchant barge?" I asked Kathleen.

"Yes," she said. "The river is fastest through the Cursed Forest and makes the journey more profitable, even if they have to pay a toll to the Bandit King."

We kept eating as I gave everyone a chance to rest.

A new ship appeared, my eye on it as it came closer. This one was a sloop, not a barge. Apart from a few cages on its deck, no cargo was visible.

"What's that?" I asked.

"Gift hunters," Kathleen said. "They specialize in taking alive those with the Gift."

"Hmm," I said. "I might have to take a closer look at them."

Not waiting for a response, I got to my feet, set down my plate and ran out onto the water. My feet struck it as if it were concrete as I sped across its surface, toward the sloop.

About twenty yards out, that was when they saw me.

An alarm went up and they responded quickly, sending arrows and bolas in my direction.

I teleported onto the ship and buried my two clubs simultaneously into the necks of two of the hunters, jumping over bola throwers. I landed with both feet on the chest of one, launching him over the side of the ship. Using my momentum from the kick, I somersaulted backwards and landed unerringly close to the ship's center. Even I was impressed!

To their credit, the Gift hunters were also good at their job, however. Fearlessly, they came for me and I was unable to analyze them which meant they weren't Gifted. They could move as fast as Gifted, however, striking out at me with long swords.

"Dominion," I said. These were skilled fighters and might be useful to keep around.

> You cannot **Dominate** these creatures. They are the results of mind shielding and are immune to all forms of mind control, domination, and compulsion effects.

Interesting. I abandoned the thought and returned all my attention to the fight, pushing out with Telekinesis and flinging two into the mast.

There came a sharp crack of bone on wood as they hit.

They had surrounded me, however, with a whirlwind of coordinated strikes. The sheer number coming at me was too many to block or evade, so I transformed into an incorporeal state, stepping through the attacks. My slashing weapons left no wounds but everyone they struck dropped their own weapons, screaming in agony as I inflicted Soul Damage upon them.

After this, approaching from the rear, I struck out again, the claws of my weapons punching through leather and steel as I tore into their backs. They turned to fight, but I teleported to the other side, ripping into them again until only five remained standing on the ship's deck.

They turned and jumped overboard.

I reached into my storage pouch to pull out half a dozen spearheads, throwing them into the air. They rotated and turning point-first, dived into the water. Red stains soon spread across the surface and I raised the bodies out, back onto the deck, the corpses flopping like limp fish.

Next, I looked at the cages, all empty except for one.

There was a sense of being watched, and sure enough, I found myself being studied by a young woman of maybe seventeen or eighteen, her pointed ears covered with fur.

She had striking eyes of saffron yellow and suddenly bared her teeth, revealing two wolverine fangs alongside normal human teeth. I cocked my head and looked her over.

Analysis revealed that she was clearly not human.

Syvia. Wolf Clan. Gifted Humanoid/Myrmidon (Wolf breed). Mortal. Rank: 8.

"Who are you?" she asked, baring her teeth.

"Can't you read my name?" I was gesturing vaguely above my head.

She squinted at me as I stepped into clear view past the bars. Gasping, she awkwardly tried to prostrate herself. "Forgive me, Warlord, for not recognizing the Champion of Kelesa," she said, her face pressed to the wooden planks of the deck.

"You can get up," I said. "Which one had the keys?"

"That one," Syvia said, pointing to one with silver accents on his armor.

Turning the body over, I found the keys on his belt and opened the cage, also tossing Syvia the keys for her Manacles.

"Dominion," I said.

The marks on her neck were different, not the usual chain pattern but looking like crossed swords.

"Why is your brand different?" I asked.

"Because I am your loyal vassal," Syvia said. "We are the Myrmidon, the people of Kelesa, destined to serve the Warlord against the champions of the gods."

"You're from a larger group?" I asked.

"Yes, I am the daughter of the Chief of the Wolf Clan," Syvia said, proudly.

"Then why are you chained up in a cage on a ship?" I asked.

Syvia spat out, "The Dragon Clan has mercenaries and bounty hunters to help in their war against us. Rather than killing us, they dishonor themselves and weaken all our clans by letting outsiders steal our gifts and take them for themselves."

"So, you'd rather they'd killed you?" I asked.

"Better to die in honor than become a breeding mare for a soft, city dweller," she said. "They would have sold me to one of their civilized lords for him to breed me like a cow."

"I see," I said. "Where is your clan now?"

"They are in the Valley of Thimara, below Mount Hegan," Syvia said.

"Yeah, that's a bunch of names that don't mean anything to me," I said. "We should get to shore. Do you know how to steer this thing?"

In the end, we crashed the sloop against the shore and I collected the weapons of the Gift hunters. Their bolas had runes engraved into them that I learned had the same effect as the sorcerer's manacles. There were also three actual pairs of sorcerer's Manacles. I stripped the bodies of their armor and weapons, piling everything into my storage pouch.

Returning to my other vassals, I brought Syvia, Morgaine, Kathleen and Jand together. The group sat in a loose circle, and the three women eyed each other warily.

"Why is there a Myrmidon here?" Kathleen asked.

"Because I brought her. She's a local, so her knowledge of the area makes her more useful than yours right now," I said.

"Sure… If you need to know how to raid a border town," Kathleen responded, obviously affronted.

"And what do you advise the Warlord on?" Syvia asked. "How to grow crops and become fat and weak?"

"I'll show you weak…!" Kathleen quickly rose to her feet, fists clenched.

"Both of you remain seated," I ordered. "I need to cross the river. I also want to gain more abilities. Syvia, is there somewhere we can ford the river? And, do you know of any local Gifted monsters or beasts?"

"This place is far from my clan's territory, but I can cast a spell to find any Gifted creature within a few miles of us," Syvia said.

"You have an ability for that?" I asked.

"Not an ability. A spell. The Old Magic has been passed down among the clans since the first warlord walked the world," Syvia explained.

"Of course, you practice blasphemy," Kathleen scoffed.

"Blasphemy?" I asked, turning to her.

"Spells were what people used before the gods gave us the System," Kathleen said. "Using the Old Magic is a way for mortals to reach beyond their station and step into what they were *meant* to have."

"We still use enchanters," Morgaine said, shaking her head as she turned to me. "You aren't going to get useful information out of this discussion. This debate is a millennium old and riddled with pointless rhetoric and hypocrisy on both sides."

Syvia and Kathleen both opened their mouths in outrage at Morgaine's words.

I silenced them with a change of subject.

"Does anyone know how close we are to the Bandit King?" I inquired.

"The ship passed a fort and paid a toll about half a day upriver," Syvia said. "I believe that is the Bandit King's lair."

"Great," I said. "Then the first order of business is to get everyone across the river while you find me some monsters and beasts to hunt for new abilities. Morgaine, try and see if you can learn from Syvia. Kathleen, you're a healer, so make sure all my troops are healthy and uninjured. Jand, take some archers, go hunting and tell the rest to forage for supplies."

My orders issued, I stood and went to the edge of the river. There may no longer be any bridges but Syvia had said there had been once, which meant they could be made again.

I found a sandbank extending out into the river and walked along it, sensing the common dirt and stone around me. "Compress Earth," I said.

I compressed the dirt and rock into a pillar, six feet around, that sank eighty feet into the earth.

"Compress Earth," I repeated.

Dirt, sand and mud flowed upwards and formed another pillar.

I kept working until I had the end of the bridge formed, though I had to take frequent breaks to let my Mana recharge. Regardless, I kept at it until I had a bridge spanning fifty feet over the water, twenty feet above its surface.

I started on another pillar, connecting it to the bridge for support. And I kept moving.

It must have been around seven in the afternoon before the bridge was completed, spanning ten feet wide and extending right across the three-hundred-foot river. I was no engineer, but thanks to the hardness of the compressed stone and earth I was able to create, I was confident this bridge could withstand whatever nature had to throw at it.

Someone could probably destroy it with an ability of their own, but that wasn't my concern.

Returning to camp, I was given a bowl of rabbit stew with broadleaf spread with a berry jam. I ate until I was full, dumping my plate and bowl by the camp's makeshift sink.

Syvia returned to camp from deeper in the forest. "I've found some," she said eagerly.

"What is it?" I asked.

"A troll, Rank 140. It's still Mortal ranked, and if we attack it with all your vassals, it will be easy for your Gifted to advance."

I shook my head. "I hunt and fight alone,"

"Are you sure?" Syvia's face was a picture of consternation. "This beast is powerful and not just some alchemically-boosted ungifted like the Gift hunters."

"I'm sure," I said. "This is how I've gained power in your world so far, and I won't veer from my course now. By my own hand and no one else's will I achieve victory. Just lead the way, and I'll take over once you've shown me where the troll is."

"It's not just one," Syvia said. "There is only one Gifted, but there are five other trolls. They are still quite powerful even if they don't have the Gift."

"They wouldn't be worth fighting if they weren't a threat," I said. "Lead the way, and I'll take over once you've pointed it out to me."

I followed Syvia through the forest. She led us northwest up numerous rises and we had to climb several cliffs until she stopped and gestured ahead. I nodded, motioning for her to stay as I moved toward the sound of heavy grunts and snarls. The source of the grunting was a group of humanoid figures, each standing over fifteen feet tall with dark brown skin and thick green hair like moss growing over their bodies. Boar-like tusks jutted out of their mouths which also contained fangs extending down past their lips. One raised his head, sniffing the air and snarling at the other trolls. This one was surely the leader, based on its size.

There was no point in trying to sneak up on them, lacking both skills and abilities in that department. So, I simply rushed at them.

The trolls jumped up and lashed out at me, their obvious surprise not diminishing their innate instincts to attack and kill.

Prioritizing my attack on the leader, I Managed to evade a huge, clawed hand, my clubs ripping into the flesh of its thigh and spraying black blood over myself and the ground.

I rolled out of the way of a swinging log as long as the trolls were tall.

The leader roared, a tremendous shockwave passing through the air as he did so, and in the next moment, I was slammed into a thick oak tree.

The troll chief charged me, his log-carved club raised to strike.

I teleported behind him, ripping into his Achilles' tendons with the claws on both my clubs. With some difficulty, the claws tore through muscle and tendon. Yet still, the troll would not fall, his body knitting itself back together almost instantly. It kicked out at me with its heel.

I took evasive action, resuming with a frenzy of strikes at the beast.

Again, black blood sprayed out, the wounds knitting themselves together.

This time, however, the skin did not fully reseal as the lacerate effect of the Nemean claws made it more difficult for it to staunch the bleeding.

I knew enough about troll lore from my world to know that fire damage would probably keep the wounds I made from closing, but I lacked the means to inflict that on the trolls.

So, I transformed into an incorporeal state as a massive foot stomped down at where I had been. I ripped into the appendage with my weapons while in Phantom Form.

The troll howled and I concluded that their regeneration abilities probably didn't cover healing from Spirit Damage. With my Telekinesis, I controlled spearheads and weapons, beginning to shred the skin of the non-Gifted trolls; while they appeared to have a level of regeneration, it was nothing compared to their leader's. With their dustbin-lid-sized hands, they covered their screaming faces as their leader swung the log club at me.

Jumping up, I landed on the log and charged toward it.

The troll roared again and the sound sent out another immense shockwave, flinging me back through the air a second time. Determined to avoid hurtling into another tree, I teleported, rematerializing above the troll and hammering down onto its mighty head with my clubs, penetrating the tough skin. The skull, however, was harder than granite, the claws skidding off the bone. Roaring, the troll bucked and swatted a hand toward me.

I backflipped off its shoulders, sending a storm of spearheads toward its face.

It held up a hand, shielding its eyes as it swung blindly behind itself.

I easily dodged the aimless strike.

As the troll was raising the club above its head, the boring log became surrounded by a black aura. The troll smashed down at me one-handed, the other protecting its eyes from my rain of attacks. My Foresight went insane, showing me dozens of ways in which I was about to be fucked with no good options to avoid taking it up the ass.

The club smashed down, sending out a wave of black energy over a hundred feet. The other trolls roared in agony as they retreated from the battle, leaving their leader to fight me alone.

The black flames flowed up my body, my skin blistering and rotting like a wound left to fester. I teleported back to down a health potion, but it did little to repair my rotting skin.

Emboldened by the success of its attack, the troll smashed its foot down and charged forward in a lightning-fast burst of speed. I became incorporeal, its club sailing through where I'd been standing barely an instant before. As I lunged forward, my clubs raked into its shoulders, and I saw it jerk back from my phantom weapons. I still wasn't sure what Soul Damage was, but its right arm dropped the club as Blavresh howled in pain.

It was fair to say I wasn't doing well, either.

The black flames still flickered over my withering, rotting form, my skinny ribs markedly protruding through my skin when I looked down at my chest.

Only Wrathful Meditation was keeping me moving now, helping to numb what would otherwise have been a blackout-inducing pain.

I teleported forward again while I still had a second remaining of active Phantom Form. The troll still distracted, I buried my phantom weapons into its thick skull, then returned to my physical form, my weapons still embedded in Blavresh's head. As the club manifested back into material form, the huge skull cracked open, sending blood and brain matter exploding over me.

---

70 rank points gained.

I felt a weight disappear from my shoulders.

You have absorbed the hide of a Nemean lion which has bonded to your Toughness Attribute and will fuel and guide your body's mutation when you pass the Mortal limit for your Toughness Attribute.

"But I liked that cloak!" I snarled at the System, a little pissed it had just taken that from me without asking.

Ability gained. Troll Hide (Rank 1): Your skin remains supple but becomes as tough as leather, increasing its hardness by 2. Whenever you are damaged, your flesh regenerates, reducing all afflictions, debuff effect and duration by 40 percent.

This is a passive ability, costing 5 Stamina/5 seconds. This ability will turn off when you are out of Stamina.

Upgrade this ability to increase your skin's toughness. Each upgrade increases your Toughness Attribute by 1.

The addition of the ability slightly mollified me over the loss of my Nemean cloak and as I looked at my body, my rotting skin was falling away, new skin growing in its place. My scars were still there, having apparently not been erased by the regeneration process. Not that I minded as the scars were just as much a trophy from my battles as the bone weapons I'd made.

It seemed unlikely there'd be any good trophies from the body of the troll; I could go kill the trolls that had run off but there were too few to make meaningful progress toward my Blood and Souls quest. They weren't Gifted anyway, so I wouldn't earn rank points for killing them. I turned to the cave behind the troll's fire where a moose was spitted over the flames.

Walking into the cave, I cringed upon seeing all the crude, smelly fur scattered about as bedding. A hollowed-out log at the back acted like a crate or chest. Looking in the log, I found a small pile of gold- and silver-flecked rocks and a few other gemlike protrusions.

Tentatively, I picked up a red ruby-like crystal. It burned my hand, and I let it fall.

Fire Ruby: Rare magical stone. Hardness: 8. Filled with the fires of creation; deals moderate Fire Damage on contact.

I dismissed the prompt and looked down at the stone with more interest, levitating it and depositing it in my storage pouch. Then, I looked over the other crystals. Only one was magical and I levitated it too into my storage pouch.

> **Frost Quartz:** Rare magical stone. Hardness: 7. Touched by the bitter cold of winter; deals moderate Frost Damage on contact.

The other crystals were merely a collection of uncommon gemstones but I picked them up to use later with Compress Earth.

I'd save the magical gems for when there was a special weapon to work on.

So, I departed the cave, sitting down by the troll's fire to meditate and rank up my new ability. "Increase Troll Hide to Rank 20," I told the System when settled in my Wrathful Meditation.

> **Troll Hide (Rank 2):** Your skin remains supple but becomes as tough as leather, increasing its hardness by 2.2. Whenever you are cut, your flesh regenerates, reducing all afflictions, debuffs effect and duration by 45 percent.
>
> This is a passive ability, costing 5 Stamina/5 seconds. This ability will turn off when you are out of Stamina.
>
> Upgrade this ability to increase your skin's toughness. Each upgrade increases your Toughness Attribute by 1.

It looked as if my Toughness increased by point two per rank.

Hopefully, that would hold true with subsequent rank-ups. The reduction for the duration of debuffs and afflictions went up by 5 percent per rank.

I skipped the next two notifications until I got the pop-up for the added effect.

> **Congratulations! You have raised an ability to Rank 5. Please select an additional effect for your ability from the list below:**
>
> - You can infuse one square inch of skin on any part of your body to have double hardness for the next 60 seconds.
> - Regeneration speed is tripled while in combat. This effect increases the Stamina cost by 2 per second.
> - Your body's regeneration also fuels your Stamina, increasing it by 5 Stamina regened per second.

I considered my options. If the amount of space I could infuse went up with more ranks, it could be useful to make parts of my body almost indestructible. The second option looked good.

It would no doubt be a Stamina hog but the prospect of having my wounds seal themselves as soon as they were inflicted was hard to pass up. The third option was good too, but I could live without it, and just upgrading my physical stats would boost my Stamina regen.

The second choice was too good to pass up.

Troll Hide (Rank 5): Your skin remains supple but becomes as tough as leather, increasing its hardness by 2.8. Whenever you are cut, your flesh regenerates, reducing all afflictions and debuffs effect and duration by 60 percent.
Regeneration speed is tripled while in combat. This effect increases the Stamina cost by 2 per second.
This is a passive ability, costing 3 Stamina per second. This ability will turn off when you are out of Stamina.
Upgrade this ability to increase your skin's toughness. Each upgrade increases your Toughness Attribute by 1.

The passive cost for the ability had gone up by two Stamina per second. I skipped the next four notifications to get to the options for the next effect.

Congratulations! You have raised an ability to Rank 10. Please select an additional effect for your ability from the list below:
• **Your body's regeneration also fuels your Stamina, increasing it by 10 Stamina regened per second**
• **The toughness of your body's hair is doubled, making your body hair an additional layer of armor.**
• **Your regeneration reduces the cooldown for all your abilities by 1 second.**

I looked over the options, finding the first one a better version of the effect seen at Rank 5. The second option was just weird! While there was certainly a lot of hair over my body, I honestly couldn't imagine how this effect could be used. The third option was tempting and would let me use abilities such as my Phantom Form more often; however, that would also mean I'd use up Mana more quickly. I selected the first option. Ostentatious effects were cool, but if I didn't have enough juice to pull them off, they would be useless.

Troll Hide (Rank 10): Your skin remains supple but becomes as tough as leather, increasing its hardness by 3.8. Whenever you are cut, your flesh regenerates, reducing all afflictions and debuffs effect and duration by 85 percent.
Regeneration speed is tripled while in combat. This effect increases the Stamina cost by 2/second.
Your body's regeneration also fuels your Stamina, increasing it by 10 Stamina regened per second.
This is a passive ability, costing 5 Stamina per second. This ability will turn off when you are out of Stamina.
Upgrade this ability to increase your skin's toughness. Each upgrade increases your Toughness Attribute by 1.

The passive cost for Troll Hide had gone up by another two points per second, reaffirming my decision.

Troll Hide (Rank 11): Your skin remains supple but becomes as tough as leather, increasing its hardness by 4. Whenever you are cut, your flesh regenerates, reducing all afflictions and debuffs effect and duration by 90 percent.
Regeneration speed is tripled while in combat. This effect increases the Stamina cost by 2 per second.
Your body's regeneration also fuels your Stamina, increasing it by 11 Stamina regened per second.
This is a passive ability, costing 5 Stamina per second. This ability will turn off when you are out of Stamina.
Upgrade this ability to increase your skin's toughness. Each upgrade increases your Toughness Attribute by 1.

I briefly looked over the changes to the ability between ranks. It seemed my Stamina regen would increase by one additional point per rank. Not a lot in the grand scheme of things but it would act to counterbalance the cost of this ability as well as my Heightened Speed.

> Congratulations! You have raised one of your attributes beyond 20, the Mortal limit. Your body will now physiologically change to adjust to this increase to keep your attribute from killing you.
>
> Your bones have gained a hardness level of 10 and resistance to breaking abilities. The cells of your body have reinforced themselves, making your whole body more resistant to damage and able to survive more serious injuries.

No 'darkvision' but with unbreakable skin, I needed sturdy bones to support it, so this was a welcome mutation for my survival. I skipped the next three notifications to get to the pop-up.

> Congratulations! You have raised an ability to Rank 15. Please select an additional effect for your ability from the list below:
>
> - Your blood acts with a life of its own and will crawl back into your body, preventing blood loss from your injuries
> - Your limbs will slowly regenerate and restore after being cut off. Holding a severed limb to the stump will reattach it in a few seconds
> - Severed limbs can act of their own accord even when separated from your body.

These effects were distinctly weird. The first and third were particularly creepy and I wasn't even sure how useful they would be. So, I went for the more obvious and less strange effect of option two: the ability to regrow body parts sounded way more effective than having them act autonomously.

> Troll Hide (Rank 15): Your skin remains supple but becomes as tough as leather, increasing its hardness by 4.8. Whenever you are cut, your flesh regenerates, reducing all afflictions and debuffs effect and duration by 99 percent.
>
> Regeneration speed is tripled while in combat. This effect increases the Stamina cost by 2 per second.
>
> Your body's regeneration also fuels your Stamina, increasing it by 15 Stamina regened per second.

Your limbs will slowly regenerate and restore after being cut off. Holding a severed limb to the stump will reattach it in a few seconds.
This is a passive ability, costing 7 Stamina per second. This ability will turn off when you are out of Stamina.
Upgrade this ability to increase your skin's toughness. Each upgrade increases your Toughness Attribute by 1.

The Stamina cost had gone up again, but the ability was now giving me more Stamina than it was taking. Thanks to the effect of my pauldrons which already currently boosted the Toughness of my skin by 12, it would have double the hardness of diamond when I hit the max ability rank.

It looked as if I might have maxed out the percentage reduction on the duration of debuffs and afflictions. It had gone from 95 to 99 instead of the usual 5 percent.

Now, my enemies' most devastating afflictions and debuffs, with which they expected to keep me down, would last only a few seconds at most.

I skipped the next four notifications to get to the last additional effect for this ability.

Congratulations! You have raised an ability to Rank 20. Please select an additional effect for your ability from the list below:
• **Your body can act independently of your head for a short period, although you are blind and deaf during this time**
• **If your body is destroyed but a part of you survives, such as a limb, your body will gradually, over the course of a year, regenerate from that section**
• **You can survive without your vital organs for double the number of time, and they will regrow if destroyed or removed from your body.**

The first effect would let me run around like a chicken with its head cut off—funny but not super useful. If I retained the ability to hear and see, it would be a great choice, since it would pair nicely with my previous effect to reattach my head almost immediately. The second choice looked good, but it was basically preparing to lose. If I died, the chances were that my entire body would be destroyed alongside it, and a year was a long time to wait!

I'd come so far in a little over a week, so losing a year would put me massively behind every other champion of the gods. The last effect would help me avoid being destroyed and killed in the first place, so I chose it.

Troll Hide (Rank 20, max rank): Your skin remains supple but becomes as tough as leather, increasing its hardness by 6. Whenever you are cut, your flesh regenerates, reducing all afflictions and debuffs effect and duration by 99 percent.
Regeneration speed is tripled while in combat. This effect increases the Stamina cost by 2 per second.
Your body's regeneration also fuels your Stamina, increasing it by 20 Stamina regened per second.
Your limbs will slowly regenerate and restore after being cut off. Holding a severed limb to the stump will reattach it in a few seconds.
You can survive without your vital organs for double the length of time and they will regrow if destroyed or removed from your body.
Final rank bonus: You can expend half your maximum Stamina to heal all injuries in your body, restoring you to perfect health.
This is a passive ability, costing 9 Stamina per second. This ability will turn off when you are out of Stamina.

Would I still be able to get scars with this ability? It hadn't removed previous scars I'd picked up, but would I still scar now? It didn't matter too much but I liked the *badges of honor* from my battles to show the pain I'd taken and that I was a survivor. It was my way of telling anyone I fought that I wasn't worried about getting stabbed, and I'd already had worse.

"What are my current attributes?" I asked the System.

Mordred, Champion of Kelesa. Gifted Humanoid/Human. Mortal. Rank: 165.			
Available rank points: 76.			
Might:	13 (+3) = 16	Mind:	27

Speed:	32 (+18) = 50	Perception:	47
Toughness:	31	Spirit:	46
Endurance:	31	Power:	50
Maximum Stamina:	159	Maximum Mana:	214
Stamina Regen:	34.8 per second	Mana Regen:	45.6 per second

Abilities:

Dominion (Rank 5), Telekinesis (Rank 20), Heightened Speed (Rank 10), Foresight (Rank 20), Compress Earth (Rank 20), Bestial Senses (Rank 20), Phantom Form (Rank 10), Storm Soul (Rank 20), Magma Heart(s) (Rank 20), Troll Hide (Rank 20).

Blessings:

Blessing of War (Mortal).

Titles:

Mark of Cain, Bloody Pugilist, Exorcist, Survivor III, Feral Barbarian, Field Alchemist III, Berserker, Beast Slayer III, War Chief, Venom Resistant III, Keytaro's Guardian III, Wrathful Meditation, Fireproof III, Visitor of Death Superhuman.

Now, I simply needed to unlock an ability for my Might Attribute and I could progress into Veteran rank. I could wait and gather more rank points but that was what everyone else did.

Becoming more and more suspicious of the commonsense strategies of the inhabitants of this world, I intended to do things my way, not theirs.

Hearing running feet, I stood and watched as a goblin riding a raptor rushed toward me. Yanking his mount to a stop, he pointed back toward the camp.

"We're being attacked by a monster, Warlord!" he shouted.

I sprinted back toward camp, my speed going from zero to a hundred instantly, each footfall heavy. I landed on a log and cracked it in half, having become a lot heavier.

My shoulders had broadened significantly too as my body had lately gained what seemed like an extra fifty pounds of mass. Bursting through the trees, my body was flying through the air, a roar of primal rage erupting from my lips as I soared into combat.

Chapter 25: River Fangs

Felrick staggered after being struck by the tail of an adult forest drake.

Jamis, in bear form, tore into the drake's back while Torvin prepared for a charge.

Helen and Mira hung back, one healing while the other supported with ranged attacks.

> **Regaris, the Drake Lord. Gifted Beast/Forest Drake. Mortal. Rank: 102.**

The drake snapped down on Felrick's shield. Its teeth were unable to penetrate the metal but notwithstanding, they clamped resolutely onto the artifact anyway.

Regaris now lifted Felrick off his feet by it, beginning to shake him back and forth.

Felrick's collarbone broke, his shoulder dislocating with a barely audible 'snap' and 'pop'.

Tossing Felrick aside, the drake had someone else in mind, slamming Torvin in the chest.

Torvin was knocked off his summoned mount just before he could finish his charge and before he managed to pierce with his lance. Torvin went flying into a tree, a sickening snap audible to accompany the shattering of dozens of his bones.

An arrow went through the drake's left eye, its head snapping back as it roared in agony and rage. In one swift movement, it threw Jamis from its back and slammed him into the ground. Regaris then turned its attention toward Mira and Helen, taking a charge at them.

Helen disappeared in a shaft of moonlight, soon to rematerialize beside Torvin; she helped him up with a quick healing spell.

Mira moved backwards, continuing to fire at the charging drake.

Regaris did not slow down at all.

"Steps of the wind!" uttered Mira, her feet stepping through the air. She broke into a run, quickly gained height, and set herself down on a thick tree limb.

The drake passed underneath her.

Mira fired an arrow propelled by the force of a hurricane.

It struck the drake at the base of its skull. The monstrous bird staggered, dazed, a massive hole through its neck. Despite the grievous wound, however, Regaris was not yet completely out of the fight.

Jamis landed on its back. His heavy claws dug deeply while his bear jaws bit into the drake's throat, holding it in his mouth like a dog shaking a lifeless bird.

A golden horse charged forward, a lance appearing in its rider's hand as a restored Torvin rejoined the fray, his lance splitting open the drake's chest.

Regaris fell to the ground as the fight left its body, soon to be followed by its life.

---

10 rank points gained, split between surviving party members.

"Any new abilities gained?" Helen asked.

"I didn't get an ability, but I got a title called Mounted Combatant. It increases my Might by 25 percent and my resistance to being dismounted by an attack," Torvin said.

"And I got an ability called Armored Hide," Jamis said. "Gives my skin and hair increased toughness."

"Bones of Iron, I got," Felrick said. "Similar to yours, Jamis but increases the toughness of my bones and ligaments."

"Another few fights like this, and I think we'll be ready to face the Champion of Chaos," Mira said. "Ready to press on toward the capital?"

"Yes," Helen said. "But first, let's find a river or stream to wash this gore off."

The others agreed, and the party set off again.

***

I landed on the back of a massive serpent, the claws slashing into its scales which deflected my blows as I clamped on with my thighs, like straddling a horse.

I held on tightly, repeatedly striking down on the basilisk. My speed was incredible, my strength less so. Only the faintest of superficial scratches had been left on the scales.

Someone else had been more successful since there were javelins and arrows sticking out of the length of the river serpent's body.

Goblins rode past, two to a raptor. The first threw a javelin while a second on the back of the saddle fired a bow. Then, each raptor turned and raced away.

It looked as if I'd suffered few casualties as the goblins harried the serpent from its front and flanks.

Izmaris, The River Prince. Gifted Monster/River Wyrm. Mortal. Rank: 145.

The serpent was very highly ranked for a Mortal monster. It had already taken damage from hundreds of different sources, so I wouldn't get many rank points from this.

However, rank points weren't my main goal.

I was more concerned at this point about keeping it from killing my vassals. The only reason it hadn't been able to get close to the goblins harrying it was Euphrates, who blocked its path. His mane rippled as he kept trying to sink his fangs into the side of the serpent.

I slowly climbed along the serpent's scales, toward its head.

Reaching out with my Telekinesis, I grabbed the javelins and arrows and pushed them downwards, sinking them into the serpent's hide.

The snake reared up like a cobra, nearly flinging me off. It opened its mouth, shrieking loudly enough to shatter eardrums. Fortunately, my body's mutation closed my eardrums to the sound, though I still felt the soundwaves traveling through its scales and into my bones.

It emerged fully from the river, the water rising like a shadow behind.

The serpent wielded an ability unused until now. The tsunami grew larger and larger, climbing one story in height, then two and it was still growing.

"Get inland!" I ordered, hoping someone could hear me.

The goblins and my other vassals started moving inland. Had they had heard my command? Well, they were moving, which was the main thing.

The serpent crashed into the water.

I lost my grip on its scales, plummeting to the ground as the now four-story wave crested above me. "Shit," I winced and prepared for the impact.

The serpent eventually spotted me and lunged down toward my prone form.

As it did so, I rolled to the side, the ground around me darkened by the shadows of the serpent and the gargantuan wave. Just as the wave was about to hit, I turned incorporeal.

Moving through the water in my Phantom Form, uninhibited by the rushing water, I struck out toward Izmaris and slashed at its face with my spectral weapons. I made only a few hits through its rainbow scales before turning physical again. Teleporting above the water as soon as I could, I took a deep breath and dived back toward the river wyrm.

Next, I grabbed onto a javelin, plunging it into its side below the base of its skull, holding on. I clutched one of its horns, pulling myself forward through the water. All around me, I could feel the water rushing back toward the river, dragging everything it could back with it.

A fish slapped into my face as it was sucked back by the current and I had to keep myself from swallowing water. Clenching my teeth, I struggled forward against the immense force of the water, grabbing another spine and pulling forward like climbing a ladder.

Izmaris was swimming forward after my retreating vassals, only noticing me again when I appeared directly above its line of vision. I gripped a club in my right hand, held on with my left, and swung down at the orange and yellow vibrant eye.

A thin, glass eyelid covered it, but it was nowhere near as hard as the serpent's scales and my club punched through. The serpent spasmed and thin, pink blood filled the water.

I continued my assault, feeling my lungs beginning to burn, the water constricting and reaching around me as if hands were pulling at me.

I didn't stop, continuing hacking until the eyelid shattered.

The remnants of the serpent's right eye spattered through the water, a terrible roar creating a tremor in the waves, traveling through it like a shockwave. The force was enough to finally dislodge me, my lungs burning for air. I teleported far above to catch my breath.

Now, the serpent reared up out of the water, her mouth opening wide as she lunged up at me.

I fell toward her open maw, moving into a dive with both clubs again in my hands. I activated Phantom Form just as the jaws snapped around me;

no longer physical, I slashed about with weapons made of Spirit, inflicting Soul Damage on the wyrm.

Izmaris roared again but didn't open her mouth this time.

I became physical again, the world twisting and shaking around me.

Attacking with physical weapons, blood sprayed over me as I cut and hacked into the soft, vulnerable flesh of Izmaris' mouth and throat. A barbed tongue wrapped around me, and my ribs strained against the constricting force. But the barbs couldn't pierce my skin, equalizing our respective abilities to penetrate the other's outer defenses.

Now, I was inside it, no scales able to protect it from my weapon.

I was a tornado of destruction, so much blood lying pooled at my feet.

Soon, the serpent would have to choose between drowning in its own blood or dying by hemorrhage, bleeding out every drop of its vivid red life force.

She opened her mouth, and a stream of water from the back of her throat hit me with the slam of a firehose, blasting me out into open air.

It stung and burned, and I felt what must have been acid eating into my skin, sending me spinning through the air, teleporting to the ground as soon as I was able to tell up from down. I landed awkwardly on my back due to my disorienting airborne journey.

As I rolled to my feet, the serpent was already slithering back toward the river.

"Oh no, you don't!" I growled and raced forward, teleporting as soon as it came off cooldown, appearing yet again directly in front of the river wyrm. My skin was falling off, but my regeneration was already replacing the lost skin dissolved by the acid.

Izmaris snapped her teeth menacingly.

This time, I did not turn incorporeal but grabbed her fangs, stepping down with my foot, straining and feeling something twinge in my back as I struggled against the serpent's titanic strength.

As I stepped forward, the teeth skidded off my pauldrons and skin so I fought to keep my legs straight, prying her jaws open and holding them wide. Lashing out repeatedly with the club in my left hand, I smashed into one of her fangs, finally breaking it off. A black substance that I assumed to be venom dripped from both the tip and stump of the broken fang.

Izmaris shrieked in pain.

I was lodged too firmly in her jaws for the sonic attack to disrupt me. I dropped my club and grabbed the broken fang, slamming it repeatedly into her jaw.

She formed a coil and tried to constrict me, locking me in her jaws. Suddenly, an arrow came flying past me into the serpent's mouth. Javelins fell in a wave, bouncing off scales but occasionally hitting in between them. A few bounced off my skin, eliciting the slightest grunt but still not knocking my focus off the task.

Izmaris' body began spasming.

As for me, I kept on stabbing.

---

1 rank point gained. The remainder will be split between contributing members of the battle.

Blood and Souls (Repeatable): Kill 5,120 monsters or humanoids. Current progress: 4,365/ 5,120. When you complete this quest, you will gain 1024 rank points. The next quest will require double the number to be completed but will award double the rank points.

One measly rank point! Only to be expected, I suppose.

Death throes spasmed through Izmaris' body.

Extricating myself from the still-writhing corpse, I pulled my gore-stained body from the battlefield.

Fish flapped on the ground, stranded by the receding tidal wave.

When they saw me, the goblins cheered and raised high their weapons in loyal salute.

"Warlord!" they chanted. "Warlord!"

Their thunderous applause was encouraging. I took the cleaning cloth from my storage pouch and used it to remove the blood, acid, and dirt that covered me. When I'd cleaned myself, I stood before my vassals. No longer did I have my Nemean cloak, attired now in only a ragged pair of acid-burned pants, boots, gauntlets, helm, and pauldrons. I towered over the goblins although I'd noticed that Juruk had grown significantly. I raised a hand to silence them.

"Bring anyone injured to Kathleen to heal. Do whatever is your custom with the dead and harvest the serpent for materials. Be ready to move by morning, tomorrow," I commanded.

The goblins and a few of the humans gave one last cry of "Warlord!" before going out to perform what I had commanded.

I looked at the sodden ground and raised my hand.

"Compress Earth," I said. Raising and hardening the ground into a flat, dry area the size of a parking lot, I created a mini-island which allowed the water to flow back into the river. I built a stone table and chairs, sat down, and closed my eyes. I drifted in and out of sleep but my eyes suddenly snapped open as I felt someone approaching.

"I'm sorry I couldn't assist you against the serpent," Syvia said.

I waved her off. "Plenty of others contributed to that fight. I only got a single rank point out of it."

Morgaine and Kathleen joined me, taking a seat at the table.

"How was your hunt?" Morgaine asked.

"Fruitful," I answered. "I got an ability to fill in one of my attributes and some rank points, so all in a good day's work. Why did the serpent attack you?"

Kathleen raised an eyebrow. "Why? You have over a hundred low-ranked Gifted now. It's like a feast for any beast wanting to get stronger. Even if we didn't all have abilities, we look like meals on two legs to most creatures in this forest."

"Hmm," I said, considering her words. "It will be night soon. I should prepare defenses for the undead attacks."

"Why are undead attacking in the first place?" Morgaine asked.

I pulled out the jeweled skull and placed it on the stone table. "What do you know about breaking curses?"

"Quite a bit, actually," Morgaine said, picking up the skull and looking it over.

"This is a minor artifact. Breaking its curse will not be easy. To do it, you would need the help of a god or the System itself," Morgaine said.

"So, I do what? Call up Kelesa and ask her to smash this?"

Syvia seemed shocked by my casual reference to her goddess.

Kathleen seemed amused and Morgaine indifferent.

"No, Kelesa wouldn't do that! If she were to destroy this artifact, it would give some other god a free shot, without reprisal, to break an artifact she had created," Morgaine explained.

"Ok, so how do you do it?" I asked.

"Why do you want to?" Kathleen asked.

"The System gave me a quest to do it," I said with a shrug. "As a quest, I have to."

"Then you need to find out why the System wants this destroyed," Morgaine said. "The System is the only entity that can destroy artifacts without reprisal. If it wants this destroyed, it probably has some purpose for it. You need to know what that purpose is."

I heaved a sigh. Really? I now had to do that as well?

"How do I find out what the System wants?" I asked. "Also, what does the System do? I've been thinking about it as if it's some automated service, but you all talk about it as if it's alive."

"Of course, it's alive," Syvia said. "The System is the only true neutral deity. The Gods of Law and Chaos created it, and its power is greater than all of them."

"So, what does it want?" I asked.

"To balance out chaos and law, of course," Morgaine said as if it was utterly obvious. "The System must view the artifact as disrupting the balance. So, it wants you to rectify that."

"Ok, but how? And why can't the System just do it?" I was full of questions.

"Even the System has some limitations," said Kathleen. "It can't spawn monsters in cities, for instance, and it can't destroy artifacts that a creature owns. It is also limited by how much it can affect our world outside of its dungeons."

"Your best bet is to find a dungeon and see if you can somehow interact with the System while there," Morgaine agreed.

"I know of rumors of a dungeon close to the castle of the Bandit King," Syvia said. "Our clan doesn't use it due to its close proximity to him. We wouldn't want an outsider to learn of it and use it to farm for power."

"That statement raises a lot of questions," I said. "First... the Bandit King has a castle?"

"He has the ruins of a castle, to be quite correct about it," Kathleen replied with a roll of her eyes. "Nothing properly fortified, so don't worry about that."

"Fine. Second question: what exactly do you mean by 'farm a dungeon'?" I asked.

"A dungeon respawns monsters and awards magical items for every completion," Syvia explained. "My clan has its own dungeon for our elite warriors. The longer a dungeon goes without being farmed, the more the odds are against the party running the dungeon, and the better rewards the System grants you."

"It also always rewards some rank points for completion," Morgaine said. "But the dangers in a dungeon are not to be underestimated: traps; dungeon beasts as powerful as a high-ranked gifted; and various 'tricks' peculiar to the dungeon."

"All right, could you lead me to this dungeon, Syvia?" I asked. "We are only a few days away from the Bandit King, so we must be close."

"Of course, Warlord," Syvia agreed eagerly. "I don't know its exact location, but I'm sure I can use my senses to sniff it out for you."

"Great. Be ready to lead me there tomorrow morning."

I began compressing walls around the stone platform I had made. Night would soon be falling, so I went and leaned against a wall. Due to my immunity to exposure, I no longer required a comfortable bed upon which to fall asleep.

***

"Ahem." It was accompanied by a cough.

My eyes snapped open: *Juruk.*

I stood up and cracked the bones in my neck, feeling and hearing the satisfying pop. After this, I jumped up, landed on the wall, and looked down at the milling crowd of zombies and skeletons. Raising my hand, I threw down a storm of stone spearheads and bone weapons, smashing through skulls and rib cages in a vast and sudden crescendo of violence.

Orchestrating my weapons telekinetically, I observed the number of undead being halved within minutes. They posed little threat behind our stone walls. When their numbers had been reduced to a quarter, I jumped down among them. Feeling the sweet rage well up, I succumbed to the desire to smash and kill as my clubs carved through the undead.

In a pathetic response, all the zombies could do was to break their teeth against my skin.

Laughing, I spun under the swipe of the zombie bear, my clubs ripping its rotten skull from its neck.

An unearthly shriek split the air as a pale woman of mist rose from the water and flowed toward me. By that point, I had fought more than one incorporeal undead, so it was plain enough what I had to do and it should prove simple enough. Teleporting forward, I transformed myself into an incorporeal state, my efficient weapons tearing into her pale, ethereal spirit.

Again, she shrieked. This time, it was not the terrifying, haunting cry of despair, but one of fear and agony. I became corporeal again and dropped my clubs.

My fists punched into the banshee.

She wailed in pain as I tore her apart with my bare hands, feeling something hot rise within me, a desire to bite and rend with my teeth. My teeth snapping almost with a will of their own, I gave in to the desire and bit into the ethereal flesh, immediately feeling the energy dissipate within the entity. Then, something within me grabbed hold of the energy, dragging it inside me.

With a final tormented cry of pain, a visceral sound, the banshee dissolved completely.

Needless to say that by this time, a sudden feeling of exhaustion overwhelmed me but the task was not yet complete. Staggering slightly, I casually summoned a wave of spearheads and destroyed the remaining two dozen skeletons and zombies.

Then I fell to my knees as notifications popped into my vision.

Blood and Souls (Repeatable): Kill 5,120 monsters or humanoids. Current progress: 4,957/5,120. When you complete this quest, you will gain 1024 rank points. The next quest will require double the number to be completed but will award double the rank points.

I was close to completing this quest again. After that, I'd have to kill the population of a small city to complete the next in the series. Dismissing the following notification, I read the next.

You have completed a hidden objective and earned a title.
Objective: Devour the ethereal energy of an incorporeal creature.

Reward. Title: Soul Eater (unique).

*Soul Eater: The spirit of vengeance inside you has reached out to draw power to fuel itself and can now influence your actions with greater impact.

Hmm, not good. I noted my possession of one other unique title, Visitor of Death, and I wasn't too enthusiastic about that either. *I wonder if you can get rid of titles? Instinct tells me no, not possible. I'll have to think about this later.*

I dismissed the notification, then removed the cleansing cloth and wiped off the rotten flesh and sweat before heading back into the fort for a night's rest.

***

Lady Emaril's arm rested atop Arthur's as they took a walk through the public gardens of
Camelot. On either side of the path were clear water ponds with golden-scaled fish, colorful water lilies and reeds. Flowers grew alongside the ponds, their open blossoms filling the air with a beautiful, natural scent while their colorful pollen dusted the soil.

"What was Viviane like?" Lady Emaril asked as they walked. "And what does her realm look like? Can you describe it to me?"

"She was as beautiful as sunset but imposing as a mountain," Arthur said. "Her realm is a massive lake, sitting inside a ring of mountains. Her gown was like a waterfall when she called me to the lake and anointed me as her champion."

"Were you afraid?"

"A little," Arthur confessed. "She is a goddess, but my family has been worshiping Viviane for centuries, ever since Arthur I. I asked Viviane for a scabbard like the one owned by our namesake back in our ancestor's home world."

"What does it do?" Emaril asked.

"It grants me resistance to mortal and lethal wounds while I wear it. I am also immune to bleeding conditions, and my Toughness goes up with my rank," Arthur explained.

"What happened to your namesake?" Emaril asked. "The stories I've heard differ so much."

"According to the stories Arthur told his children, our namesake had many offspring and died peacefully, passing his kingdom down to his eldest son."

"I've heard other versions where he died in battle," Emaril said. "The man who told me said it was the first version of the story that Arthur I ever told."

"Well, it's not the one he told us," Arthur said. "Besides, how would that man know? The first Arthur died three hundred years ago."

"You're right," Emaril agreed. "Besides, who would be strong enough to kill the great Arthur?"

Chapter 26: Tunnel to the Grave

Mira, Jamis, Felrick, Torvin, and Helen broke out of the Cursed Forest at midday. They had completed another battle against a Gifted beast that morning and were making straight for the capital. Grabbing their horses, they rode through the night, arriving at the palace gates early in the morning. Their horses were exhausted. They all dismounted, and Helen led the way inside.

Servants were bustling to prepare the way for them and in half an hour, the Queen arrived. Her hair was combed back but not done up. She had obviously just woken.

"How was your quest, Helen?" the Queen asked. "You return while it is still night… is everything all right?"

"We have received a quest to slay a Champion of Chaos," Helen said. "There is one in the Cursed Forest. They already have a large force and we have come to gather troops to crush them before they become a threat to our kingdom."

"It will be difficult to raise the army at such short notice," Queen Lunara said, sitting in a high-backed chair with elegant poise despite the ungodly hour.

"Not as difficult as you might think," another woman said, her voice high and clear.

They all turned to face the woman entering the room. She wore bright silver scale armor with a white and blue tunic, a gambeson, and a silver cape. She carried a long rapier at her belt and a long horsehair-plumed helm in her hand which she held at her hip. Her silver-blonde hair was plaited and ran down in a braid, reaching almost to her waist. Pale skin framed piercing blue eyes. Her features were as smooth and beautiful as freshly fallen snow.

"My entourage arrived with me to visit you, your Highness," she said. "Two hundred men in total. All at least in Veteran rank."

"Princess Guinevere," Queen Lunara said. "I thought you weren't supposed to arrive for another five days. Nor have my scouts sent report of you entering our land."

"We took a shortcut through the Cursed Forest," Guinevere said. "I wanted a chance to increase my rank and those of my guards."

Jamis looked at her, his mouth growing dry as he read the notification over her head.

> **Guinevere the Winter Lady. Gifted Veteran. Humanoid/Human*.**
> **Rank: 255.**

"We would indeed be pleased to have such a powerful warrior with us," Jamis said, flashing white teeth at her.

"Ease off, Jamis!" Helen said, rolling her eyes. "She's betrothed to the Crown Prince of Camelot."

"Then he's a lucky man," Jamis said, chastened but still smiling.

Guinevere laughed. "I'm glad. It would please me greatly to help rid the world of one of the Champions of Chaos. As soon as you have gathered as many warriors as you feel necessary, we can set off."

"Are you sure you have the power to authorize this?" Queen Lunara asked, skeptically.

"When it comes to killing the chaos spawn, all our lives are secondary," Guinevere said. "You can send a missive to my father if you feel the need."

"Very well then," Queen Lunara agreed. "I shall call for my lords and gather the royal knights."

***

I stepped into the ring of warriors. All around me, torchlight glinted off metal. A hulk of a warrior rushed toward me.

Our weapons met. I ducked and dodged in a desperate fight to stay alive. Afterwards, I could recall no details of the combat except for terror and rage in the struggle to avoid being cleaved in two. At last, I felt the cold stab through my heart and fell into the darkness.

Again, the cold laughter echoed all around me, an unknown force hungrily reaching out and grabbing onto my spirit. I felt it being dragged down into the blackness.

***

I awoke with a start. The ominous, looming visions of my dreams were still fresh in my mind. The beating of my hearts slowly faded and my mind, at last, convinced itself I wasn't in the void. I sat up slowly, stretching, then ventured into the woods and returned to the sight of everyone packing and lining up to cross the bridge.

Immediately, I made my way to the front to lead the procession. We crossed the river and entered the forest on the other side. Here, Syvia jogged up beside me and began sniffing the air. With a sudden jolt, she darted ahead without a word.

It felt as if we were moving ever closer to the castle of the Bandit King.

Syvia rushed back eagerly, almost barreling into me.

"I found it!" she said, pointing enthusiastically.

"Great," I said. "Show the way."

I easily kept up with Syvia as she ran down animal trails and leaped over logs. After half an hour of running, she came to a stop near a small brook feeding into the main river. Recessed into the cliffside by the brook was a small, unremarkable cave.

As I approached, a cold rush of air emanated from it, bearing a rotten, earthy stench.

"This is it?" I asked, stepping into the cave and activating my Bestial Senses.

The scent of rot and death slapped me in the face, while the noises of animals in the forest outside were like a gun going off next to my head.

"Yes," Syvia confirmed. "The smell is how I found it. The stories I heard said it was an undead dungeon in a cave by a small river, the smell of death flowing out of it."

"Very good, then. Keep watch on the others and scout for them. Make sure no one sneaks up on them."

"You don't want any help clearing the dungeon?" Syvia asked, sounding both disappointed and afraid.

"I told you, Syvia, I'm going to win by my own strength, no one else's."

I could sense Syvia waiting outside for several minutes as I ventured deeper into the cave and squeezed into a side tunnel. Using Compress Earth, I widened the tunnel to enable me to comfortably walk down it, heading deeper into the pitch darkness. My Perception mutation allowed me to see in the blackness, and I traveled underground for what felt like at least two miles. Finally, I emerged onto a platform where steps on either side led to an enormous cavern.

You have discovered a never-completed dungeon: Cavern of Death's Vengeance. This is an unexplored dungeon and you will be given the title Dungeon Finder if you complete it.			
Since you are the first to find it, completion of this Dungeon will give increased rewards.			
Dungeon Rank:	Mortal	Max Party Size:	6

Pillars with interconnected walkways and platforms rose high into the air. Hundreds of skeletons in ragged chain armor with chipped weapons patrolled the ground and platforms.

Focusing on one of the skeletons, the System sent me a notification.

Red Fang Skeleton Warrior. Dungeon Creature. Mortal. Undead/Skeleton. Power Level: 80.

Looking at one of the archers on the platforms above, I got a separate notification.

Red Fang Skeleton Archer. Dungeon Creature. Mortal; Undead/Skeleton. Power Level: 75.

They have a pathetically low power level in relation to my own high rank, but there are hundreds of them! Collectively, they might put up quite a fight.

Teleporting onto one of the platforms, my clubs tore the skull off a skeleton archer. I leaped at another, my foot plunging into its chest and smashing it into the railing, shattering it into dust and bone fragments. My Foresight showed me every attack in advance, but I didn't bother to dodge the arrows as they bounced off my skin without leaving even a mark.

I swept the archers off the platforms before jumping down into the throng of skeletons below, each one thrashing in its eagerness to get to me. A rusty sword shattered on my pauldron and I backhanded it, removing the skull from its owner as I spun using my Speed and Toughness to push me forward. My Stamina was dropping, so with a flip of my storage pouch, I dropped out a hundred spearheads and let them loose. Spinning with my clubs, the spearheads fanned about me like a whirlwind's vortex, shredding the ranks of skeletons.

1,024 rank points gained.

A colossal roar shook the cavern, making me turn and roll as my Foresight warned me of the threat. I became incorporeal just as the mass of bone and shadow passed through where I'd been.

Red Fang Bone Behemoth. Dungeon Creature. Mortal. Undead/Bone Guardian. Power Level: 115.

I teleported forward, landing on the behemoth's back and beginning to tear off layers of its armor with my twin clubs. Black shadow oozed out between the cracks of its armor, like blood. The Bone Behemoth soon bucked and threw me from its back.

I hit the ground in a roll, coming up to meet its charge again and jumping to the side, grabbing onto a spur of bone as the bull-like creature passed.

Swinging onto its back, I pulled my maul out of the storage pouch and slammed it down with my Telekinesis into the cracks made before. A two-foot-wide section of armor opened and I felt a terrible hunger infuse with my rage. Before I could stop myself, I snapped forward, my face biting into the shadow substance.

The behemoth roared.

In a ravenous frenzy, I shook my head like a dog, tearing off sections of its shadow essence and devouring them into my spirit. Another roar rocked the cavern, three more behemoths rushing me as the pile of bones I stood over collapsed.

The energy that had animated it moments earlier now drained into the spirit of vengeance inside me. I answered the Bone Behemoth's roar with an echoing call of my own.

I teleported forward, my emotions wild and rampant as the fury in me told me to *kill, kill, kill!* My maul and spearheads lanced forward, smashing one behemoth to the side as the other impaled me on its horns. My emotional state was too chaotic to focus on my Foresight and predict the attack, so it slammed me into a stone pillar.

I felt and heard the terrible cracking of ribs and bones breaking inside me.

My rage numbed the pain to almost nothing, the twinges of the pain only serving to fuel my ire. I turned incorporeal and phased through the undead, my spirit form lashing out at its insides, and I bit chunks out of its essence as I passed through while the behemoth roared in agony.

I appeared on the other side, only to be struck by the third behemoth and sent crashing into another pillar. My regeneration slowly pulled my bones back into place as I stood up. Then, I teleported above the first behemoth as it tried to gore me with its horns. Landing on its back, I ripped through its armor, then dipped my head into its body cavity and tore into the shadow essence, gulping it back in a mad, desperate need to consume.

Heedless of their ally, the other two behemoths slammed into its side, cracking the bone armor plating and flipping it like a car on the freeway.

Dropping to the ground, I howled in pain, rage, and frustration at the meal being stolen from me. My veins were throbbing under my skin, glowing red like coals as my Magma Hearts fed off the pain and misery. Rushing forward, I grabbed the behemoth by its bull horns and flipped it upwards to land on its back. Then I summoned my club to my hand with Telekinesis, beginning to rhythmically bash into its skull.

The other behemoth charged at me and my mount but my maul came in from the side, hitting it square in the head and sending it reeling. I had broken a hole through the skull of the behemoth I was riding and pressed my mouth to it, inhaling the shadow ichor as my spirit drained it in mad desperate gulps. Beneath me, the behemoth roared and bucked, but my legs were wrapped around its neck and wouldn't be dislodged.

It stumbled, finally collapsing into a pile of empty bones from which I drained its shadow completely. Phantom Form ended and I teleported away, waited for a moment and then reactivated it. Rushing back into the fight, my brain was a mess and my legs unsteady, sending me stumbling as if drunk toward the last remaining behemoth.

It staggered to its feet, cracks spiderwebbing across its skull from the impact of the maul. It roared defiantly and charged at me, but lacking the force it had held before.

Now, I was able to grab onto its horns and twist its head, biting down into a weakened section of its neck and spitting away bone fragments. The behemoth was now of undead essence, so I threw back my head and released a roar of transcendent triumph.

> **Blood and Souls (Repeatable): Kill 10,240 monsters or humanoids. Current progress: 149/10,240. When you complete this quest, you will gain 2,048 rank points. The next quest will require double the number to be completed but will award double the rank points.**

Starting to come down from my battle high, I dismissed the quest update.

> **You have completed a hidden objective and earned a title. Objective: Devour the ethereal energy of an incorporeal creature.**
>
> **Reward. Title: Soul Eater II (Unique).**
>
> ***Soul Eater II: The spirit of vengeance inside you has reached out to draw power to fuel itself and can now influence your actions and emotions with greater impact.**

The notification sobered me up from the rush of adrenaline and euphoria. I didn't like this title or the fact it had advanced.

"This can't be good," I said, reading it over, not even having thought of the title during the fight, having been so utterly consumed with bloodlust and the need to feed.

I sighed and rose to my feet, activating Bestial Senses but unable to hear anything, so I pressed forward. Exploring the giant cavern, my gaze cast down several passages, but they were all dead ends. Finally, another tunnel was leading me to a set of stairs which appeared to entice me further down. And so began the descent into the next section.

At a large doorway, its arch engraved in a seemingly illegible script, I pushed open the stone doors carved with reliefs of a great battle and stepped into what looked like a cross between a crypt and a throne room. Ghostly torches cast spectral blue light over the area.

A wizened, skeletal figure sat on a throne on a dais two hundred feet from me.

I was met by another prompt.

> **You have entered the boss room of the Dungeon. Your party cannot leave until one of you is dead. The rank of the boss will equal the highest rank of party members or the maximum rank for a Mortal. You will not all receive equal portions or rank points upon**

> **completion; instead, points will be awarded based on contributions. Points will also be deducted to pay for loot drops.**

Looking back, I saw a blue barrier had popped into place, blocking any retreat. I turned to look at the figure on the throne.

The boss stood up.

> **Tadris, King of the Barrow Wights. Gifted. Dungeon Boss/Undead. Mortal. Rank: 120.**

He held a long sickle in one hand and a tattered book in the other.

I charged forward.

Tadris opened the book, muttering some incomprehensible gibberish. All at once, glowing white, flaming skulls appeared from the tome in his head and flew toward me.

I dodged to the side and a skull exploded, the force tossing me against the wall. I rolled to my feet and cracked my knuckles, a feral grin forming.

"Right then! Let's see what you're made of," I said with a mad laugh.

***

Lancelot surged forward and the Troll King's sword skidded off his breastplate.

The Troll King stood fifteen feet tall and had dark, steel, armored spikes jutting out like tusks all around its edges.

Kay jumped forward, a burst of wind sending him straight up like a bottle rocket. His sword ripped through the Troll King's helmet as he let out a battle cry.

"Armor Rend!" Kay shouted, activating an ability.

The Troll King staggered backwards, clutching at his face and deflecting a follow-up attack from Lancelot and Kay with his mace.

Arthur fell from the ceiling, Excalibur raised high above his head.

"Bypassing Strike!" Arthur shouted, bringing Excalibur down on the gorget protecting the Troll King's neck.

Excalibur sheared right through the heavy steel armor like wire through cheese. It passed through the thick muscles of the neck and spine. The huge troll head dropped to the floor.

"Anyone get any abilities from that fight?" Arthur asked.

"Just rank points," Lancelot said.

"Same here," Kay seconded.

"Me too," Arthur said. "Better luck next time."

"We should go out hunting," Kay said. "Fight some real monsters out there, get some fresh experience, and hopefully, a few more exotic abilities."

"I'd love to, but I need to stay in Camelot and prepare for the Dragon Tourney for when Guinevere gets back," Arthur said.

"I'm not talking about a long hunting trip... Someplace close... Maybe we could meet up with Guinevere in the Cursed Forest and fight some beasts there," Kay argued.

"What do you mean meet Guinevere in the Cursed Forest?" Arthur asked, his head whipping around to look at Kay.

"You didn't hear?" Kay asked, surprised. "She decided to take a shortcut to Lunara and went through the Cursed Forest."

"And she was allowed to?" Arthur asked, his breath coming heavier.

"Calm down, Arthur," Lancelot said. "You know Guinevere. It's not as if anyone could have stopped her! Plus, she's Veteran rank. She'll be fine."

"She's deliberately putting herself at risk," Arthur snarled. "Why wasn't my father or I informed about this earlier?"

"I assumed you knew," Kay said, shrugging. "But even if you had known it, what could you have done? Guinevere is the responsibility of her father, not of you."

"I am her betrothed," Arthur said. "Our marriage is of vital importance to Camelot's wellbeing; she should never have put it at risk."

"I worry how you two will get along when you are married," Lancelot said, shaking his head.

"I love Guinevere," Arthur said. "Which is why it's my duty to protect her, even if it is from herself. What if she runs into one of the Chaos Champions?"

"Come on, Arthur!" said Kay, exasperated. "Now, you're just being paranoid! What are the odds of that? The only way she's going to run into one of the Chaos Spawn is if she deliberately heads toward one."

"The way she's been acting lately," Arthur muttered, "she just might do that."

Chapter 27: A Final Resting Place

Guinevere stood and surveyed the camp, her long silver-blonde hair braided down her back. Nearly a thousand warriors had been summoned from across the kingdom. She and her retinue stood apart from the main force; yes, they were allies in this fight but not subordinate to the Lunarens. Helen approached and the two noble ladies curtsied to each other.

"I haven't seen you in several years, Princess Guinevere," Helen said.

"It's just Lady Guinevere, Princess Helen," Guinevere said, stepping forward and hugging her distant cousin.

"You and Arthur have yet to marry?" Helen asked.

"As soon as I get back from this quest..." Guinevere responded with a sigh.

"That's great news!" Helen exclaimed. "Why do you seem so uncertain?"

"I don't know," Guinevere sighed. "It's just that Arthur is the same man he's been for years, dedicated to three things: practicing with his sword; hunting; and flirting with the ladies of court. Even though we're betrothed, he still entertains every court girl. He goes on long walks with them and is always buying them various gifts."

"He's just a natural flirt," Helen said. "You know he'd never betray your trust in him."

"You're right, cousin." Guinevere sighed and took her cousin's arm. They walked together among the tents. "I don't know. Ever since he became a champion, he's been more distant with me. We haven't been spending as much time with each other as before."

"Spending time together?" Helen asked playfully, bumping her hip into Guinevere's. "Have you been playing with the royal treasury, Guin?"

Guinevere laughed and blushed. "You've been spending too much time with your friends, Helen! No, we haven't been 'playing with the royal treasury' as you put it; we're waiting until marriage."

"Then you definitely need to get married sooner," Helen said. "There is no way I'd wait that long, especially not with a piece of meat like Arthur dangled in front of me."

"Helen!" Guinevere gasped.

"What?" Helen laughed. "You're the luckiest woman I know, marrying Arthur Pendragon: handsome, strong, a great warrior, poet and heir to the throne of Camelot."

"We'll see after we take care of this chaos spawn," Guinevere said. "Thanks for the talk, Helen. I needed it."

"Anytime, cousin," Helen smiled.

"What about you?" Guinevere asked. "I know you're not engaged but are you seeing any young men I should know about? Maybe one of your companions?"

"Of course not," Helen said. Her cheeks flushed.

"I sense a weak spot!" Guinevere said with a grin. "Is it your bodyguard, the knight, or that bear of a man? You did always like your suitors hairy."

"Certainly not!" Helen protested. "And Jamis sees far too many women to be tied down."

"Maybe he just needs the right woman," Guinevere said as they arrived at her tent. "I'll see you tomorrow, cousin. Let's get some rest for the hunt."

***

The impact from being tossed against the wall cracked another rib. Whilst my skin gave me immense protection, it didn't do much against the force of raw collision as I slammed into the wall and floor. I teleported forward and appeared next to the Barrow King, simultaneously activating my Juggernaut helmet. My size doubled and my physical stats increased by 30. I grabbed Tadris and slammed him into the floor, cracking the stone beneath him.

I grabbed my enlarged club, now the size of my maul, and pounded him into the ground.

Tadris turned to mist as I brought the hammer down where his skull had been.

He blinked away and a stabbing pain assaulted the back of my knee, making me whirl to see Tadris with his sickle, its edge now coated in blood.

"Turnabout is fair play," I hissed.

I felt weakness in my body, shocked by the realization I must have been poisoned or afflicted with some kind of curse.

On raised my hand, stone spearheads shot out, encircling Tadris from all directions.

He launched another wave of exploding skulls at me.

This time, my spearheads intercepted them, and they exploded before they got too close, knocking Tadris back in the process. *Friendly fire!*

Tadris' bellowing roar rattled my teeth.

Thirty skeletons dropped from the ceiling. They wore leather armor and lunged at me with long spears. One struck me and I felt it pierce my skin; although it only penetrated half an inch, the fact they could pierce my skin at all was alarming.

I caught one of the spears with my club, smashing the shaft to splinters; then, I lunged forward, crushing the skull of its handler. My Foresight warned me as I dropped to the ground, six spears plunging into the spot I had just occupied, another plunging into my back. I rolled over, snapped its shaft, and pulling its wielder close, ripped off his skull with my gauntleted hands. My larger frame, whilst an advantage physically, also made me a bigger target.

I took evasive action and rolled under the spear shafts which sprang up like sharks lunging out of the water. Three skeletons were soon under my bulk, their bones turning to powder.

I rolled again, a phantom spear quivering in the ground beside my head before turning to smoke.

Tadris raised his tome again, chanting some new spell.

I lifted my hands, and the remaining skeletons rose into the air as I crushed their bones with my Telekinesis. Their deaths fueled my Magma Heart, and my Stamina skyrocketed. I grabbed one of their spears and threw it.

It impaled Tadris against the wall and he writhed on the wooden shaft.

His spell interrupted, Tadris again transformed into mist.

I dodged to the side as he tried to backstab me. My warhammer was already swinging back and caught him across his skull.

Tadris stumbled backwards but did not fall.

A word I could not understand fell from his mouth.

I began to shrink to normal size. Knowing I would be too weak to take him on in this state, I activated the speed boost on my boots, charging forward while still shrinking.

Turning incorporeal, I began slashing. A maelstrom of blows with my now-ethereal clubs ripped into the Barrow King's soul, shredding it like wet paper.

It lasted only a few seconds before I sagged and fell, my body drained of energy, hit by the backlash of the Juggernaut Helm.

I slumped to the floor, breathing heavily, Tadris lying crumpled before me.

Job done.

Congratulations! You have cleared the Dungeon 'Cavern of Death's Vengeance' solo. Due to this feat, you have received a bonus to your rewards and gained a new title.

Title, The Commando: You deal a minor amount of extra damage when you are fighting by yourself.

Now, this is useful!

Ring of Stoneskin. Type: Jewelry. Rarity: Rare. For the cost of 40 Mana, you can infuse your skin with granite-like qualities. For the next 3 minutes, you will take half damage from physical attacks, and your skin's hardness is increased by 6.

Can only be used once per hour.

Weight:	<1 lb	Durability:	25/25

A perfect addition to my magical items. This would pair excellently with my pauldrons and Troll Hide, not just increasing my skin's hardness but also halving any physical damage I take.

Divine Focusing Crystal. Type: Magical Stone. Rarity: Epic. Hardness 10. A shard of a once grand piece of glass that belonged to one of the godly realms but is now useless on its own. This crystal can be used in item creation to help focus raw energy or Mana into different effects.

It was pretty, appearing like a broken prism and the blue light from the torches danced inside it. I placed it in my storage pouch and dismissed it for now.

Bonus Reward: Tadris' Tome of Grave Spells (Epic Tome). A tome that can be absorbed to learn the old magic known by Tadris, King of the Barrow Wights. This is a one-time item that will be consumed on use. This item can only be used by you.

Typical of the System! A tome to learn Old Magic spells that first requires prior knowledge of how to use the Old Magic before I can even use it! Putting the tome in my storage pouch for now, I read the last notification.

25 rank points gained.

Not amazing, considering I had just attained over a thousand rank points for completing my quest, but every bit helped.

I looked around the throne room/crypt for what was here. The System's hint led me to believe there was some way of breaking the curse, or at least find a way to continue somewhere here. I walked up to the throne, but it didn't seem that special. Looking around at the outside of the room, there seemed to be only alcoves with desiccated corpses interned within.

Since this was a dungeon created by the System, I wasn't even sure if the corpses had been real people or just 'decorations' fabricated to mimic the appearance of bodies. Turning to leave and search the rest of the dungeon, I looked at the doorway out of the throne room. The blue light barrier was gone, but my eye caught something not previously noticed. Small shelves were cut into the stones around the doorway, skulls resting in each one.

A small candle of blue light illuminated the sockets and gaps in the teeth.

I had an idea. With no expectations that it would work, I jumped up, catching the lip of the archway with my right hand. Using my left hand, I reached into my storage pouch and pulled out Gravecaller. I tossed out an old skull from its alcove and set the new one in its place.

Nothing happened. I sighed, jumped back up and reached for the skull.

The dungeon has accepted your gift and bestowed upon you a blessing as thanks.

Blessing of Tadris: You have offered tribute to a fallen champion, and as thanks, his spirit will allow you or any creature you designate to enter the dungeon without being attacked. If you or an ally attack any creature while in the dungeon, this effect will be removed until you leave the dungeon.

I pulled back my hand, looking over the notification. This was only the second blessing I had ever received. It was not a title, and it was strange it did not provide any mechanical benefits to me, but nevertheless, it was still interesting.

I've given the skull to the dungeon. Does that not mean the quest is complete?

As if in response to my thoughts, another notification popped into my vision.

Quest completed. Death's Curse: You have found a way to restore balance, not by removing the curse or destroying the artifact but by giving it to an undead dungeon. The curse will now fuel the dungeon, turning it from a dungeon suitable for Mortal-ranked Gifted into a challenge for Veteran-ranked creatures.
Reward: Knowledge of the Old Magic.

There it was… the notification I had been looking for and the reason I had come here. Thoughts alien to me entered my mind and found places to settle in my memories.

Looking at the runes along the doorway, I could now understand them.

'This is the resting place of Tadris, Champion of Kelesa who fell on the plains above and was buried here by his followers.'

Interesting. If this was to be believed, Tadris hadn't always been a Dungeon Boss but had once been a Champion of Kelesa, like me. How would he have ended up as a Dungeon Boss?

Was it something he wanted? Or was he cursed to remain here for failing to win the game? Could he even remember his old life?

I doubted I'd ever find out.

Pulling out the tome acquired as loot, I opened it up, perusing it. I wasn't sure how to use it but based on everything else encountered with the System, I just thought, absorb tome.

I fell to the ground as something slammed into my head, raw knowledge being shoved into my skull. I groaned as if I had just put six ranks into Mind at once.

After three minutes of agony, I sat up, not possessing a new list of abilities, but at least able to recall ancient words. I muttered a short incantation, a spectral spear appearing clutched in my hand. When I threw it, it struck the wall, then after a few seconds, disappeared.

Going through my new spells, it was apparent that each would cost Mana but not how much. I had Tadris' ability to cast exploding skulls and could raise corpses as minions. I was now also able to perform a spell to resurrect to full life a creature fallen in battle. That last spell didn't seem very on-theme with Tadris, but it was useful.

The only drawback was the required components for the spell, some type of flower called a Grave Lily and a pure black diamond the size of a robin's egg.

With nothing else to do, I left the boss chamber for the cavern above, in which the remains of the creatures I'd fought still littered the ground. Levitating all the skeletons' weapons toward me, I dumped them in my storage pouch; they were all crude and rusty, but the metal would be useful to use with Compress Earth. I stepped from the dungeon, greeted by another notification.

Time until dungeon resets: 2 days, 23 hours and 59 seconds.

I found my army camped half a mile inland. There was no need to create any fortifications since the curse had been handled, so I rested my back against a tree and went to sleep.

***

Arthur sat beside his father at the round table.

Almost sixty feet in circumference, it was massive. Carved into the wood of its surface was a map of Camelot and the surrounding lands and kingdoms.

"These raids on the northern border are a clear and present danger to us all," Lord Gareth said, pointing to the pewter figure of a myrmidon on the edge of the northern border between Camelot and Dracon. "They have been increasing their raids over the past few months and lately, they seem to have become more daring."

"Could it be the result of the guidance of a Chaos Champion?" asked Baron Sordren.

"Unlikely. The timing of these escalations and the start of the gods' game doesn't quite correlate," said Archduke Merlin.

"We need a clear response to these attacks," Lancelot said. "These raiders are coming over from Dracon, then easily retreating behind its borders. If Dracon will not secure its own border, then we must."

"Agreed," King Arthur said, speaking for the first time. "Both Lunara and Camelot have been favored by the gods with champions chosen from among both royal families and those of the nobility. But Draconians, despite their pride and arrogance do not have a single Champion of the Gods among them. We can only conclude there is some reason for this. The kingdom of Dracon has turned from the path of law. It is well known how they treat their people, and for generations, we have been unable to do anything about it. Until now. I am interpreting the attacks by these raiders and Dracon's refusal to do anything about it as a declaration of war."

"This is a massive escalation," Merlin said, looking at his brother, eyes narrowed. "One might think you had been merely looking for an excuse to invade."

"People may think what they will," King Arthur responded, dismissing the veiled accusation. "My son has been made a champion and he will lead our army and kingdom to a new and glorious age."

"As you command, my King," Arthur said as he bowed to his father.

Chapter 28: The Bandit King's Lair

Helen and Guinevere rode at the head of the procession of armored, mounted warriors as they headed for the Cursed Forest. Three more champions joined them: Felecia, Champion of Seshera, Goddess of Fertility & Abundance; Chritor, Champion of Sabre, God of Swordsmiths and Blades, and Ishtor, Champion of Heshribia, Goddess of Growth & Expansion.

Felecia was a dusk fey; her ears were pointed, and her pale skin turned to a light blue at the tip. Her hair was charcoal gray, her eyes a gray-blue.

Chritor was a djinn with metallic bronzelike skin and four arms, constantly stained with soot from his forge. As if he felt the need to further prove his identity, he carried a magnificent hammer and sword at his waist. His eyes were coal black too, his frame large and muscular, and his head either naturally bald or shaved.

Ishtor was a masia, looking similar to a human but with eyes three times as big. His skin had a glossy, wet appearance, and pale, barely perceptible scales covered his body. His hair was dark green, and his eyes were yellow with a large pupil, making him look perpetually surprised.

Behind Helen and Guinevere rode Jamis, Felrick, Mira, Torvin, and the three newest champions. They talked amongst themselves, getting to know each other and what they could do.

"Which champion do you think it is?" Helen asked Guinevere and the others.

"There are only fourteen options," Felrick said. "Fewer, if any have already been slain."

"I have heard of no such report from any other kingdom," Guinevere said.

"Then it could be any of the fourteen," Ishtor said.

"It isn't as random as you think," Guinevere answered. "The Cursed Forest is unsuitable for many chaos spawns, so we can rule them out. The Pantheon of Deception, for instance, places most of their champions near cities where they can work on their quests since their powers are based on interacting with or killing other humanoids, something not well suited to the forest."

"If we rule them out, that only leaves seven champions to choose from," Felrick said.

"Are any unlikely to make their residence in the forest?" Chritor asked.

"Kashtu, God of Plague and Illness," Helen said. "No point unleashing diseases on wild animals when you could do it to a city or town full of people. The same goes for Helria, Goddess of Famine and Starvation, so we can probably rule her out."

"The other five seem as if they could make their residence in the Cursed Forest," Felrick said. "I didn't encounter any of the chaos spawn in the trial. Did anyone else?"

"I did," Felecia said.

"Which one was it?" Jamis asked.

"The Warlord. His name is Mordred," Felecia said.

"That name seems familiar," said Guinevere, cocking her head. "How hard was he to kill?"

Felecia hung her head. "We didn't kill him. He was unbelievably fast, and I couldn't even hit him. He killed my companion and me. We tried to use a mini-boss to distract him, but he was just too powerful and overwhelmed us. I couldn't even tell his rank. He was too high above us."

"I think I heard about him from another champion," Ishtor said. "He killed around forty other champions singlehandedly outside one of the safe zones."

"Figures. He must have set an ambush and taken them out," Torvin said, shaking his head in disgust.

Ishtor also shook his head. "If the story is to be believed, he taunted them to come out and killed them all at once, one against forty."

"That has to be exaggerated," Mira said.

Ishtor shrugged. "I'm only telling you what I heard."

"What do you think the chances are that this is the same chaos spawn?" Helen asked.

"One in fourteen," Chritor said dryly.

"Or one in five if our process of elimination is to be trusted," Jamis added.

"I'd say plan for the worst," Guinevere said. "If it is the Warlord, be prepared for the battle of your lives. The Warlord is a master tactician, and his abilities will let him move his army like pieces on a board. His every move will be calculated as if a room of generals were at his side."

***

"You can't just march up and kick in their door," Morgaine protested.

"Why not?" I asked irritably. I had just had the same dream as the past three nights, and it was getting on my nerves.

"Because it's suicide," Kathleen said.

"I think it's a great idea," Syvia said. "You can definitely take them all."

I looked at her sidelong, but couldn't detect any sarcasm in her voice. "Thanks."

"You're not helping," Kathleen said, pointing a finger at Syvia.

"Wasn't trying to," Syvia said, sticking her tongue out.

"Girls, enough!" Morgaine snapped. "My Lord, we are in these woods because you dragged us here. We rely on you for our safety, so trust me when I say that your plan of simply going up to their front door and challenging the Bandit King is suicide."

"And what do you suggest?" I asked.

"I suggest killing him in his sleep." Morgaine sighed. "But I know you won't pick that option."

"Where is the fun in that?" I asked with a shrug.

"Then, I suggest you sneak in under cover of night and find a way to force him into accepting your duel," Morgaine said.

"Fine," I agreed reluctantly.

Her plan made sense, but my dreams of late had put me on edge. I could feel the existential dread of them looming over me like the Sword of Damocles.

"Syvia, guide me to the bandit's hideout. I'll find a spot to watch while we wait for nightfall,"

The following day, Syvia led me for half a day upstream. The land rose, and we broke through the tree-line to behold the castle ruins. It sat on the edge of a two-hundred-foot cliff, looming over the river. Ladders, scaffolding, and stairs ran down the cliff to wooden docks where longships sat in the water. Around the castle's ruins, wooden buildings had been constructed, along with a crude, wooden palisade to keep out attackers or the local wildlife.

I sat on the limb of a thick oak, watching. Smoke drifted up from the houses, and what had to be several hundred people milled around doing various tasks. I had activated Bestial Senses and could hear conversations about the weather, how many merchants were coming down the river, and who was bedding who. The last bit got a bit awkward, and I quickly shut off the ability, wincing from everything I'd just overheard.

I took off my gauntlets, which had been looking a little worse for wear, and examined them.

Gauntlet of the Soldier (Left hand). Type: Armor. Rarity: Uncommon. Increases damage with one-handed weapons by a minor amount. When paired with another gauntlet of the same type on the opposite hand, it will increase damage with two-handed weapons by a moderate amount.	
Made from common steel and empowered by a novice enchanter.	
Durability:	1/10.

Gauntlet of the Soldier (Right hand). Type: Armor. Rarity: Uncommon. Increases damage with one-handed weapons by a minor amount. When paired with another gauntlet of the same type on the opposite hand, it will increase damage with two-handed weapons by a moderate amount.	
Made from common steel and empowered by a novice enchanter.	
Durability:	2/10.

I was surprised by how much their durability had decreased. While they looked a little battered, I hadn't expected them to be that bad. I turned them over again, considering what to do, thinking it might be possible to use Compress Earth to fix them.

At Rank 20, it had gained the ability to affect enchanted stone and metal. I pulled up the description of the ability to view it again.

Compress Earth (Rank 20, max rank): You can fuse dirt and stone into a more durable, heavier material that can be shaped. You can currently fuse a 524,288-square-foot section of earth, common stone, and metal. Your compressed stone has a hardness rating of 14; your compressed earth has a hardness rating of 12. The detail with which you can sculpt is based on your Mind & Perception Attribute..
You can now use uncommon stone in your fusions. The rarer, denser, or more exotic the stone, the more it will affect the final product.

> **You can now use non-magical metals in your fusions. The rarer, denser, or more exotic the metal, the more it will affect the final product.**
>
> **You can now use rare and magical stone in your fusions. The rarer, denser, or more powerful the stone, the more it will affect the final product.**
>
> **You can now use rare and magical metal in your fusions, the rarer, denser, or more powerful the metal, the more it will affect the final product.**
>
> **Final rank bonus: You can now affect magical and enchanted objects made of stone or metal. Cost: 1 Mana per square foot**
>
> **Upgrade this ability to increase the amount you can compress, its durability, weight, and the materials on which you can use it.**
>
> **Each upgrade increases your Mind Attribute by 1.**

I was not sure if or how it would affect the enchantments. I had two gauntlets, so decided to experiment with the left. It only had one durability point remaining.

If I messed it up, I could just leave the right one alone.

I took out an orb of uncommon metal/stone which I had picked up from the magma elementals back in the Event. I closed my eyes, feeling the metal as I merged them with my compression, noticing trace lines of rare stone already mixing with the steel. Opening my eyes, I looked where I had felt the rare stone, still able to feel it in the rune markings and sigils.

Was this part of how an enchanted item was made?

I was excited, considering this a significant breakthrough. As I looked at the runes, I could understand what they said and represented, realizing This was Old Magic.

Enchanted items were something that had not been created, or at least invented by the System. I had assumed the System granted some sort of ability that would allow a person to enchant an item. Now, however, I could instinctively tell that it was more like being a blacksmith.

Anyone, Gifted or not, could learn to do it.

I returned to my task, fastidiously skirting around the rare stone, being careful not to affect the scarce gemstone. I spread the uncommon metal/stone through all the gauntlet pieces, also taking the utmost care not to fuse together the articulated sections.

I used only half the orb on it, but even that added two pounds to the gauntlet.

Examining the gauntlet, it had gone from bright steel to a storm-cloud gray.

Gauntlet of the Soldier (Left hand). Type: Armor. Rarity: Uncommon. Increases damage with one-handed weapons by a minor amount. When paired with another gauntlet of the same type on the opposite hand, it will increase damage with two-handed weapons by a moderate amount. Hardness: 14.	
Made from a compressed metal alloy and empowered by a novice enchanter.	
Durability:	25/30.

The effects of the enchantment hadn't been changed at all, but the item now listed its hardness, and its current and maximum durability had also jumped up.

It didn't seem as if I'd fixed it, but I had bumped it up way past what I had found. With its new hardness, it was doubtful it would go down much in durability again.

Picking up the right-handed gauntlet, I closed my eyes and began the process again. I finished and looked at the almost black gauntlet. The dings, dents, and scratches in it were gone, and it was as smooth and glossy as a pool of oil.

Gauntlet of the Soldier (Right hand). Type: Armor. Rarity: Uncommon. Hardness: 14. Increases damage with one-handed weapons by a minor amount. When paired with another gauntlet of the same type on the opposite hand, it will increase damage with two-handed weapons by a moderate amount.	
Made from a compressed metal alloy and empowered by a novice enchanter.	
Durability:	26/30

The sun was beginning to set, but it was still light, so I sat back and waited again. The sun crept down below the tree-line, and the world was plunged into twilight, then total darkness. The castle was still lit by torches, making it stand out at night.

The sight of it triggered memories of the visions in my sleep, an ominous, looming dread filling me. Shaking off the fear, I jumped down from my perch and stealthily crept through the tall grass and bushes. Finally within 120 feet of the wall, I teleported to its base and looked through a crack in the stonework. Finding a suitable spot and doing the same again, I was inside.

Darting into a building, I looked around; women slept on cots along the wall and some cloaks hung on hooks beside the door. I grabbed one, threw it on, tossed up the hood, and then exited the building, moving carefully toward the castle, using dark paths and back alleys.

Men in armor sat around bonfires, women bringing them food and drink. Raucous laughter echoed about the place.

To my left, a man stumbled out of a hut and I stepped back, my Foresight preventing the oaf from barreling into me. He looked up drunkenly and squinted into my face.

My Foresight also showed me various things that could happen next, none of which I wanted to deal with. So, stepping forward, I plunged a knife upward, right under his chin before proceeding to drag him around the corner of the building and drop him in the shadows.

I kept moving, leaving the body and scene of the crime behind as I continued toward my goal of reaching the castle. The alleyways and back passages came to an end, forcing me to move onto the main street. I made my way quickly through the torchlight toward the double doors of the castle. There, two men stood guard, wearing plate and chain armor.

Crossing their spears, they blocked my path.

"I don't recognize you, stranger," said the one on the right. "Who are you, and when did you arrive?"

"Dominion," I said, using my ability to enslave rather than answer them.

White brands of chains appeared on their necks and wrists. They cried out, dropped their weapons and reached for the marks on their flesh. Their loose spears clattered noisily.

People turned toward us but did not attempt to come closer.

Whip and Chains (Repeatable): Conquer 320 monsters or humanoids by bringing them under your Dominion. Current

> **progress: 16/320. When you complete this quest, you will gain 64 rank points. The next quest will require double the number to be completed but will award double the rank points.**

"Let me pass, then go back to your duties and continue as if nothing has happened... and tell no one of me," I ordered the hapless guards.

The two men immediately picked up their spears, opened the doors and closed them behind me.

I entered into an enormous feast hall.

Men sat around long tables with wooden plates in front of them as women served them food and refilled their tankards and drinking horns with ale and mead. No one noticed me in the commotion, and I slipped into the shadows in the corner of the room.

I surveyed the room carefully, observing the many lanterns hanging about the hall, giving light but casting dark shadows everywhere, hiding the grit and disrepair of the castle.

The hall was at least 115 feet in length, and the stonework of the ceiling stone curved up like the inside of a barrel. At the far end of the hall on a raised, stone stage sat a table positioned at a ninety-degree angle to the others. There, large men, each at least seven or eight feet tall, sat at the table being served by equally tall but beautiful women. In the center of the table on a heavy throne laden with furs sat a man wearing thick, heavy armor.

He had ash-white hair and eyes as dark as soot.

> **Lord Kaleb Dragonbreaker. Gifted Veteran. Humanoid/Human. Rank: ???**

Lord Kaleb Dragonbreaker looked as powerful as everyone had described. Fear was trying to grip me, but I kept it at bay, looking instead looked at the others, analyzing them in turn.

The man to Kaleb's right had dark brown hair and a short beard.

> **Jeriah Dragonbreaker. Gifted Veteran. Humanoid/Human. Rank: ???**

His son, judging by the look of him. I looked at the man on Kaleb's left, one with fine blond hair, a short beard, and piercing blue eyes. He too resembled Kaleb.

Tobias Dragonbreaker. Gifted Veteran. Humanoid/Human. Rank: ???

Also his son. I looked over the seven others at the table; they were all his sons. None was Mortal-ranked, and they all wore similar heavy armor to their father.

My eyes were absentmindedly drawn to one of the serving girls.

Lillia Dragonbreaker: Gifted Mortal. Humanoid/Half-elf. Rank: 8

It looked as if Kaleb's daughters served their father and brothers personally. The other girls were all Gifted, but it didn't look as if any resources had been put into ranking up the other girls. I scanned over the rest of the feast hall but did not see a single other Gifted.

Apparently, Dragonbreaker and his sons were all the bandits needed.

I made my plan and stepped forward, letting my spearheads fall out of my storage pouch and clatter to the ground. A crowd turned their heads at the commotion, but they flew out before anyone could move a muscle.

Spearheads hovered before everyone in the hall, pressed to their throats.

Dragonbreaker and his sons had caught the ones sent their way, surprising me with their speed. Kaleb altered the course of the spearhead, his strength ripping it out of my control as he stood up.

He scanned the hall and locked eyes with me as I strode forward, standing in the center of the hall. "Well, Mordred, you have my attention," said Dragonbreaker, rising to his feet.

Chapter 29: Death Foreseen

"I've come to fight you," I informed Dragonbreaker.

Kaleb laughed and his sons chuckled in unison. "You're not even Veteran rank, boy!" Kaleb said after his fit of mirth had subsided. "You want to fight me?"

I shrugged. "Why not?"

"Because you'll die if you do," he said with a vicious grin. "A good reason, no?"

I gave another shrug. "We'll see... Do you accept?"

"Why shouldn't I and my sons just kill you now?" he asked. "Tell me one reason."

"Because every one of your men will die if you do. I offer you this, Lord Dragonbreaker. Face me alone in single combat. If I die in our fight, all your men will be freed, and my vassals will belong to you. They reside in a cave along the bank of a river nearby. If I win, all your sons will swear their allegiance to me. Clearly, you have nothing to fear as you know I will lose."

There was a long moment of silence before Dragonbreaker nodded.

"I accept. This should not take but a moment. I give you my oath on my power that should you win, my house shall serve you."

"And if you win, my vassals become yours," I said. I pulled the spearheads back but kept them hovering above, ready to strike again at a moment's notice.

Tables and benches were pulled back to the side as torches were brought out to better illuminate the area. No one entered or left the feasting hall, the dense throng shifting to create a central arena, a dueling ring some sixty feet in diameter.

I pushed back the existential dread as my fateful vision seemed to move closer to the here and now. And before I knew it, Kaleb stood in front of me.

A sword was brought to him, its blade an inch thick, fabricated of steel so heavy it looked capable of inflicting as much blunt force trauma as cutting damage.

A hush fell over the assembled warriors as we stood at opposite ends of the circle. A red handkerchief was tossed into the circle and slowly began drifting downwards.

As the cloth floated down, Kaleb and I stood for a moment facing one another, neither of us moving a muscle. The handkerchief struck the stone floor and we both charged at each other.

We launched ourselves at each other's throat.

I twisted through the air and bent around his thrusting sword, my clubs swinging. They caught his armor, making the sound of nails on chalkboard. The clubs left long deep scratches in the metal but could not pierce through the quarter-inch-thick steel armor.

We both landed, I light as a cat on my feet and Kaleb like a meteor, the stone cracking beneath his force and weight. We turned to face each other again, circling warily. He hadn't seen any of my abilities except for my Telekinesis and as far as I knew, I'd yet to see any of his.

"You're quick on your feet, I'll give you that!" Kaleb said. "I believe you might be faster than me!"

"You too are faster than I expected," I admitted. "Is that all attribute or do you have an ability? I would expect someone as heavily armored as you to be a little slower."

I continued to circle him, examining his armor for vulnerable points.

"Many before you have made that mistake," Kaleb boomed.

His body blurred, distorting the area as an explosion of thunder hit me and he broke the sound barrier.

I teleported fifteen feet ahead as the foreseen attack came.

Dragonbreaker's sword struck downwards, the colossal force of it hitting the floor, shattering the stone into gravel and powder. The power that would have pulverized my body instead warped the blade of Kaleb's sword.

Despite its thickness, the great iron blade had not effectively withstood the sheer force of the strike. Its edge was now dulled and I could see a slight bend in the blade itself.

I moved in again, activating the speed boost to my boots and blurring forward. I did not, however, break the sound barrier, launching my attack at the back of Kaleb's neck.

He whirled and a translucent barrier of blue force appeared between us. The claws of my club bounced off of it.

I twisted to the side as his sword stabbed forward and the shield dropped. Using my power of telekinesis, I made the spearheads hovering above strike down from all directions.

Kaleb raised his fist and a burst of kinetic force blasted out, knocking back any of the spearheads going for his face, neck, and shoulders.

The rest struck with the sound of hail on a roof of metal, pinging off, leaving tiny dents and divots all over the steel plating, unable to punch through the thick armor.

Kaleb lunged forward, his sword sweeping horizontally.

Then, he twisted in midair to strike the blade forward like the stinger of a scorpion. Flames danced along its edge as he activated another ability.

I was able to foresee his action and twisted and dodged within his guard. Sliding past him, I grabbed his left knee with my hand.

"Compress Earth," I said.

The ability was slow, but I didn't need anything big or precise as I pinched in the metal, merging the articulated joint to keep it from moving.

Kaleb stumbled as his leg refused to respond properly. With a scream of metal, he straightened his leg and whirled to face me.

By this time, I had opened my storage pouch and pulled out my other weapons.

Kaleb turned just in time to take my maul in the face. He jerked his head to the side barely enough to avoid a full hit, but the glancing strike was still adequate to send him staggering and leave a nasty dent in his visor. The right side of his helmet had caved in from the force.

Dragonbreaker reached up, tearing off the helmet, a stream of blood running down from his right eye, staining his beard and face a bright red. Gritting his crimson teeth, Kaleb grabbed my maul as it swung around for another attack. Dropping his bent sword, he took the maul and gave it a heft. He raised an eyebrow and looked it over.

"Where did you pick up a weapon like this?" he asked.

"I made it," I said nonchalantly, mostly true even if I'd just modified a previously existing weapon.

"Then I wouldn't have expected the Warlord to be a craftsman," Kaleb said, pacing around me like a stalking mountain lion.

"Well, I did used to work in construction," I said with a dismissive shrug.

Dragonbreaker tensed his muscles for a millisecond, then leaped forward, swinging the maul and striking the ground. "Shatter Shock," he said, barely loud enough for me to hear him.

The maul struck the ground and a cone of shrapnel launched at me.

There were no good options presented by my Foresight.

The cone took up nearly all of the dueling circle, the only area not affected being directly behind Kaleb, but I foresaw instantly being attacked if I entered it.

With no way out but through, I covered my eyes and hunkered down for the four seconds it would take for the shrapnel to hit and pass me. My skin was diamond hard, but the stone seemed enhanced by his ability and still left abrasions and paper-thin cuts where it hit.

Blood squeezed out before my skin resealed, leaving my body decorated with hundreds of tiny red rivers as they cascaded down my skin.

Kaleb's sons lowered their hands. A blade barrier dropped, identical to their father's. It had been used to protect those outside the circle from their father's attacks.

I began circling Kaleb, studying how he moved, in particular the awkwardness of his left leg. I tightened the circle, watching his grip on the maul, seeing how he held it to give himself maximum reach.

Kaleb tried to strike at me.

I rolled inside his guard to blunt the force of his attack.

He slammed his head forward.

I twisted, taking the blow on my shoulder and taking the opportunity to briefly grab his wrist.

"Compress Earth," I said.

"Form of the Volcano," Dragonbreaker demanded, almost simultaneously. His armor and skin began to glow.

I tried to take a step backwards. My Foresight caught up and I saw that I wouldn't be getting out of this attack.

Fire and molten stone gushed as if from a firehose from Dragonbreaker's body.

I became incorporeal just before the attack, striking his body with my spectral weapons.

Kaleb snarled and the onslaught of fire continued.

The duration of Phantom Form ended and I had six seconds before I could use it again. The fire raged on and my skin was scorched, parts of my body having begun to melt!

Exposed fat, flesh and muscle dripped from me.

Finally, the flames stopped and I teleported to the opposite side of the circle to let my skin regenerate and my burns heal.

Dragonbreaker approached me with labored, cumbersome movements. The knee joint I had messed up threw him off balance and his grip on the maul was weakened thanks to the fusion in the armor of his wrist. He built up speed as he came for me, the maul now beginning to glow red hot as he activated some ability without a verbal component.

I stepped forward, teleporting past him in a blink. Now beyond his clumsy attack, my right club lashed out at the back of his right knee, puncturing through the chain and leather.

He stumbled and whirled to face me.

Suddenly, I caught a flicker of movement from the shadows as Syvia leaped down, claws extended to take off Dragonbreaker's head with a strike from behind.

He started to move, but it was already too late.

Syvia froze in midair as I held her. "I said," I growled at her. "That you were to remain back unless called upon!"

"We cannot risk your death, my Lord…"

"I do not require your help!" I roared at her.

The brands along her wrists and neck grew white hot as she paled.

"You will stand back and not interfere or I swear by my goddess it will be my own hand that kills you."

Syvia dropped to the ground and scurried back, retreating into the circle of onlookers.

And I—I turned back to Dragonbreaker.

"Sorry for the interruption," I apologized, bowing my head to him. "It won't happen again."

We faced each other like two lions, one slowly surveying the other as we let our Stamina and Mana regenerate.

Kaleb blurred forward again, another clap of thunder destroying the sound barrier. The maul swung out in a one-handed grip in a spinning twenty-foot radius.

I ducked under the maul, lunging forward in an attempt to get inside Dragonbreaker's guard.

Kaleb's stance changed. He caught my clubs with the haft of the maul.

I was close and he took advantage of that, using the maul more like a quarterstaff now as he spun, striking at me with its shaft, pommel and head. Kaleb's hands were a blur as he attacked with a flurry of strikes, each one an attempt to pulverize me.

I sidestepped, seeking to hit the back of his knee again.

Instead, he caught me with the haft of the maul and shoved me backwards, my boots skidding on the ground as I struggled to maintain my balance.

There was a sound behind as Dragonbreaker lunged forward. Kaleb caught the edge of a greatsword with the spike of the maul and tossed it up.

His son fell back as his father stood over him.

"You shame me, son," Dragonbreaker said. "I accepted this duel and put my honor on the line, yet you intervene… even after my opponent already showed his own honor to me?"

"You are lord of these lands! We cannot let some upstart…" His son tried to defend himself before his father's fist caught him across the jaw.

"There is only one rule that is absolute in this world, boy," Dragonbreaker said, looking down at his son now sprawled on the ground. "The rule of strength! If I am not able to fight, then I am underserving of what I have, even if it is my own life. Do not dishonor me again."

Dragonbreaker turned to me, bowing his head to me in respect. "Sorry for the interruption. It will not happen again."

We stood apart, studying each other, no longer circling.

Kaleb raised the maul and lightning sparked along its head.

Then, he darted forward and struck the ground with it.

I rolled to the side, directing my spearheads and weapons to target Kaleb's face.

A blast of electricity flowed out in a thirty-foot radius from the strike. There was no way to avoid it within the circle.

I went incorporeal.

Dragonbreaker opened his mouth. A laser beam of light shot from it, cutting across my form.

Even with my Berserker title, the pain of the light was immense. I could tell instantly it was one of the types of damage to which this form was most vulnerable. I ended my incorporeal state and teleported behind Dragonbreaker, just as he struck again with the maul, shattering the stone where I had stood.

"I see you have talent, but you only have a few tricks." Dragonbreaker hurled the maul at me.

I rolled to the side, then ducked as the maul went flying back and slapped into Kaleb's hand like a boomerang.

He gave me a lupine grin. "Did you think you were the only one who could manipulate objects at range?"

In response, I launched two hundred spearheads at him.

They merely bounced off his shield and Kaleb lowered it.

I suspected it had some sort of cooldown period but couldn't stake my life on that.

"I can tell you are a great warrior, but I see that you have stagnated here," I said, eager to return his compliment in kind. He looked most aggrieved, understanding the insult that it was.

"Stagnated? No!" Dragonbreaker growled and lunged at me.

Sidestepping, I said, "You've been here for years," and then ducked under the maul to attack Kaleb's arm at the elbow, unable to make a palpable hit on it. "So why have you done nothing to repair this castle, or make any claim to these lands, or even return to where you came from?"

"I will retake my lands in time," Kaleb snapped.

He struck the ground, sending up a cloud of shattered stone. I easily bore the impact of the shrapnel and allowed my skin the opportunity to knit itself back together.

"When? This century?" I was taunting him. He had more attributes, abilities and experience in fighting than me. My best chance was to get right under that armored skin of his and get him so pissed that he made a mistake.

Kaleb snarled and swung low at my legs.

I easily jumped over the strike, able to stay out of his range now that his leg was crippled. I tried a sneak attack with my spearheads from behind, but he blocked them with his shield ability again. If it did have a cooldown period, it wasn't a super long one.

"You've grown fat from shaking down merchants. You have reached the limits of your potential," I goaded.

He stumbled as the joint in his armor malfunctioned.

I thought now was a good time to strike.

Suddenly, he shocked me by doing something about which my Foresight had failed to warn me. A blinding burst of light exploded from every part of his body and he lunged toward me as fast as a bolt of lightning... too fast, in fact, for me to predict or dodge.

His hand wrapped around the gorget of my pauldrons and lifted me off my feet.

He swung me into the ground.

I cracked my head against the stone, my skull ringing like a clapper in a bell within my helmet. My vision swam, nausea assaulting my guts, bringing bile to my mouth.

Kaleb raised the maul high, the spiked end facing toward me.

Despite my harder-than-diamond skin, it was clear that this blow would kill me. I reached out with my Telekinesis, grabbed Dragonbreaker, and begin to squeeze. He resisted, and I felt his Might fighting my Spirit as our attributes and abilities clashed.

Blood ran from his nose, ears and the corners of his eyes as the veins along his body bulged.

With my right hand, I swung up my club and slashed Kaleb across the throat. His skin was as strong as a steel breastplate, but the Nemean claws carved through it, slicing grooves three inches deep like engravings by a master carpenter in a block of softwood.

Kaleb's blood fountained out over me, but his eyes hardened. I felt him break through my Telekinesis. I tried to turn incorporeal but Kaleb's hand around me was glowing now, and I could not transition. The maul descended, the spike driving through my hearts.

A hole the size of my fist had been punched right through my chest.

Kaleb collapsed on top of me.

My vision dimmed.

You have been affected by an ability that prevents wounds from closing and healing. Damage stage is reduced from insta-death > mortal wound > lethal. Close the wound and stop the bleeding before you die. Time until death is 10 seconds.

   9...

I tried to shift Kaleb, but could not move his weight.

   8...

I tried lifting him with my Telekinesis, momentarily securing some kind of traction until my mind fuzzed over, and I lost contact.

   7...

The darkness began to creep in all around.

   6...

Every shape lost its distinctive edges, becoming blurry and indistinct.

5...

I tried reaching out again, but couldn't get a hold. I started forward, giving up on shifting Kaleb off me and trying to access my satchel.

4...

At least I went out on my own terms.

3... 2... 1

Guinevere lunged forward, her rapier deflecting a strike from the scorpion's tail.

She darted in and her left hand shot out a blast of ice which struck the creature's shell, freezing it solid. Then, she struck forward and broke through the shell, plunging her rapier deep into its body. She yanked it out.

King Scorpion. Gifted Beast/Scorpion. Veteran. Rank: 192.

The scorpion chittered and snapped at Guinevere with its pincers.

She teleported, leaving a silhouette of frozen vapor where she had been. She reappeared above the scorpion, her rapier wreathed in ice and wind as she plunged it inside the wound of the gargantuan arachnid.

The scorpion struck down with its pincer.

Guinevere deflected it with a strength that belied her slender frame.

The scorpion spasmed and then fell to the ground, its body continuing twitching for several moments.

Guinevere walked away from the corpse, wiping her blade on a white cloth before sliding it back into its scabbard.

19 rank points gained, split between surviving contributors.

"You did it again, girl!" Guinevere's instructor said, crossing his arms.

"What?" Guinevere sighed. She already knew the answer.

"You left your team behind," said Instructor Jarrek, a gnarled, burly old warrior.

"They were busy helping Karish get back to his feet," Guinevere argued. "So, I kept the monster occupied while they tended to him and finished the battle to minimize risk."

"Karish is your tank," Jarrek said. "And you left your healer too far back to support you. What would you have done if you'd got hit?"

Guinevere had had enough. It had been a long day, and this tired, old lecture was the straw that broke the camel's back. "I didn't need them, Jarrek! Ok?" Guinevere spat back. "We were attacked, and I stepped up to do my job. I was obviously capable of accomplishing it alone."

"This time," Jarrek said. "But what happens next time if you face something Hero-ranked? Do you think you can beat something of superior rank on your own? You'll need your team, but you won't have the teamwork and trust built to prevail. This is your team. You need to act like you want to be part of it."

"They aren't my team," Guinevere said, lowering her voice so only Jarrek could hear her. "They are my father's team. He picked them for me."

Jarrek sighed. "I know you wanted to choose your own party and I think you would have been better for it but sometimes, we just have to play the hand we are dealt. Think of this as a test of your leadership: to guide and direct them. Focus as much on that as you do the fighting."

"I'll try." Guinevere sighed.

Mira walked up to Guinevere who turned and gave her a tired smile. "How is everyone? Did you handle the rest of the scorpions all right?"

"We're fine. Only two casualties in total," Mira said. "How did your fight go?"

"We defeated the King Scorpion with no casualties, so everything is fine," Guinevere said. "Is there something you wanted to say to me?"

"I've just been meaning to ask," Mira said. "Do you know Sir Lancelot? It's just that he's from Camelot like you, so I thought you might be acquainted."

"Of course, I know Lancelot! He's my cousin," Guinevere said. "How do you know him? I didn't think you'd visited Camelot yet."

"I met him in the Event," Mira said. "I didn't have a chance to properly say goodbye to him after the final boss."

Guinevere took Mira's arm and walked with her. Their feet crunched on the dry leaves and sticks of the forest floor as they took a stroll. Behind them, scorpions were being cut apart for meat and their shells dissected to be used as material for a variety of crafting.

"So, I assume you like my cousin?" Guinevere asked.

Mira nodded, blushing.

"Don't be embarrassed! Strangely enough, all the women who meet Lancelot like him," teased Guinevere.

"Is he...you know, seeing anyone?" Mira asked.

"Not that I'm aware of," Guinevere said. "But he is a very private man. I can enquire discreetly for you if you would like, and maybe arrange another meeting...?"

"I don't know... that seems so...."

"Passionless and businesslike?" Guinevere asked. "Welcome to my world! That is simply how relationships usually are for people like us."

"Like us?" Mira asked.

"Gifted women," Guinevere said and gestured to the army behind them. "Look behind us. Over 70 percent of this army is male. That's not because there are more Gifted men than women but because there are different things expected of us."

"You seem pretty at peace with it," Mira said, seeming uncomfortable.

"Oh, I've grown used to it," Guinevere said with a shrug. "I'll give you a warning, Mira: you are very valuable, but you aren't valuable for the reasons you would like to be. Please do not delude yourself into believing that your extreme power is in the God-given abilities that make you a great archer, tracker or warrior. Your real value lies in the fact that any children you have will share in this potency. Kings will want you to marry their sons so you can breed them stronger heirs. And what's more, they really won't be interested in your view on the matter."

"That's pretty dark," Mira said, looking around. "Why did you want us to be alone before telling me this?"

"Because I don't trust those around me," Guinevere said. "I am betrothed to the Crown Prince of Camelot and there are those who want to prevent that marriage. The words I have just spoken to you could easily be used against me."

"Then, thank you for trusting me with them," said Mira.

"I'd like us to be allies," Guinevere said. "Friends, even."

"I'd like that." Mira extended her hand and the two shook. "To friendship."

Chapter 30: Bearer of Death

I hung from the ledge and dangled over the void, already feeling my fingers slipping. Hungry laughter surrounded me. Something pulled at me, like invisible hands dragging me into a grave. Finally, my fingers lost their grip on the edge and I fell.

A white, burning hand caught my wrist, keeping me from plummeting into the darkness.

"I won't let you destroy me a second time." The voice of Karnen rang out in the blackness.

The Spirit of Vengeance was dangling over the edge, his hand wrapped around my wrist.

"Pull yourself up!" Karnen commanded. "I don't have the strength to pull you out of this place."

The laughter intensified as if to mock the idea of escape. As I tried to pull myself up, a wave of lethargy overcame me, making me feel so very tired and heavy, losing track of Karnen.

My eyes began to close.

You're the reason I never got anywhere. If I hadn't been tied down with you and your mother, I could have made something of myself.

The old hateful words were never far from my mind, a painful memory filled with bitterness and resentment that had haunted me for as long as I could remember.

I pushed down the child's pain and latched onto the resentment, the only thing I had left to hold on to in this place and the only thing given to me by my parents.

The resentment burned in me, and my eyes opened again.

An icy hand latched around my leg, its touch seeming to chill the blood in my veins. Pushing past the frozen agony, I reached out to Karnen with my hand.

He grabbed it and held on.

Briefly, I stopped slipping downwards, still hanging precariously from the edge over the blackness. Suddenly, something clung on to my legs and started pulling me down.

Furthermore, Karnen was being pulled down with me.

"You cannot leave!" Something below me spoke, its voice reverberating through my mind.

"Like fuck I can't!" I gritted my teeth and tried to kick whatever it was off my leg.

"You have escaped us long enough, the voice said. We are hungry, and you are so filled with emotions for us to dine on."

Another hand latched onto my other leg.

I could kick out no longer.

Karnen slid closer to the edge, his wiry spirit frame unable to hold my soul as we were dragged toward the black abyss.

You are a failure. Just accept it and give up.

The voice of my father echoed again in my head, not the exact words he had used but the voice was the one that had plagued me all my life.

"I am not you," I growled as my fury built. "I am not a failure."

Something hit my legs, the weight doubling and I began to fall as Karnen slipped. Then, the hands around my legs let go.

"He was mine!" the voice growled in frustration.

"He is mine now. His anger and rage are intoxicating. He will fuel our little star," said another voice as cold and hungry as the first but with a softer, feminine tone.

"But he is so weak! How will he feed her?" whined the other voice.

"It will feed her, or it will die," said the feminine one.

A sharp, stabbing pain ran through my chest in the place where Kaleb had impaled me. A cold pressure seemed to take hold of me, giving me upward momentum. After a few seconds, I broke through the darkness and into the light.

---

172 rank points gained.

Ability gained. Black Rage (Rank 1): Every kill you make increases your Might Attribute by 0.5 for the following 2 minutes. Multiple kills may be stacked together to intensify your singular desire to kill.

Cost: 1 Stamina/sec while active.

Upgrade this ability to increase the amount of Might increased by this ability and its duration. Each upgrade increases your Might Attribute by one.

You have completed a hidden objective and earned a title. Objective: Become the host for a Spirit of the Void. You have survived death itself and returned. Now, you are not alone. Inside your spirit now resides a Voidling, a child of the denizens of the Void. It will feed on your pain, joy, sorrow, pleasure, rage and exuberance. It will also feed on the emotions of those in close proximity.

Reward. Title: Bearer of Death (A unique title that replaces your title Visitor of Death).

*Bearer of Death: You are now the host of a Voidling inside you. Its presence may affect your emotions and the abilities that you receive.

You have completed a hidden objective and earned a reward.

Objective: Survive death itself. Reward: Unknown.

Blood and Souls (Repeatable): Kill 10,240 monsters or humanoids. Current Progress: 150/10,240. When you complete this quest, you will gain 2,048 rank points. The next quest will require double the number to be completed but will award double the rank points.

Kaleb's body lay on top of me, pinning me to the stone. I could not shift his weight and felt him slowly crushing the air out of me. Closing my eyes, I fell into Wrathful Mediation.

I needed strength and I needed it now.

"Raise Black Rage by 10 ranks," I whispered to the System.

Black Rage (Rank 2): Every kill you make increases your Might Attribute by 0.6 for the next 2 minutes and 30 seconds. Multiple kills may be stacked together to intensify your singular desire to kill.

Cost: 1 Stamina per sec while active.

Upgrade this ability to increase the amount of Might offered by this ability and its duration. Each upgrade increases your Might Attribute by one.

I could feel the hole in my chest had shrunk by half already and was slowly closing.

Black Rage (Rank 3): Every kill you make increases your Might Attribute by 0.7 for the next 3 minutes. Multiple kills may be stacked together to intensify your singular desire to kill.
Cost: 1 Stamina/sec while active.
Upgrade this ability to increase the amount of Might offered by this ability and its duration. Each upgrade increases your Might Attribute by 1.

The fragments of my ribs slowly pushed out of my hearts, bubbling out of the frothy blood as they were expelled from my chest. My spine cracked as muscles I didn't even know I had begun to swell and expand on my back.

Black Rage (Rank 4): Every kill you make increases your Might Attribute by 0.8 for the next 3 minutes and 30 seconds. Multiple kills may be stacked together to intensify your singular desire to kill.
Cost: 1 Stamina per sec while active.
Upgrade this ability to increase the amount of Might offered by this ability and its duration. Each upgrade increases your Might Attribute by 1.

Muscle and bone knit back together, leaving raw flesh exposed before skin slowly began to regrow over it. The changes from Rank 4 were processed. It was time to pick my first addition to this ability before I progressed with its upgrade.

Congratulations! You have raised an ability to Rank 5. Please select an addition to your skill from the list below:
•   **The damage from your attacks and abilities is increased by a minor amount while Black Rage is active.**
•   **You feel less pain while Black Rage is active, enabling you to fight on through difficult or life-threatening injuries.**
•   **Your mass is significantly increased, making you heavier and harder to move while Black Rage is active.**

I looked over the options, settling almost immediately on the first one. My priority was damage output. I could fight through pain, and it was already covered by my Berserker title.

Being heavier and harder to move might have its perks but, for me, still didn't compare with massive damage output.

Black Rage (Rank 5): Every kill you make increases your Might Attribute by 0.9 for the next 4 minutes. Multiple kills may be stacked together to intensify your singular desire to kill.
The damage from your attacks and abilities is increased by a minor amount while Black Rage is active.
Cost: 1 Stamina/sec while active.
Upgrade this ability to increase the amount of Might offered by this ability and its duration. Each upgrade increases your Might Attribute by 1.

My legs and arms were swelling, the fingers in my gauntlet expanding so painfully against the confines of the metal. Then, they began to shrink and contract like a deflating balloon.

Black Rage (Rank 6): Every kill you make increases your Might Attribute by 1 for the next 4 minutes and 30 seconds. Multiple kills may be stacked together to intensify your singular desire to kill.
The damage from your attacks and abilities is increased by a minor amount while Black Rage is active.
Cost: 1 Stamina/sec while active.
Upgrade this ability to increase the amount of Might offered by this ability as well as and its duration. Each upgrade increases your Might Attribute by 1.

My neck bones cracked as muscles expanded and retracted all over my body. My muscles swelled, then shrank but on each occasion, I grew a little in mass, height and width.

Black Rage (Rank 7): Every kill you make increases your Might Attribute by 1.1 for the next 5 minutes. Multiple kills may be stacked together to intensify your singular desire to kill.

The damage from your attacks and abilities is increased by a minor amount while Black Rage is active.
Cost: 1 Stamina/sec while active.
Upgrade this ability to increase the amount of Might offered by this ability and its duration. Each upgrade increases your Might Attribute by 1.

My body felt lighter, and I could barely tell I was wearing my gauntlets or pauldrons anymore as my physical strength went higher and higher.

Black Rage (Rank 8): Every kill you make increases your Might Attribute by 1.2 for the next 5 minutes and 30 seconds. Multiple kills may be stacked together to intensify your singular desire to kill.
The damage from your attacks and abilities is increased by a minor amount while Black Rage is active.
Cost: 1 Stamina/sec while active.
Upgrade this ability to increase the amount of Might offered by this ability as well as its duration. Each upgrade increases your Might Attribute by 1.

With that upgrade, my Might finally passed its Mortal potential.

Congratulations! You have raised your Might Attribute to 20, the Mortal limit. Your body is undergoing changes to help you survive the adaptations to your attribute.
Your slow-twitch muscles have increased in durability, density and power and your joints have been reinforced to handle rough and heavy motions and weight without strain or tearing. You can lift x10 your body weight without straining.

I felt ants crawling under my skin and the twisting of serpents through my muscles.

After what felt like hours but what had in reality been less than a few dozen seconds, my writhing metamorphosis finally ceased.

Congratulations! You have raised all your attributes beyond 20, the Mortal limit. You have reached Veteran rank. All damage done to

> you by creatures of a lower ranking than you is reduced by one damage stage. Damage dealt to a creature of a lower ranking is increased by one damage stage. You will now only get a quarter of rank points from creatures of a lower ranking than you.

> **Blessing of War (Mortal) has become Blessing of War (Veteran).**
> *Blessing of War (Veteran): You are the mortal embodiment of war and carnage. You regen 10 Stamina and 10 Mana per second to fuel you as you carve your way through the battlefield.

I had reached Veteran rank. Its benefits were not bad, but nor were they spectacular and world-changing. The main difference was the penalty to rank points that I would get but I had already known it was coming.

> **Black Rage (Rank 9):** Every kill made by you increases your Might Attribute by 1.3 for the next 6 minutes. Multiple kills may be stacked together to intensify your singular desire to kill.
>
> The damage from your attacks and abilities is increased by a minor amount while Black Rage is active.
>
> Cost: 1 Stamina/sec while active.
>
> Upgrade this ability to increase the amount of Might offered by this ability and its duration. Each upgrade increases your Might Attribute by 1.

With Rank 9 passed, I had only one more choice to make.

> **Congratulations! You have raised an ability to Rank 10. Please select an addition to your skill from the list below:**
>
> - Your mass is increased, pulling in the shadows around you, obscuring your form. This makes you more difficult to hit and is magnified by every point of Might you gain while in Black Rage.
> - Each of your kills heals you for a minor amount, regrowing bits of lost body mass and sealing up wounds.
> - While Black Rage is active, you are immune to mind controlling effects but also have difficulty in recognizing those around you. As a consequence, on

> **occasion, you may find yourself accidentally attacking allies.**

Again, the first option seemed the most interesting and practical.

Whilst healing was useful, it was only on kills and not on each strike, so its usefulness would be nonexistent in fights like the one I had just had. Furthermore, my regeneration was already a passive and more reliable version of this addition. Being immune to mind-controlling effects was very tempting but the side effect was just not worth it.

Black Rage (Rank 10): Every kill you make increases your Might Attribute by 1.4 for the next 6 minutes. Multiple kills may be stacked together to intensify your singular desire to kill.
The damage from your attacks and abilities is increased by a moderate amount while Black Rage is active.
Your mass is increased pulling in the shadows around you, obscuring your form, making you more difficult to hit. This is magnified by every point of Might you gain while in Black Rage.
Cost: 1 Stamina/sec while active.
Upgrade this ability to increase the amount of Might offered by this ability and its duration. Each upgrade increases your Might Attribute by 1.

I pushed Dragonbreaker off me and stood up, a shroud of inky black mist surrounding me. I could just see my veins glowing red under my skin as the effects of Magma Heart(s) were apparently still active. How long had I been dead? I guessed it had not been long as a ring of people stood around me, looking extremely perplexed and unsure of what to do.

"I have won the duel," I said, my voice hoarse from whatever I had gone through. "I will accept your oaths to me now."

The son who had tried to stab me in the back stepped forward. "Our father is dead. I say we finish what he started and avenge him."

"That's enough, Tobias." Jeriah, another of Kaleb's sons, stepped forward. "You will not disgrace the word of our father."

Tobias turned on his brother. "You would give your oath to this murderer?"

"To kill in battle is not murder," Jeriah responded, emanating calm, immovable seniority.

"Who are you?" I asked him. I already knew his name, but wanted to hear his answer.

"I am Jeriah Dragonbreaker, eldest son of my father," he said.

"Tell me what you want, Jeriah."

"I want what my father promised me," Jeriah said boldly. "That my family's lands would be returned to us. You were right in what you said to him; he had stagnated and grown too comfortable here."

"You would talk about our father like that when his body hasn't even cooled?" said Tobias, almost spitting with indignation.

"You weren't even born when we were driven out of our lands," Jeriah replied. "You don't remember the splendor of our castle or the beauty of our orchards. I refuse to live in this ruin and raise my children here. I want more."

"And I want vengeance for my father," Tobias said, turning to me. "What would you do if one of us killed your father?"

"I'd thank you," I replied dryly. "I have no love for my father. I tried to kill him myself when I was seven."

For once, Tobias had no retort and fell silent.

"I will make a pact with you, Jeriah," I said. "I will put you under my Dominion either way, but if you enter my service willingly, I promise I will restore your father's lands to you. I will also ensure the return of any land you have had stolen from you by others."

Jeriah extended his hand.

I reached out.

He clasped my wrist, and we shook. "I swear allegiance to you, Mordred, Champion of Kelesa."

I turned to Tobias and extended my hand.

He glared at me before he lowered his eyes and grasped my forearm. "I swear allegiance to you, Mordred, Champion of Kelesa," Tobias promised.

One by one, each of Jeriah's brothers stepped forward, grasped my arm and swore allegiance.

When they were done, I raised my hand like a priest performing a prayer.

"Dominion," I said. The word echoed around the hall with resonant gravitas.

Jeriah, Tobias, and their eight brothers all reached up as marks appeared along their necks. They were not of the chain pattern but the crossed sword design akin to that of Syvia.

> **Whip and Chains (Repeatable): Conquer 320 monsters or humanoids by bringing them under your Dominion. Current progress: 25/320. When you complete this quest, you will gain 64 rank points. The next quest will require double the number to be completed but will award double the rank points.**

"Put three ranks points into Dominion," I told the System.
Settling into my rage, I skipped past the next three notifications.

> **Dominion (Rank 8): Several times per day, equal to 640 plus your Spirit Attribute, you can, as a spoken command, force a creature not bound by another creature into your service. You can dominate a number of creatures at a time, equal to 40 plus your Spirit Attribute. A creature may choose to serve you willingly or may attempt to resist by opposing their Mind Attribute against your Spirit Attribute. You can, at will, see the abilities and attributes of any creature under your Dominion. You may have a maximum number of creatures under your Dominion equal to your Spirit Attribute multiplied by 9.**
>
> **The larger your Dominion, the more it grows in power. All attributes of your vassals are raised by 1 when they are in a group of 50 or more. Every further 50 vassals increase this bonus by 1 to a maximum possible attribute score of 20.**
>
> **Cost: 1 Mana per 5 creatures.**
>
> **Upgrade this ability to increase how many creatures you can dominate per day as well as the multiplier for how many creatures you can dominate at a time. Each upgrade increases your Spirit Attribute by 1.**

I considered the increase in how many people over whom I could hold Dominion and raised my hand.

"Dominion," I said again.

Every other man in the room dropped to their knees as the brand of chains appeared around their necks and wrists.

> **Whip and Chains (Repeatable): Conquer 320 monsters or humanoids by bringing them under your Dominion. Current progress: 296/320. When you complete this quest, you will gain 64 rank points. The next quest will require double the number to be completed but will award double the rank points.**

"You now serve me," I said, projecting my voice so all could hear. "Rest. Tomorrow morning, those of you without abilities are to go and gather as much stone as you can and bring it here. It is time to turn this ruin into something defensible again."

I turned to Jeriah. "I need somewhere to sleep."

"My sister will show you to your quarters," he said, gesturing to a tall, blonde woman.

I turned to Syvia. "Go back to the cave tonight and protect the others. Bring them back here in the morning."

"As you command, my Lord," she said, bowing her head and not daring to meet my eyes.

Jeriah's sister led me through the least dilapidated part of the keep. I focused on her until a prompt appeared.

> **Katlyn Dragonbreaker. Gifted Human. Mortal. Rank: 8.**

She led me into a large room. In the center stood a king-sized bed in a wooden frame of stained pine, covered with furs. Katlyn closed the doors and then proceeded to undress.

"What are you doing?" I asked.

"My brother instructed me to warm your bed and keep you company tonight," she said.

"That won't be necessary," I said with a tired sigh.

"Do you not find me attractive?" Katlyn asked, seeming somewhat hurt.

"It's not that." I felt a strange need to reassure her. "I'm just not ready to get involved in romantic entanglements."

"Is there anything you need, then?" Katlyn asked.

"Yes," I admitted. "Could you please help me out of my armor? I think I'm stuck."

After an awkward ten minutes, I was finally free of the armor.

Katlyn curtsied and left the room.

A wooden tub filled with hot water had been prepared for me. I stepped into it. Dried, congealed blood floated off my skin. The water was pleasantly warm and I sank back and let it soak away my aches and pains. But I still had something to do before I could fully relax.

"What are my current attributes?" I asked the System.

Mordred, Champion of Kelesa. Gifted Humanoid/Human. Veteran. Rank: 188			
Available rank points: 1,219.			
Might:	23 (+3) = 26	Mind:	27
Speed:	32 (+20) = 52	Perception:	47
Toughness:	31	Spirit:	49
Endurance:	31	Power:	50
Maximum Stamina:	171	Maximum Mana:	223
Stamina Regen:	44.2 per second	Mana Regen:	54.4 per second
Abilities:			
Dominion (Rank 8), Telekinesis (Rank 20), Heightened Speed (Rank 10), Foresight (Rank 20), Compress Earth (Rank 20), Bestial Senses (Rank 20), Phantom Form (Rank 10), Storm Soul (Rank 20), Magma Heart(s) (Rank 20), Troll Hide (Rank 20), Black Rage (Rank 10).			
Blessings:			
Blessing of War (Veteran), Blessing of Tadris.			
Titles:			
Mark of Cain, Bloody Pugilist, Exorcist, Survivor III, Feral Barbarian, Field Alchemist III, Berserker, Beast Slayer III, War Chief, Venom Resistant III, Keytaro's Guardian III, Wrathful Meditation, Fireproof III, Superhuman, Bearer of Death.			

I closed my eyes and drifted off. With a curious inevitability, I sensed a familiar presence. My eyes snapped open. I was not in the castle anymore but atop the ziggurat.

Kelesa sat facing me on a stone block, and I was still in the bath which had obviously shifted realms with me. "We need to stop meeting like this," I said.

"Please, Champion!" Kelesa scoffed. "I have beheld thousands of your kind in their nakedness before. There is nothing you have that I have not seen or in which I am interested."

"I have not heard from you in a while. What do you need from me?"

"Nothing," Kelesa said, giving me a shark-toothed grin. "You have done quite well, better than I had even hoped. I knew you were an excellent candidate."

"And what makes me so great?" I asked.

"Why, your hatred and desire not to become like your father," Kelesa responded.

I stiffened at her words but forced myself to relax.

"What do you want from me?" I asked, coolly.

"I have a new quest for you," said Kelesa. "Something to help subtly guide you and increase your power."

"You have not been guiding me at all, so far. Why change now?"

"Every time we gods intervene with our champions, we give our rivals a free chance to do the same," Kelesa explained. "Warning you about an attack would give the right to one of the other gods to warn their champion you were about to ambush them, for instance. I've been stockpiling freebies and you haven't needed any help. Here you are, conquering a castle full of warriors without a word from me!"

"So, what's changed now?" I asked.

"I won't say. It would allow one of the other gods to speak freely without consequence."

"An answer in itself," I mused. "Someone is coming after me. That is the reason you're speaking to me now. You got a free pass to speak to me now because they interfered with one of their champions. Quid pro quo."

"Perhaps," Kelesa said with a shrug.

"What's the quest then?"

Quest gained. Conquer (Repeatable): You have been tasked with conquering your first region. Take control of the Forest of the Ancients by defeating the 8 powers of the region and preventing any other faction from forming a presence there.	
Current progress:	1-8.
Reward: A Rank 4 Artifact of your choice or creation.	

"I look forward to watching your progress," Kelesa said.

Act I Epilogue

Arthur splashed a full bucket of water over his head and washed away the sweat from his sparring practice.

"You always have to show off to the ladies," Lancelot said, joining him at the water barrel and pouring a bucket of water over himself too, to cool off. Unlike Arthur, his shirt remained on.

"There's no harm in looking!" Arthur said with a brilliant smile.

"I don't know if Guinevere would agree with that," Lancelot said, toweling his hair. "She can be pretty jealous as I remember."

"Then I should show off as much as I can before she gets back from her diplomatic mission," Arthur said with a shrug.

"You didn't hear?" Lancelot asked.

"Hear what?"

"Guinevere joined up with the Lunaren Royal Army to track down one of the Champions of Chaos in the Cursed Forest," said Lancelot.

"What?" Arthur's easygoing expression was now replaced by a scowl. "It's bad enough she decided to take a shortcut through the Cursed Forest. Why was she allowed to go running off after a chaos spawn? And why was I not informed about this?"

"The Lunaren Princess needed aid. Guinevere's father approved it. I only heard about it myself this morning," Lancelot said. "She can take care of herself, you know. She's a whole grade higher than you, remember!"

"She isn't a champion," Arthur reminded him.

"Don't bring that up with her," Lancelot said. "I know she'll never say, but she's still bitter about not being chosen by any of the gods."

"The gods choose who they will," Arthur said with a sigh. "And Guinevere has always been too rebellious for her own good. Don't tell her I said it, but I'm glad she wasn't chosen. She'd throw herself into every fight if she had been. I want her in Camelot where she'll be safe."

"She'll settle down after the wedding," Lancelot assured him.

"I hope so." Arthur picked up a sword as long as he was tall and slung it across his back.

The two cousins walked together out of the training ring and into the grassy tourney fields as knights on horseback jousted and trained.

"When will Guinevere return to Camelot?" Arthur asked.

"She was ordered to return directly after dealing with the chaos spawn," Lancelot said. "She has almost ten champions with her and an army of royal knights from both Camelot and Lunara. I expect she'll be back home in less than a month."

"As long as she doesn't throw herself at another of our enemies," Arthur said. "I love Guinevere, but worry for her. She needs to accept her place in Camelot and embrace her duty."

"She will," Lancelot said. "I heard as soon as she gets back, her father will hold the Dragon Tourney for you to perform for the crowd and 'win' her hand. After that, we'll have the wedding, and everything will be as it should."

"Thanks, Lance," Arthur said. "I suppose we should rest up and get ready to run the dungeon again?"

"Good idea," Lancelot agreed. "See you in three hours."

"Make it five," Arthur laughed. "Lady Lionor wishes to take a walk through the gardens this afternoon."

Lancelot let out a sigh of exasperation. "Arthur, you're betrothed!"

"I'm not married *yet!*" Arthur said. "Besides, I'm just going on a walk with her. A man does not need to be married to take a walk."

"Whatever," said Lancelot. "I'll see you at the dungeon entrance in five hours then."